STROKE OF DEATH

A Psychic Visions Novel
Book #17

Dale Mayer

STROKE OF DEATH
Beverly Dale Mayer
Valley Publishing Ltd.

Copyright © 2020

ISBN-13: 978-1-773362-86-1
Print Edition

Books in This Series:

About This Book

Cayce's art is well-known and respected among her peers, and, as such, has spawned forgers, copycats ... and enemies. But when her favorite model and best friend is murdered—the masterpiece painted on her skin cut off her body—Cayce knows she's up against a collector of a very different sort.

Detective Richard Henderson doesn't know much about art, but he knows what he likes. Of all the art mixed up in this case, it is the artist, Cayce, who fascinates him the most. While he understands her work contains an element of something extraordinary, he just doesn't know what that is exactly or how she embodies it in her creative works of art.

But, when other models show up dead, with more souvenirs taken from their bodies, both the artist and the detective realize much more is involved in this than just Cayce's art ... It's all about Cayce's soul.

Sign up to be notified of all Dale's releases here!
https://geni.us/DaleNews

CHAPTER 1

C AYCE CORMONT DIDN'T want to rush her work today. She didn't want to rush any day but definitely not today. This was the fifth day she had put into this commissioned art piece, her static part of her art. She had finished the backdrop. Today was all about getting the presentation of the model incorporated in just right, merging perfectly with Cayce's background art. That she'd been feeling unwell the last two days only made her job harder.

To add to her pain and frustration, the "perfect model" whom the set director wanted was the worst model for the job. Cayce had only found out about the change in the model yesterday. She'd been putting the final touches on the backdrop, when the company brought in the new model to show her. Cayce's normal approach was not to let others dictate her models to her, not even the client who had commissioned the piece. But this time the client's representatives had pulled a fast one on Cayce at the very last moment.

To top off that insult, Cayce had taken an instant dislike to the new model, Naomi. Something about the sly curl to her lips and that look in her eyes combined to say that she knew exactly what the world wanted, and she was prepared to give it up—for a price. Cayce had really struggled to find anything good about her. And, in Cayce's work, that bonding and blending was everything.

But Cayce was a professional and did what she needed to do. Today was no exception. Besides, the sooner she was done, the sooner she could move on. She walked from her vehicle to the art installation, putting down her large cases and turning to study the work she'd completed the night before.

Finally, after a few moments, she stepped back and nodded. "It looks good."

"Looks darn good."

At the sound of footsteps, she turned to see her replacement model saunter in, dressed in a bikini and not much else. Cayce nodded in acknowledgment of Naomi's comment, then said, "Okay, so right back to the same position we set up last night," she said, motioning to the wall— Cayce's artwork—where the model herself would disappear into the actual painted background.

"And good morning to you too," Naomi said in a snide voice.

Cayce shrugged it off. She was short on time as it was and couldn't afford to waste more by slinging words with Naomi when Cayce needed to be slinging paint. It was hard to be creative if she had adverse feelings for the whole scenario. She wished she had her regular model because Elena would have been absolutely perfect for this job.

Cayce had worked with Elena just two days ago on another art show, highlighting different masterpieces, and it had worked out stunningly, but that had been for a fancy house party, where Elena had been the artsy centerpiece of the ballroom. She had done a phenomenal job, and, when Cayce had told her best model to go home and rest, Elena had laughed at her and said, "Now that I'm off duty, I want to enjoy the party and mingle with the guests." She had given Cayce a gentle hug, then turned and walked away.

Elena's happy energy was so very different from the critical scowl Naomi wore, as Cayce tried to sort out what she
needed to do next, other than deflecting Naomi's negative
energy.

"You can start anytime now," Naomi said in a bored
voice. "At this rate we'll be here all day."

"I won't be," Cayce said. She bent down, opened up her
cases, brought out her palettes and paints, mixing the first
color she wanted. When she was ready, she pulled on the
energies around her, looking for that creative light, that
rainbow, which she wrapped around her, almost like a
blanket of good luck, spreading out into all the different
colors. She was a firm believer in the colors of sound and the
colors of nature.

When she reached for a certain color, Cayce always
called out to Mother Nature to help her make a true
representation.

Finally she stood up with her palette and walked over to
Naomi and got to work. Cayce started with Naomi's left
shoulder and arm, working down her elbow; Cayce's strokes
were sure, fast, and accurate.

Naomi watched her in surprise. "Wow, when you get
going, you get going."

Cayce didn't say a word. What could she say? It was beyond her to talk at this point because all the possible colors
of the spectrum surged through her heart, through her mind,
wrapping around her body and soul. She needed the same
energy to wrap around Naomi, to help her model attract and
pull in, to blend with the same colors, to blend with the
same energy. Only there was no blending with Naomi. Her
energy was impatient, irritated—edgy.

Yet Cayce's work entailed a magical element, and she firmly believed it was due to the energy that she utilized. Something she'd accidentally discovered after practicing her healing lessons with Dr. Maddy, a physician well renowned for her energy work in the healing arts.

When the magic happened naturally, it was great, easy, wonderful. Sometimes Cayce could also make it happen; she was a pro at that. That would desperately be needed here with Naomi. Because otherwise, the art would look flat and feel … off.

Cayce worked relentlessly for two hours, before she finally took a step back. She had the preliminary body-painting on the top half of Naomi, the background blending beautifully into the foreground. Although Cayce still had the other layers to work on, Naomi's hair was pulled back into a tight braid down her back, and Cayce had to blend Naomi's face and that hairline yet. She walked closer to the model. "Do you need a bathroom break or some water?"

Naomi nodded. "Yeah, that'd be good." She walked toward the hallway, disappearing around a corner.

Cayce took a deep breath and let it out, gently twisting and stretching her spine and neck. Then shook off Naomi's negative energy she'd been working to bypass. When she heard hard footsteps behind her, she stiffened. She hated on-site visitors when she worked. She just wished they'd wait to see the finished piece at the opening event. Not to mention that the energy preceding her visitor had a dark, disruptive influence attached. She pulled in her aura, then turned to face the coming threat.

When she saw a man in a suit walking toward her, her eyes opened wide. His chiseled face was his most striking feature—but a model in a suit with a crisp hard attitude seemed incongruous here.

"May I help you?" She studied his aura, seeing it snugged tightly against his body. A barely visible white line of energy surrounded him. Except it resonated with anger—lots of anger. Yet controlled. She raised her eyebrows slightly.

"Why would you think I need your help?" he asked in a tight, hard voice.

Although he might not be aware of what his aura was doing, he clearly didn't want her aware of it either. Because now his energy had thinned even more. "It's just that you look angry," she said. She waved her hand at the installation. "I'm kind of busy."

"You are Cayce Matlock?" At her nod, he continued, "And you worked with Elena Campbell?"

"Yes, all the time. We did a piece together two nights ago," she said, her face softening at the reminder. "She's a really good friend of mine."

Just then Naomi returned, instantly shifting the energy in the room. She took her position against the backdrop wall, as she eyed the new arrival with a pretty smile on her face. "Oh, perfect. Somebody to come and watch me," she said, as she bounced her bare boobs a bit.

It was all Cayce could do to hold back her sigh of frustration.

The man looked at her, then looked at Naomi. "So do you know Elena too?"

"Sure," Naomi said. "Models in this business usually know each other. She's pretty decent. I'm better." She indicated her sleek body. "That's why I'm here, and she's not," she said smugly. "I'm Naomi Star."

The stranger's gaze narrowed.

On the side, biting back her caustic response, Cayce

watched Naomi's energy. The deceptive fluffy lights flitting off in a million different directions hid something dark inside, but everybody had something dark inside. Because Cayce had taken an instant dislike to the woman, Cayce had put up barriers, so she wouldn't have to deal with Naomi's energy on a firsthand basis, but that also made her painting process go a bit slower, as she had to bypass the barriers to make this work. It would never be as good as with a better model, but, given Cayce had no choice this time, it's what she would have to do.

While Naomi seemed to think that Cayce was fast and on target, today wasn't really going as smoothly, as timely, or as well as Cayce would have liked. And she didn't have time for interruptions. She turned to the stranger. "You haven't identified yourself," she said in a cool tone. "What's going on?"

"I am Detective Richard Henderson," he said, pulling out a badge.

She frowned, reading the name on the badge. "What do the police want here?"

"Doesn't matter what they want," Naomi said with a throaty laugh. "They can send all their hunky detectives my way anytime."

Naomi's words gave Cayce everything she needed to know, without even turning toward Naomi to see the same darkness oozing from her pores. *Nerves. Fear. Uncertainty. Insecurity.* Cayce studied her model for a long moment, then faced the detective, noting no change in his energy. He was completely unfazed by Naomi. Neither was he attracted to the mostly naked woman.

Interesting.

"Detective, why are you here?"

"Because we found your friend," he said with added emphasis on that last word.

"Which friend?" she asked, not understanding where he was coming from. "What do you mean, *found?*"

"Elena Campbell," he said. "Remember her?"

Frustrated now, she gave a quick nod. "Yes, I already told you that she's a good friend of mine."

"Her body was found in a dumpster yesterday morning." His gaze was hard, angry. "What do you know about that?"

Cayce took the blow almost viscerally. Her body bowed against the pain. Her knees sagged, and her heart crushed from the horrific pressure of the shock. "Are you serious?" she gasped out. "Oh, my God." She sank to the floor, shutting her eyelids, as if that would somehow stop the assault on all her senses.

Her mind was completely overwhelmed, as shards of pain splintered through her. Was that why the last two days had been so rough? She'd fought the headaches and the nausea, and, when a darkness had enveloped her, she'd really wondered what was going on. When she found out Elena had been replaced in this installation, Cayce hadn't been happy—as in seriously not happy—and had figured the ugly energy was due to that. That, in part, had been behind her bad mood.

Although her being forced to use Naomi hadn't helped. She liked to choose her own models. Not deal with the ones who were sleeping their way to the top. Naomi hadn't fit the bill yesterday. She hadn't fit the bill today. Cayce's models had to have that extra something.

Naomi didn't have it.

Elena had it ... in spades. No, ... *had had* it. *Past tense.*

The grief crushed her, and she couldn't get air into her

lungs, as she stared at the detective.

The detective squatted in front of her. "Breathe."

She struggled, then gasped, and drew in a deep breath, her gaze wide and painful as she stared at him. "How? When?"

"She had already been dead for several hours," he said softly, as he studied her. "Her throat was cut."

The shocks just kept reverberating. Her body shook involuntarily. Then she added her own headshake. "Oh, my God, dear God, no." She continuously shook her head, her lips firmed into a straight line, her eyes filling with tears. "Please, no," she whispered again, turning to the detective. "Elena was special. Why would anybody want to hurt her?"

"You body-painted her, correct?"

She nodded, her gaze still locked on his, searching for anything to say, but her throat had closed, her heart shutting down at the terrible horrors filling her mind's eye.

"And what did you paint on her that night?"

She stared up at him, and sadly, she whispered, "A masterpiece. I painted her into a masterpiece."

"Well, guess what?" he said, his voice hardening. "A collector found something else to collect. Her skin."

At his last words, her body automatically took a fetal position, rolled over, where her stomach revolted, and she vomited all over the floor.

In her heart of hearts, she knew the murderer hadn't just collected a masterpiece of art. Something was so very special about Elena. Her energy was pure gold.

When her killer took her life, her painted skin, he'd also taken a part of Elena's soul.

HE STARED AT the beautiful painting in front of him. It would be a challenge to preserve this. He'd taken multiple photographs, and he'd already stretched out the canvas. The stretching bars were ever-so-gently tightened in order to fine-tune the tension to get the look that he wanted. It was a stunning picture—sunsets and an eagle—but something was just luminescent about it. He was desperate to capture that luminescence. He quickly coated it with yet another layer of preservative, trying to keep it as it was, trying to keep that something special. He looked at the discarded masterpieces he had worked on before.

Most of them were no good, but he'd taken photographs and had them blown up, just as a reminder. But they were something. They were a memory, faint, just a shadow of what they should be, what they could be. This one, however, he had high hopes for. He studied the piece again carefully, analyzing the stretchiness of it. And then quickly tightened just one millimeter on one of the top bolts to stretch that one portion back out again. Satisfied, he sat back and took more photos. He was obsessed with the painting. It was just so good, so stunning. He'd hadn't realized she'd become so big, until he'd seen the artist at a huge installation.

She had created a great big wall painting and was doing an incredible job of taking people from their normal reality, dropping them right into the fantasy world she wanted the observer to experience. He'd watched the artist work, as she painted a doorframe and walls, all the way down, giving it a 3-D effect, as if you could walk right in, and yet into what? And that was the thing that she invited you to play with— into the world beyond, into the world within, into the world that you had yet to explore. He'd spent most of the day there, absolutely enthralled with her work.

And he hadn't been alone. A lot of other people busily worked, standing and staring in surprise, shock, and wonder. He couldn't leave it alone. He'd become obsessed, knowing he had to own a masterpiece himself. Only she didn't sell them—at least not at a price he could afford. But so much life existed in her paintings. So much life force.

He'd painted at her side for a time, but she'd taken off, and he hadn't.

He pondered the idiosyncrasies of fate that left him here in this dreary hidden space, while she was queen of the art world.

When he realized he'd never own a Cayce masterpiece, he'd become inspired to pick up his paintbrush again. He'd been an artist for years. Surely he could copy her work. Make something so similar that he'd be happy. But it hadn't happened yet. Those failures had fueled his determination to not only own one of hers—now something he'd succeeded in, even if it was only a tiny piece of Cayce's art—but it was here beside him for him to copy, so he could become the king of the art world.

Through his phone he heard his mother yell out.

"You were supposed to bring me milk for my tea," she said in that querulous voice.

"I did bring you milk, Mom," he said ever patiently. "I brought it to you yesterday, and I brought it to you again today."

"Well, I'm out," she said, in that sad voice, denying the evidence in front of them, which she couldn't remember anything.

"Open the fridge, and you'll see the milk in the left-hand door."

He heard her shuffling across the room, heading to the

fridge, and the small *click* that said she had opened it.

"Oh, you're such a good boy," she said. "The milk is here. I just didn't realize you came and went without stopping to visit."

He closed his eyes, pinched the bridge of his nose. "Mom, I came and had lunch with you."

"Are you coming today?"

He looked over at the clock and frowned. "If I do, it'll be late."

"That's okay," she said in delight. Her words were followed by the *click* of the phone.

It made him really sad to think of the bright fresh mind of his mother, now reduced to an old lady who couldn't even remember if he'd brought in the milk. He knew he wasn't alone in this scenario, and he knew that maybe a good son would have brought his mother in to live with him. But no way he could. No way she'd understand the obsession with his artwork.

He stepped back from the piece he'd been working on, moved the canvas under the lights, nodded, and set up his own easel. People had been capturing and imitating the great artists of the world since time began. He was determined to do the same with the work of Cayce Matlock. The woman was a genius. If he could just figure out how to capture that very essence that made her paintings so special.

He picked up the paintbrush and made his first stroke.

CHAPTER 2

C AYCE SAT ON the bench in the police station. She kept checking her watch because, damn it, her appointment was twenty-five minutes ago. She understood that they considered themselves busy, and this was important, but she was the one who just had to wait. In her world, she had things to do too, and twenty-five minutes late was unacceptable. She shuffled once again on the hard bench seat. She looked up for the tenth or thirtieth time and searched around her. She swore she was being watched, but she couldn't see anyone. Finally she pulled out her phone again and checked the time yet once more, groaned, and sat back. She'd already told her assistant she would be late. She just hadn't realized how late.

"Cayce Matlock?"

She looked up to see the detective, Richard Henderson, staring at her. She bounced to her feet and frowned at him. "How long will this take? I'm already late."

He gave her a slight tilt of his head, his gaze hard and assessing. He motioned for her to follow him. She was okay to do that but wished she knew what this was all about. She was led into a small interview room.

He motioned at a chair on the opposite side of the table and said, "Please, take a seat."

She sat down, dropped her oversize purse on the floor

beside her with a *thunk*, put her folded hands on the table, and said, "I hope this won't take long, Detective. I'm really late."

"It'll take as long as it takes," he said in a mild tone of voice, as he opened up a file folder in front of her.

The flash of a photograph before her had her breath catching in the back of her throat as she stared at it. She snatched the headless picture, just a torso shot, her other hand covering her mouth in shock. "Oh, my God," she whispered. "Is this Elena? Is this what he did to her? He ruthlessly hacked away at her body like that?"

He looked at her, then down at the picture, and she shook her head wordlessly. Tears flowed down her cheeks. He grabbed a tissue box she hadn't seen and switched out the photograph for the box. She quickly plucked several from the package and covered her eyes with them, as the tears flowed in an incessant stream.

When she finally regained her voice, she asked bitterly, "Did you do that purely for shock value?" She closed her eyes again, more tears flowing, trying to stop them with tissues again. "She was my best friend, you know?" When she had dabbed her eyes enough, she looked up, catching just a hint of regret on his face as he stared down at the photograph.

She sniffled, wiping her nose, still taking short, halting breaths. "Did he mutilate her back too?"

Richard frowned.

"The painting continues on her back."

Richard shook his head. "How did you identify her?" he asked quietly.

She swallowed hard, clenched her fist around the tissues, then reached for the photograph again. "See this portion here? He didn't take all of it. At the collarbone it's much harder to paint. I have to take a lot of extra care when we get close to the surface of the bone because the light hits it differently as she moves." She pointed out the deep purple color still along the top.

"I know it's probably an impossible thing to ask, but is there any way to know if that color was changed or altered in any way?"

"You mean, other than the fact that it's been brutally and haphazardly cut off?" She stared at him suspiciously.

He nodded. "We need to know anything that might help make sense of this."

"My best friend was skinned by some crazed hack," she said softly. "There is no making sense of this."

"No," he said, "but there's a reason. It made sense to somebody."

"A psycho," she said immediately.

"That's because, in your mind, you can't see any real value to skinning somebody, I presume."

"I'm sure there are cultures where it's done for either reasons of tradition or revenge," she said, "but no."

"We do it to animals all the time," he said mildly.

She raised her head in shock, looked at him, saw the note in his gaze, but couldn't pin a description to it. Then she glared at him. "Is that some kind of a joke?"

"It's not," he said, "but, of course, we have to consider cases in the past where people have tanned the hides of people. Turning them into atrocities, like little purses and things."

She could feel the bile rising up in the back of her throat at his words, her right hand instinctively going there. It was hard to consider.

"Don't pass out on me," he snapped at her.

She swallowed, blinked rapidly, pushed back her chair, and dropped her head into her hands. Just the thought of somebody doing something like that to such a beautiful and vibrant woman like Elena made Cayce want to scream and rail at the world.

"Why do you paint?"

Stunned at the question, she turned to look at him and asked, "Pardon?"

"I asked, why you paint?"

"Because I'm an artist," she snapped. "Is that really the question you wanted to ask me?"

A ghost of a smile appeared as he shook his head, picked up a pad of paper, and said, "No, you're right. We do have specific questions. So tell me. When did you last see her?"

"At the installation. I already told you that."

"And how long was she there with you?"

"We'd been working all day," she said. "The show opened at seven o'clock in the evening."

"So she was there from seven until when?"

Cayce had to stop, took several deep breaths, corralled her brain cells that were already firing off in a million different directions, most of them in horror. "I think she was there until ten. And then I'm not so sure. At ten she walked around, separated herself from the installation, and became a moving art piece."

"What does that mean?"

She groaned. "One of the things that I do a little differently at times," she said, "is I paint the installation behind her, then I paint her, but this time I carried the image all around to the back, so, when she walks, she's covered."

He stared at her. "Covered?" he asked delicately.

She glared at him. "It's a very intimate process. It's a

very intimate job. Elena felt naked if she wasn't 100 percent painted, especially if she was expected to walk around and to visit with people."

"Being covered by paint is hardly being covered," he said.

"It's covered enough," she said with a sigh and sat back. "Look. Each model feels a very different way about being painted. For Elena, as long as it wasn't her bare skin, she wasn't nude. So, when I knew that she would be walking around, and not just going home afterward, I made sure that her back was fully covered as well."

"And is that normal?"

She shook her head. "No, not at all. A lot of artists don't want to use any more paint than they have to, and, to a lot of the models, the special artistic ones, it's like that two-sided part of their personality, as in, the front is covered, and the back is not. It shows the two sides to who they are."

"So, they're exhibitionists?"

"That's a judgment call, Detective," she said tiredly, as she pressed her fingers through her long strands of blond hair. "Elena was not an exhibitionist."

"She appeared nude in all kinds of art pieces for you," he said. "How is that not being an exhibitionist?"

"She's an artist."

"You're the artist," he corrected.

She shook her head. "I am the artist, but to say that the model isn't also an artist would be to minimize what their role is."

"I don't get it," he said, shoving back his own chair slightly. "What does the model do except be still?"

"Sure, being still is one thing," she said, "but consider the fact that she has to be still for hours, that she has to maintain the exact same position, and that she has to find that same position again, no matter what. She has to hold it. She has to know which muscles to engage, which facial expressions she was in, in order to regain that exact same look."

"And can they hold it for hours?"

"Yes," she said. "Every hour, or every couple hours, we give them a break, but we definitely keep it going."

"And you have to paint the models for hours too?"

"Depends on how complex the installation, yes, but what I'll often do is I'll paint, say, her legs, and then I'll do something else, so she can walk around and take a break. Or I'll paint her torso and carry on. I do the last layer when she's in place, in position, and I tune her right into the background painting itself."

"So, she's a part of the bigger masterpiece, is that it?"

"Yes."

"Isn't this about hiding? Isn't this about not seeing what we're seeing?"

She stared at him thoughtfully. "You mean, body-painting?"

He nodded slowly. "I'm trying to understand the mind of the killer."

She winced at that, her gaze darting to the photo and back again. "I so wish we didn't have to," she said sadly.

"But that's not helpful," he said. "This person has taken the life of somebody you care about. But the why of it is what I need to know."

"I have no idea," she said.

Then realizing she hadn't answered his other question, she took a deep breath and said, "I don't think this body-painting artwork is about hiding anything. I think it's about making you look deeper."

He stared at her for a long moment, then slowly nodded. "Do you think maybe somebody looked deeper and found something they liked?"

"Obviously." The tears choked her again. "Why don't we get off those kinds of questions before I start bawling again?" she asked. "Can you ask the rest of your questions, so that I can leave?"

"Yes," he said. "I have some information that I need to confirm."

They went through some of the basics in her world. Quickly they ran through Elena's address, phone number, and circle of friends, which was so vast that she shook her head at that one. "Elena was a butterfly. She had a lot of social connections. A lot of people wanted to be in with a model, especially Elena. She had a lot of surface relationships, but I'm not sure that she had very many intense, deep ones."

"Other than you?" He hesitated before continuing, "Just how deep was your relationship?"

She stared at him for a long moment. "If you're asking if we were lovers, the answer is no. But did I love her? Yes. I loved her like a sister. I loved her like an inspiration." She hesitated, not quite sure how to make him understand. "The thing is, an artist has something inside them that helps to keep them inspired. Elena was that person for me."

"And was your love maybe a little more than just platonic?"

"Absolutely not." She smiled. "Elena loved men. But again, she was that social butterfly. She would have a relationship, and she would leave. She would slide into somebody's life and leave. Unfortunately she left a trail of broken hearts." She understood he didn't like hearing that. "She was light," she said, trying to explain it. "She was a good soul."

At that wording, he froze, slowly raised his gaze, and looked at her. "Interesting wording."

"No, she came from the heart. Everything Elena did was to help bring light and laughter to the world," she said sadly. "And, if you can't understand that, I'm sorry."

"I understand very well," he said. "Unfortunately."

RICHARD WALKED OUT of the hallway door and into the lobby, watching Cayce as she strode away, her tall, lean frame moving rapidly, as if she couldn't get away fast enough. He understood that, for it was a reaction he saw again and again with suspects. Though she wasn't really high on his suspect list, except that, in her own words, she had loved the victim. Who knew exactly what had been behind that love?

He'd asked her about a few of her own relationships, but there hadn't been anything major or recent, according to her. Now, if only he had somebody else to confirm that. That just meant losing Elena was all the more heartbreaking, if she'd been the main friendship in Cayce's world, but it didn't answer the question of whether Cayce had had a hand in Elena's murder. Being within a masterpiece, maybe Elena had done something to ruin it. Maybe she'd upset the artist somehow, or maybe she had done something with somebody else, gone to another artist?

More questions to ask Cayce.

She had disappeared from sight now, but he pulled out his phone and quickly called her. "Did Elena model for anybody else?"

"Yes," Cayce said, on the other end. "Several people."

"Email me that list," he said in an urgent tone. "I need to contact them as soon as possible."

"As soon as I get back to the office," she said in a resigned tone, "I'll send it to you."

"And, if you think of anything else, of anybody who might have had something to do with this, let me know."

"That's your job, Detective," she said. "I'm a busy person too."

"Unless, of course, there is some reason why you don't want to help the police," he said, his voice hard. He walked outside the police station, his gaze quickly scanning the crowds, moving rapidly up and down the streets.

She groaned. "If I don't cooperate, I'll look suspicious, and, if I do cooperate, I have to keep reliving everything to do with my friend's death."

"Yep, that's about the way it works," he said. "Deal with it or don't. But I'm not going away until I solve this."

"Nobody wants you to solve this more than I do, Detective," she said.

"Then prove it," he snapped. He hung up the phone, walked across the street to a food vendor, and checked out the huge pretzels they had. He smiled, reached for one, and said, "How much are these?"

"Two bucks."

He quickly paid him. It was wrapped up with a paper napkin because it was still quite warm, and Richard stood here, studying the gray morning. Seattle was many things, but it typically wasn't exactly a bright blue sunny day. It was gray, cloudy, and threatening to rain. Just like yesterday.

This new case was bothersome. Something about it was

wrong on so many levels. And not just about the skinning.

When his phone buzzed, he looked down to see a text from one of his team, saying they were pulling the next meeting ahead twenty minutes and asked if he could be there.

He messaged back, saying he was on his way. With half a sigh at the crazy dark world around him, he headed back inside. He needed to find answers, and he needed to find them soon. They'd already missed the crucial twenty-four-hour window. Hell, he had already missed the forty-eight-hour window as well.

CHAPTER 3

C AYCE RETURNED TO her gallery, deeper within, toward her small dingy office that she deliberately kept cramped and crowded, in order to force herself in and out as quickly as possible, so that she could go paint again.

As she walked in, her assistant looked up with her eyes full of tears. She got up from her desk and came racing over, throwing her arms around her. Cayce wasn't terribly demonstrative, but, if she understood one thing, it was grief. She hadn't allowed herself to feel the pain of losing her friend yet, and it hurt her already to know how many other people would be affected.

"I can't believe what they're saying. Please tell me that it's wrong."

"It's not wrong," she said sadly. "Elena is dead."

"But not just dead." Anita stepped back, tears pulling the mascara all the way down her cheeks, like streaks of rain on a windshield. "But murdered, skinned apparently," she snapped.

"Where did you hear that?" she asked.

"The news."

She frowned at Anita. "The news shouldn't have had those details."

"Well, you know what the news is like," she said. "It's a cutthroat business."

"That may be, but that doesn't mean they couldn't pass on rumors."

At that, Anita gasped, stepping back. "Do you think they're wrong then?"

"No," she said. "They're not wrong at all. But we don't want to keep spreading that information for shock's sake."

Anita nodded and smiled. "We need to do something to memorialize her."

That thought alone caught Cayce in the back of her throat, because, of all the things, that was the hardest about Elena's death, the fact that somebody had taken her skin, and they'd already planned to memorialize her in a way nobody else would understand. "If you want to come up with some ideas," she said, "I'm in." She reached up and rubbed her face.

"Oh, my God, did you get any sleep last night?"

She shook her head. "No, it was a pretty rough night."

"I heard Naomi was pretty blasé about the whole thing."

In defense of the replacement model, Cayce shrugged and said, "We were at an installation, and she was doing a job when we found out. She was definitely calmer than I was."

"I am surprised she wasn't cheering at the news," Anita said with a waspish tone. "That would be more in character."

Naomi was a very different kettle of fish in terms of personality. Where Elena had been lightness, sunshine, and butterflies, Naomi was darkness, storms, and shadows. She had a graspy greediness to her. But she'd never been a top model, and she was trying to gain in rank. With Elena's position now open, it gave Naomi another spot to climb into. And that made Cayce frown. Was that a motive for murder?

Cayce made her way back to her small crowded office in her gallery, wondering if that attitude put Naomi on the detective's watchlist. Or if Cayce should add Naomi to his list if it hadn't. Somehow that felt completely wrong too. As if she were betraying the other model. She shook her head and decided that it was definitely not a road she needed to go down.

As soon as she sat down at her desk, her phone rang. She groaned as she realized business intruded into her day once again. The problem with being an artist was the fact that she didn't get to be an artist all the time. The business aspect remained there always; people who wanted things from her, that she didn't always want to give. But, since they provided the avenue for her to make a living with her artwork, she was forced to deal with them. It sucked big-time.

She lifted her head a little while later and wasn't at all surprised to find that two hours had passed.

Just then Anita popped her head around the corner. "Hey, how you doing?"

She shrugged. "Doing. Whatever that means," she said, "but everything is going ahead for next week's installation."

Anita's face broke out into a smile. "They finally went through with it?"

She nodded and returned the smile. "Yeah, they just returned the signed contract."

"Yeah, right at the last minute of course," she snapped, shaking her head. "Good God."

"I know, but, hey, … it's work, right?"

"The trouble is," Anita said, "that's really tight. Do we have enough paint?"

"That's what I'm about to find out," she said. "Plus that installation design was done with Elena in mind."

Anita's eyes immediately filled with tears. "Wow," she said. "She will really be missed."

"In many ways," she said. "I don't even know how to express what her absence will mean."

"But we can do this."

"We can," she said with a smile, "but I'm not sure I want Naomi in this one."

"Who are you thinking then?"

Cayce sat back and thought about the models that she'd used recently. "Why don't we see if Candy is available? But I'll want the hair gone right off."

"Skullcap?"

"I can't paint that either," she said, frowning. She tapped her pen on the desk. "Unless we can find a way to make her hair fly out off to the side."

"Part of the wind, you mean?"

"Something like that. Leave it with me while I figure it out."

"That's fine," Anita said, "but you have a whole twenty minutes to figure it out."

She glared at her, then snapped, "You're wasting my twenty minutes."

Anita chuckled and left.

"And put on some damn coffee," Cayce yelled behind her.

"Will do," she said.

With that, Cayce went back to looking at the diagram for next week's installation, wondering which model she needed. She could try somebody new. It would certainly be a way to go forward after Elena. Cayce had seen an interesting model a few days ago.

She quickly went through a portfolio that she kept on

various models. *This one.* Her name was Hartley, which was unusual in itself, but her looks were even more unusual, with a very angular jawbone, angular cheekbones. Somewhat masculine, but not quite. Determined maybe. Cayce didn't have any problem with determination. That was a requirement of life.

"THE BITCH IS gone," the woman cried out, dancing and laughing through her apartment. "A spot opened above me," she said with a chuckle. "Who knew?" She stopped, looking at herself in the mirror, then smiled, reached a hand through her long luxurious black locks, and said, "I'll make it to the top! Yeah!"

Behind her, her best friend and coconspirator, even though he had no clue, Derek called out, "You know what happens to people at the top?" he asked.

"They fall," she said, "but that's got nothing to do with me."

"You keep saying that," he said, "but it really is something you need to keep an eye on."

"Well, I didn't kill her," she snapped.

"Of course not. That would be too easy."

She turned and glared at him.

"You're just happy she's gone."

"Well, of course I am," she said. "Why wouldn't I be?"

"Well, you could be a little more conservative in your joy."

"Yeah, that's not happening," she said with a laugh.

He sighed. "I'm heading out with Benjamin soon. Are you coming with us for breakfast?"

She looked over at her friend, then smiled and said,

"Sweetie, you go eat. I'm eating on the fruits of my emotions right now."

"Those are the emotions," he said, "that will choke you."

"They can try," she said, "but, honest to God, I'm just too happy to be worried about it right now."

He frowned, nodded, and said, "Yeah, and that's a little disturbing too."

"You know exactly who and what I am," she said with a smile.

He nodded. "I know that," he said. "You've never been anything but what you've appeared to be."

"So stop being so glum about it."

"I'm not." He straightened his tall slim frame, dressed in a beautiful three-piece gray suit.

He always looked elegant, never a hair out of place. She was a little more on the rough-and-tumble side and had to work out to look like he did, but his look was effortless. He was that role model ahead of her on her path, who made her just want to be him, only in female form.

He gave her a gentle hug and said, "Stop for a moment and just enjoy living instead of always conniving for your next step."

She smiled, kissed him gently on the cheek, and said, "You go meet Benjamin for breakfast and enjoy."

He nodded, and, as he headed to the front door, he turned and looked at her. "Don't let other people know how you feel, right?"

"Of course not," she said. "I'm not that stupid."

He nodded, and, though he was obviously a little worried, he headed out the front door.

She could hear his footsteps as his long, lean legs ate up the yards. Something about Derek almost set her teeth on edge. They'd known each other since they'd been little kids, and he'd been warning her about her scheming ever since.

She'd often asked him, "Why are you even friends with me?" His response had shocked her the first time, and now she feared it was just a joke because he kept saying it was his job to keep her on the straight and narrow.

She often told him how he was failing terribly on the job. He would nod and say he was, indeed. But he was working on it. She didn't understand half of what he said, and Benjamin appeared to be just the same. But Benjamin couldn't stand her, and she couldn't stand him, which just added to their animosity. The fact was, her longtime friend had somebody in his life who was the polar opposite of her. Again it made her wonder why she and Derek were even friends.

Benjamin was another one of those well-dressed, smooth, clean, always perfect-looking guys, but the difference between the two men was obvious. She couldn't stand the one. Now Derek had often told her that she had a serious case of jealousy and that he would be her friend no matter what. But she'd already seen a change in his attitude, a change in his affection, and a change in the amount of time he spent with her and his willingness to talk with her.

She knew Derek was tired of listening to them fight, but it didn't matter to her because anything she could do to keep that asshole away from Derek would be good for her. Yet she already knew that she couldn't do it directly; otherwise Derek would turn on her. Hence her wanting to send him off to have breakfast with his lover.

Why the two of them didn't live together, she had no idea. But that only helped her out, as she was the one who had crashed at Derek's place last night. She needed an alibi, and she needed what he could give her—that little bit of stability. Which was often.

She needed her wits about her for what was happening next. She somehow had to maneuver herself into a position to take over the modeling world.

She had no intention of being a body model for long, but, for now, it provided an excellent opportunity for everybody to check out her personal assets and to make sure they were in prime condition for whatever was needed next.

One of the clothing designers she'd really admired had told Naomi that she was too heavily endowed. She'd been horrified, but he had refused to let her wear any of his creations on the runway. Heartbroken, she had seriously considered getting her breasts reduced, but Derek had stopped her, saying she'd been given that beautiful body, and it just wasn't the right market for her to show her wares.

She had agreed, then promptly did her best to disrespect the designer. She carefully started rumors that caused the designer to break up with his current lover in a most unbecoming public display causing the designer to be removed from the current fashion show, and she realized just how much power she had. Since then he had bounced back, but she didn't care. She had made her point. And, just in case he hadn't understood that she had done it, she'd sent him a little note saying, *Thanks for nothing, from Well-Endowed.*

She didn't know if he would recognize that as being her because he saw so many models all the time. But it had given her that sense of satisfaction nonetheless. Still, she didn't want to go too far. Not only did she not want Derek to know what she was up to, but she also didn't want anybody else to know either because that would impact her ability to model. And that would never happen, if she could help it.

She reached for her bottled water and her morning meds.

"Pretty soon," she said to the empty room, as she popped two of the pills that she needed. "Pretty damn soon."

"HOW IS THE case going?" Andy asked, standing beside Richard. "Any new leads?"

"No," he snapped. "You?"

Andy shook his head. "No, I've just come back from setting up witness interviews for everybody who was there at the end of the evening. Unfortunately, well over two hundred attended. So that's a lot of phone calls. I can't get hold of about sixty of them, and we don't have names for a bunch of them."

"There was a guest list," he said, looking at Andy in surprise.

"And apparently a lot of the guests brought guests," he said.

"Are they talking?"

"No, and they're not only not talking but, in many cases, they're saying stuff like, 'You know? It was just a friend of a friend.'"

"Great," he said. "That's not helpful."

"No, it's not. What did you find out?"

"Only that Elena was there as part of the installation, and, when she stepped away, the guests were all shocked to realize that the painting continued on her backside. She had been painted all the way around. But those who knew Cayce's work said it was fairly common in some cases. I don't think any of them realized it was only common in

Elena's case."

"Was Elena with anybody?" Andy asked.

"She had several glasses of wine and enjoyed mingling and talking with various people," he said, "but she didn't appear to be *with* anyone."

"Did she leave alone?"

"She called a cab and stepped out as soon as the cab pulled up."

"Anybody see her get in the cab?"

"Apparently somebody pulled up, who she must have known, and offered her a ride instead."

"So, we don't have an actual cab that delivered her anywhere?"

"No, but I did track down the cabbie," Richard noted. "He said that he had been called for the fare, but then she gave him a twenty and told him that she had another ride."

"Shit," Andy said. "So we still don't know who she left with. No video cameras?"

"Tons of them," Richard said. "Steven is running through them right now." He groaned and sat back. "I'm about to reach out to some of her other friends again."

"Nobody answering?"

"Either not home, not at work, or not answering."

"Are they ghosting you?"

"It's possible," Richard said, "but deliberate? I don't know." Just then his phone rang. He picked it up and said, "Detective Richard Henderson here."

"You've left several messages on my phone," a tired male voice said. "I'm Mr. Johnson. What can I do for you, Detective?"

"Have you heard about Elena?"

After an awkward silence at the other end, Mr. Johnson

spoke, his voice hoarse from tears. "Yes, that's why I haven't been taking calls. I was very good friends with her."

At that, Richard launched into his list of questions.

"No, I didn't see her that night at the installation."

"Why not? Wasn't it a big deal for your friend?"

"Of course, and I was delighted for her, but I've been to many, many of them, and that night I wasn't feeling well."

"When did you hear from her last?"

"Just before the installation. I sent her a good luck text."

"When did you hear the news?"

"Through the news media yesterday," Mr. Johnson said, and then he broke off to clear his throat. "There's no good way to hear it, but a personal message would have been better. A lot better. Hearing it like that was … horrible."

"It's taken us some time to track down who she was close to in her world, and we still haven't found any family members. Does that sound right?"

"She didn't have any family that she was close to," Mr. Johnson replied.

"Well, I'm sorry you had to hear it that way. It shouldn't have gone to the media until the family was notified, or at least not until the next day anyway," he said.

"I think her father lives in Switzerland," he said sadly. "They didn't have anything to do with each other."

"Siblings?"

"No."

"Mother?"

"She took off when Elena was just a child."

"Do you know her name?"

"No. I don't think I've ever heard it mentioned."

He provided the father's name. No location other than Switzerland, but it was a start. "What about other friends?"

"Well, there's her artist friend, Cayce, of course, and Elena had several other modeling friends." He provided those names as well. "And one of them was a male."

Richard studied that male name and circled it. "Do all these people do the same kind of modeling, the body modeling?"

"They all do all kinds of modeling," the man said. "I used to do body modeling myself."

"Under your current name of Johnson?"

"Yes. I used to model as Joe Johnson. And, yes, that's my number you called," Joe said drily.

Richard made a mental note, jotting that down. "Was there ever anything creepy about this body modeling?"

"Any time you take your clothes off for art," he said, "it depends on how the artist presents it. Cayce is always very, very clear about a celebration of the human body, looking within, looking deep within to her art, in order to see what it was. It isn't just a gimmick for her."

"A gimmick?"

"Yeah. Her art involves almost like a trick of the eyes, you know? A trick with the lighting or an optical illusion somehow. That kind of stuff. But she's done installations where she had multiple models, and nobody knew until they moved."

"That takes some talent."

"Cayce is extremely talented," Joe said.

"Is there any reason to think she might have had something to do with Elena's death?"

A gasp of shock came, then silence at the other end. "No. I can't imagine that there would be. No."

"A falling-out among friends, a business relationship gone bad?"

"No, not at all," Joe said, his voice much stronger. "You're barking up the wrong tree there."

"Do you know of anyone Elena was afraid of, ex-boyfriends or anything?"

"She's had a lot of boyfriends," Joe said. "But it's not—I can't even call them boyfriends really. She was somebody who made friends easily. She loved and lost just as fast."

"Cayce called her a butterfly."

"That describes Elena exactly," Joe said sadly. "She flitted through life, adding a little bit of light and love everywhere, every time."

"Do you think anybody would have wanted to kill her over a relationship like that?"

"Everybody wanted more from her," he said instantly. "And that was the thing about her. She was light itself. The kind of light you can never hold on to. It slipped right through your fingers. You want it, but you can't hold on to it. So, anybody who thought that they could touch her and keep her was heading into any relationship with Elena in the wrong way."

"Does anybody come to mind who may have wanted to do something like that?"

"She's had trouble with two men in the last year," he said instantly. "The guys were best friends. She went out with the one, who then told his friend about what a great time he'd had, so the second friend worked it, and Elena decided to give him a run. After that, the two friends hated each other and constantly vied for her attention."

"That doesn't sound like a good dating system," he said.

"No, not at all," Joe said with a chuckle. "The thing is, in her case, I don't think she did it for anything but fun, but it ended up ruining a long-term friendship, and both of the men never quite let it go."

"Okay, and who were these guys?" Richard asked.

"One is Eric Cross and the other …" His voice trailed off. "Hang on. I'll think of it. Um, … it's … Gerard. Yeah, Gerard, but I don't know his last name. Oh maybe Bagota."

"That's good enough," he said. "I'm sure we can get it from Eric."

"I probably have Eric's phone number too."

"And how do you know him?"

"We used to be buds."

"Until?"

"Until he slept with Elena and wanted to use me to get to her."

"Sounds like she spawned some really deep emotions."

"Absolutely," Joe said. "And that's not necessarily a good thing."

"Got it," Richard said. "I need you to think about the friends, the circumstances, anybody in Elena's life over the last year who might have a reason to kill her or who might have wanted to take her out in revenge."

"It's a competitive business," Joe said. "It's one of the reasons I left it."

"In what way?"

"People like Cayce, they can put your name on the map. So Elena was considered one of the best because she was Cayce's personal model of choice."

"So anybody else who worked for her, then what?"

"Well, that's the question, isn't it? Anybody else who works for Cayce now has an opportunity to move up."

"What about a model named Naomi?"

"She's okay, but she aggressively wants to climb the ladder."

"I met her. She was working with Cayce."

"Yeah. She's been doing a little more, trying to get higher up."

"But does that not give her the same cachet?"

"Not necessarily, no," he said. "It depends on how often Cayce uses her. Whoever Cayce chooses to replace Elena with now will determine the repositioning within the modeling world."

"What if Cayce chooses somebody completely different?"

"If she's smart, she will," Joe said. "Like pluck up a brand-new talent, make all those old ones go away."

"Why would that be the smart thing?"

"Because they will all fight now, and, if Cayce didn't use them before, she won't want to use them now."

"That makes some sense." After ascertaining that Joe was with people the night Elena went missing, and the following morning, having slept over with a partner himself, getting names and contact information for them, Richard said, "But, like I said, if you think of anything else or anybody else, anybody who might want to do this or who held some sort of grudge or ill will, please contact me."

"Will do. Oh hang on, here's the other number. I just found it."

After he hung up, Richard looked over to see Andy sitting at his desk beside him, pondering cell phone records. "Anything there?" he asked his partner, as he wrote down the two men's phone numbers on his calendar to call as soon as possible. Then dialed the first one as he listened to Andy.

"A lot of hang-ups," Andy said.

"Meaning, they called, and Elena didn't answer?"

"In the beginning, she answered. We've got calls lasting

ten seconds, fifteen seconds, and then she didn't bother answering."

"How many calls after that?"

"Another five, ten, fifteen," he said, counting off the sheet.

"Those are fairly determined hang-ups," Richard said.

"Absolutely, but I'm not getting any trace on the phone number."

"It'll be a burner phone," Richard said. Just then a man answered the number he was calling. "Eric Cross?"

"Yeah, who's calling?"

"Detective Richard Henderson."

"Damn, this is about Elena, isn't it?"

"Sure is." Richard then proceeded to ask him similar questions to the ones he'd asked Joe.

"I haven't seen her in forever. I wish I had, but I had one night with her, and that was it," Eric said wistfully. "I'd have done anything for her."

"Including kill her?"

The shocked silence was followed by a blast of "*Noooo.* Never. I loved her." And, with that, he burst into tears and hung up.

Richard groaned. It was always rough dealing with those left behind to suffer through the aftermath of death. And murder made it that much harder on everyone. He looked at Andy, even as Richard dialed the second number. "Have they cleared her apartment yet?"

"Yes. You want to head over there?"

"Yeah, I do. I was there once, but they were already working on it."

"That's because George got there ahead of you."

Richard stifled the words threatening to jump from his

mouth. George was part of the team but liked to think he was the lead on all cases.

"And don't forget. George had just come off a couple heavy cases. He charged in the same as you and I would, if we had been there."

"I know," Richard said in exasperation. "I just wanted to be first on scene." He lifted his phone as a voice answered. He identified himself and explained the call. The response was almost identical to Eric's, just without the tears.

"You have to understand, Detective," Gerard said in a whisper. "Everyone wanted to be with her. I can't imagine killing someone like that. The world is a much darker place today."

As soon as he hung up from the call, Richard said to Andy, "Let's go. Getting out for a bit will help clear my head."

The two men hopped up, grabbed their phones and keys. Andy smiled. "I'll drive."

The two of them joked and laughed as they headed to Andy's small pickup truck. As Richard climbed into the front seat, he looked around. "Why do you even keep this thing? It's not much bigger than a can opener."

"That's not the point," Andy said cheerfully. "It's my rig. And I like it."

"Only because you're not as tall as I am," Richard retorted, as he shifted so his head didn't bang the ceiling.

They drove the short distance to Elena's apartment and got out to find she had one of the converted artist lofts down in the commercial district.

"Wow," Andy said, as he stood outside. "I've always wanted to go into one of these."

"Exactly. This is our chance."

Laughing, the two of them headed in. Using the manager, they got into her apartment, closing the door nicely in his face. Richard turned to look around and whistled. The loft had a soaring double-height ceiling, with a loft section off to the right, long lights hanging down low, big exposed rafters in the ceiling. "I wonder what it's like to heat this place."

"I doubt it's that bad," Andy said, "because every one of these places are sold as soon as they become available."

"And that just brings up another question," Richard said. "We've seen murders done for less, but what are the chances that somebody wanted this loft?"

Andy looked at him, pulled a notebook from his pocket, and said, "You know what? Unfortunately that's just all too possible. These things are expensive, and it's quite a bit more to get them in the first place. But they turn over instantly as soon as anybody has one free."

"Well, guess what?" Richard said. "One is about to come free."

"And, if it doesn't, we need to find out who stands to inherit."

"Yeah, if it isn't a lover who gets to gain." As he stood and looked around at the beautiful white and silver high-end loft, Richard realized that this model wasn't just a model but she was also wealthy. "Do you think these body models make this kind of money?"

"I was just thinking that," Andy said. "This has got to be worth what, a million?"

"But it's also decked out to be worth like a million and a half," he said. "You don't see anything quite like this everywhere. I thought these were working people."

"But then it goes along with what Joe Johnson told you, about how working for the high-end artists could put these models on the map. In this case, apparently that artist is Cayce."

"So what would somebody do in order to make sure they got to work with Cayce? And they can't work until there's a spot?"

"Which brings us back to that whole point of this maybe being all about competition."

"Let's take a look."

They headed to her bedroom. If there was ever a place to find out what really went on in a person's life, it was in the bedroom.

CHAPTER 4

C AYCE HAD BEEN working three hours already. She had this massive, expansive wall—twenty by sixty feet. It wasn't that she particularly liked this size, but it was something she was certainly capable of doing. She put the roller back down and relaxed her shoulders, rotating them and her neck to ease up the tension. She had a base color on the back wall, and she had the sky with the clouds working in. She was doing the foreground in this one, and that was tougher—a fantasy forest winter design.

"That's quite a job," a man said behind her.

Cayce stiffened, then turned to look at Detective Richard Henderson. "Are you back to bug me some more?"

"Do I bug you?"

She narrowed her gaze at him. "What do you want?"

"I have a few more questions," he said. He looked at the many trays of paint all around her. "Good Lord," he said. "Are you really doing this whole wall?"

She shrugged her shoulders several times, again feeling her muscles cramp. "Yes, and I have to do the background first, before I start doing any of the fine detail."

"And how long does something like this stay up?"

"Weeks, months sometimes," she said. She walked to where she'd placed her coffee, realizing it was lukewarm at best right now. She took a big slug, nearly spitting it out.

"Back to the questions, Detective," she said pointedly.

She was caught by the way the light played along his cheekbones. Just the way he stood there. She moved a little to the left, so she could take a look at him from a different angle. Her mind immediately filled in all the details of this man and realized he had unforgettable features. But, of course, that sent her mind spinning, only to wonder what the rest of him looked like. Just from a model's perspective, she assured herself.

He frowned at her. "What are you looking at?"

"Your cheekbones," she said bluntly. His eyebrows shot up, and she grinned. "I *am* an artist."

He shrugged uncomfortably and said, "Well, I won't be part of your installations anytime soon."

She nodded, smiled, and said, "That's fine too, considering you weren't invited anyway. So, questions?"

He glared at her. "Joe Johnson."

"Good model," she said instantly. "I really like him."

"Personally?"

"No," she said. "Not personally. But he's a very good model. He could hold the position and stand for a long time, but he wasn't cut out for the actual cutthroat part of the business."

"Isn't that a little hard to believe?"

"Every business is cutthroat, if somebody stands to gain a ton of money," she said. "There are always markers that define success, fame, or wealth. But knowing that your face will be on every magazine is a thrill for a lot of people."

"True," he said, "and Joe wasn't cut out for it?"

"No, not at all," she said. "But that didn't stop him from being damn good at what he did."

"Would you use him again, if you had a chance?"

"I don't body-paint men very often," she said, "but, yes, I would."

"And did Elena have anything to do with him?"

"You'd have to ask him," she said. Cayce hated talking about her friends, particularly the ones who were no longer here to answer any questions.

"We have to pry into Elena's life," he said gently. "Somebody took it from her. No way I'll let that happen to anybody else."

Her eyes widened as she thought about that. She took several steps forward, her voice dropping as she whispered, "Do you think other models are in danger?"

"I don't know," he said. "You tell me. Was this dedicated just to her, or is there something about her that somebody wanted?"

"It depends if they were trying to kill her for revenge," she said, "or if it was because of the masterpiece."

"Why do you keep calling it a masterpiece?"

"Not because I'm an egotist," she snapped, "but because it was a copy of a masterpiece that she was in."

He stopped, stared, and said, "Really?"

She nodded. "A van Gogh."

"Oh, God," he said. "That adds a whole new layer of shit to the case."

She nodded slowly.

"We have to get to the bottom of this and fast. Do you have any other masterpieces coming up?"

She stared at him in horror; then she nodded slowly. "Tomorrow night," she said. "I'm doing one tomorrow night."

He waved at the wall behind her. "This one?"

She shook her head immediately. "No. I'm doing one at

the big art museum," she said. "It's different. We're bringing in the canvases that will be the backdrop, and then the models in the front. So, I'm doing them in pieces."

"Not that I even begin to understand that," he said, "but I'll have some added security on the place."

"You can do that," she said, "but will you look after my model too? I don't want her to turn out to be a second masterpiece for some creep collector who's found something new to collect."

RICHARD HAD INTERVIEWED as many people as he could and had spoken to many others from his share of the list of attendees at Elena's last installation, yet he had a whole lot of nothing. Names, dates, figures, and absolutely none of them were artists themselves, and that concerned him. A lot of them were collectors, but it took an especially unstable mind to want to collect a masterpiece painted onto a woman's body. But he also knew that it gave him insight into the mind of the collector.

He picked up the phone and called a friend of his. "What was the name of that doctor you went to?"

Sarah, on the other end, laughed. "Well, I'm not exactly sure what doctor you're talking about," she said, "because I just had a pap smear done by Dr. Watkins."

"No, no, no," he said hurriedly, and then realized she was laughing at him. He groaned. "You're right. I deserved that," he said. "That doctor dealing with children's issues."

"You're talking about a child psychologist?" she said curiously. "You do remember that I don't have any kids, right?"

"I'm not explaining myself really well," he said, frowning as he stared down at the list. "And maybe that's who I should be talking to—a psychologist. Maybe then I might come to understand this. But it's really weird stuff."

"It depends what you mean by *weird stuff*," she said. "I know you're a cop, and sometimes you have to deal with really strange cases."

"This is quickly becoming the weirdest of all," he said.

"Well, I'm a nurse, but I don't think I have anything to offer you."

"Actually, you do," he said, thrumming his fingers on his desk for a moment. "How hard is it to skin somebody?"

An instant of silence passed on the other end; then she gasped softly. "You're serious, aren't you?"

"Partially," he said. "Only the skin off the torso was taken."

"But not dismembered?"

"No, just that portion of her body was skinned."

"Well, it isn't technically all that difficult," she said. "But to keep it, to preserve it somehow, would be very difficult."

"And, if they were to use something to preserve it, presumably it would damage anything on the surface of it."

"If you're thinking fingerprints, I would assume so, yes." She spoke slowly, as if trying to feel her way through his meaning. "What did you think this psychologist could do for you?"

"I don't know," he said in frustration. "I've done all the legwork I know to do at this point, and I need some insight into who and why somebody would want to do this."

"Sure, but I think I know who you're talking about. She doesn't deal with normal issues."

"This isn't a normal issue," he said drily. "And it's not me who has the problem. It's one of my cases."

"Well, you must have a specialist who you can talk to on staff."

"And I have an appointment with him this afternoon, yes," he said. "Anyway, forget about it. I'll rethink my ideas." And he quickly hung up on her because one of the things that he had wanted to speak to that specialist about went beyond the norm and into what he called the woo-woo factor. He just couldn't remember what her name was.

His phone buzzed. He looked to see a text from Sarah.

Her name is Dr. Maddy. And she does that woo-woo stuff.

He smiled, wrote the name in his notebook, then headed to his appointment with the shrink.

As soon as he explained the case to the department shrink, Dr. Willoughby sat back with a long, slow sigh and said, "Wow."

"I know. A little bit complicated, a little bit off to the left, a whole lot weird, and very, very sad."

"But, at the heart of it all," he said, "it's simple. Somebody wanted something, and he took it. So you've got a collector who knows there's no other way to get this, except to do what he's done. What you don't know is whether he wanted to collect this because he wanted to own it, wanted to stop somebody else from owning it, wanted to potentially duplicate it—"

"You're thinking art forgery?" Richard asked, frowning. "I hadn't considered that."

"I'm not sure it's even viable in this instance. It's just one of the factors that has to be dealt with in the art world."

"But to kill somebody for it?"

"It means that the person, the victim, is no longer human. They've become a piece of art," the shrink explained.

"So, whether they wanted the person to die or not isn't even an issue here. They'd been relegated to an art object, and this is what had to be done in order for that object to be taken."

"So, somebody who's on medication, somebody who is a sociopath and/or psychopath, somebody who doesn't care, and would he likely do this again?"

"Absolutely," Dr. Willoughby said. "Think about it. If it gave him what he wanted, then he'll repeat it. On the other hand, we could be looking at this in a way that is far too complicated. It could just be a serial killer, and that is his souvenir. Maybe he is targeting these models, and that's the souvenir he wants to keep as a reminder of his kill."

"Right," Richard said, sitting back. "I wasn't thinking along that line at all either because I had focused on the artwork."

"Exactly. But, in this case, I'm not sure that's something you can do because, in many cases, we know that they take a souvenir. This just happens to be a big souvenir and a very specialized one."

"Very specialized. So, what are the other options then?"

"Well, it's simple. You're right back down to the psychopath who doesn't care about anybody else's feelings, doesn't care about anybody else and what they want. It's all about what he wants. And really, it doesn't matter if it has anything to do with this individual victim. For all you know, that art piece or souvenir was literally just something that he could look at and remember his victim by."

"That's not helpful."

"Nothing's here that you don't already know," he said. "We've worked on multiple cases for well over a decade. I understand that this one is a little more disturbing."

"Is cannibalism a potential motive?"

"Was any of the underlying flesh gone with the skin?" the psychologist countered. "Or an organ removed?"

Richard shook his head. "No, everything is intact."

"And how clear and concise was the job?"

"Decent," he said, "according to the coroner anyway. Not surgical precision but by someone who was decent with a knife. But he also said, that could be anyone. No training required, just practice."

"And the woman, being a model, was presumably lean. Was the fat left on the skin or left on the torso?"

"The bulk of it was left on the torso, and there wasn't much at all."

"And that's to be expected. What you really have to consider is what does he do with that skin now? It's not something that he can keep easily."

"So freezing is an easy answer, but it won't keep the masterpiece intact, if that's what he wanted."

"Exactly."

The shrink talked a little bit longer, but Richard didn't gain a whole lot here. It's not like he could ask for a profile when they didn't have very much to go on. He'd already checked on similar cases and had come up blank. He'd also done a run on cannibalism and had come up blank. At least not in the last twenty-five years, which, as far as he was concerned, was a *thank God* all the way around. But now he was wondering what else to even check out.

Still musing, he pondered his way back to his desk. When he got there, Andy sat at his desk nearby, frowning.

"We didn't find anything in her apartment," he said, "on our first walk-through, but maybe a second is needed."

Richard nodded. "That was the next thing on my list to go back to. We're so short-staffed right now, it's like we only get halfway into a case. Then we're pulled off to a dozen other cases."

"We did a quick search on her place but not any deeper than that. I'm not sure we need to go back honestly," he said.

"You don't have to come with me," Richard said, "but I want to take another walk-through."

Andy hesitated and said, "Honestly, I should go to Southside and take care of that gas station report. I've got a few more questions to ask the second attendant who came on late."

"You do that," Richard said, reaching for his jacket. "And I'll head over to Elena's apartment again."

"Any idea what you're looking for?"

"No, I just hope I recognize it when I see it."

It took a little longer than he wanted to get out of the police station and over to the loft, but, as he had tons of potential witnesses to contact, her apartment could theoretically wait. Still, something nagged at him. He really wanted to take the time to sort through and make sure they didn't miss anything this time around. As he walked into the loft, he stopped once again, amazed at the light and the airiness. "A prime piece of real estate for sure."

He did another quick walk-through the living room, but not much was here. A coffee table, without drawers. A couple couches but the other guys had already lifted the cushions and looked underneath.

He checked the kitchen—one of those ubercontemporary everything-hidden-away-and-not-on-the-counters kitchens with chrome, gleaming glass, and white wood and walls. He opened all the drawers, but she didn't even have a junk drawer for manuals or where you'd stick things that you didn't know where to put otherwise. A place for all the items that just never seemed to have any regular home in a kitchen. She didn't have a drawer like that.

Frowning, he stopped and looked at the kitchen. "It's almost like it's unused." He frowned, pulling up his records to see when she'd purchased the place, which was about six months ago.

Noting that, he headed into the bathroom, and definitely items were there, but it wasn't full of makeup. It wasn't full of what he would have expected. He had commented on it the last time he was here. Andy had wondered if she had been away or staying with friends or if this was a secondary house.

"We didn't find another piece of property when we did a run on assets, so, if this isn't where she lived full-time, where did she live?" Richard asked out loud to nobody but himself. "We'll need to keep looking at more property. If we could find her Last Will and Testament, that would help."

He opened all the doors and drawers in the bathroom and found feminine products, cleansers, a stack of towels, and spare toilet paper. Nothing, absolutely nothing out of the ordinary.

With that, he headed into the bedroom. And again noted a massive queen-size bed, perfectly set up like at a hotel, with six pillows, as if she were a movie star. Well, she was a model, but did she live this lifestyle? It looked so darn perfect.

He walked into the closet to find clothes, but it wasn't stuffed with clothing. That led credence to the fact that she potentially didn't live here full-time.

Then he stopped, and something hit him. It was almost like the place was staged. Was she planning on selling it?

Had it gotten that far and not gone any farther? He called Cayce. "Elena's apartment is sterile. As if she didn't cook or even sleep here."

"It's the way she liked to live. She was a free spirit in relationships, but she kept her home immaculate."

"So she wasn't planning to sell it? It looks staged."

"No, she was creating and living the life she wanted. That was just her."

After the end of that call, the manager of the building called him. "I have the records you were looking for," he said.

"All her visitors in the last six months?"

"Yes," he said, "and there's a lot."

"Email them to me, please," he said.

"Will do." The manager hung up.

Richard refocused on the bedroom. He checked under the bed, under the mattresses, between the mattresses, behind the headboard, but nothing was out of the ordinary. It was just way too clean.

He checked the night tables, under and around them, but nothing. On the wall were great big paintings, all of herself. And they were stunning. He didn't know who the artists were who had painted her various portraits, but three were very, very similar, and he'd bet his next week's paycheck that they were Cayce's work. He took photos of them and then carefully lifted them off the wall, checking to see if anything was behind them, but again found nothing. Frowning, he went back into the closet and moved the hangers, and, sure enough, he discovered a small hidden cover. He opened that to find a safe. He immediately sent Andy a message and a photo.

We've got to get into that pretty fast, Andy texted

back.

Contact her lawyer, he typed. **See if we can get the combination. Otherwise we'll bring in somebody to break this lock.**

How are your skills?

They suck, he said.

Don't you know somebody who has magical abilities pertaining to locks?

No.

The thing was, he did know somebody, and he'd lied twice just now to his partner because Richard was that somebody, but he wanted it on record with his texts that the safe was here, without giving away Richard's special skills. He looked at the dial and sighed.

"Well, we said we wouldn't do this again, but we pretty well have to."

He reached up with his fingers, already gloved. Using his inner eye, with his acute hearing locked down on this point, he turned the dial, waiting for the tumblers to *click*. He'd learned to do this a long time ago, but he couldn't do it very often with very many things. He'd often wondered if possibly he could do more with his secret abilities but, ... so far, nothing yet.

He followed the energy. And, when that little pin dropped, he could hear, see, or feel when it went. By the time he turned the dial back the other way, he found the next one, and then the last. In less than two minutes. He smiled, stepped back, and pulled it open. Inside was money, as in megabundles of cash. He whistled, pulled them out, took a look at how much was here, and realized hundreds of thousands of dollars were in her safe.

He turned to look at the place and then at the safe. "Did

you really make that kind of money?" He needed to double-check her income tax and see just what the hell she was claiming.

Underneath the money was an envelope. He pulled that out to see the label, Last Will and Testament, affixed to the envelope, not sealed. He pulled out the document and quickly glanced through it and froze.

Half of the entire estate went to Cayce. He stared at that damning motive for murder and shook his head. "Wow."

He quickly put everything back, checked that nothing else was here, and locked up the safe. When the phone rang, he picked it up and said to Andy, "Well, that took you a while."

"Hey, I know you cracked a different safe that we had to get into before."

"Yeah, and I just did it again," Richard said. "But I'm not allowed to, as you well know."

"I do know that," Andy said, "but we are allowed to try. And, having done that, I already contacted the lawyer. He has no idea about a safe."

"Of course not," he said, "but what's in here is hundreds of thousands of dollars, in cash, and a will."

"Could you get into the will?"

"Absolutely. Half of it goes to Cayce."

"The artist?"

"Yeah, the artist."

"That's easily half a million dollars. That's motive," Andy said. "Who gets the other half?"

"Five other people," he said. "I don't know who they are yet, but I took a photo of the will. And I'd say it's way more than one point five million dollars in Elena's estate."

"Well, we've got clearance from the lawyer to open it

because he needs to deal with the estate. He's pulling up his copy of the will and needs that one to compare to, in case she changed it."

"Good enough. You can tell him that we'll get this to him as soon as possible. I think I'll photograph everything as it is."

"How is it you always see that stuff before anybody else does?"

"Just lucky, I guess," he said in a noncommittal voice.

Andy snorted and hung up.

Richard went back to the safe, using the same method he'd used before to see the slight energy around the edges. What he saw best were small thin lines because they lit up for him, almost like a flashlight would. Anyway, he reopened the safe and carefully unloaded everything, took it out and placed it on the bed, and photographed it all—the money just as bundled but with a close look at the topmost serial number, noting the second one and the last one. All sequential. Then he put it all back into the safe and locked it up again. He wrote down the combination for others, if they needed to come in here and access it, because the lawyer would have to deal with the contents before the property transferred over.

With that job done, Richard checked again in the bedroom, but nothing else was here. Taking a few photographs, he headed back to the station. What he wanted to do was check with the artist and see if she knew who were these other five people in the will, and he wanted to have a talk with her about how she ended up being the main beneficiary.

He walked back to his vehicle with one final look at the loft standing prestigiously alone in the setting sun. He shook his head. "That's a crapload of money for a body model."

CHAPTER 5

C AYCE STOOD BACK from the same large installation where she'd been working on the design for the last couple days. The background was about 85 percent there. Frankie's work was improving as he helped her install the backdrops and did an initial layer of painting.

Anita walked in and said, "You haven't taken a break, have you?"

Cayce looked over at her, smiled, and said, "You know what I'm like when I get in the zone."

"You also booked your schedule way too tight," she said. "And you're getting stressed out."

"Nothing to do with the painting though," Cayce said with a sad smile. "I can't stop thinking about Elena."

"I know. Do you think what we're hearing about souls and stuff was real?"

"No," she said instantly. Of course some of it was, but she wasn't in for a long-drawn-out conversation with someone who didn't understand.

"Remember that weird guy who came to one of the shows a few months back, saying you shouldn't be painting the models like that?"

"Yeah, but he was a whack job," she said defensively. "A panhandler wanting the free food. Security got him handled pretty quickly." The fact that this guy had been weirdly right on also bothered her.

"He said something about you stealing their souls."

"And yet what I was doing was trying to enhance their bodies," Cayce said with a smile. "How could I be stealing souls?" She smiled at her assistant. "It's words from a nutcase."

"I don't know. It freaked me out."

"But he said a lot of stuff," she said. "We can't let everything anybody says freak us out."

Anita nodded, turning her attention to the painting. "You're really talented," she said in amazement, as she stared at the massive wall. "I couldn't even begin to paint something like that on a small scale, and here you are doing these massive walls."

"It's not just me though." She pointed to several laborers, who were doing the backdrop for her.

"I know they do a lot too, but, jeez, look at this."

"Starting to look really good, isn't it?"

"It really is." She shook her head. "Good thing this installation isn't for at least six months."

"We were talking about two years maybe."

Anita looked at her in delight.

She gave her a small smile. "See? Sometimes it does work out."

"It's not the models at all, is it?" Anita noted.

"Not really, no. Only for opening night," she said absentmindedly. "It's just what I'm known for."

"Still though—"

"Still," she said with a nod, "just because I lost Elena doesn't mean I stop doing what makes me feel good."

"Does what that guy said ever bother you?"

"No, not really. He was kind of weird."

"Did you tell the police about him? They should probably know."

Cayce was about to tell her not to worry about it, when a man spoke from behind them.

"Tell the police about what?"

Her shoulders sagged as she recognized Detective Henderson's voice. The fact that she could already see his form in front of her as soon as their energy connected was yet another weird and wonderful fact of the way her mind worked. It wasn't just her mind; it was her energy that reached out to these things that, to her, were incredible art objects that she desperately wanted to paint. With a heavy sigh, she turned to face the detective. "Good evening."

He nodded, his gaze on the painting. "It's come a long way since I saw it last."

"When was that? This morning?" she asked in a caustic tone.

He turned slowly to look at her. "A lot has happened since then."

Immediately hope surged. "Did you find Elena's killer?"

"No," he said quickly.

Her hopes dashed, she nodded mutely and turned back to the painting. He'd come for more questions, obviously, and that was something she didn't really want to deal with. "I'm behind schedule," she said, "so, if you have any questions, please direct them to my assistant." She looked toward Anita, but her assistant was backing away, her hands up, as if to say, *Don't include me in this conversation.*

"Well, I would," he said, "but she can't answer these."

"Fine. What's the question?" She turned to look up at him, surprised to find that he was taller than she remembered.

"Did you know that you were in Elena's will?"

She felt a jolt to her heart, then sadness and tears. "That's so like Elena," she whispered.

"And how is that?"

"Elena felt that I was the reason she ended up doing so well as a model," she said. "Plus we've been friends forever. She's in my will too." And that reminder depressed her.

"Did your work really put her on the map as a model?"

She shrugged. "In many ways, yes. So, if I'm in the will, I'm sure it's just a token thank-you."

"How about 51 percent of her estate?"

She turned slowly to look at him, the shock still reverberating through her heart. "Why would she do that?" she asked curiously.

He shrugged. "That's the question I would ask you."

"Because she's a very generous and caring friend," she said, opening her arms wide. "And she has no family to speak of."

"I understand she has a father in Switzerland, who we have yet to run down."

"*Step*father. Good luck with that," she said. "You might want to check the criminal system first. If he's not in jail, he needs to be. She was a foster kid."

"Interesting," he murmured.

She watched as he wrote something in his notebook.

"So can you tell me why Elena left you the money?"

"Obviously because she wanted to," she said, looking at him in surprise.

"Obviously," he said, his tone turning sarcastic. "What about these people? Do you know them?" And he went on with five other names.

She nodded. "I've heard about all of them. Are they in

the will too?"

He watched her closely as he nodded. "The five of them share the other half."

"Well, that's interesting," she said. "She should have updated her will."

"Why is that?"

"Because two of them are dead for sure."

He stared at her in surprise.

She gave him a wan smile. "Lanen and Arnold were in a terrible car accident, and neither of them survived. Are you sure you even have her current will?" she asked. "Her lawyer should have that stuff."

"That's what we're trying to confirm," he said. "Maybe, maybe not."

Almost a sense of relief flowed through her at that. She nodded. "Well, maybe check that out before you try to contact everybody first."

"I do know how to do my job," he said in a mild tone.

She smiled, nodded, and said, "Of course you do," but she kept the rest to herself.

He asked her a few more questions that she had no trouble answering, then he asked one more zinger. "So, what was that about, with your assistant, when I came in?"

She looked at him in surprise, then shrugged. "At one of my art showings," she said, "we had some guy come up and made some comments that were a little unsettling."

"What kind?"

"It was nothing," she said with a shake of her head.

"I want to hear. Especially if this was connected."

She stared at him in frustration. "It was obviously somebody who wasn't well," she said. "He just kept talking about how I was stealing souls."

"What kind of souls?"

She glared at him. "He said that, by painting over the body models, I was stealing their souls, and I should be setting them free instead."

HE PAUSED AS he considered her words. He knew a little about energy and souls. What were the chances she did too? And was hiding it? Then why wouldn't she? Most people considered the entire topic nuts. He was no pro on this stuff, but he wasn't comfortable discussing it either.

Richard studied her carefully. "Can you describe him?"

She stared at him in surprise. "Are you taking him serious?"

"No, but how do I *not* investigate him when it might be pertinent to the case."

Shocked, her eyes wide, she shook her head. "He's a panhandler. We see him around every once in a while. He carries religious texts and wears dozens of crosses. But I haven't spoken to him again."

He nodded, looking for deception, but couldn't see any. "Any truth to his words?"

Her jaw dropped. "I can't imagine," she finally whispered. "He was obviously struggling with mental issues."

He nodded. "I'll track him down and see what he's about. If he comes back, let me know."

And, with that, and a final glance around the cluttered space, he headed outside to the fresh air.

The street was busy, being the middle of a business day. He didn't see the man she'd mentioned, and the pretzel seller at the next intersection hadn't seen him either.

Neither had the hot dog vendor.

Nor the burrito vendor.

But the coffee vendor had.

She looked at him and smiled. "That's old Halo. We call him that as he's always trying to save souls."

"Ah, so that's normal for him?"

Her smile was bright and yet wry. "For him, on his good days, yes. On his bad days it's way worse." She leaned over the counter. "He's harmless though. Doesn't weigh ninety pounds. Is all about saving a world that's dying to kill itself off with greed." Her smile dimmed. "On his good days he's as normal as you and me. But he's had more bad days than good lately. You can find him over there ..." And she pointed in the direction of a small park. "It's an old favorite haunt."

On that note he thanked her and headed in that direction.

"I doubt he'll be there," she called out, after he'd gone a few feet.

"Why is that?"

"He moves around all the time. He's likely miles away from here. Haven't seen him in a week at least. He said something about an artist last time, and he wanted to get away from her. Said she was dangerous. And would bring devastation down on us."

He froze at the word *artist*. He turned around. "Do you think he intended to harm the artist before she could do that?"

The woman looked at him in surprise. "Oh, no. He was planning on leaving before it got any worse."

HALO HEARD HIS name from the other side of the coffee

truck. He froze, then slowly sidled backward. He could taste the brew in his mouth. Hildie was always good for one cup. Especially if he timed it right.

His hand clutched the cross hanging close to his heart. Evil was everywhere. He could see it in people. All kinds of people.

Nowhere was safe in this world. He watched a woman with a small child stroll down the sidewalk, giving him the stink eye. But he wasn't the one she should be worried about. It's the other one of him who was dangerous.

Keeping the world safe was impossible.

Not when evil lived everywhere. Especially inside.

CHAPTER 6

A NITA WALKED INTO Cayce's office, leaving invoices for her to review before signing the attached checks. "Detective Henderson asked for the details on the installations that Elena was in." She stopped for a moment to collect her emotions before she continued, "Is it okay if I give him the invoices with the contact details?"

Cayce stared at her assistant, as her mind tried to shift from the art design laying on her desk in front of her to Anita. Cayce gave a slight head shake as she tried to corral her brain and turn it back to the business aspects. "If he's asked for it, I'm not sure we have any choice," she said, "and we don't want to appear obstructive to the case. We want to do anything we can to help them solve Elena's murder and to bring her killer to justice."

"So, I guess that's a yes," Anita said drily. She nodded. "I'll scan it all in and email it to him."

"Good, and the sooner, the better," Cayce said. "Otherwise he'll just show up on our doorstep again."

"Are you sure that's a bad thing?" Anita asked. "I know this whole business is terrible and outrageous but the detective? ... Well, there's just something really raw about him."

This wasn't the first time Anita had said something unusual and different and very accurate like that. Cayce looked at her assistant, her lips twitching into a smile, and said, "Agreed. I'd love to get my paintbrush on him. But I'm not sure what setting I'd put him into."

"A storm." It came out immediately. "Something wild, untamed. He's pretty sexy," Anita added on a laugh.

"If you like that kind of thing," Cayce said with a dismissive wave.

"We *all* love that kind of thing," Anita said. "Even you." She turned and left the area.

Cayce stared at her assistant's back as she walked away. *That's not quite true*, she thought. She didn't love that kind of thing. It made for an interesting relationship, but she tended to stay safe, away from relationships, so things didn't blow apart in her world. Enough was in her world that she needed to be calm to focus on, so blowing her world apart with a sexual relationship was just not appealing anymore.

She stared down at the paperwork Anita had given her. Cayce had to get out of here, and she had to get out of here fast. She'd been up late working, but she was already behind schedule. Nothing pissed her off more and upset her creative flow more than being behind on her artwork. Other than paperwork.

Anita's voice called from the other room. "Don't forget your schedule."

She groaned and stood, as she checked the clock, her body already moving. "I'm leaving."

"Sorry, sweetie," Anita said. "I'll be there in a couple hours."

"Bring breakfast," she said.

"A thermos of coffee and food. Got it."

Cayce walked over, grabbed her big satchel, packed up the last of her art designs, and decided that walking was about the only way to clear her head.

She headed out her gallery entrance to the main street and took a right. This installation was only about four blocks away. The walk should have helped, but somehow it didn't. It did give her a few minutes to breathe in the fresh air, if the air in these clogged city streets qualified as fresh, and just having a moment to regroup from her office and the startling reminder of the detective's striking looks helped.

She should have slept well last night, but instead her night was haunted with dreams of energy and souls. Her grandmother's age-old voice slipped through her mind. *Remember. When you connect on one level, you connect on another.* The problem was that she and Elena had connected on many levels. On a soul level too. She was easy to work on because it was like working on herself. Cayce knew everything that mattered about Elena and the same in reverse.

They'd been friends years ago and had found each other again through the modeling world. Most people didn't know they had an ancient history. But she'd helped Elena many, many years ago; and Elena had turned around and had helped Cayce too. As had a few other people. People she'd lost contact with over the years as she refused to dwell in the past.

But now she had this ragged hole, a sense of loss of something very special being removed from her life, and it was devastating. When she thought about Elena, the tears burned in the corners of her eyes. She didn't dare let them drop. She didn't dare let herself focus on it. She had to just keep moving. She *had* to just keep on going.

Especially since the next couple weeks would be pretty hectic. She didn't know how she had gotten herself into these problems, but schedules were what they were, and people often didn't stick to them. They expected the artist to pull shit out of their creative hat, even when nothing was there or even when things were too pressured to even access creativity. And this thing with Elena was enough to run Cayce off the rails for a long time. But she couldn't let it.

As she walked into the installation, her heart sank because Naomi was already here, throwing a fit. The room was chaotic and full of colors she didn't want to work in. Cayce shook her head, tried to walk in quietly, and failed.

Naomi spun, saw her, and glared. "You're not the only one whose time is important," she screeched.

Cayce stared at the model, hating the angry sparks flying around her, and tried to keep her own tone mild, as she pulled her aura protectively tight against her body. This was *not* the creative environment she needed. "You're getting paid by the hour, so what do you care?"

Naomi tossed her hair. "I care. I don't want to just stand around doing nothing."

At that, Cayce snorted, and her lips quirked at the irony, since that's precisely what the body model did. She walked over, completely unconcerned about Naomi's impatience, and stood in front of the installation, studying it. The backdrop was done; all the front pieces were done. Today was all about Naomi; then this one would be over. Cayce had already done everything else except for touch-ups. Now she just had to do the models.

As she looked over, she saw two little children. She smiled because the little imps were going into the installation too, and that would be a challenge. But a fun one. They would be painted to represent beach balls, lively jitterbug balls. Their childish energy already zoomed around them with excitement. That also meant Cayce needed to do them last. And she'd have to paint them fast, as she didn't imagine their attention span would last very long. And they were earlier than she'd have liked.

She took her satchel to the side, setting out her paints, and heard Naomi in the background, still screeching.

"You can start anytime," Naomi said.

"Get a coffee and relax," she ordered her model.

Naomi glared at her, her feet tapping the floor, her hands on her hips.

Deliberately Cayce turned. She was supposed to be the temperamental artist, but it seemed like all she did was deal with temperamental models. Another reason Elena had been absolutely perfect.

Not only had she got it, but she *really* got it. She'd been quiet, unassuming, and she blended into the pieces as she was intended to do, whereas Naomi was desperate to stand out, and she wanted the art to revolve around her. She didn't understand she was just a tiny piece of it. And, if she did understand, she'd never accept it because, of course, in her world, there couldn't be anything but her.

Finally Cayce was ready. She grabbed her small cup, put it atop her palette, grabbed her brushes, and motioned at Naomi. "Bottom first."

Naomi sighed, slipped off the beach cover-up she had on, revealing a nude pair of panties. She still had a sports bra on top, which would be fine until Cayce got to the upper half of her body. Naomi stepped forward, tossed her hair back, and said, "I hope I don't have to put up my hair yet."

"Nope, you don't," Cayce said, and, reaching for the paintbrush, dipped it in the paint, and made the first of many long strokes to come.

Richard opened his email, saw the one from Anita, immediately clicked on it, and printed off the invoices. When he picked up those pages from the printer, he added them to the file, and, as he did so, he sat down to study the summary on top.

"Something interesting?" Andy asked, as he plopped a heavy mug of coffee on his desk and threw himself into the chair beside Richard.

"Not likely," he said, "just the invoice of who paid for the last installation where Elena had been."

"Right," he said. "We still have to cross the *T*s and dot the *I*s."

"Always." He picked up the phone and contacted the number on the other end. When it rang, it went to voicemail, but no company was identified. He figured a lot of the wealthy art patrons around the city didn't necessarily order these installations directly, and it mostly would be under company names, but Richard couldn't be sure. He quickly left a message, hung up, and then brought up the company name on his desktop, only to find absolutely no information about it. He sat back in his chair, thrumming his fingers on the desk. "So the company doesn't come up on Google."

"What's the name?"

"John Hallmark," he said with a tilt to his head. "Interesting business name."

"Probably thinks of himself as an artist. It's likely another one of those artsy niche boutique companies," he said.

"That could be. Did you have any luck getting ahold of the remaining three people in the will?"

"Some, but one more is dead," he said.

Richard slipped his head around the corner of the monitor. "Seriously?"

"Yes, but that person died quite a few years ago," he said.

"And does the lawyer have a more up-to-date will?"

"The lawyer is not returning our phone calls," Andy said in a dry tone.

At that, Richard's growl was thunderous. "Well, in that case, we need to have a little visit."

"I'm always up for rattling lawyers," Andy said with a laugh, "but this guy appears to be out of the country."

"Well, somebody must be left behind."

"Small outfit, small firm, just him. Answering service that handles several businesses."

"A new lawyer?"

"No, I think the opposite," he said. "An old one."

"Great. We'll send him a message that we need to speak."

"I did a while ago. Let me check in case he wrote back." Tapping the keys as he signed onto his computer, he said, "Sweet, there's a response," Andy said. "Let's see what he has to say." A few more clicks. "He says he can do a phone call later this afternoon," Andy said, tapping his email on his desktop. "That just came in about two minutes ago."

"Good. We need to resolve that issue to make sure we've got a current will, and we need to know who these other two people are."

"I know."

"Any connection between the three dead ones?"

"Yes, they all died a while ago," he said. "But the two who died in the car accident together were deemed an accident. Drunk driver hit them. He's been convicted and long gone."

"Okay, so that wasn't anything suspicious. What about

the other one?"

"Breast cancer."

Richard let out a slow breath. "You're killing off all our possible suspects."

"I know," he said. "I don't think it's anything to do with the will, but I could be wrong. Apparently a ton of money is there."

"Well, now two are left who stand to inherit a hell of a lot more."

"And, if those two aren't around, then somebody else stands to inherit an even bigger portion." Andy paused. "Do we have anything that suggests there's more to the relationship between Elena and Cayce?"

"Not that I've found," Richard said, "but I didn't ask her specifically." He reached for his phone and called Cayce's gallery. When Anita answered, he said, "This is Detective Henderson."

"I sent you the invoices this morning, Detective," Anita said.

He could hear the strain in her voice. She was one of the more bubbly type personalities who was suffering right now from the loss of Elena. "Yes, thank you," he said. "We don't have very much information from that. Nobody's answering the phone on that order for Elena's last installation. Of course, it's early on in my investigation, but the company name isn't showing up."

"He's a private collector," she said, "and he's been fascinated with Cayce's work for a long time. They've talked about him doing something multiple times, but this is the first time it's come to pass."

"What's his name?"

"Hallmark," she said. "John Hallmark."

He wrote that down. "Do you know if Cayce and Elena have any history together?"

When she answered, her voice was stiff. "If you're asking if they had a relationship, outside of being friends and business associates, the answer is no."

"That's not what I'm asking," he said. "I'm truly asking about whether something more than just working together was involved. Like, were they friends a long time ago, or did they both get their start together, or how did they meet? Was it just as a model and an artist?"

"I believe they were childhood friends," she said. "Then they lost track of each other before reconnecting as adults."

He nodded. "That makes more sense."

"Well, if you think it does, maybe it does," she said, "but I don't see how." Her tone was filled with doubt. "You have to understand that, even if they were the best of friends, if she didn't fit the installation, no way Cayce would have put her in there."

"Right," he said. "So it just happened to be that a lot of the installations were perfect for Elena?"

"Well, you must understand one critical thing," Anita said. "Elena knew what her place was in all this."

At that, Richard straightened. "What do you mean by *her place?*"

"The model isn't supposed to be the object of the art," she said, as if instructing somebody who didn't understand how art worked. "She's supposed to be an element to temporarily enhance the actual piece, but isn't the actual piece itself."

His mind took a moment to sort through it and said, "So she was not the art piece itself?"

"No, not every time. But at this last show, because Cayce

had body-painted all of her—her back as well—when she separated from the actual installation, she became an art piece on her own. Cayce doesn't do it for the other models."

"Why is that?"

"She would tell you that it's because the others don't have the same panache or the same ability to step out of the actual piece and become something on their own."

"And yet, say, this other model, Naomi, when she steps out, is she not an art piece?"

"She isn't in the sense that she isn't part of the piece, then separated as a unique art piece on her own," Anita said. "Besides, Naomi is far too brash to allow herself to be part of the installation. She wants to be *the* art."

"So then why does Cayce use her?"

"It depends on who's paying for the installation. Sometimes they determine the artist," she said.

"Ah, and so Naomi is getting requested for some recent ones?"

"Yes." But Anita's tone was disapproving, as if Naomi wasn't the model Cayce wanted.

"And what does a model have to do in order to become somebody who's requested for these types of jobs?"

"Just do what people have been doing since forever. You either rise to fame because you fit and work the art world or because you have a way of getting people in power to request you." At that, her tone turned businesslike. "I have no intention of gossiping about any of the models," she said. "So, unless you have any direct questions, I need to get back to work."

As she started to hang up, he said, "Wait."

"What?"

He sighed and said, "Can you tell me if anybody had

specifically requested that Elena be at that installation on the last night she modeled?"

"Yes," she said, "because that collector, that artist who has helped us with many installations, was a big fan of Elena's work. He preferred that Cayce use her whenever she could."

"So, she was requested to be there that night?"

"Yes, but that's not uncommon," she said. "It's happened many times."

"And it would be the same company who requested her?"

"Well, that's one of his businesses," she said. "The philanthropist who ultimately pays us is John Hallmark. We call him *R. John* because he's—" And then she stopped and said, "I guess that's a fairly inappropriate joke. But it was a joke between us because he was always helping us. You know? Intentionally trying to help Elena and Cayce make their mark in the world."

"And what was the prior relationship between them, between Elena and Cayce?"

"I don't know what it was," she said, her tone turning flat. "Detective, I'm not happy answering these questions. If you have more, please direct them to Cayce." With that, she hung up.

When he put down his phone, Andy looked at him. "Uncooperative suspect?"

Richard gave a laugh. "That was Cayce's assistant," he said, "and she is fairly open and responsive, yet defensive at the same time."

"She's probably protecting Cayce, isn't she?"

"Yes, but I don't think it's about protecting her because she's done something criminal, just protecting her employer and a friend," he said. "You can't fault her for that."

"It depends whether she knows something else is going on or not."

CHAPTER 7

C AYCE STRAIGHTENED, JUST barely holding back the groan as she felt her back creaking. She would have to find a better way to work when she was on these installations. Maybe having the models up on a higher pedestal or something, but she knew that would just make Naomi way too happy.

"I need a bathroom break," Naomi said suddenly.

Cayce stepped back and said, "Not a problem. I'm done with the bottom half anyway."

"Finally," Naomi said with a note of disgust. She turned and walked away.

One of the two men who had worked with her many times on the big jobs shook his head. "She really doesn't get it, does she?"

"Oh, Naomi gets it," Cayce said with a smile. "What she gets is that she's the center of the universe."

"She doesn't even realize she's a part of something much bigger," he said, "and this one is particularly wonderful." He stood back in admiration, as he studied the massive painting going on behind the scenes.

"I'm behind on time," she said, looked at her watch. "I've got what, eight hours?" She could feel the stress cramping her stomach, her chest seizing too.

"Not really," he said. "I think you've got an extra hour

and a half. It's not opening until seven o'clock, right?"

"I don't know," she said. "I won't have a ton of time."

"Do you want to paint some base on the kids?"

The kids came racing over when she stood there, palette in hand, without the model in front of her. Their beautiful faces beamed up at her. "Is it us next?"

"Well, I can do a layer," she said gently, "if you think you can keep still and keep clean until later tonight."

Their mother walked over and said, "Hi, Cayce. I didn't want them to disturb you, but—" she waved her hand helplessly toward the little bouncing girls.

Cayce smiled at them and said, "I just wanted to match up a few things," she said, "and then, if you're okay, come back this afternoon to let me finish. I don't want them to be painted for too long."

"They'll love the paint," she said, "but if you think it's not good for their skin or something?"

"It's a special paint for the little ones," she said, "but, no, we don't paint all of them in order to keep them nice and healthy." She smiled down at the sweet guileless smiling faces of the girls. "I'll just be doing their fronts. Meaning, I'll mostly be painting the nude-colored leotard they'll be wearing, which gives them all the requisite big belly we need here."

The mother seemed relieved. "You don't normally add children to the art, do you?"

"No, but, in this case, it's pretty important," she said, "and I'll have some help. This afternoon you have four children in all, and Frankie here"—she motioned at the tall twentysomething man smiling down at the kids—"will give me a hand. That way we can get it done faster, and the kids won't have to stand still for so long." She looked at her watch and said, "Maybe you can come back in, let's say, four hours?"

"Will do." She turned and looked at the girls. "I told you that we'd stop in, but I didn't say we would stay. Cayce wants us to head home and get some lunch and come back later." She cocked an eyebrow in question at Cayce. "Then we'll come back."

The girls groaned immediately, but Cayce crouched and said, "It'll be fine. We just don't want you to have to stand around and to get bored for too long. When you come back, it'll be straight down to business."

The girls laughed and nodded and headed off.

Frankie stood at her side and said, "That'll be a fun challenge."

"It'll be beyond a fun challenge," she said.

"If we have to make the painting mobile, it'll be a challenge," he said. "And I'll have to work really fast."

She walked over to the big installation. "We need to work on the set of trees over here," she said. "The picnic area is looking a little on the flat side." Absentmindedly she reached out with her paintbrush, brought over the ladder, and started working.

"Well, I'm back," Naomi said, her tone exasperated. "I just said I had to go to the bathroom, not that I needed to, and now my lunch break has already come."

"Doesn't matter what you need," Frankie said in a disgusted tone. "It's not about you."

Naomi tossed her hair. All Cayce could hear was the disgust in her tone. Those two never got along. She understood it because they were both, in their own way, egotists, but at least Frankie was much more about the large-picture scene; he wasn't all about himself.

Cayce came down the ladder, looked at her touch-up, and said, "That'll work. I think this is done. What do you think, Frankie?"

"I think it's great," he said. "This is one of the most vibrant pieces you've ever done."

"I hope so," she said. "The kids will only be a small part of it but a fun part." She turned to look at Naomi. "Okay, the bottom is good. Let's get to work on the upper."

"Finally," Naomi said, and she quickly pulled the rest of her clothing from her upper half. "Where do you want to work?" Naomi walked around, deliberately showing the world her breasts and her beautifully trim figure.

But Frankie had seen it all many times before, and he couldn't give a shit. As far as he was concerned, she didn't belong here at all.

As for Cayce, well, she'd worked on dozens and dozens of male and female bodies as part of an art installation, and that was the extent of her interest.

She grabbed her paints, rotated her neck slightly, and said, "Let's get to work." She walked Naomi over to a pure white backdrop, where Cayce could see what she was doing and put on the base.

As soon as she was done with that, she walked Naomi back to the installation, set her where she had been before, stepped back, and said, "Okay, now we'll get into the details."

She closed her eyes and took a deep breath. This was the part that people didn't understand. In order to make her model one with the backdrop, Cayce had to make her model one with herself. In order to make Naomi one with herself, Cayce had to deal with the things that she didn't like about Naomi and then cover them in such a way that Cayce could hide the part of Naomi that didn't belong in the installation, which was her greedy, self-serving need to be famous. A lot about Naomi wasn't nice.

Then Cayce picked up her paintbrush and also mentally reached for the threads of anger and darkness, using her energy to pull them from Naomi, so she could be a part of this installation without leaving that stain. It was work at the soul level. No darkness allowed.

Closing her eyes again, she checked in on the energy of her colors and of nature. Then went to work.

WOW, HE WHISPERED to himself as the show opened.

He stared at the installation in shock and amazement. He'd made it just in time. The crowd was hundreds deep here, but he'd found a ladder left behind one of the curtains against the back wall and climbed up just a step so he could see what was going on. The installation was on a platform, but it wasn't high enough for anybody else to have seen quite what he was seeing. Not only was the installation incredible but, just as he managed to get a decent view, Naomi had stepped forward, and nobody had seen her until then. Cries of delight came from the audience as they watched her do her pirouette, before stepping back and blending in once again. This was typical for the Cayce installation reveals. But the audience was due for another surprise.

Suddenly a child came bouncing out of the middle, doing cartwheels. Painted as a great big beach ball, she turned like a pinwheel across the stage. Immediately the crowd broke out in cheers, clapping, and laughter. The little girl immediately spun backward, and, with a little bit more difficulty, set herself back into the painting.

If that wasn't enough, three more children, all at the same time, came bouncing out and did exactly the same thing. When they were almost done, the fourth little girl joined them, and they did one complete revolution, running around, dancing, and laughing. They came up to the front of the audience and did a bow, before they walked back to the painting and reset themselves into the actual art installation.

He stared in amazement, whispering, "Dear God! Cayce had outdone herself this time."

And, just like that, Cayce, in a long flowing white gown, something smooth and sleek, yet simple, stepped forward and raised a hand of thanks to the entire crowd. Everybody jumped up, cheered, and laughed, crying and screaming in joy.

She smiled and said, "As you can see, I added something a little special this time."

And they clapped and cheered. When it finally died down, only the waiters moved among them, with large flutes of champagne and trays of hors d'oeuvres. Cayce herself walked over to the kids, popped them out of the painting, and took them up to the front of the stage again, introducing each one to the audience. Then she gave the four little girls a little glass of something bright pink and bubbly and headed them off to the two sets of parents who had brought their kids.

Then she walked to Naomi, reaching out a hand. Naomi took her turn in the spotlight, as she felt she always should, the stupid bitch. Then they parted, and Cayce moved back into the crowd.

He watched Cayce join the guests with that same elegance she put into her paintings, that same life, that same verve, and yet she herself was so controlled, as if she had a way to blanket it, a way to keep it under control, and she only allowed that life when she did an installation—and in the party afterward. As if she had been turned on, and the rest of the time, she was turned off.

He wondered about that. He'd known it for a long time, but she was simply stunning. His heart made a happy sigh as he slipped off the ladder and walked through the crowd, grabbing a flute of champagne as a waiter walked past, until he could see Cayce. She never really spent any time with him, never really saw him, not like she used to, but he was determined to make her see, one day, that he was worthy of her attention. It couldn't be yet, but one day she would see that he was worthy of being beside her.

But just being here was special. Just seeing an artist at the top of her game was beyond special. Even being in her aura, well, that was something else yet again.

He reached out to touch her, then pulled back just in time. He didn't want to draw attention to himself but wanted to feel who she was as she walked by.

He wasn't sure if she noticed or not, but she stiffened. He loved that too. She was so responsive; she probably had no clue what she was reacting to, but he did, and that made him feel even more special, more connected. With a happy sigh, he watched as she walked from person to person, talking to them, smiling with them, just being herself. Which was, in essence, perfect.

HALO HUDDLED AGAINST the brick building, as the rain poured steadily only a few inches from his toes.

Rain, God's tears.

Someone bad was out there.

God wasn't happy. A sob broke free, and he burrowed his head against his knees. He wanted a hot coffee so bad. But he'd been too scared to go back to Hildie. He wanted the rain, his brain hurting as it always did. But the rain made the rest of him hurt too. His knees creaked as he pulled them closer to his chest.

His punishment. For being bad.

But he tried to be good. Always had. Only bad things happened when he was around.

His mother had said he was one side of the coin. The other had to be kept secret. Hidden.

Is that why Mom hadn't loved him? Tears flowed on his cheeks, as they did inside his soul. Some hurts never went away.

Neither did some wrongs.

He tried to warn the pretty woman with the paints. But she hadn't understood.

His mother's voice whispered in his head, as she always did, *Good boy. Bad boy. Good boy.*

CHAPTER 8

C AYCE WOKE UP the next morning, tired and sore, realizing it hadn't even been a week since learning about Elena's murder. Felt like an eternity. And here she was, still aching inside and out, the pain so acute it was heartbreaking. She had no idea how she was supposed to get through the rest of her life without Elena at her side.

When her phone rang, she didn't want to answer it. She just let it ring. When it stopped, there was no voice message. She sank back into bed and muttered, "Good."

Her mind drifted through what she had to face throughout the day. There would be news media and press releases that she would try to avoid. Last night had been a monumental success. The children had added such life and verve to the installation that she had never seen before, and she was thrilled.

But she had another one to do next week. And that one was lagging behind schedule, adding to the pressure on her. However, for the moment, she was in bed, completely snuggled into multiple pillows and under a huge down comforter, as she allowed her body and mind to relax the day after a presentation. Surely there had to be some rest for those who worked hard. The trouble was, every time Cayce relaxed, Elena filled her thoughts. Elena, who had never complained, had always showed up early, had stayed late, and always did her utmost to make Cayce's design world come to life any time it was an installation she was involved in.

Naomi, on the other hand, tried to be the prima donna all the time. And she never wanted her back painted so she could give shock value with her beautiful form, completely exposed on her backside, as she wandered through the installation. As it was only adults at that point, it was fine, and Cayce wasn't in the position of having to body-paint Naomi's back, like she did with Elena because Elena was an art piece all unto herself. And Cayce had always given Elena the respect that an art piece deserved and had finished the job, meaning, doing her front as well as her back.

Unfortunately Naomi was absolutely nothing like Elena.

The phone rang again. She groaned, rolled over, looked at her screen, and saw it was the detective. She picked up the phone. "Now what?"

"Good morning. So your installation last night went off beautifully."

"It did," she said warmly. "The children added so much life."

"I was there," he said easily. "And it was pretty special. I've never seen anything like that before."

"It was a bigger background than I would have liked to do," she said, "but it was part of the scope of what the patron wanted," she said.

"Well, it was certainly something to see."

"Do you have any update for me, or are you just bothering me with more questions?"

"We talked to Elena's lawyer last night," he said. "He's traveling, but we did catch him by phone."

"And?

"We spoke about the will," he said, "and you are definitely inheriting half."

Her heart stilled and warmed at that. "God. I've cried so many buckets of tears, I don't want to cry anymore."

"What relationship did you have with her outside of the art world?" he asked abruptly.

"You already grilled Anita," she said, "so why are you asking me this all over again?"

"Because Anita said I should ask you," he said mildly.

She sighed. "Right, so we were friends way back when," she said. "She was having a tough childhood, and I reached out to her. Many years later we reconnected when I was in a bad spot, and she reached out to me. When we came together in the art world, it was just a natural meeting of minds, energy, and souls."

"Interesting phrasing," he said. "Do you believe in that energy stuff?"

"Everybody believes in the energy stuff," she said drily. She shifted herself in her bed so she was sitting up, leaning against the headboard, staring out at the fast city around her. "It's just that no one likes to talk about it or to explain it because it gets into the woo-woo territory."

"You saw Dr. Maddy many years ago, didn't you?"

She froze. How did he know? Or was something like that in her medical file? She'd never considered the information to be something to hide, but that didn't mean she wanted everyone to know. She let out a long, slow breath. "Interesting barb, Detective. But then, that's what you do, isn't it? Detect, I mean. I'm sure that seeing one of the most prominent healthcare officials in the world could not be construed as a crime, even by you."

"Well, it wasn't a crime," he said, "but it was definitely

interesting."

"And why is that?" she asked.

"Because, of course, Dr. Maddy works on energy."

"She does, indeed," she said mildly, rubbing her temple.

"I spoke with her."

"What? You spoke with Dr. Maddy?" she asked, clearly surprised. She leaned forward. "I haven't seen her in years. How is she?"

"She seemed to be quite fine," he said. "She wouldn't tell me much."

"There is that pesky doctor-patient confidentiality business," she said snidely.

"True, that's why I'll ask you point-blank, just what the relationship was."

"You mean, between me and Dr. Maddy?"

"Yes."

"I had a health problem," she said, "and so did Elena. I paid for both of us to see Dr. Maddy."

"So, Elena didn't have any money back then?"

"No. Since then she had a relationship with someone wealthy. He passed on and left it to her."

"So, why did you both go to see Dr. Maddy?"

"Because she was abused early on in her life, and she endured a lot of trauma."

"That's hardly Dr. Maddy's forte, is it?"

"I'm not sure there's anything that Dr. Maddy can't do," she said. "But, at that point in time, I had heard that she had the ability to help with various things, and I knew that Elena had more than the usual physical disturbances, and I wasn't sure what that meant," she said. "Somebody I knew suggested Dr. Maddy. So we went, and it was incredible. She helped Elena, and then she helped me. She'd also been instrumental in showing Elena how to protect herself from toxic people by not allowing that energy into her own space relationship-wise and how to use her own energy to blend with her job as a model and an artist to make the paintings more alive. Although that last part she'd figured out on her own and had perfected her skill even more."

"Is that where you learned to deal with the energy?"

"Any artist feels connected to the world in a way that's well beyond the norm," she said, "so to not feel anything, to not feel that connection—which, in this case, means energy—just means an artist isn't connecting with their subject."

"So it's just terminology to you?"

"What are you getting at, Detective?" She hated that he was questioning all this because she had no idea where his beliefs were, but, if the media ever got a hold of it, they would have a heyday at her expense. She didn't tell anyone about what she did. It wasn't secret, but it was private.

"Just asking questions."

"I guess you've got to dig into the dirt, don't you?"

"No," he said. "I'm just trying to find out who killed Elena. That means I have to understand everything in her life. And that means *everything*, … whether it makes sense or not."

"And what does her seeing Dr. Maddy years ago have to do with anything?" she cried out. She leaned forward, wrapped her arms around her knees, pulling them tight to her chest. "Or me, for that matter?"

"Maybe nothing," he said, "but do you really want me to *not* turn over every rock to find out what's going on?"

"No, of course not." She threw back her covers, frustrated and upset, hopped out of bed, and said, "Now that you've destroyed my early morning peace while I lazed about in bed, which I was really looking forward to in order to recover from last night, is there anything else you can upset me about?"

"Maybe," he said mildly. "I just wondered if you knew anybody in your circle of the world who has any medical skills, enough to have done that to Elena."

Her breath caught in the back of her throat, before she let it out slowly. "I hadn't considered that," she said. "And I really don't want to. Although what they did to Elena's body could never be called *surgical*. However, to answer your question, several medical people are in my world, but that doesn't make them criminals."

"Of course not," he said. "That doesn't make them innocent either."

She winced. "Fine. One of the philanthropists is Dr. Hilltop. He's a surgeon. You can talk to him. I'm sure he'll be just thrilled to see you." She smiled at that because Dr. Hilltop was definitely blustery and left no doubt about his opinions.

"What about Dr. Maddy?"

"What about her? Would she have those surgical skills? I imagine the answer is yes. But then so would millions of people around the globe. I haven't spoken to Dr. Maddy since my last appointment with her years ago."

"So you don't see her outside of your doctor-patient relationship?"

"I've sent her invitations to a couple art shows, but I don't know that she's ever shown up to one."

"Actually, she has shown up to several of them," he said.

She groaned. "And, of course, I didn't see her to say hi." She shook her head. "Sometimes I'm just so blind."

"Any reason she wouldn't come up and say anything to you?"

"Dr. Maddy likes to stay fairly unobtrusive in the public eye," she said. "It's not an easy life for her."

"Meaning?"

"She's famous, and the world is a sad place today. A lot of people want what she has to give."

"What is that?"

"Hope," she said. "Simply hope and healing." There was a silence at the other end. She smiled and said, "I know that's not what you were looking for in terms of an answer, but I'll have Anita send you a list of anybody else I might know of."

"Good," he said. "I'd appreciate it."

"Anything else, Detective?"

"No," and then his voice deepened as he said, "Go back to bed and enjoy your morning. You worked hard for last night, but it was worth it." And he hung up.

She stared down at her phone in surprise. But his words left a smile on her face, and the tone of his voice left a smile in her heart.

IT'S NOT THAT Richard wanted to wake her, but, now that he had, he couldn't get past the idea that she had been lying in bed, and his mind immediately filled in a tiny little silk negligee as she was surrounded by heavy down comforters and pillows, looking dreamy-eyed and still half asleep. He shook his head and swore.

"Now what's your problem?" Andy asked.

Richard shot him a hard look. "Nothing. What's up?"

He shrugged. "We have another case. Sketchy details at the moment."

"Dammit," Richard said. "Don't we have enough problems to be working on without getting another?"

"Oh, absolutely, but that doesn't stop the crime in this town from carrying on."

"True enough," he said. "Let's go. What is it we're doing?" Richard asked, as he reached for his jacket yet again.

"Visiting a body in a dumpster."

"Wow. And why is that a surprise?" Richard shook his head. He followed Andy outside to his small truck. "How far away?"

"Not," he said. "Just a couple blocks away from where Elena was found."

Immediately he shot him a hard look. "Any connection?"

"Not that anybody's aware of yet," he said, "but who's to say?"

"Right," he said. "Something to consider."

"Absolutely."

It wasn't long before they pulled up at the scene, already cordoned off with crime scene tape, police all around.

Richard looked at the crowd and asked, "No coroner yet?"

"They're on the way," somebody said at his side.

He turned to see another team member. "Hey, Thomas. What have we got here?"

"A young man," he said, his tone grim. "And there is a connection to your other body."

"Which one?"

"The one who was skinned."

Immediately Richard froze. "Was this another body-painted model?"

"No," he said. "Not at all. At least not that we could

tell."

"Do we have an ID on the victim?"

"Not yet. The face is intact though, and I've got photos." He brought it up on his cell phone.

Richard took a look, shook his head, and said, "I don't know him, that's for sure."

"Might be interesting to know if your artist knows though," he said, "because this guy had his torso skinned off too."

"That makes no sense," he said, frowning.

"Says you. Always some copycat is out there."

"Well, that makes more sense than anything. Send me the photo, will ya?" He stepped a few feet away, picked up his phone, and called Cayce back.

When she answered the phone, her tone exasperated, she said, "I've just barely had a shower, dammit. Now what?"

"We have a new body," he said tersely.

Silence. "And that means what to me?"

But he could hear the horror underlying her tone. "It may mean nothing," he said, "and it might mean everything because his body was also skinned."

"Everything?" Her voice rose in horror.

"No. Just the front midsection." He stared at the alleyway. "I have a photo I want you to look at."

"Do I have to?" she asked.

"Yes. I need to know if you recognize the victim."

Her voice was soft as she said, "Okay. Send it to me." And she hung up.

He quickly sent the photo to her. He waited all of one minute; then he called her back. "Do you know him?"

"Yes," she whispered, her voice breaking. "He's one of the men who worked on painting the backdrops on the big installations."

"When did you last see him?"

"Yesterday afternoon. I think maybe four-ish," she said. "I'm not really sure. I was already working on the children then."

"Would he have been there last night?"

"Well, he could have been," she said. "How am I to know? A lot of people attended last night."

He nodded, giving her that point.

"Was he skinned the same as Elena?"

"Yes," he said. "Can you explain why?"

"How the hell would I know?" she cried out. "I never body-painted him."

"Is there any reason that he would have something that would appeal to somebody doing this?"

She took a slow, deep breath. "Meaning?"

"Do you know if he has a tattoo? Something that some-body might have taken for a collection? That's what I was thinking," he said honestly. "But anything that could possibly make sense out of this would help."

"I have seen him without a shirt, yet I don't recall any tattoos to speak of," she said, "but I'm not certain."

"No, of course not," he said. "Do you have any other relationship with him, other than him painting your backdrops?"

"He works for a company called Mediacorp," she said, "and they work with me on a lot of my big installations. Other than that, I can't tell you any more. He was a lovely young man. I think his name was Thorne. Thorne, *hmmm*, Watson, maybe. No, Matson," she said with relief, as if finding that piece of information was everything.

And he understood because he heard suspects, or other

people who he had to interview all the time, trying to be helpful, coming up with something that would hopefully make a difference. "I'll follow up with Mediacorp. See if we can find out his last movements last night. I'll need a list of who was there."

"Anita will get you the invites list. But that won't tell you about everyone who was there." Her voice broke, and she whispered, "Please tell me that they're dead when this is being done to them."

"I haven't got an autopsy report on them yet," he said, "so I can't tell you for sure, but, yes, I would dearly hope to God they were."

He could hear the tears choking her voice when she said, "Detective, is somebody targeting me or the people around me?"

"That is something we have yet to figure out," he said.

"I just don't understand," she whispered. Then she paused and said, "Unless he's trying to do something similar."

"As in, body-paint, like you do?"

"Yes, but that wouldn't make much sense in Thorne's case."

Her frown was easily picked up through the phone. But that didn't mean he didn't wish he could see her face. Matter of fact, he wished he could see her regardless. "What do you mean?"

"Thorne was hairy," she said. "And, even shaved, it's very hard to get a smooth stroke of paint. A lot of models go through laser hair removal in order to have the skin that we need to paint on."

"So, as far as you were concerned, he wouldn't have made a good model for what you do?"

"No," she said, "and laser surgery would take quite a while."

"What about if he was freshly shaved?"

She frowned at that. "Potentially, but the hair comes through within a few hours."

He thought about that, nodded, and said, "Okay, if you think of anything else, keep in touch."

"I wish I could say the same to you," she said, "because this is driving me nuts. Now that there's another victim I know, that just feels so very wrong. When it was just Elena, I thought maybe it was one of her friends or somebody who would target her because she's so beautiful, but what purpose could Elena's killer have for targeting Thorne?"

"I'm not sure," he said, "but I guarantee you that we'll get to the bottom of it." He thought she'd hung up, and then she said in a broken whisper, "Thanks." He winced as he hung up his phone. But he turned to face the others and shook his head. "She knows him. His name is Thorne Matson. He worked on the installation, through a company called Mediacorp. Actually on several of her installations." He looked at his phone. "I forgot to ask if he worked on the same one that Elena was the model for. I'll send her a quick text. She has no reason why or how, but she did say that he wasn't a good candidate for body-paint modeling because he was quite hairy."

The two men looked at him in surprise, then nodded. "I guess that completely changes the paint medium."

"She also said that most of the models with aspirations for this body modeling work, or any like it, do laser hair removal. She said, for her, if she's doing something where the hair fits her needs, then she would use them. However, that's a fairly rare occurrence, so generally it's not a model that she would use."

He sent her text now. **Had Matson worked on the same installation as Elena? And do you ever use male models?** It seemed like there were always questions that he never thought to ask at the time.

When he didn't get a response right away, he figured she had probably put down her phone and wasn't willing to talk to him right now. He motioned at the team. "Let's get going on this one as much as we can. I can stop by her work later today and get these answers if I don't hear back from her soon."

Andy walked over and said in a low voice, "Just don't get too attached."

He looked at him in surprise, before motioning at his phone. "To her, you mean?"

"Something is very compelling about her presence. I don't want you to get sucked into that."

"Why would I?" Richard asked in astonishment.

"Because she's the kind you like."

He stared at his friend and coworker in surprise. "She's a suspect," he said. "I've never crossed that line before."

"What about when she's cleared from being a suspect?"

"Then what difference does it make?" he said briskly.

"I don't want you added to the body count. People around her are dying."

"I'm hardly involved in her artwork."

"But we don't know what's going on," he said. "That could be just where it starts."

"Maybe. I hope not," he snapped, more interested in Cayce than he was willing to admit. And pissed that Andy had seen signs of his interest. Because, of course, he *was* interested. What the hell was not to like? She was talented, beautiful, lean, and the creativity that she expounded, the things that she managed to create? Well, they were just astonishing.

"Just remember," Andy said, as he walked away.

Richard took his place up close to the dumpster, studying the area, studying the location. The trouble was, it was just another damn alleyway and just another damn dumpster. If he had a dollar for every dead body that somebody had thought was just garbage and had thrown away, he'd have been a rich man, and he could have retired. He stared at the scene and knew that very little forensic evidence would be found to go on.

Just then the coroner arrived, bustling forward and shooing them all out of the way. Dr. Bankster was a pro. Efficient, super diligent, and somebody they could trust. He took one look at Richard. "What the hell are you doing here now? I don't want any more bodies like this."

"Neither do we," Richard snapped.

"Then get the hell out of my way, and go find the asshole who did this," he said, as if Richard wasn't already on it.

"We're still checking out the crime scene," Richard said in a soothing tone, but the doctor waved his hand at him.

"Nothing here to find. If there is, we'll find it. Just go." And with a final dismissive look from the coroner, Andy, Richard, and Thomas turned and left.

"We still have two more names on the will list to track down," Andy said. "The lawyer gave us the last known addresses, but they are no longer current."

"When was this will made?" Richard asked Andy.

"Ten years ago, and she updated it a couple years back. She didn't make any other changes. She added power of attorney for Cayce in there."

"Always back to Cayce?" Thomas asked.

"Absolutely," Richard said. "Apparently they were best friends when they were young, and I believe she said something about Elena helped her out, but she had helped Elena out earlier on. Then they came back together again as adults, and now they were best friends again."

"That's an interesting way to go through life," Andy said. He asked Richard, "Where are you heading now?"

"To the installation where she'll be working," Richard said, "but first I'll stop off at her gallery, get a list of everybody she works with there, then find out from Anita who else from Mediacorp might have worked on that installation last night and any others they are currently involved with. We need to know if there are other suspects but also other potential victims."

"Okay," Andy said. "I'll head back to the station and call Mediacorp to confirm what Anita tells you hopefully, about Thorne and any others assigned from Mediacorp, and make some more calls off the attendee list from Cayce's assistant as to Elena's installation. Then, if there's a moment of free time, I'll start tracking down those other two people in the will."

"Ten years is a long time."

"The lawyer said Elena didn't care about changing the other beneficiaries. She apparently knew about some of their deaths but didn't want to wait to make the signature changes that were required to take them off, something about, *if they're dead, they're dead. We can't do anything about it. Cayce can have it all.* So, as far as Elena was concerned, if it went to these other people, that was fine. If not, it was all okay for Cayce to have the whole shebang."

"Apparently, Cayce didn't even know that she was in the

will in the first place, so I would assume she doesn't know about the power of attorney either," Richard said.

"Do we believe her?" Andy asked.

Richard turned to see Thomas already heading out to his vehicle, going off on another case. "I'm not sure," he said, "but, at this point, I'd have to give her the benefit of the doubt."

"Like I said, watch your step."

"Will do," he said. "I'll stop at her gallery first."

"Well, it's walking distance almost." He pointed in that direction. "Or do you want me to drop you off?"

Richard turned and looked that way, saying, "Go on. I'll walk." He started in that direction. He didn't really want to piss on her day any more than he had already, but they were well past the point of being polite. He would just rip her world apart until they found out who was killing the people in it.

HE SHOULD HAVE known they would find the body so fast. It was disappointing in a way because, if it had been any other body, they wouldn't have. He could have dumped it any place, and nobody would have given a shit. But because it was his body, they were all over it. Not that he was concerned about the police, but he was concerned about not having enough time to solve the problem currently vexing him.

He turned to look at the new sample that he had stretched out. The hair was an interesting quandary. He hadn't really thought about it, until he started cutting. A rookie mistake. Cayce never would have made it. He was green compared to her.

He wasn't even sure what the hell he was doing with this canvas right now, but it fascinated him. He ran his hand over the hair and smiled. It was still soft.

He expected it to go hard and bristly. But then, why would it? It did appear to be slightly longer though, and that concerned him, until he'd looked online and realized that it wasn't so much that the hair was longer but that the skin had shrunk back in, and the hair follicles were out more. And, as he worked on the backside with the softening moisturizer that he was putting on both sides, it pushed the hair out farther and farther.

How would paint look on it?

Instinctively he knew he should have stuck with females. But something had been really appealing about the young man, and having spent the night with him, the opportunity had presented itself, and he couldn't refuse. His young lover had no idea how his night would end. He'd hoped, and he'd certainly worked the angles enough that his lover had gotten what he wanted, and lots of it, so he certainly didn't feel bad about taking a young life after giving him such a pleasurable evening.

He heard something in the other room. "I'm coming, Mom. Hold on. I need just another minute to finish this."

Damn, she needed him, but that need was pissing him off.

Another sound came again from the next room.

He turned to face the door, then groaned as he returned to his creation.

The fact remained that this was not the morning-after that young Thorne had hoped for. But it also alerted him to the fact that he had allowed his own personal issues to interfere or to get in the way of what he should have been doing. If it was business, it should be just business. If it was pleasure, it should be just pleasure. Now having crossed that line, he had to make sure he had alibis set up so he wouldn't be on any suspect list, at least not for long.

He looked at the canvas in front of him and reached for the moisturizer once again. He had tried several different kinds of treatments for the underside, but, so far, the oil seemed to be preserving it the best. The moisturizer on the top and different oils on the bottom were a good mix. He had tried a lot of oils, from coconut to olive to walnut even. He'd gone to a tannery supply house and gotten an odd mix as well. Because he hadn't been such a fool as to get it from the tannery house in person, he'd ordered it online. Have to love that. Everything was available for a price, and, in today's world, that price was too damn cheap.

"HOW DID IT go last night?"

"It went wonderfully. Of course it went wonderfully," she snapped. She groaned, cradled her head, and said, "Sorry. I appear to be a little more hungover than I thought I'd be."

"I thought alcohol was something you weren't supposed to have," Derek said.

She glared at him. "Really? You'll lecture me?"

He just shrugged. They were sitting inside a coffee shop. He was eating breakfast; she was having coffee.

"On the other hand, the installation was a wonderful success," she said. "I was brilliant."

"I did show up, but I didn't stay for long," he added apologetically.

She shrugged.

"You probably couldn't have given me any more connections than I made for myself anyway."

"And I suppose you came with *him* too." She knew that the bitchy side of her was coming out more because of the alcohol and her lack of sleep and a little bit of disappointment because she had really planned on going home with somebody last night. Instead she'd ended up alone. Like how did that happen? She never slept alone, if she didn't want to. But then she'd been a little too drunk, too upset, with too many choices. Maybe she hadn't made a decision fast enough and had lost the two who were on the hook.

She shrugged, looked over at the toast, picked up a piece, and took a bite. But the melted butter on the top made her stomach curdle and her throat gag. She hurriedly threw down the toast, reached for her coffee, swallowing the thick black brew several times, forcing down the butter and toast.

"That bad?" he said with a twinkle in his eye.

She glared at him. "Yeah, that bad."

"When is your next job?" he asked, as he worked away on his crab omelet.

He was the only person she knew who ate seafood with eggs. The thought just made her sicker, but he loved the good life, and he had the money to afford it. She, on the other hand, didn't, and it pissed her off. "I think I have another one next week, but I'm not sure. I'm up against somebody else," she said with a sneer.

"So, in other words, it's your job. You just haven't officially been given it yet," he said with that bright confidence that she loved and so needed.

"I'm not so sure about that," she said, "but I sure hope so."

"You're not broke again, are you?"

"No, not broke yet," she said, "but that apartment of yours is eating me alive."

"That's because you put yourself into a world full of expensive trappings that you have to maintain. If you would just step back a bit and live in a place more reasonably priced, you could save money."

"Why would I?" she asked, her voice strident, attracting attention from other restaurant customers. "It's what I'm meant for. You know that."

He gave her that sad smile and said, "Remember not to keep grasping for what you can't have."

"But I can have it," she said. "You and I both know that. Elena had it, and I can have it."

"But Elena had money behind her," he said.

"Maybe. She also made very good money, more than I'm making right now," she snapped, "and that's not fair. I should be getting paid more for these huge art pieces."

"Why is that?"

"Well, if it had been Elena there with me," she said, "you know she would have been paid more."

"Maybe," he said, "maybe not."

"No," she said, "there's no *maybe* about it. Elena didn't ever stand still for less than ten thousand dollars."

He looked at her in surprise.

She shrugged. "You know that she was the favorite. You know that they kept paying her a lot of money, even though she had millions of other jobs."

"Maybe something else was between them?"

She sneered. "I'd sleep with the bitch too if I thought it would get me that kind of money."

"Depends if the bitch wants you," he pointed out with his words, at the same time as he pointed his fork at her.

Her glare fell off his shoulders as he laughed. "You have to remember. A lot of things go on between two people, and it's not always about what they can get out of the relationship."

"All relationships are what people can get out of them," she snapped. "Don't ever forget that."

He smiled, picked up another bite, and popped it into his mouth.

Recovering, she asked him with a faint smile, "What are you doing today?"

He nodded, put down his knife and fork, pushed away his half-eaten omelet, and said, "I'll be gone all day, possibly all night."

"New boyfriend?"

"No," he said. "Remember? There's more to a relationship than what people get out of it."

"You're an idiot there," she said. "You've been going strong for a couple years now. Isn't it time to move it up?"

"Not necessarily," he said. "If you think about it, we have everything we need."

"Not really," she said. "You have each other, and that's only part-time."

His face closed down slightly because they'd had this conversation repeatedly. "Maybe," he said. "It's good enough for us right now."

"Unless he gets jealous again," she said slyly. "When he sees you with a potential lover. Or an old one, ... like Kenneth, wasn't it?"

"Not likely," he said with the patience that she knew he'd worn out when dealing with her. "It's not about what you get out of a relationship."

"The only reason you're still with Benjamin is for the

time that he deigns to give to you," she snapped, shoving her face across the table. "And don't you forget that." She pushed her chair back. "I'm heading home to collapse."

"You do that. Maybe you'll wake up a sweeter person."

"Not likely." With a wave, she walked out of the restaurant.

The two of them knew each other inside and out. She didn't understand why they were friends and how that friendship had even remained, and sometimes she wondered if she was just a curiosity for him to study and to ponder. But, at the end of the day, it worked, and he was a necessary part of the fabric of her life.

She didn't have to be anything special with him, just herself. And if there was one thing she highly valued, it was just being her nasty self. And her friendship with Derek was the place to do that, to be that. Fully. Without condemnation.

When she was a model, she had to be the perfect model. Not only the perfect model, but she had to actually become whatever it was that these people expected of her. Whether she liked it or not, she had to grin and bear it—or stand completely still or tear up or do this or that. She followed instructions and orders, and it chafed at her. It bit at her. It snapped the bounds of what was and was not acceptable. She did it anyway because she needed the money, and she wanted, desperately craved, the fame that went with it.

Now that the damn bitch Elena was gone, she was prepared to take her rightful place at the top of this modeling world. It was still a relatively small world, but it was the path that would lead her on to so much more. And no way anybody else would take that from her.

CHAPTER 9

TIRED AFTER A rough night and a crappy morning at her office in her gallery, Cayce had just packed up her stuff in her cramped office, ready to head out the door to work on an installation, when the detective walked into her gallery. Her feet stopped, and her heart stopped. Her whole body sensed his presence as the main door opened. She knew it was him, even though she couldn't see him yet. Something about that energy field of his as he moved toward her. The thing was, outside of him, she only saw the energy of her models.

Transfixed at her office door, she waited for him to appear and watched the phenomenon she'd only noticed last time. The closer he came to her, the more his energy leaned eagerly toward her.

He stopped near her office doorway and looked at her, inclined his head just slightly, and said, "Going somewhere?"

"To work," she snapped. "Remember? I do have a job."

"As a lot of people have spoken about, if your reputation is anything to go by."

She frowned. "You want to explain that?"

"No," he said. "I've just been doing a lot of research, and people sing your praises all over town."

She shrugged. "Good. I put value into my work, and I put my heart and soul and energy into it," she said briskly, using the same word that he had questioned her about.

"And you still won't tell me what you went to Dr. Maddy for?"

She stiffened slightly, forced out a smile, and said, "Not more than I did already. It's personal."

"If it had anything to do with why Elena was murdered, it definitely is my business."

"I can tell you clearly that it didn't. I told you why before. It's personal. I have no hidden agenda about this."

"What about Elena's husband?"

"He passed away. You should check your records," she said. She took a step, expecting him to move out of the way, but he didn't. She sighed and said, "Could you please let me go? I'm late."

"Maybe. I need a list of everybody else who's worked on the installations with you over the last year."

Her mouth dropped open slowly. "Oh, shit," she said. She rubbed the back of her neck, slowly turning her head to release some tension bottled up in the back. "Talk to Anita. She should have that information." She looked at him with a cold glare. "Did you find out anything new?"

He shook his head. "No, but obviously it's somebody connected to you."

"Not necessarily me," she said. "I was thinking about that. It could just as easily have been connected to the art world. It's small but not that small."

He looked at her in surprise.

She shook her head. "Why does that surprise you? Elena's a model. She needed more work than I could give her."

"She was rich," he said bluntly.

She looked at him in surprise. "Elena?" Then she

shrugged. "I guess she was. It wasn't part of our relationship, so it's not something I think about."

He nodded. "Do you have no idea how big the estate is that you're inheriting half of?"

She shook her head. "No. Why would I?"

"Well, because you were friends," he said, emphasizing the word *friends.*

It gave her a queasy feeling in her stomach. "Yes, we were friends," she said slowly. "Not lovers, and we weren't necessarily the girls'-night-out-to-catch-up kind of friends either. There was a bond between us that went across time and distance."

On that note, she brushed past him and stepped outside of her gallery and onto the street. She needed her car for this next job, and she was grateful because she really wanted to run away. From him and her thoughts. And especially from that way-too-attractive energy of his.

RICHARD STEPPED OUTSIDE and watched her retreat, but it was obvious that she was grateful for an escape. He called out, "Where are you going?"

She turned and frowned at him. "I told you. I have to go to another job."

"Address?" He made sure his tone of voice gave her no chance to argue.

Her shoulders sagged, but she gave him the address.

He recognized it. Close enough to walk from here, which as he had no wheels right now was perfect. "I'll be there in a few minutes." There was no doubting the heat in the glare she shot him before she stormed off.

He stood there with a smile on his face, watching her

long legs eat up the sidewalk. She was gorgeous, and she was so … alive, and that was something he couldn't quite get his mind past. Something was just so mobile, so action-oriented about her.

"Do you always stare at her like that?" asked a twentysomething man standing beside Richard.

Richard looked at him, frowned, and asked, "Who are you?"

"One of the backdrop artists who works for her," he said. "Name is Frankie." He held out his hand.

Richard reached over and said, "Detective Henderson."

"Ah," Frankie said. "You're barking up the wrong tree if you think she had anything to do with Elena's murder."

"And why is that?" He studied the tall, lean man, wondering if maybe this was yet another suspect. Or a possible victim. Because Frankie worked with Cayce, that automatically put him in both categories.

"Because the two of them were inseparable when they were together."

"And yet they didn't spend much time together except at work?"

"Some people are like that," he said. "If you ever saw them together, you'd realize that something between them went well past what words would describe."

"And yet not lovers."

"No, not in any possible way," Frankie said. "Elena was good people. Cayce is even better people," he said. "I would not be happy if anything happened to her."

"Well, we've discovered somebody else who worked on one of the installations who has also been murdered," he said. "Have you heard about him?"

"Thorne, yes," Frankie said with a grimace. "He was a

good worker. I'd say that was more copycat than anything."

"That's only if you know the details." He glanced at the back of the room, then looked at Anita's guilty face.

"I heard the details already," Anita said. "So Frankie knows them too."

Richard pinched the bridge of his nose. "I get that you all think this is something to gossip about," he said, "but we're really trying to keep the details out of the media."

"Got it," Frankie said. "Interesting that Thorne was the next victim though."

"Aren't you afraid for yourself?"

Frankie looked at him in surprise. "Why? I'm not a body model, and I haven't pissed off anybody," he said. "It's not my style." He waved at Anita and said, "Thanks for the check." Then he looked over at Richard. "Anytime you need to talk to me or to ask questions, feel free. I've worked with Cayce for a couple years now."

"In what capacity?"

"I help her do some structures, set up scaffolding, paint lots of the background stuff with her, for her, generally in on-the-spot forming." He shrugged. "I'm the one who gave it that title, so, if you ask her about her forming, she'd be completely confused who you are talking about."

Richard nodded and tucked away that note in the back of his mind. "Good to know. Did you know Thorne personally?"

"Yeah. I worked with him the last two years. I'm not sure exactly what job Thorne came in on, but he was a good kid."

"Know anybody who would hate him enough to kill him?"

"Interesting you'd say *hate enough to kill* because I think that lovers tend to love enough to kill."

"Were you two lovers?" Richard asked bluntly, wondering at the artistic minds he was surrounded by and how differently they seemed to take his words.

"No, we weren't," he said. "Thorne often went both ways, but he fell in love with the person, not the body."

"And did he have a current lover?"

"Not that I know of," Frankie said. "I didn't know him that well outside of work though. We'd have a couple beers on the job, as we had dinner to carry us through another evening of working overtime, and we'd talk about whatever installation was happening at the time, talk about Cayce's artwork and how it was just so unbeatable and impossible to replicate. Then we'd have a good laugh and carry on back to work," he said with a shrug. "As for Cayce, she's one of a kind."

"Do you love her?"

Frankie flashed him a bright smile. "I absolutely do love her," he said. "She's very lovable. She's *not* very approachable. And, no, we're not lovers, never have been lovers. We don't intend to ever be lovers. It's not that kind of a relationship." And, with that, he waved goodbye and walked on.

Richard turned to look at Anita through the huge plate glass window. She immediately dropped her gaze and pretended to be busy at her desk. She wouldn't get away from him that easily. He stepped inside the office, approaching her. "I'm looking for all the artists you've hired and staff of any kind you've worked with for the last two years."

She looked at him, and her face fell. "Two years?"

He stared at her steadily. "And just how many people are we talking about? It surely can't be that many."

She looked at him, shrugged, and said, "No, it's probably not more than thirty, forty, fifty, maybe."

"I want all the names, phone numbers, and contact information."

She stared at him, chewing on her bottom lip. "I don't even know if I'm allowed to give you that information."

He gave her a strong, hard smile. "You're allowed. It's actively encouraged that you do. And, even if you don't," he said, "I can get a warrant, and then you'll have no choice."

"But see? That's the thing. If you get a warrant, then I won't have any choice," she said, "so it won't piss off anybody."

He walked into her office, sat down on the single chair across from her, and asked, "Who would be pissed off at our efforts to find out who murdered two people in the industry?" He leaned forward, adding, "I really want to know who those people would be."

She stared at him in surprise. "How would I know?" she asked.

"I don't know," he said, "but you seem to be concerned about people being upset. And I want to know what people you're concerned about."

She frowned at him, looked down at her desk, then back up. It was obvious that she was either nervous or didn't have a clue how to take him.

Now that was something he was used to. And it didn't bother him in the least if he was disturbing her sense of calm. He smiled at her and said, "Seriously, I would like to know who would want to hurt Cayce."

"I don't know anybody who would want to hurt her," she whispered. "You don't understand. Cayce isn't—" She stopped and stared out the window for a moment. "It's not that she's not lovable, just that she's not cuddly. She's somebody who you stand back and admire from a distance. She's not the good-old-coffee-klatch friendly type because I think she lives in her own world of art. She keeps to herself and has a reserve that naturally keeps people away. But, when she smiles at you and when she includes you in something, you feel like you're special," she said simply. "Just because you're part of her world, you're special. And I love that. I love knowing that I'm helping her do what she does. Because she is so very talented."

"Agreed. I'm already sold on her talent," he said. "I saw the installation with the little kids, and I've never seen anything like that in my life." His face just beamed.

"Wasn't that wonderful?" she said. "You should see the art critic reviews. They're just raving about it."

"I'm sure they are," he said. "However, you're getting off the topic. I want to know about the people who would be upset at the success of the installation. I want to know about the people who would be angry that she's at the top of the news again. I want to know who hates the fact that the media loves her."

Anita stared at him for a long moment. "Fenster, Gruber, and Naomi." Then she shrugged. "For sure on those three, but I'm not sure how many others."

"Fenster, Gruber, and Naomi. Who is Fenster?"

"Somebody who worked with her a couple years back. She fired him because he was telling people that her designs were his designs."

Richard quickly pulled out his notebook and jotted down notes. "Gruber?"

"Gruber was stealing from her," she said, in a disapproving tone. "I'm talking like paper and pencils, some of her old designs, cans of paint, anything, and then we found out he was selling them as pieces of her. It was disgusting that he was capitalizing on her name and her reputation, and people were loving it, lapping it right up, while he turned a profit."

"Okay, well that certainly warrants being fired," he said. "And what about Naomi?"

"It's not that Naomi hates Cayce," she said, "because that would be really sad, but I think it's more of the fact that she really wanted Elena's top position. And even now that Elena is gone, I don't think Naomi realizes that she won't get the top spot. There was something special between Elena and Cayce, and Cayce would say it wasn't the reason why she gave her the jobs," Anita said hurriedly. "She would say that Elena fit the bill perfectly."

"Do you think she drew designs that fit Elena properly, maybe better than others?"

Anita nodded with relief. "That's it. I think she saw the beauty that was in Elena, and certain art installations just worked perfectly for her. Naomi? She doesn't like working with anyone, and she doesn't like listening. So Cayce has to block her out. She can't stand the greedy miserable persona behind who Naomi is. But I don't know that Naomi is so black-hearted that she would have killed Elena."

He nodded slowly. "I met her once."

"She was also in the installation with the children. Even when she stepped out to take the applause, it's like it was only her. She's not supposed to be the piece that gets the applause," Anita said waspishly. "She's supposed to blend in and be just a part of the art, but she won't. She insists that the art is a part of her. A slight difference but one that's very important, if you get what I mean."

"So, she's a little on the arrogant, egotistical side, and that can cause problems."

"A little?" Anita shook her head.

He motioned at the computer. "Keep pulling names."

She just groaned. "I'm pulling them from the accounting system. It'll be everybody we've had to pay, and you'll have to sort it out from there."

"Or we'll sort it out together here," he said mildly, "because I don't need to know everybody you bought paint from."

"Why not?" she asked darkly. "Some of them weren't very happy with Cayce either."

"Seriously?"

Anita shrugged. "She has a certain cachet about her, so, if she buys from somebody, you can bet that the others want her to buy from them."

"Professional jealousy."

"She doesn't like to take any advertising for suppliers," she said. "Cayce would say that takes away from the art itself. She's not promoting the paint. She's not promoting where she got the brushes or any of it. Believe me. She buys everything purely for her art alone. She doesn't promote anything or anyone, except for whoever it is she is doing the job for. You know what? In some cases, we do art for big charities, so she'll help promote those charities, and she'll do it for the art piece itself."

"So she's all about the art?"

"She is."

"What about the masterpiece that Elena wore as her body art?"

"That was a special show for a collector who wanted copies of all the masterpieces on his wall to come to life, and he really wanted Elena to wear one."

"And who was that?"

"I gave you his name earlier," she said. "He's the company that isn't really a company."

"Right, John Hallmark Company."

"Yes that's him. I don't know that I've ever called him. I only have the invoices."

"I have, and it'll just go to a voicemail that I'm sure no one ever listens to. So how does he pay your invoice?" the detective asked.

"Usually bank drafts."

"That's an odd way, isn't it?"

She turned and smiled and asked, "How much do you think she got for that painting?"

"Which one?"

"The one with the children."

"I have no clue."

"Seventy-five thousand dollars," Anita said.

He stopped and stared.

She smiled, nodded, and said, "So, when you think about professional jealousy, you also need to understand that she did that one for a fraction of her normal price because it was raising money for charity. She really doesn't do anything for under a quarter million."

He had been in the act of standing up, but, when he heard that news, he sat back down and said, "Okay, that opens up a whole new level of motive."

She gave him a fat smile. "Doesn't it?"

HE PICKED UP the paintbrush once again and made a stroke. He knew that was where the stroke belonged, but somehow it was wider, thicker, and more defined than the stroke he had wanted to place. He stared in frustration at what was supposed to be his masterpiece, but instead it was coming out clunky, like a caricature.

He'd been painting for decades but had stopped multiple times, frustrated with his lack of success, but he had been so damn sure this would work, and he felt like he was staring a monumental failure in the face right now. Something he had never wanted to see. This was his swan song. This was the way he would make it back to the lost soul that he was. He'd done everything right, so why wasn't it working? He looked over at the stretched-out frames of the various paintings that had led him here.

He could see the progress; he could see the improvement. But this? This was nothing.

Angrily, he stood and kicked the frame off to the side, dumping paint and throwing his palette. He didn't care about the mess. He didn't care about his art when the damn art wasn't working. Of course, something was behind that damn art too, but, so far as he could tell, that wasn't working either. Cayce had her art and there was something special behind her art. So where the hell was his something special?

He stormed around his apartment, pouring more coffee, then dumping it down the sink without tasting anything, pouring a glass of water instead and throwing it back, and then poured himself a second one. He stormed back to where his stacks of paintings were, staring at them and wondering how he was supposed to make this leap to become the artist he wanted to be.

It seemed like every stroke he did was careless, even though he was fine-tuned in his efforts to place it exactly as he wanted to. But it never quite looked the way he envisioned it in his mind.

Maybe it wasn't about working on these paintings.

Maybe he should try a new medium. Maybe he should be trying a new life. He groaned to himself. Frustration ate at him. He would have to go out, get away from here, and rethink what he was doing. Because, if there was one thing he did know, it was that he couldn't continue this way. It was driving him crazy.

He sat back down with a second cup of coffee and stared around the small apartment and then back out to the dreary, rainy, cloudy day outside. He'd never been a big proponent of everyone saying Seattle had coastal weather and how it was rarely sunny, because he'd seen lots of sun in his life here, but this last week? Man, the dismal days had really gotten to him. He was depressed, uncertain, and frustrated.

Finishing his coffee, he got up, checked that he wasn't covered in paint, grabbed his light jacket, and headed outside. Anything was better than sitting here, hating who he was, while he admired everybody else around him. Surely there had to be a better way to get what it was he needed from each of these paintings. He knew what he was doing and why he was doing it. He just didn't want to express it. He'd rather run from it than acknowledge that he felt empty inside. Some things were just too hard to refill, and, without these paintings in his world, in his life, this artistic bent, what did he have? And the only answer that would come to mind is *nothing*. And that was unacceptable. He needed to refill his own well to be something, to be someone. But it just wasn't working.

"HALO," HILDIE SAID with a happy smile. "I haven't seen you around lately." She handed him the hot take-out cup. "It's the last of the pot, so it's on the house.'

Gingerly he took the cup and sniffed the aroma. She said the same thing every time he was here. She was a good person. Some people were. Until life dished them something they hadn't seen before, … that was bigger than them, … then they let all the bad out.

Sometimes the bad stayed out.

He eyed her carefully, looking for signs of the bad. But she looked the same as she always did. Then so had his mother. *Good boy. Bad boy. Good boy. Bad boy.*

The litany continued in his head, long after he'd finished his coffee.

CHAPTER 10

CAYCE SAT ON the floor, glaring at the four white cans, each a different shade, different color, different temperature, and not one of them was right.

Frankie walked in just then and said, "I'm not sure what it is you're looking for," his tone helpful, in a calm and relaxed way.

She looked up at him with that glare still in place. "Not these. This isn't what I ordered."

He pulled out the manifest and checked. Bending down, he checked the numbers from the lids of the cans to his manifest. "Well, these are the numbers that you ordered," he said slowly, as if dealing with a child, afraid she would blow up and throw a temper tantrum.

She reached over, checked the numbers, then tapped the manifest. "No. See? This one is off by a number."

He looked at it in surprise. "You're right. So what color was this one supposed to be?"

"Winter white," she said instantly. "I need a blued white for that permafrost look."

He nodded, looked up at the large brick wall that they were doing. "How much of it do you need?"

She glanced at the manifest and said, "Well, if they've got four gallons there, that might work."

He said with carefully hidden relief, "Okay. Do you

want me to run and get them?"

"Take these back or get somebody else to do it," she said, "because we're short on time again." She put a heavy emphasis on those last words. "I can't keep up with my usual speed since …" Her voice trailed off.

It was hard to even sleep at night anymore. The loss of her friend, someone she kept close to her heart, was eating away at her insides. It just was so unfair that a beautiful light like Elena should be snuffed out without a care, tossed into a dumpster, like human garbage. That Thorne had joined her in a different dumpster by the same hand was so unacceptable. Cayce didn't even know how to operate. So, she focused on her work, tried hard to keep the momentum going.

She groaned, as she stood. "I'm not sleeping well," she said. "Sorry if I'm short-tempered."

He looked at her warmly. "You have reason to be," he said quietly. "You've lost a close friend. But we do have to keep going."

She nodded as she glanced down and said, "Get me four cans of the right paint, and I'll start in the top-right corner with the clouds."

"You'll have to blue under them though."

"I can probably blend it at that corner," she said.

He shook his head. "Why not just give me a chance to get the paint? You probably haven't even had food today, have you?"

She looked at him and groaned. "I don't even know when I last ate."

He pulled out his phone. "I'm calling to have something brought to you. Go sit over there, have a cup of coffee, and relax."

"But—"

"No buts," he said immediately. "I'll be back in thirty minutes with the right paint."

She stared at him. "Surely somebody else can do that."

"This is what happens when somebody else does it," he said, tapping the manifest in his hand. "We can't afford any more screwups."

"No, you're right," she said. "Thank you."

He gave her a brief smile, touched the back of her hand, and said, "Go sit. I'll get coffee and food to you in about ten minutes."

She started to protest, then realized it wouldn't do any good. She got up, walked away from the paint that was driving her crazy, and flopped down onto a large settee that sat in front of one of the big floor-to-ceiling windows. She loved this space and loved this area in it. It was classy and cold, which was why the art piece would be a reflection of that same space. It was a winter scene—snowflakes, frosty trees, and shiny crystal-clear snowdrops. But she had to have the correct whites.

As she sat here, musing over her designs, she was startled to hear, "Good morning."

She looked up to see the detective, and her hopes sank once again. "I was sitting here," she said tiredly, "trying to regain some of my verve for the day. And look who I see instead. Somebody to take away all my spirit and wreck me emotionally again."

He sat down at the end of the settee with a hard *thump*. "I'm sorry," he said.

For the first time she could hear the empathy and the pain in his voice, and she realized how much of her own frustration she'd attributed to the man, when he was just doing his job. A job that she desperately wanted him to succeed at. Tears once again formed in the corner of her eyes, and impatiently she rubbed them away.

"It's not your fault," she said, hating the fatigue in her voice, "but this is a never-ending nightmare. I'm a creative person, and it's hard for me to look at a huge painting I have to do and to get in the mood, where I get to paint what's on my design, when instead all I want to do is throw up blacks and reds and pour out my pain and my anger and rail against my loss." He stared at her, and such an odd look came into his eyes that she realized she probably came across as completely crazy. "I am *not* going nuts," she said crossly.

"I'm sorry," he said. "I didn't mean for you to feel that way at all. Grief is something that we all have to process in our own way. And, if throwing blacks and reds on a canvas does it for you, then maybe that's what you need to do."

She studied him thoughtfully for a long moment. "You know something? That may not be a bad idea. Maybe when I get home, I'll give it a try."

"You have a studio at home?"

The corner of her mouth tilted up. "Detective, this is what I do. I live for my art," she said. "I have a room that doesn't get to be cleaned because it's got paint on the floor and paint on the walls. It's a studio, my studio. I own the space, and, if I ever want to sell my apartment, I'll have to get the entire place repainted. But it's my creative chaos, and I need that as much as my soul needs it." She watched his own energy contract and bend at her words, yet it still leaned toward her. She studied him curiously. "Every time I say *soul*, it bothers you. Why is that? Have you any energy experiences? Psychic experiences? Strong religious leanings you feel I'm stepping on?"

"No religious leanings, and no," he said, "I've never had

a psychic experience. Not personally," he clarified quickly, "but—" He took a deep breath. "A couple odd occurrences in my life made me wonder if more was out there than I knew about."

She leaned forward. "I've wondered that too, and Elena did as well. It was our connection that came from one of those. So, if you can imagine what it's like to lose something that has been inside your space for a long time, that's how the loss of Elena is for me."

His gaze was steady. "Have you ever worked with psychics?"

"I know of a few energy workers," she clarified. "And I've had readings done a couple times," she admitted. "Dr. Maddy was not my first venture into woo-woo land."

He nodded slowly.

"What about you?"

He shrugged. "In the world I'm in, we do have some psychics we work with every once in a while."

Her gaze lit up. "That's Maddy's friend, isn't it? Stefan?"

"Stefan Kronos, yes. I've heard their names linked a couple times."

"But not romantically," she said. "They both have partners." She stared absently out at the world, wondering what it would take for her to have a partner. Or did she just not give a shit anymore.

"Have you seen any of his paintings?"

"I haven't gone looking," she said, "but I do know a couple other people in his sphere that paint."

"Right. Isn't that Ronin?" he said thoughtfully. "I thought I saw an installation or a huge painting like yours."

She nodded and smiled. "Absolutely. And his artwork is really incredible."

"And always uses his wife as his model, I believe."

Her smile lit up. "Isn't that something?"

"Does that make you feel good or bad?"

"Good." Her joy dimmed somewhat, and she glared at him. "That's the problem with your mind," she said, "you have to analyze everything."

"It's a problem that comes with being a detective," he said, "because think about it. We have to do what we have to do in order to solve problems, and one of those is to ask a million questions that upset people. I don't mean to upset people, but I have no other option."

She nodded and smiled. "What do those two people have to do with me?"

"Because I suspect something is slightly different about your work," he said. "Something ... special. It's as if lit from inside ..."

Inside her something froze. "I don't know what you're talking about," she said smoothly, *so* not ready for the discussion as to why her work lit up.

"See? You just changed right there," he said. "You're not a liar. You're somebody who believes firmly in the truth in your own hand, but that hand is through the expression of your art. You don't want to explain how you do it though."

"Very perceptive," she said, sounding slightly sarcastic, hoping she could throw him off.

He shook his head and smiled at her gently. "But something is very luminescent about your art. A light that others can't quite copy, and I don't know why."

She just smiled at him and stayed silent. No way she could explain how she touched on souls with her work. "What about you?" she asked. "Do you find that you use anything like that yourself? Psychics or any kind of energy work?"

He shrugged. "I see energy around people and objects. I'm told it's auras, but I have never put it to any good use."

"I've heard that from a lot of people. If you look just to the side, out of the corner of your eye, people can see things that we wouldn't have expected, like the energy around an object."

"But what good does it do us?" he asked, with a smile.

"Well, if you see something different than the normal white energy," she said impulsively, "it's supposed to tell you something."

"Well, if I look at you," he said, "I do see the white border around you. But I also know that, before I come, it's usually wider, and then, when you see me, it shrinks."

She looked at him, smiled, and said, "Well, yours changes too. It does that when you approach people." Of course she didn't add in what happened when he approached her. The trouble was, she loved that his energy was all over her. There wasn't anything threatening about it. It was almost protective.

He looked at her in astonishment. "Why would it happen with me?"

"I'm not sure," she said. "It happens with a lot of people when they come toward me. I figure it's because they don't like me. Maybe it's the same way how people view you."

He settled back on the bench and shook his head. "I don't have any reason to not like you," he said, "so that doesn't make any sense."

"Nothing makes sense in a lot of ways," she said tiredly. "Like a beautiful light such as Elena being snuffed out before her time."

"What was her aura like?"

"Calm, beautiful, soothing. I felt at peace when I was near her," she said abruptly, not sure how to explain how special Elena's energy was.

"As if somebody had been through the shit and had come out okay on the other side?"

Again she felt that start of surprise at his perceptiveness. "Somebody who'd been through the worst in life, found herself, made it to the other side, and was comfortable, regardless of what accusations, criticism, or jealousy was thrown at her. She was centered. And nothing seemed to faze her."

"If she was in the room right now with us," he said, "what would her reaction to you be?"

"She would tell me, *C'est la vie*," she said instantly. "She never expected to live long, and she always said that the good went early. She'd lost several friends throughout the years and found it easier to almost ignore their deaths than deal with it."

"Interesting," he said. He glanced around. "Have you ever considered going to a medium to see if they can contact her?"

She leaned forward and asked, "Have you?"

He frowned at her.

"If you've got connections in the police department, why don't you bring Stefan in on the case?"

"Because we don't have budget money for it because it's not yet high profile," he said, emphasizing the *yet*, "and it's hard to get permission for things like that. Stefan does a few pro bono cases, so I figured it wouldn't hurt, but ... all his cases for us can't be free of charge."

"Right," she said with a smile. Just then her phone rang. She put it down on the bench between them and said, "I'm not answering that."

"You might want to see who it is," he said.

She tapped the top of her phone, letting her in, and they both stared when they saw Stefan Kronos's name show up on her phone.

He gave her a hard glare. "I thought you didn't know him."

"I don't," she said, puzzled.

"If his name is showing up, it means he's in your Contacts."

She shook her head mutely.

He tapped the Answer button, putting it on Speaker. "Go ahead and answer."

"Yes, do answer, please," Stefan said, his humorous tone coming through the phone. "It's already a trick to do this. I could reach you in other ways, but it takes more energy than I have to spare right now." And, indeed, fatigue was evident in his voice, but it was mingled with humor.

"Hello, Stefan," she said. "I know of you from Dr. Maddy, but I've never spoken to you before."

"No, you haven't, and of course you have Detective Henderson sitting there with you, right?"

Shocked, the two looked at each other.

Henderson, his voice hard, snapped, "How did you know that?"

"Because of energy," Stefan said. "I don't really have a ton of time or my own energy to expend trying to convince you of this. I do not know Cayce and haven't spoken with her before, but it's important that both of you realize a darkness is around you, around both of you."

"What kind of darkness, and why do I care?" she asked in confusion. "This makes no sense." She studied her phone, wondering how the hell that trick worked and what the specific energy was that he spoke about.

"There's a killer, not targeting you but targeting your work, your life, your soul," he said.

"This makes no sense," she murmured. She stared down at her phone in shock. When she raised her gaze, she saw the doubt and disbelief in the detective's gaze as he stared at her. She glared at him. "I had nothing to do with this."

"No, she didn't," Stefan said, his voice quiet. "Henderson, you need to check into my files if you don't understand that."

"I know of you," Richard said, "but I don't know you. I've never worked with you."

"Well, you can talk to a couple people," and he named off a few names.

She didn't know either of them, but, based on the look on Richard's face, he did.

He nodded. "Okay, fine. So you have some woo-woo magic trick that has you showing up in her phone. Even though she supposedly has never spoken to you, and you're giving us this vague warning about some darkness. Obviously somebody is targeting her or her work because we've got two people dead who are linked to her."

"I know," Stefan said, his voice growing stronger. "And I can't tell you very much about it, but it's connected to the art. It's not so much about the victims. It's about the art," he said.

"My art?

Stefan's voice was calm but crisp when he said, "No, his art."

"And what does my art have to do with his?"

"He's trying to get back to his art. He's frustrated and

angry. Those are the emotions I'm picking up. And it's connected to you."

"I don't understand," she said curiously. "Is he jealous? Is he trying to imitate? To emulate?"

"I don't think so," Stefan said. "It's really all about getting his own art back, his own passion, his own sense of worth in the art world."

"Interesting," Richard said. "You're busy saying *he* and *him*, but you don't have a name for us, right?"

"I never have names," Stefan said with a humorous note. "There's a reason that the cops have their jobs. It's not like I can give you all the details. You have to go out and do the work."

"You haven't given us anything I can go on," he said in exasperation. "I have two bodies in the morgue, and both of them have had their torsos skinned."

"Yes," Stefan said. "I saw that." There was a moment of disturbed silence as they absorbed that information. "It's not the first time," he said.

Richard leaned forward. "Not the first time that he's skinned somebody?"

"No, it's not. It's not a perfect job though. So he could be just practicing and getting better as he goes along."

"Meaning he may have started with animals and moved over to people? I don't understand the people part," he said.

"That's why I'm not sure it was animals either," he said. "But it's very much connected to the body art."

"Meaning, he's a body-painting artist?"

"No. I don't think so," Stefan said. "I know I'm being extremely nebulous, and I'm sorry about that," he said, "because I can't pinpoint who or when or where. What I can tell you is anybody connected to one of your next pieces is in danger."

"You want to give us a little bit of proof here," Richard demanded, "like what would her next piece even be?"

"Ice," Stefan said immediately. "It's a huge winter scene, correct?"

"Yes, that's the one I'm sitting here looking at the start of right now," she said. "And I just had an argument over one of the white paints this morning."

"Whites are definitely hard to do," he said. "It has to be the right whites."

"And I created these colors on my own," she said sadly, "and people still don't follow instructions and make it up the way I need it."

"I'm surprised you even trust people to do it for you," Stefan said curiously.

"But consider the size of my canvas to your own," she said with a smile.

He chuckled. "Good point. You're also utilizing something that somebody else wants," he said abruptly. "You know it. The murderer thinks it. The detective is sure of it. The audience has no clue. But it gives your pieces that extra something. I admire that. In fact, I'm fascinated by it."

"Your pieces are pretty fantastic yourself," she murmured. Why she was seeing flashes of his paintings, as if she had researched it, but she didn't think she ever had. "Even though I'm seeing images right now, I have no clue when I may have seen them before."

"And you probably didn't," he said cheerfully. "The minute you open yourself up to energy work, other energy comes toward you."

"Of which you're making no sense," she said cautiously. She'd started energy work a long time ago without any effect before, so why now?

He chuckled. "I'm making lots of sense. You're just not understanding. But you will," he said. "Now that you've opened up that energy channel, you need to be careful because of the connection with you and Elena. A connection that you both trusted and bonded, loved, nurtured, and now that that bond is gone, you're hurting."

"Of course I'm hurting," she cried out. "My best friend was murdered."

"On an energy level, you've slammed a door shut," he said, "but that's just a door to the pain, so you don't have to feel the same agony that you did before. This is an entirely different thing. You had a line of energy between the two of you. That energy is what the killer wants because something special was between you, so, when you painted Elena, she became something special. When he stole part of Elena, he thought he was getting that something special for himself. That he could use it for his own work."

She shook her head, not even beginning to understand. Then the phone crackled. "Stefan?"

"Have to go," he said.

AND, JUST LIKE that, Stefan was gone.

They stared down at the phone. Richard snatched it off the bench and first checked what the last number was, and it came up as a local number, different than he expected. He held it out and said, "Whose number is that?"

She shook her head. "That's Anita's number. Where the hell is Stefan's call?"

Richard checked through, looking for recent calls, recent conversations. And then stared at her. In a hard voice, he said, "There isn't any record of the call."

Shocked, she could only wonder, "So did he do that himself?"

Richard sagged in place. "I'm not sure what the hell just happened."

"You at least have people you can go talk to," she said, "to find out just what he's like."

"Yes," he said, "I can. I have lots of work to do."

She smiled. "Don't let me keep you."

Somebody called out, "Delivering coffee and croissants. I'm looking for a Cayce Matlock."

She looked over, smiled, lifted her hand, and said, "That's me."

The courier walked over and placed the box on the bench for her. "Breakfast," he said cheerfully, and he disappeared.

Richard looked over at her. "Did you not eat?"

She looked at the croissants that her stomach already didn't want and shook her head. "I've been struggling to eat since Elena."

"Not good," he said. "You need to keep up your strength." He motioned at the croissant. "Go ahead. Eat up."

She sighed and picked up the coffee instead.

He shook his head. "No," he said, "you don't eat right now because you want to. You eat now because you have to."

She stared at him.

He pointed at the wall and said, "You can't do this, and you can't do it to the level of what you want to do unless you immediately start eating. You've lost weight just in the last few days."

"That's no surprise," she said, sipping her coffee. "I often lose weight when I'm doing these big projects."

He leaned forward and said, "So, how do you think Elena would feel if her death caused you to lose focus and to stop taking care of yourself to the point that your art suffered?"

She glared at him. "That's a low blow," she snapped.

He nodded slowly. "It is, and, for that, I'm sorry. But you do need to remember to look after yourself."

"I thought you figured I was the killer," she murmured, eyeing him steadily.

He shook his head and smiled. "No, of course not."

She hated to feel the relief settle inside, but it was definitely a relief to hear that she wasn't considered a suspect. She took a sip of the hot coffee, lifted her gaze to see him studying her with a note of amusement in his eyes, and she said, "At least tell me why."

"So, now you're upset that you're not on my suspect list?"

Her lips quirked. "I know it's perverse of me, but you have to consider the fact that I was, at least initially, and I don't know what's changed."

"It's easy." He leaned forward, touched her hand, and said, "You painted the masterpiece on Elena, correct?"

She nodded slowly.

"It's your artwork. It's that piece of you that makes everything so special."

She shrugged at that but murmured, "Yes, it's a piece that I cared about on a model who I cared about."

"Exactly," he said. "And, if there's one thing I've come to understand, it's that you would never ruin your own artwork."

Her eyes widened as she stared at him. "Oh."

He chuckled. "Surprises you, huh?"

"Yeah," she said. "It does actually."

"It shouldn't. One thing that you are through and through is an artist."

"What if she ruined the painting," she said, "and then maybe I got angry."

"If that was the case," he said, "you would have ordered her to take it off, using whatever means that you guys remove the paint from human skin. You never would have cut it off her."

She settled back, smiled, and said, "You do know me."

"Have you ever ordered somebody to take off the paint and never used the model again?" He watched as she made a tiny wincing motion and then nodded slowly. He leaned forward, "Who?"

"Trish. She kept ruining the paint. On purpose. I stopped and ordered her to clean up and to not come back."

He stared at her in shock.

She smiled and nodded. "Nothing is quite like having a model who believes she knows more than you."

"Wow," he said. "That takes a lot of balls."

"Not sure that's quite the right answer," she said, "but I wouldn't tolerate it. And I refused to paint over it, on a model that undeserving. So I fired Trish, brought in a new model, and started over."

"Do you always have a choice? If so, why do you use Naomi now?"

"I wouldn't if I had a choice in this case," she said carefully, "but sometimes the people who pay for this work see or know the models, and they make the request for that model."

He studied her for a long time. "And why would somebody request her?"

She stared at him in surprise. "She's beautiful."

"A lot of beautiful women are here. But why would one of these philanthropists request her?"

A smile played at the corner of her lips as she said, "Maybe as a favor."

He sat back and said, "She sleeps with them, doesn't she?"

The beautiful woman across from him shrugged and said, "She might. I have no proof of that, but I've heard rumors."

"That's a lot of sleeping around."

Her gaze twinkled back at him. "Naomi does love life, and she lives it to the hilt. That usually means she enjoys a lot of different partners. Particularly if they do something for her."

"Do you like her as a person?"

"No," she said, "but that has nothing to do with it. I have to live with what I live with, and that is all there is to it."

"Do you get to pick out any models yourself from now on?"

"I'm working with four different ones over the next few weeks," she said. "I'm hoping to find that I enjoy working with some of them."

"One or more?"

"It's a new era for me," she said sadly. "So more. Definitely more."

"NEW MODELS?" HE stared at the notice on the door. It was a call for models for Cayce's projects. How he'd love to see the models. It was unusual for her to even advertise this much. Although a simple sheet on the entrance to her gallery was hardly advertising. He couldn't contain the whisper of excitement deep in his belly. Was this the chance she'd find another Elena? He wanted to watch. To see whom she chose. To see the lineup and to pick his own. Surely it would be his time right now, wouldn't it?

When the best-of-the-best put out the call for new models, you could damn well be sure he would be there. Now he just had to make sure that he was on time and was prepared for his best performance.

CHAPTER 11

W HEN CAYCE GOT home that night, she could feel the
throbbing in her gut and her temples. They were both
pounding out a planet Earth drumbeat as old and primal as
time itself. Tension had coiled deep within her veins, pulsing
with the added pressure of everything going on in her world
right now. When she finally unlocked the door to her
penthouse and stepped inside, she sagged against the closed
door. Even as she reached behind her and shut the bolt
home, she stared at her absolutely wonderful, peaceful
sanctuary and knew that tonight it might not be enough.

She kicked off her shoes, gathered up her strength, and
wandered slowly into the living room. If she collapsed on a
couch, she'd never get back up again, and she desperately
needed a shower. She looked down at the dried paint that
she was inevitably covered in, but instead she veered off into
the kitchen, opened a bottle of wine, and poured herself a
decent-size glass. She wanted to immediately fill it to the
brim, take a big gulp, and refill it but kept it at two-thirds
full.

She opened the fridge, looked inside to see if anything
was even close to being edible. She sighed, shut the door.

She walked over, pushed the button to turn on her gas
fireplace, and sank onto the huge couch, sitting right in front
of the fire. She took a sip of the wine, put it safely down on

the coffee table, and then punched the pillow lightly to the side of her and curled up against it, resting her head.

As she lay here, dozing, she knew she needed to get up to have that shower, but she needed this rest time first. The alcohol wouldn't likely help with the headache, but it would help with the soul ache. Working on Naomi today had been heartbreaking—because every stroke reminded Cayce that Elena was never coming back.

Naomi had been short-tempered, impatient, and bitchy. But then, when wasn't she? As it was, Cayce herself had been off her strokes, a little less sure, her arms a little more awkward.

Finally, even Naomi had said, "Why didn't you just take the day off?"

But how does one take the day off when she has back-to-back shows? What she needed was somebody who fed her energy, not rattled it like Naomi always did. Cayce wrote a mental note to contact Anita to see the photos of the new people, so she could pick one to work with the next time.

For Naomi, this was the last project she was contracted for, so it wasn't a good day to be bitchy. Regardless Cayce couldn't afford to be with people who upset her or unsettled her. When her creative juices were going, she needed to move with the flow, not get rattled. And Naomi was all about rattling. Cayce would cancel any job going forward if Naomi was the model. Cayce had to. It was twice the work to use Naomi. Cayce had to add so much light energy just to make today's session passable. It wasn't close to being her best work.

But, without Elena, Cayce had no idea what that piece would look like now.

One of Naomi's last jabs of the day was, "I hope I don't

die like your other models."

Cayce hadn't frozen at the time. But she had packed up her stuff, hearing Frankie's hoarse, furious whisper behind her as he ripped into Naomi, and Cayce grabbed her jacket and left.

Outside she'd taken several deep breaths and then forced her feet to head home. No doubt it was because of her that Elena was dead, and that was yet another heartbreak. Cayce was far too exhausted to handle the guilt on top of this ultimate loss in her life.

She must have dozed off and on because, when she checked the clock next, an hour and a half had gone by. Her stomach rumbled, and she knew that she should eat; otherwise she'd wake up in the middle of the night, hungry. She managed to get herself upright, took another sip of the wine, carried it into the kitchen, and once again stood in front of the open fridge.

Nothing seemed to be anything that she wanted or needed.

When her doorbell rang, she froze, staring at the door like it were a viper about to explode, intent to let the demons of hell inside. The last thing she wanted was anyone in her space. Not now. Not ever. When it rang again and again, she wondered how the hell the person had gotten past security. Then she knew. She could see the energy tendrils reaching for her.

She walked to her door, took a look through her peephole, and confirmed it was Detective Henderson. Exhausted, but knowing he had no intention of going away until he got answers from her, she opened the door and stared at him. "Do you ever do anything but bother people?"

He looked at her, frowned, and asked, "Are you ill?"

"Sick of life, yes," she snapped back.

"Good, get angry," he said, as he glared back at her. "It's putting some color in your cheeks. You look like death warmed over."

She gave a broken laugh. "Of course I do," she said. "Trust you to remind me of it."

He pushed his way inside, closed the door and bolted it, grabbed her gently by the elbow, and walked her to the nearest kitchen stool, right beside her glass of wine, and sat her down there. "Have you eaten?"

"No," she said. "What are you doing in here? I didn't exactly invite you in."

"Given a choice," he said, "you wouldn't invite me anywhere but to the grave." At that, tears welled up in her eyes. He made a strangled exclamation, spun her around on the stool, wrapped his arms around her, and said, "Do you ever break down? Do you ever just give in and let the soul release?" And he wrapped her up tight and held her close.

Maybe it was the unexpected shock of his actions. Maybe it was just being held by somebody who understood. Or maybe it was just the sharing of human comfort, but her tears broke loose, and the deluge she'd been holding back ran free.

He didn't say anything; he just held her close, murmuring something against her ear, gentle soothings amid the silent sobs. When she finally exhausted her supply of tears, her eyes burning hot against his chest, she wasn't even surprised or shocked anymore. It was like something inside her had broken. She didn't think she could ever put it back together again. She tried to push away, but he wouldn't let her. She wasn't sure he could, with the way their energy had wrapped around the two of them.

"Just stay here for a minute," he said, his own voice thick.

She sniffled several times and then said, "I need a tissue."

He gently released her, walked over, grabbed a box on the coffee table, and brought it back to her. He slipped a finger under her chin, tilted her head up so he could look into her eyes. "You know it's okay to let go sometimes, right?"

She reached for the tissues, blew her nose, and, with another one, dabbed at her eyes. She motioned at his shirt. "Your shirt is covered in mascara."

"It'll wash," he said without a care.

She stared at him, startled. "You don't care that I ruined your shirt?"

He walked over to the sink, opened the cupboard beside it, pulled out a glass, and filled it with cold water, placing it in front of her.

She stared down at it, wondering at his thoughtfulness, but picked it up and took a long drink. It helped ease the coarseness in her throat. "It's really hard."

"It is," he said, his voice firm, yet gentle. "Anytime we lose someone close to our heart, it's hard. It's always hard to say goodbye."

Her eyes filled with tears again. Patiently she brushed them back. "It seems like all I do is cry."

"It seems to me like all you've been doing is holding back the tears," he said, pointing out what she'd been trying to ignore. He opened the fridge and said, "What about food?"

"I don't think I can eat," she confessed. He turned to look at her and frowned. She shrugged. "I had the croissant at breakfast, but that's it."

143

He whistled, turned back to the fridge, rummaged a bit, and pulled out vegetables. She watched in dulled surprise, her mind sorting out what he was doing.

When he grabbed a knife and started chopping, she said, "You're cooking?"

He nodded. "You need to eat."

She half smiled. "Is this what you always do for all your suspects who come off the suspect list?"

"I'd spend my days cooking then," he joked. "This detective work is what I do in life. Remember? It's the seedy, dark side of life, and there's no good way to tell people that they've lost somebody they cared about. It's always left up to us to try to handle the ugly details."

She thought about that and nodded. "That sucks."

"It does," he said, "until I can also bring closure by finding out who did this."

She watched silently as he chopped broccoli, cauliflower, carrots, and onions, then rummaged in her cupboards for a pan.

"Are you looking for a frying pan?"

His head popped up, and he glanced out of the pan cupboard. "A wok, actually."

She pointed to a long cupboard off to the side.

With a smile he bounced in that direction, crouched before the cupboard, found a small wok, and brought it out with a smile. "Glad to see you have one. Do you cook?"

She shrugged. "I used to. I don't really have time anymore."

"Good food keeps up your energy," he scolded lightly.

She shrugged listlessly. "I don't think I care."

"And that's right now," he said. "Any chance you have any protein in the fridge? I didn't see any."

"No, I don't think so," she said. "There are eggs, although I don't know what you'd do with them."

He looked over at her with a smile. "Well, watch and learn." He pulled out several eggs, whisked them in a small bowl, put a little bit of oil on the bottom of the wok, and heated it up. He poured a bit of egg in it, swirled it into a pancake crepe-looking thing. As soon as it was done, he flipped it onto a plate and did several more. As he took them off, he rolled them up, cut them in half, and arranged them on the side of a plate.

She looked at him with interest. "Now what?"

"You have to have some protein," he said, and he turned the heat on under the oil again and asked, "Do you have any nuts?"

"Cashews," she said cautiously.

He followed her instructions to get the cashews, nodded when he saw they were raw, and said, "Perfect." With the oil smoking in the bottom of the wok, he lifted it, swirled the oil around gently, and dumped in a mess of cashews. He roasted them very quickly, then put them off on a plate, and he added more oil to the wok and tossed in all the veggies. While they sautéed in the pan, following her further directions to where he'd find other ingredients, he added a little bit of starch, water, and spices. Stirring, he heated the mixture into something.

She watched with interest, her stomach grumbling with joy when she saw real food heading her way. "I'm sorry that I don't have chicken or beef or something like that."

He nodded. "The eggs will do for the moment."

As soon as all the veggies were done to his liking, and the sauce had thickened a bit, he tossed the nuts back in and stirred quickly to coat them. Then he served up two platefuls, and he laid all the egg crepe things in a series of rolls on the side of each. He handed her a plate with a fork. "Now eat." He brought his plate around next, sat down beside her, and forked up a bite.

She took one taste and stopped with her fork midway to her plate. "That tastes wonderful," she said.

"It's what real food tastes like," he said with a smile.

She shrugged. "I'm just so busy."

"That's no excuse for not taking care of yourself."

"Yes, *Mother*," she said in a dry tone. She focused on the food, picked up one of the little egg roll things, and took a bite. "What makes it taste so different?"

"The sesame oil."

She quickly ate up the food on her plate. Not until the last couple bites did she realize just how full she really was. She managed to get down those final bites, but, when she pushed away her plate, she said, "Now I'm stuffed."

"So you should be. It's a lot of vegetables and a little bit of protein," he said. "You should sleep well on that."

She picked up her glass of wine and wandered to the couch, where she'd been napping earlier, and sat back down, but this time she didn't collapse quite so badly. She looked at him, looked at the wine, and said, "Pour yourself a glass, if you can."

"I have a long night, so I'll hold off," he said. "Do you mind if I put on the teakettle?"

"You drink tea?"

He shot her a look. "I drink coffee, tea, herbal teas. I drink a lot of things," he said, "and, yes, red wine is one of them, although I do like a whiskey at night."

She laughed at that. "Sure, put on the teakettle. I'll take a cup of tea up to the shower when I go."

"Is that a hint that I'm not to stay?"

"It's a hint that I can't keep my eyes open much longer," she stated. "And you had a reason for coming by. What is it?"

"Can't I just come to check on you? Make sure you're okay?"

"Well, you can," she said. "But, chances are, that wasn't the reason."

"No, it wasn't," he said. "Just more questions."

"Of course. Such as?"

"Fenster and Gruber."

"Both men I fired," she said. "I presume Anita told you?"

"Yes," he said, "she did, and that's the information we need to know."

"Have you gotten anywhere following up on them?"

"No," he said. "I was hoping you could give me some contact information."

"I have no clue," she said with a shrug. "They came from the same company that Frankie works for, so maybe ask him?"

"I can do that," he said. "Was there any ugliness over the firing?"

"I wouldn't say so. When people are caught dead to rights in doing the wrong thing, it's hard to walk back from that."

"Okay. Anybody else but more along a relationship angle?"

"Not really," she answered. "There have been people over the years but nobody recent."

"Did you ever see that strange man who said those weird things to you again?"

"No," she said. "I haven't."

"Nothing else has happened these last few days?"

"Except for the fact that I really struggled to work today. Then I couldn't focus, and Naomi was bitchier than usual, but maybe that was because I was more tired than usual." She shook her head.

"I wanted to ask about the new models that you're trying out. Have you contacted them?"

"I believe an email went out, yes," she said. "Why?"

"And did it go out to just the four?"

She shrugged. "I have no idea. You'd have ask Anita. What has this got to do with anything?"

"I just don't want them to become targets."

She stared at him. As his thoughts slowly filtered in, her heart constricted. "Is that what you think will happen?" She put her wine down, hopped up to her feet, and paced. "Am I supposed to stop working?"

"No, because I don't think that's the answer."

She spun on her heels and glared at him. "Answer to what? Some psycho is out there skinning torsos off people who he's murdered. What's to understand about any of this other than he's just plain crazy?"

"No doubt he'll probably claim insanity as a defense when he goes to court," Richard said quietly. "However, he is doing this because of his own logical-to-him sequence of ideas and beliefs. And we need to figure that one out so that we can stop him from doing it again."

She took a deep calming breath and said, "As far as I know, Anita contacted the four models, but I can't be sure that she didn't contact a few others. I gave her four names and two other possibilities, so she may have contacted them as well."

"And have you heard from Fenster or Gruber at all in the last couple years since you fired them?"

She shook her head. "No, but you've got to understand there's a line of defense to keep that world away from me so I can work. So again, you'd have to ask Anita."

"Any association with Frankie?"

At the quick spin in conversation, she stared at him. "What about Frankie?"

"How long has he worked for you?"

She shrugged. "A couple years maybe. I don't know. Ask Anita."

He gave a warm chuckle. "When you go into your art, you really don't see anything else, do you?"

"Possibilities," she said. "Endless possibilities. But that's all."

There was silence for a moment as the two stared at each other, and abruptly he said, "I'll go now. I want you to get that shower and go to bed."

"Yes, after you leave." She tried to keep her tone less sarcastic than normal, since really he had come in and taken care of her with actions that left her reeling from the compassion she'd seen in his gaze. And had felt in his arms. "But I'll take a shower and go to bed because I want to, not because you told me to."

He flashed her a grin. "Good. As long as you do it, I'm fine with that." Just then his phone rang. He looked down, saw it was somebody that he needed to get answers from, but it wouldn't be pleasant.

She could tell from the odd look in his expression.

He lifted the phone and said, "Richard here. What's up?" He nodded, his gaze zinging toward her. "Yeah, I'll tell her. I'll be right there."

"What's the matter?" she asked, when he hung up.

"Naomi was attacked in an alleyway tonight." He held up a hand as she gasped and jumped to her feet. "She'll be fine."

"Was it the same guy?" she cried out, her hand going to her mouth. How horrible. Naomi might not be her favorite person, but no one deserved what happened to Elena.

"I'm not sure yet," he said. "I have to go interview her."

"Where is she?" she asked, looking around. "I should go with you."

"No," he said. "This is for us to do. You need to go to bed and to get some sleep."

"After this?"

"For all I know, it's a plain old mugging," he said. "She went to a bar. We don't know that it has anything to do with you."

She took a slow calming breath and started to relax. "That's a good point. Naomi does hang out in a lot of bars. Not necessarily nice ones either."

He nodded. "Exactly. Now go to bed." He walked over to her, wrapped his arms around her, gave her a very gentle hug, and said, "And please look after yourself."

Touched, she gazed up at him with misty eyes, saying, "I will. I promise."

He chuckled. "You'll promise, but you still won't do enough of it. However, I'm hoping, after tonight, maybe you'll do a little more." He reached down and kissed her gently on the temple. "A lot of people are counting on you. Remember that." And then he disappeared out her front door.

She stared at the closed door, wondering how her life had just suddenly gone off-kilter. Or maybe it had already gone off-kilter with Elena's death. But something about his actions tonight, his words, that little kiss on her temple, had helped move things back in the right direction again. Either way, she felt measurably better.

And it was definitely time for her shower and then bed.

RICHARD STRODE AWAY from Cayce's door, wondering at his very uncharacteristic inclination to mother her. But something had just been so endearing and so broken about her when he'd seen her at her doorway that he couldn't do anything else. But now, as he stared down at his phone again, double-checking the information he'd received, he hated that he was suspicious, but what the hell was going on with Naomi?

He finally made it across town to the hospital twenty minutes later. As he walked in, Andy met him at the entrance. His face was grim.

"What does she have to say?"

"Apparently she was at a party," Andy said, "drinking and having a good time, when somebody told her about a job he wanted her to work on, and he coaxed her outside. She thought she was going out the front door but admitted that she'd had a lot to drink, and he took her out the back door. She didn't see the blow coming, but she took one punch to the jaw and went down."

"And then what?" Richard asked, as he strode inside the emergency hallway heading toward where he assumed Naomi was waiting for them.

Andy said, "Apparently another couple was having sex outside, and, when Naomi's guy hit her, the other couple screamed, and Naomi's guy took off."

"I can see that working too," he muttered.

"Right?"

"So, did she have a lucky save because she's not the third victim in our possible trio here, or was it something completely random?"

"We don't have any way to know at this point," Andy said. "She's not looking like her normal self."

"Well, that leads credence to there being an attack."

"I know. I had the same thought myself. But, just because she comes off brass and brutal, it doesn't necessarily mean she could have set herself up for something like this."

"No, of course not."

As it was, she was getting up and walking toward them. Richard frowned. "Should you be leaving?"

"Like hell I'm staying," she growled.

"Isn't it early for you to be at a bar?"

She gave him a hot stare. "I like to live at the bars," she said smoothly. "You got anything to say about that?"

"No," he said. "What time did you leave the art world tonight?"

She shrugged. "It was mostly an afternoon get-together leading to an evening drink thing. I left at nine, and I was at the bar maybe forty-five minutes when this guy approached me."

"Can you give us a description?"

"Well, if you two would talk to each other," she said, "you would know that I already gave Andy a description."

Richard looked at Andy.

Andy held up his notepad. "Six feet tall, red hair, heavy makeup."

"In other words, you couldn't identify him."

"I've never seen him before in my life," she said. "I like

men. I know men. And this was one I hadn't seen before."

"Do you think he was just a whack job? Do you think he had another reason for hitting you?"

"I don't know what you're talking about."

He glared at her. "Tell me exactly what happened in the conversation between you two."

She gave a negligent shrug. "He said he had a job for me. I assumed it was art because that's my world. I followed him. I thought we were going to the front door, but instead we headed to the back door. And that's when he clocked me."

Something about her words didn't ring true. He turned to look at Andy. "Did you get a description of the guys who stopped the attacker?"

"I have their contact information," he said. "They were also pretty inebriated. They may have forgotten by the time we get to them," he said.

"I was thinking of that too. Let's head over and grab them first."

"What about me?" Naomi said sarcastically. "Or does what happened to me just not matter?"

Richard turned and looked at her. "I presume you already told everything to Detective Ganderwahl—that's Andy. You'll need to come to the station to file a report."

She faltered at that and frowned. "I don't think I want to file a report," she said. "It'll impact my ability to get work."

He stared at her in surprise. "And why is that?"

"Because people who cause waves," she said, "are not people who others want to work with."

He could understand that, but, at the same time, if she had been attacked, they needed to find the perpetrator. "We can't catch him," he said, "if we don't have your cooperation."

"I'll think about it," she said. "Right now, I just want a drink."

"A drink?" They let her walk between them, and she headed toward the exit.

Richard frowned. "Shouldn't you go home?"

"I am going home," she said. "I have booze there too."

"Can we give you a lift?" Andy asked, concerned.

She waved him back. "I'll take a cab." She was dressed somewhat. And looked a little bizarre, being half painted and half not. But she disappeared out the front door with the casual, confident stride of somebody who wasn't fazed by her appearance.

"We need to contact those two people who saw and heard them," Richard said.

"Yeah," Andy said. "I've got messages from both." He called the first name on his list. "This is Detective Ganderwahl. I'm calling about the incident that you witnessed this evening at the bar." He listened for a few minutes. "And then you scared him off, I understand." He listened some more.

On the outside of the conversation, but hearing just enough to keep him in the loop, Richard stood there impatiently, until Andy ended the call.

"So, that changes things a little bit," he said.

"In what way?"

"Apparently this guy had a job for her, but it was a different kind of job." And Andy waggled his eyebrows.

"Ah, shit. So I presume she resented it, struggled, it got ugly, and he knocked her in the head."

"When Naomi and her man came outside, they were laughing and giggling, having a good time, lots of kissing and cuddling going on, but, when he mentioned a price, she got furious and hit him, and he hit her back."

Richard barely held back a smile. "Yeah, slightly different story and definitely not connected to our killer."

"We hope," Andy said. "We know what assumptions can do to our cases."

"Yes, I hear you," he said. "Good enough. We'll follow up, but I'm not sure how we'll find a guy who may have hit her in self-defense."

"Which is most likely why she didn't want to make a statement."

"Exactly."

Andy stood for a long moment and asked, "You were talking with Cayce?"

Richard nodded, keeping his face deliberately blank. "Yes, trying to get more information on Gruber and Fenster. I need to run Frankie down, as I'm still looking for contact information for both of them."

"No luck looking them up?"

"No luck finding them with those last names or anybody with those last names," he said with a look at Andy. "Something about the nature of the art world."

Andy nodded. "Well, I'm heading home," he said. "It's been a damn long day."

"Yeah, I'm following." He sent a quick text to Cayce, telling her that Naomi was her usual self and not to worry.

He headed on toward his home. The problem was, even though his mind should be on the case, all he could think about was Cayce. She'd looked so vulnerable, so different from the woman that he'd seen up until now that it gave him an insight into who she was as a person. The one she never let anybody else see—although he suspected that Elena had

had many chances to see it. He really wanted to know what was in the two women's backgrounds.

As soon as he hit home, he brought out his laptop and researched the two of them. He went back twenty years. Cayce was thirty-two. Elena was thirty-one. And then decided he needed to go back twenty-five years, maybe even twenty-seven.

It took him a while, but he finally found a case with Elena's name. Her last name had been changed when she was ten. She had been sexually abused by her stepfather. Only one mention was in all the articles, even in the case files he'd managed to find, of the one friend who'd saved her, sneaking into her bedroom that night and half dragging her from the house to the hospital and safety. That one friend had been Cayce. Elena was put into the foster care system and hidden away. Which explained why Cayce had lost touch with Elena for so many years. A trial date on the rape of Elena had been set, but the stepfather had disappeared before it got underway and hadn't been heard of since.

Richard sat back, stunned. "Cayce was right. Something like that went way past all normal relationships."

He could understand now why the two had been so close. Their kinship covered decades. Cayce had mentioned something else in later years, of having come together and Elena saving *her* that time. He wondered if it was a similar situation. And, though he hunted, he couldn't find any information. So, even if Cayce had also suffered abuse, it hadn't gone criminal, and he didn't have an old case for it. And he found nothing on the internet about it at all.

He shook his head and thought about the lives of the two women who only had each other, but, once they found each other, it was something more precious than gold. And then he realized just how devastated and alone Cayce must feel now. With Elena gone—that one light in her life, that one person Cayce could always trust—Cayce had no one.

SO MUCH LIGHT was in her work. Halo stared through the window at the wall mural. So pretty. Too pretty. Must be bad. Evil.

He shoved his hands deep into his oversize coat and hunched his shoulders. His mother's words were ever-present in his head. *You can't paint. You can't draw. That's the devil's work. He chooses his minions by the skill he gives them. No one should create such works without his permission. Remember that.*

How could he forget? His art had been part of his soul. The evil part.

Good boy. Bad boy. And the litany carried on.

CHAPTER 12

W AKING UP THE next morning, Cayce could feel some
of her vigor returning. She didn't understand how or
why, but it was almost as if that breaking of the dam last
night had helped. She hated that she had fallen apart with
Richard though. She should have been strong enough to deal
with it on her own.

She reached out a finger, trailed it across the familiar face
of Elena on one of the big pictures she kept on the wall close
to her bed. Elena had been so photogenic. So easy to body-
paint, so easy to turn into something special, and it would
just be that much harder to find a replacement for her.

Cayce thought about Stefan and all that weirdness with
him calling her via the sound waves or whatever to speak to
her and Richard, wondering just how weird it really was.
Something was incredibly odd and unique about Stefan too.
But it was more than that. His unique gift or ability, or
whatever the hell that was, made that telecommunication
happen. And the fact that he knew about the way she dealt
with energy and how he knew that the luminescence found
in her art was made by blending her energy with that of her
subject, the model, and why Cayce couldn't ever make
Naomi be Elena, no matter how much Naomi wanted to
become the next Elena, because something was really wrong
about Naomi's energy.

As far as Cayce was concerned, she dealt with people who were full of love and light, people who wanted to do good and be good—not people who were full of bitchy, cranky miserableness and who wanted to step on others in order to move up because that was just so wrong.

Cayce could do so many things with the right person, but she was seriously crippled when she had to deal with the wrong person. And, after yesterday, she knew that she was done with Naomi.

She picked up the phone and called Anita. "I'm just now waking up. I know I'm late, but can you make sure Naomi is no longer on any of my schedules?"

"Let me check," Anita said. "Did something happen?"

"Nothing more than usual," she said. "I just can't deal with that woman anymore."

"I'm surprised you ever could," she said. "She's brutal."

"I know, but some things just—"

"I know. You can't do it. Okay, she's booked for one more next week."

"Have we paid her, or is it a contract that we have to honor?"

"No, we haven't, and, no, it isn't," she said. "I can cancel it."

"Please do. We won't be using her again."

"Good," Anita said. "She's nasty and greedy, isn't she?"

"She is at that, and that's the nice way to say it," she said. "Anyway, I'll be in soon."

"Okay, I'll see you in a bit."

Cayce got up and headed in to take a shower. Just standing under the hot water, getting the dried paint all off, the little bit that she had missed getting off last night, wouldn't be enough. She obviously needed a good scrubbing to get herself clean of the toxins used to remove the paint initially. This time she did a full-on scrub with the intent to soothe and to ease her skin, instead of last night's hard scrubbing, when she had been too impatient and too tired to do anything else.

As soon as her shower stopped dripping, she put a one-minute conditioner on her hair and let it soak in, then gave it a quick rinse before wrapping it up in a towel. She stepped out of the shower and into the bathroom and coated her body in moisturizer. One of the handicaps of being a full-time artist was dealing with elements that stripped her skin of its natural moisturizers. And that was something she had to watch out for.

When she was done, she walked back to her bedroom, pulled out white capris, some little flat shoes, and an elegant long tunic top. It was simple cotton but made her feel good and look good too.

Downstairs she put on coffee and rustled up some eggs and toast for her breakfast. The one thing that Richard was right about was how she wasn't taking care of herself. She had allowed her work schedule to interfere.

Before Elena's death, Cayce's lack of self-care had been a problem; now, after her best friend's murder, Cayce had mentally compensated, trying to put that soul-deep loss in the right perspective, and she had again just let her own self-care slide.

While she ate, she made a simple list of things she had to do, and on top of that list was to move some of these potential artist models forward. She really wanted to find somebody she could connect with. Not necessarily as well as Elena—that wasn't realistic—but someone who was unique and fresh, different, with some sort of connection between

Cayce and the new model.

Cayce would have to use her energy in a different way today. Something that she used to do all the time after being put in the hospital by a boyfriend—make that fiancé—where she had mentally corrected because she had this problem with distancing. She always tried to distance to the point that she didn't even acknowledge what the relationship originally was. He was her fiancé, the man who she would marry and spend the rest of her life with. Until he got mad because she chose to go to an art show instead of spend time with him. The end result was that she spent time in the hospital.

Elena had moved Cayce out of the very difficult situation she'd been in and had helped her set up her life again. She had been consoled by the fact that somebody had threatened her fiancé to disappear quietly—or else.

She would be forever grateful to that person. She didn't know if that person was still around because of Elena, who had a lot of those kind of people as friends, whereas Cayce just had Elena, making Cayce's loss all that much more heartbreaking.

With Cayce's to-do list well and truly locked in, she nodded, realizing that this failure to take care of herself was causing all kinds of chaos in her world. *I'll do better now*, she thought, as she headed to work.

When she walked into the next project, the big icy one, she stood there, looking at it, when Frankie came up.

"Hey, how are you doing today?" he asked.

"I'm doing fine," she said with a smile. "At least I'm doing better than I was."

He looked at her intently. "You do look better," he said. "Brighter skin, a little happier."

"It'll take time," she said. "There's really no other answer for grief."

"I understand," he said. "At least you're in the position where you can keep moving forward."

She motioned at the backdrop behind him. "How's this going?"

"You tell me," he said with that big grin of his.

She smiled, loving the energy that came with Frankie's smile. He was always calm, upbeat, energizing to be around. She studied the icy backdrop and smiled. "Those areas there need a bit of work," she said, pointing. "That series of icicles hanging around the cave needs a bit of work too," she murmured.

He nodded. "I knew you'd catch those two areas," he said. "Look at the bottom far corner. I don't think the trees are quite right yet."

"I can finish those," she murmured. "I just want to make sure we've got a really good solid foundation before we even attempt to find models."

"Not Naomi?" he asked in surprise. "I thought she was booked."

"If she was booked, she just became unbooked," she said briskly.

"Got it," he said, nodding. "Can't say I'm sad to see her go."

"You and me both," she said with a smile. "Just being around her is terrible."

"True," he said. "This a good thing."

"Says you," she said with a smile.

"And you too," he said. "Otherwise you wouldn't have done it."

"I had to," she said. "It was just too impossible."

"You'll never hear me argue that point," he said. "I'm all

for it. I do know a couple potentials, if you're interested."

She looked at him in surprise. "Friends?"

He nodded. "Yeah, friends."

Something odd was in his voice. She looked at him, smiled, and said, "Lovers?"

He flushed. "Yeah. I love her."

"Send me her photos, and I'll see," she said, "but I make no promises."

"Good enough," he said. "That's all any of us can do, you know? Is take a look and see."

"Okay," she said. "Now let's get to work." And she quickly pulled her long smock over her clothing, kicked off her shoes, rolled up her capris a little bit higher, and walked over the canvas cloths littering the floor. "I'll work down here first," she said. "I'll fix these trees and then work my way up this side."

"Good enough." And they got started.

When she turned around a few hours later, somehow she wasn't surprised to see Richard standing in front of her.

He eyed her critically. "You do look better."

She shrugged self-consciously. "Thank you. I didn't expect such kindness from you last night."

"We tend to have that initial negative effect," he said, "but we're not mean people."

She nodded. "No, it's just that you're involved in an ugly job."

"That we are," he said.

She looked at him and asked, "Do you have any more details about what happened last night?" She gave a slight glance over in Frankie's direction.

"It's not connected," he said.

She sighed in relief. "Well, thank God for that."

"Exactly."

"Not to worry," he said. "You can carry on with the next installation. We'll probably have some undercover cops around, just to make sure we don't have a third victim."

"And yet I don't think Thorne was at the last installation, was he?" She frowned and looked at Frankie. "Frankie, was Thorne at the last installation the night that he died?"

Frankie nodded. "But we were done easily by four o'clock in the afternoon."

She turned to look at Richard. "So I don't know that added security at that show would have made any difference."

"What you really mean is," he said, "that somebody could be watching during the day, if they pinpointed Thorne."

"That's not what I meant to say," she said, "but, now that you brought it up, it is quite possible."

"Good enough," he said. "Maybe I'll just hang around, walk a few blocks, take a look at what's going on around you, while you do this," he said. "A fair bit of attention is out there."

"Of course," she said. "It's a big project, lots of activity, and I think I need to put a sign or two outside to say what is coming."

"Okay, I'll just blend into the background and see what I can see."

"You can also get video cameras," she said. "You might see the same person at the same installations."

He smiled at her. "I am a cop, and I've been one for a really long time. I do know what I'm doing," he said. "And honestly, we have asked various people for those feeds. And we have several people at the station culling through all those

165

that we've received to date."

"Oh," she said, flushing. "I didn't mean to be rude. It just occurred to me that maybe the same person, if he was stalking Thorne, could also be stalking someone else."

"Exactly," he said. "Go and do your work. Let me take a look around and do mine." And, with that, he turned and walked away.

Frankie walked over and asked, "This is still about Elena?"

"Elena and Thorne," she said sadly. "Two young lives that had no business being cut short."

"I know," he said. "There's been some talk on the set too."

"Anybody quit because of it?" she asked him, stepping back slightly. "Does it bother you?"

"It doesn't bother me," he said, "but I also have a black belt in karate. Killing me won't be quite so easy."

"No," she said, "but the minute you think that it's almost a guarantee, somebody will find a way around your skills."

He chuckled. "Come on. Let's get back to work. It's the only time you are ever really happy."

She thought about it, nodded, and said, "Boy, you are right there."

RICHARD WANDERED AROUND the area, checking out her work, checking out Frankie—and her relationship with him—seeing a bond, and, although Richard had told her that he saw auras, he saw a little bit more than that.

A stranger's voice at his shoulder said, "It's pretty amazing, isn't it?"

He turned to look at the speaker, only to find nobody there. Frowning, he spun around and then turned to look back in the direction he'd been. "What the hell?" he whispered.

"It's Stefan," the voice said at his shoulder.

He turned in an ever-so-slow loop again. "Where are you?"

"I'm here," he said, "but, while you're studying the energy of those two over there, you're not looking at my energy."

"I can't see anything."

"Go back to the position where you were standing originally," Stefan ordered.

Obediently Richard turned to study Frankie and Cayce, who were standing and discussing a corner of this massive painting. "And?"

"Now look out of the corner of your eye."

He turned a bit, looked out the corner of his eye, and, sure enough, there was a yellow glow. "Is that yellow goldenness yours?"

"Yes," he said calmly. "I'm outside. I dashed in to take a look. I'd like to talk to you."

"And you didn't have another way to do it?"

"You seem to need proof," he said, "so—"

"I'm coming," Richard said, and he walked out the front door. "Where am I coming to?" Then he turned and up front was a sports car, with a man in a beautiful suit leaning against it, who stared at him. Richard walked up and said, "Stefan?"

Stefan gave a clipped nod. "I am, indeed."

"What did you want to talk to me about?"

"An energy is all around her," he said. "And it's not all hers."

"And that means what?"

"You see? You're one of those guys who uses instincts, gut feelings, and that little bit of energy that you can see as a way to do your job," he said. "*But*, if you would open your eyes and see what's really there, you'd be incredible at your job," he said.

Immediately Richard could feel the anger sparking. "Who the hell are you to tell me that?"

"Just Stefan," he said. "Somebody who sees a whole deeper level than most people are expecting."

"Okay," he said. "And what is it that I'm supposed to see?"

"The energy that's not hers."

"Is that normal?" He turned to look back at the building. "You could have told me this while I was in there, so I could look."

"Yes, but you have to separate it by shades. I counted no less than seventeen people."

"Jesus. That seems like a lot." He stared at Stefan. "And yet you don't seem terribly shocked."

"I'm not," he said. "I'm saddened, but I'm not shocked."

"Saddened?"

"Because it's much harder for her to function if she's also carrying all these people."

"And who are they?"

"In most cases, I would say that they are likely to be people who she cares about, with a few more unsavory energies in the mix."

"I'm not sure she cares intimately about anybody in her world, now that Elena is gone. Is there anybody else?"

Stefan smiled and laughed. "It's one of those things that we do unconsciously in any relationship, intimate or not," he said. "Generally, if you have more than a cursory relationship, their energy is attached to you. That will include people you work with, who you knew growing up ..."

"Okay," he said. "So, is it wrong for her to have these seventeen people?"

"Not necessarily all are wrong, but some of them? Yes."

"Such as?"

"You'll never convince her that carrying something of Elena's energy is wrong."

"I doubt anybody would feel that way," he said. "Doesn't it help to keep them close?"

"Yes," he said, "it definitely does. And, whenever she did a bit of work with Elena, they would mix their energies. Cayce would use Elena's light in order to make everything glow around the model. And then, as Elena would step away, it would be almost like a light dimmed the painting behind her. Elena used her own energy in the painting to make it glow as well."

"And that was part of the artistic show that the model herself would put on?"

"Absolutely," he said, "and now, without Elena, Cayce can't do that. Or at least not as well, not as easily."

"Which is why her last few have seemed different."

"Yes. And nobody'll understand why," he said. "But she understands, and she's looking for another source, so she's trying out other energy relationships. Seeing if she can work with them."

"Is she hurting them?" He turned to glance back in her direction.

"No," Stefan said emphatically. "In no way is she hurting these people."

"So Cayce's requesting these energies?"

"Most of them, yes," he said, "but not all. And it's the other ones that worry me."

"Why is that?"

"Because a couple of them are very dark, and I think that's what makes her tired and is holding her down, making it hard for her to sleep."

"What can she do about it?"

"She has to toss those energies," Stefan said quietly. "But she has to do it in such a way that she doesn't scare them, so there's no backlash. She has to keep herself safe at all costs."

"How dangerous is it?"

"Very," Stefan said. "The ultimate worst-case scenario is the loss of her life."

That message was bad enough, but then Stefan added one more cryptic message. "One energy is there that—" and he stopped his words abruptly.

Richard leaned forward. "You can't stop there."

Stefan shrugged. "I can't be sure it's the problem."

"Can't be sure of what?" Richard bit off.

"I can't be sure," Stefan said, measuring his words carefully, "but something about that one energy I recognize."

Richard sank back on his heels, crossing his arms over his chest. "In what way?"

"An old case," he said. "The problem with this is, energy changes, but the signature is always the same. This signature is different."

Confused at the new terms, Richard just stared at him. "Meaning?"

"Meaning," he said, "that I'm thinking, and I can't be sure right now, but I'm thinking that this might be somebody who's related to somebody who I encountered in an old case."

"Are you saying, something like a criminal's son?"

"Or brother or father or mother, et cetera," Stefan said. "But I haven't seen this before, so I can't define it."

"An awful lot of vagueness here," Richard said.

Stefan gave him a beautiful smile and said, "In energy work, nothing's definite." Stefan added more cryptic layers to the conversation. "They would have been attracted to the bright energy she's putting out."

"That doesn't make any sense," Richard said in confusion.

Stefan continued, "She's looking for the same energy she had with Elena, so she's asking the world around her for that same energy. From people who are close to or very compatible, loving, and caring. She's bringing them into her world so she can find one, two, three, or more models she can work with. I think, at this point, she doesn't want to rely on just one."

"Well, that makes sense, having just lost *the one*," Richard said, "but that doesn't explain why this other energy would be attracted."

"Because it's seeking something. Most dark energy is emptiness. Evil is empty inside. They try to fill it. Because they can't reach and access the good energy, even though they try really hard, they generally fill it with the negative energy, because that's easy. That's what they're used to. It's readily accessible. It's much easier to go rob, rape, murder, to refill their well, than it is to turn around and do an about-face of their basic character and reach for these good energy feelings, like doing something good for others. You know? Helping people, really sending love out to the world instead of hate."

"So, by the extension of her requesting this good loving

energy, she's attracting negative energy?" Richard wanted to be clear because this was freaky stuff.

Stefan nodded. "That's exactly it."

"So again, it's not her fault."

"You need to stop thinking guilt, blame, fault, responsibility," he said. "She does enough of that."

He leaned against the car and studied Stefan. "What is that supposed to help me with?"

"It means, you need to look at the people around her," he said, "and those who come into her world in the next week or two because they're coming for a reason. She has a void in her life now with the loss of Elena. Cayce's trying to fill it, and all these people want to be that person. And it won't matter what means to an end they use to get there."

"Right," Richard said. "You know what? On that note, I think I'll head back inside and keep an eye on her."

Stefan straightened and said, "I'll do a little more digging into old cases, see if I can figure out that connection."

"You do that," Richard said. He turned and walked away.

"Don't forget," Stefan called behind him.

Richard spun and looked at him. "Forget what?"

"To look at the energy," he said in a low tone. "And that means, your gut needs to come into play. Your instincts need to be sharp. Something's going on."

"Right," Richard said. "Got it."

WHO THE HELL *were those guys,* he wondered. He studied the two powerful men, leaning against the car. They were the kind he hated. They were the kind who knew what they could do. They were pros and had that arrogance that made his back go up. They always thought that they were better than him, even though he was the one making his world happen, and they were just taking paychecks and doing whatever life dictated to them.

Not him. No, not him. He was making his world happen. He smiled and turned, walked out of the building and away from them. They wouldn't notice him. Chances are, they weren't even looking in his direction anyway.

He darted through the moving vehicles and headed across the road. He picked up a coffee and a hot dog from a vendor and kept on going. He'd be back in a little bit. He had a right to be back, after all. But more than that, he needed to be back. There was just something magical about watching her work, and he couldn't let that go. No way he could let go of anything to do with her. It was an interesting problem, and one he was fully prepared to work on. He needed to touch that light, to have that light, to make it his, so that his art could be that—all of that.

He took a bite of his hot dog, smiled down at it, and mumbled, "You might be cheap, but you're definitely what I want right now."

And everyone needed comfort food now and then.

CHAPTER 13

I T WAS ANOTHER long heart-curling day. Was that because Cayce was trying desperately to get her emotions under control? Still, she managed to get the bulk of the Arctic Ice installation done.

As she stared at it, a proud smile on her face, Frankie came up behind her and said, "This one is extraordinary."

She laughed at him. "The last one with the kids was extraordinary," she said, "but this one is definitely classy."

"It's a tie with the other one," he admitted. "It's really stunning."

She smiled up at him. "Thank you."

"What about the models?"

She frowned. "I want to let this dry, have another day, two maybe, and then I've got to pick a model."

"So definitely not Naomi?"

She shook her head. "No. Definitely not. Tomorrow morning I'm taking a look at some models in person."

He hesitated.

She looked at him. "I never did get the pictures from you."

He looked at her in surprise, quickly pulled out his phone, then grimaced. "Sorry. It's in my Drafts folder." He hit a couple buttons, then said, "Okay. I've sent them."

"It might be too late for this one," she warned.

He nodded. "I know. Just if you could think about it."

"Will do." She took off her smock, set it aside to dry, and said, "Remind me when we are back in the office that it might be time to order another half-dozen smocks."

He chuckled. "How about if we don't? If you would wash them in between …"

"But, by the time they have the paint on them, and they have all the other mix of paints on them," she said, "they don't really wash."

"That one is stiff now," he said, pointing out the way the fabric wouldn't hang.

"I know," she said. "That's why I need to order another batch."

"I presume that's something Anita does for you?"

She nodded. "They should be on reorder, or whatever, that automatic ordering system. Is that what everybody uses these days?"

"You're right, one delivery a month."

"It is what it is," she said. "The cost of doing business."

"You make good money," he said. "You should order what is needed. Then, at least, you don't have to put one on if it doesn't make you feel good."

"How did you know that was often the determining factor, as to whether I wore the one I had or went to get a new one?"

"Because you're all about feelings," he said. "Now maybe you'll listen to me and go home and get some food and make it an early night."

"I had a good night last night," she said. But she nodded, looked down at her paint-covered hands, even though she'd washed them several times already, and shook her head. "Definitely time for a shower with a big scrub brush again."

He grinned. "You could paint your nails. Then you would look like it was part of it," he said.

She looked at her nails that, even though she had scrubbed them, still had bits and droplets from splatter. "My hair is covered anyway," she said.

He turned, looked at her intently, and then chuckled. "It is, indeed."

She rolled her eyes at him. "And, on that note, I'm heading home. We'll see you tomorrow."

"Aren't you coming back here again?"

She shook her head. "No, I've got appointments at the gallery with the models first thing in the morning, and then I'll be back here, probably eleven-ish, to see what else we need to finish up."

"When is this live?"

"Next week Saturday," she said.

"Right. So my model has probably not got enough time."

"I'll look when I get home. That's the best I can do," she said.

He smiled, nodded, and said, "I just appreciate you taking the moment."

She gave him a small finger wave and headed to where her raincoat and purse and boots were.

When she quickly dressed in her outer layers, it covered up a little bit of the paint. But not much. When she turned around, purse in her hand, she came face-to-face with Richard.

He frowned at her, his gaze on her painted hair. "New fashion?"

"I'm setting the trend," she said blithely. "And obviously this is my look."

They both laughed, and, for that, she was also grateful. When he smiled, something spontaneous went through him, and she realized that was one of the same elements that she saw in Elena. The trouble was, with Richard, he didn't let that part of him out all that often, whereas Elena lived in that spontaneous world, and her darkness didn't come out very much.

They all had the darkness. Everybody either hid it or reveled in it, but everybody had it.

"Come on. Let's get you home," he said.

She looked at him in surprise. "You don't have to escort me home," she said.

"I know I don't have to," he said, "but I want to." He held out his elbow.

Surprise was the only reason she allowed herself to react, she followed her instincts, and she slipped her arm through his. She stepped forward and walked beside him. Feeling an intense gaze on her back, she turned to see Frankie staring at the two of them. She gave a half shrug and a smile, saying, "See you tomorrow, Frankie." He lifted a hand, and she turned and walked out.

"Is there something between you and Frankie?"

"I already told you there wasn't anything between us," she said, "but I haven't done something like this in a long time. So, of course, Frankie's surprised, and especially that it's you. Frankie's now figuring out if it's personal or business."

"And have you worked that out?"

She stilled, but he dragged her forward another step. She continued to walk at his side. "Are you telling me there's a choice?"

"If you haven't figured that out already," he said, "you're

slow. And I know for a fact that you're not slow."

"You don't know me that well," she said defensively.

Once outside, he laughed.

"How do you know I didn't drive today?" she asked.

"I was here this morning. Remember?"

"Right," she said.

He led her toward a conservative-looking sedan. Surprised, she asked, "Ghost car?"

He looked at her, grinned, and said, "No, it's my own."

"This is not what I envisioned you driving."

"This is my work vehicle," he said cheerfully. "I do have a Jeep for weekends and playtime."

At that, she couldn't help but burst out laughing. "Now that would make more sense to me. Please tell me that it's some ultrabright color that's the complete antithesis of this sedate conservative vehicle in front of me."

"Lime green. Does that work?"

She stared at him in fascination. "Actually, that's perfect! The artist in me definitely approves."

"When is this arctic showing?"

"Next week Saturday," she said. "My current problem is I need to find a model."

"Even in a pinch, you won't use Naomi?"

"No. Not even in a pinch. I will no longer use Naomi. Ever."

"And what about finding the others?"

"I'm definitely interested in some. I'll see them all in person tomorrow."

"I guess you need that, don't you?"

"People in pictures are one thing. Pictures can be tweaked, some more than others. In this case, I need to see the models. I need to see their skin tone. I need to see scars. I need to see tattoos," she said with a one-armed shrug. "People hide all kinds of things, and, when you get to what they're really like, we'll deal with it. I don't want to deal with it at the last minute. I want to know what I have going in."

"I presume you can cover it all up?"

"Absolutely I can cover it all up, but it takes time, accuracy, and I may have to alter pictures. And, yes, I can do that in the moment, but why should I have to?"

He helped her into the vehicle, closed the door, walked around, got in on his side, and started the engine.

"Sorry," she said. "I sounded a little defensive there, didn't I?"

"With good reason," he said. "You're the artist. You're well-known for the quality of the special work you do."

They pulled away from the curb. She sank back into the leather seat, loving the little bit of luxury that was available in the seating. Maybe it was more the fact that somebody was taking care of her.

She couldn't even remember the last time that had happened. She had staff who looked after her to a certain extent, but it was obvious that they were staff. This was something different. She didn't know what he wanted, and that part of her was being judgmental. Of course he wanted something. Everybody wanted something. But, at the same time, she didn't know what it was.

She pointed at the corner light coming up. "If you turn right here, it's the fastest way home."

He nodded. "But, if I take you home, you won't eat, will you? Remember? We ate most of your food last night."

She turned to him in surprise. "Well, I would have a shower and then eat."

"I'm taking you for dinner."

"Oh no, you're not," she gasped in horror. "Look at me."

He looked at her, smiled, and said, "Believe me. You'll be very welcome at this place."

"No, no, no," she said. "I'm not going anywhere with paint in my hair!"

"Do you realize that you almost always have paint in your hair?" he asked with an affectionate chuckle.

She was still protesting when he pulled up outside a small brick restaurant. Italian from the looks of it. She shook her head. "Nope, nope, nope, no way, not happening."

"Yes, yes," he said. "Absolutely yes. Come on. It'll be fine. You'll see."

At the end, her voice rose in a wail.

He laughed, got out, and circled to her side, where he opened her door and held out a hand. He said, "Remember who you are."

She shook her head. "I'm an idiot, apparently," she said. But nevertheless, she placed her hand in his, wondering at herself for doing so, and stepped from the vehicle. "You do realize my clothes have paint on them, and I've got paint on my fingernails." She held them up for him to see.

He didn't even look at them.

"Why is this so important?" she asked.

"Because you don't look after yourself," he said. "I'll take you home afterward. You can have a shower and get a good night's sleep."

Feeling embarrassed and horribly put out, she somehow allowed him to lead her into the restaurant. As soon as they entered, she realized that the lights were dim, and the ambience was much more subtle than what she had expected. That was still no excuse for his behavior though. She gave him a good frown to prove it. But his teeth flashed white in the smooth, silky atmosphere. They were immediately led to a corner in the back of the room.

She shook her head. "How do you get that kind of treatment?"

He leaned down and whispered, "I have connections."

She just rolled her eyes at him.

Cayce was seated in the dark corner, so just he could stare at her hair. And she realized he'd also done that deliberately. "Well, you get points for consideration," she said, "but not for *not* allowing me to come out in my best."

"If you were really hungry, would you have cared?"

"I've been known to go to a coffee shop," she said cautiously, "but not anywhere else if I looked a mess."

He nodded. "This place won't care. They already know who you are. They're absolutely thrilled to have you."

She shook her head. "They don't know me. Unless you just told them, they wouldn't have known either."

"I told them a while ago."

Just then another woman appeared with two menus. She placed them down, held open her arms, and he hopped up, gave her a big hug, then turned and introduced Cayce to Rosita. The woman beamed.

And yet poor Cayce felt terrible. She immediately apologized for her appearance.

The woman in front of her shook her head. "You honor us with your presence. The fact that you have just come from yet another masterpiece is also an honor. You must never feel that you need to put on airs or be anything other than who you are here. We have known Richard for decades. Now, what can I get you to eat?"

Cayce hadn't even had a chance to look at the menu.

Richard looked over at her and asked, "Do you have any objection to spaghetti and meatballs?"

She shrugged and said, "This appears to be your show. Go for it." Her tone was dry.

Rosita laughed with great merriment. "At least you understand Richard. That's good." She quickly removed the menus and disappeared, coming back a moment later.

They hadn't said a word to each other while the woman returned with a basket of what appeared to be fresh sourdough bread, the aroma wafting up from the basket and making her stomach growl. And then Rosita came back with a pot of whipped butter.

Richard picked up the loaf, slicing off thick slabs. He took one for himself from the center and left her the rest, for whatever choice piece she wanted. She couldn't help herself. She reached for a crust, buttered it, and took a bite, then sank back and ate it slowly in complete silence. She just loved the warm, yeasty bread, as it slid down her throat wrapped up in fresh butter. "That is delicious," she said.

"I'm glad you think so," Richard said. He left her to just sit and enjoy.

When she had a second slice of bread now buttered, she put down her knife, and then ate it with a smile.

He leaned forward and asked, "Feel better?"

She nodded. "But now the fatigue is setting in, and I'm a long way from home."

"You're only a few blocks away, and I promise that I'll get you home again."

She smiled at him. "It's not your job to look after me."

"Well, somebody needs to," he said gently. "Obviously you're distracted and aren't doing such a great job of it.'

"It's just ... this business with Elena," she said, getting

her friend's name out with great difficulty.

He nodded. "I know," he said, "and you're allowed to feel this way."

She nodded. "But it's still not your job."

"Everybody needs help sometimes," he said.

They sat in comfortable silence amid the candlelight, and she realized just how much like a date this was. Not that it made her necessarily uncomfortable. She certainly hadn't been dating much in the last six months—or however long it was. But she was just having that odd sense of having somebody care enough to look after her. However, she was still fighting it.

"Stop," he said. "You're trying to wrap your mind around this, trying to figure out the details, trying to see if there's an underlying issue. There isn't. So just stop."

"Meaning that you're just being a friend, making sure I don't collapse?"

"Absolutely," he said, and his tone was sincere. Then he flashed her a bright grin. "If it makes you feel better, don't think of this as anything too intimate," he said. "Just think about it as me looking after my case."

She rolled her eyes at that. "I highly doubt you take anybody else out for a meal."

"I do for dates," he said.

She studied him quietly for a long moment.

"And we can consider this a date," he said, "but I'd much rather take you out when you're not quite so exhausted."

"That brings us back to the personal-versus-business conversation," she said slowly.

"It does," he said.

Just then Rosita appeared with two large plates of spaghetti and meatballs. When she placed one platter in front of Cayce, she stared at it in shock. "I'll never eat all this."

"You'll eat what you can," he said, "and we'll take the rest of it home for tomorrow."

She looked up at Rosita, who held up a block of Parmesan, asking her if she wanted some. She nodded mutely as a generous sprinkling went over the sauce. When Rosita was gone again, Cayce stared down at the food, looked over at his plate, and said, "Is it my imagination, or is your serving even bigger than mine?"

He laughed. "They know me here," he said, "so my portion is probably bigger."

She looked down at the four massive meatballs in the center of her platter and saw that he had five. "If you can eat all that, I'll be amazed."

"I'm likely to work all night," he said, "so it's one of those things, you know? I eat when I can."

"Ah, so you don't look after yourself either," she said immediately.

RICHARD CHUCKLED, STARING at Cayce, loving the wit that she mustered, even though she was obviously exhausted, and yet she had been game to come here. Although obviously not pleased at first, now that she was here, with a hot meal in front of her, she wasn't throwing a fit. He knew lots of women who would never have stepped into the restaurant at all. He'd warned Rosita ahead of time, so she'd been extremely discreet but happy that Cayce was here.

He took a bite and moaned. "You need to try it." He watched as she slowly twirled a few noodles onto her fork, lifted it up, and took a bite. She stared at him in surprise. He nodded. "They do absolutely divine spaghetti here."

She didn't bother answering. She bent her head to work on the food on her plate. And when she finally put down her fork, he noted the amount left on her plate and estimated that she'd eaten about 40 percent. Adding in the French bread, that was a fairly decent meal for her.

He nodded. "We'll get Rosita to put the rest in a to-go container."

"And I'll need to go soon," she said.

He could hear the fatigue in her voice. Black shadows were under her eyes, and she looked very droopy. He nodded. "I can take mine to go too."

"No, no, no," she said. "You eat. I'll be fine."

He laughed. "If we leave that plate in front of you for more than another five minutes, your head will fall right into it."

She looked at him, laughed in delight, and said, "Can you imagine the mess?"

"A new form of art," he said.

Rosita appeared, almost as if by magic, but she'd seen the conversation from a distance and was extremely astute. She quickly removed both plates and came back a few minutes later with their take-out boxes.

Thanking Rosita before she disappeared again, he looked over at Cayce. "I should have offered you a glass of wine," he said, "but I completely forgot." He chastised himself for that. Not very smooth.

She waved a hand. "I wouldn't have had it anyway because it would put me to sleep."

"That might not have been a bad thing."

"The pasta and the bread are doing that alone."

"I'll get you home in five minutes. I promise. Just stay

upright a little while longer."

Rosita came back with the check, which he quickly snagged and paid with his credit card, and then stood. He held out a hand and helped her from the bench seat, as he said, "Come on. Let's get you home."

She looked at the to-go boxes. "That's coming with us, right?"

He snagged both containers. As they headed for the exit, Rosita met him at the door with a bag. They carefully put the take-out boxes in it, and he stepped outside. His car was just a few feet away, and she stumbled even getting that far. He put the take-out bag on the hood of the car, walked around, and helped her inside. Then came back, sat behind the wheel, giving her the bag. "You hold that."

She clutched it like it was gold.

He chuckled. "It was good, wasn't it?"

"It was delicious," she murmured. "And, as exhausted as I am"—she gave him a half a smile—"my mind is already putting this in my stomach for breakfast."

"You could do a lot worse," he said.

He pulled up in front of her apartment a few minutes later. He hopped out, even though she was busy protesting that she didn't need him to. He opened the car door, helped her back out again, grabbed the leftovers, and said, "You'll learn one day that no way will I leave anybody, especially a woman, alone outside in the city at night. I'll take you up to your apartment. Just to compound all this, please remember a crazy wacko is out there."

At that, she subsided.

He tucked her arm into his elbow, and, as she walked up to the front entrance, the door opened automatically, and the doorman smiled at her. "Did you have a good evening?"

And with the same elegance that he expected from her at all times, she nodded and smiled. "Despite my looks, we just had a wonderful spaghetti dinner."

The doorman's face split in two with a great big smile. "Did Rosita look after you?"

She stared at him in surprise. "Do you know her?"

"She has the best Italian food anywhere in the city," he said with a big grin. "Besides, I saw the bag."

She chuckled and waved at him. "Any messages or anything I should know about?" she asked.

He shook his head. "All is quiet."

"Thank God for that," she said. As they walked into the elevator, she looked at her purse.

"Forget about it," he said. She glared at him. "Yes, I know you're thinking about checking your phone."

"I absolutely am," she said.

"Don't," he said. "Not right now, not until tomorrow morning."

"But things can blow up in that time period," she said in protest.

"Then let it," he said. "You need to look after you. Remember?"

Suddenly they were at her front door, and he could see she felt awkward. He took the key from her, unlocked the door, and pushed it open, ushering her in. He put the leftovers into the fridge and then did a quick search of the flat.

She stood beside the front door, staring at him in confusion.

"Just making sure," he said. He turned to walk to the door, then walked back in a very long, slow, unhurried pace, tilted her chin up, and kissed her on the lips. It wasn't one of his out-of-the-park kisses, but it was definitely a way to impart that he cared, that he was really worried about her, and that he really wanted her to take care of herself. And that he really wanted to spend more time with her.

When she stood there dazed, swaying on her feet, he kissed the tip of her nose and said, "Now off to bed." He turned and walked out, closing the door behind him.

It was all she could do to walk over, throw the bolt, and drag herself upstairs. As soon as she got into her bathroom, she took one look at the mirror and shrieked.

"GET OUT OF my way, loser," the beautiful woman snapped, as she walked past him on the sidewalk. Halo shrank back against the wall. He knew her.

She'd been in one of the paintings.

She was marked.

Needed to be warned. To be saved.

"Your soul is at risk," he cried out, his voice hoarse.

Caustic laughter wafted toward him.

"There's no saving me, asshole. And I don't need your help. Look at you. Just a homeless bum on the street. You wouldn't know good or evil if it came and bit you in the ass." And she walked away, strutting her stuff.

But she was wrong. He did know. He'd learned at a young age that evil came in male and female forms. That it came in the form of those who said they loved you the most. And sometimes in the form of complete strangers.

You couldn't let down your guard.

Good boy. Bad boy.

CHAPTER 14

"**O**H, MY GOD," Cayce said to her mirror. "He dragged me out in public like this? How could the restaurant even let me in?" She alternated between laughter and fury, and then realized it was already an after-the-fact thing. No wonder Graham, her doorman, had been grinning.

She shrugged, stripped out of her clothes, let them all drop where she stood, and stepped into the shower. She leaned over, putting her hands against the shower wall, and just let the water sluice down her hair and back. She wanted to moan and cry for joy, but that took effort.

It took three times washing her hair to be able to run a comb through it without snagging on dried paint. Her fingers took a little bit longer to scrub. By the time she was done, she stepped out, grabbed a towel, wrapped it around her hair, and another around her body. She quickly dried off and walked into her bedroom.

She stared out the window, wondering how quickly her life had changed. She'd lost Elena, and then, all of a sudden, there was Richard. She didn't know what to think. She didn't know how to act. It was like he'd completely taken over, not as if she were a suspect, but as if she were a dear, dear friend. Something that Elena would certainly have done, if she'd been here. If it had been anybody else who had affected Cayce the same way, she might have known how to handle it. Not that she had to handle anything, but it felt like she did.

Then she realized she was just too damn tired, too tired to think, too tired to stand here any longer.

She walked over to the bed, dropped her towels to the floor, and completely collapsed under the sheets. Her last thought was that he had put all the leftovers in her fridge. And then she closed her eyes and let the world of darkness take her away.

And if her dream world had just taken her for a nice gentle stroll, it would have been fine. Instead it led her through a nasty maze of nightmares, of artists being hacked apart, arms being skinned, legs being skinned to go with the torsos. She knew that she could count on Richard to do the best he could, but, so far, two were dead, and, from the way he acted tonight, it was obvious that he thought she may be in danger too.

All of this filtered through her mind throughout the night, so, when she woke up the next morning, she lay exhausted, even while still in her bed. Her eyes opened. Instead of her almost perfect bed, as if she had slept solidly in one place, her bedding was twisted and turned, with the blankets and pillows everywhere. She groaned, shifted so that she sat up, leaning against the headboard, and pulled her knees to her chest.

Just then the phone rang. She stared at it, almost hating to answer. When she picked it up, Richard was on the line. "How did you know I just woke up?" she asked, feeling confused.

"I didn't," he said, "but it's ten o'clock."

She gasped in horror. "Oh, my God. I'm late."

"I don't think so," he said. "Remember. You're the boss.

You're the artist. And you're supposed to be eclectic, creative, and on your own time frame."

"I also run a business," she said. "Other people depend on me, and, therefore," she added, "I pride myself on being on time."

"Wouldn't that be nice?" he asked with a smile. "But today is an exception."

"Did you get some sleep last night?" She couldn't help asking.

"Actually, I did," he said brightly. "Have you had a shower?"

"No, but I had one last night." She held out her splayed fingers, studying the paint residue critically. It looked like she had done a pretty decent job.

"Good. Tell Graham to let me up then."

"You're here?" She bolted from bed. "I'm not dressed."

"I wasn't planning on coming in and attacking you," he said with a note of humor. "Get dressed by the time I get there. We can have breakfast." And, with that, he hung up.

Her intercom rang a few moments later. She hit the button. "Yes, Graham, you can send Richard up."

His voice was full of laughter. "You've got a live one," he said. "I approve." And he hung up.

She stared at the intercom in shock. Did everybody feel that she was in need of companionship? She raced back to her bedroom, pulled out a sundress that didn't need a bra, stepped into white cotton panties, ran a brush through her hair, and quickly twisted it into a knot at the nape of her neck. By the time she was done, there was a knock on her door. She walked over, threw it wide open, and glared at him. "A little more warning next time?"

"If I have time to give you warning," he said, "maybe."

And he walked in, taking a good look at her face. "Doesn't look like you had the best of nights though, huh?"

"No," she said. "Definitely not. Full of nightmares and demons, and, you know, nasty people who cut up others."

"To be expected," he said. "Have you got coffee made yet?"

"No," she said with exasperation. "I haven't had time."

"Well, you start warming up the spaghetti, and I'll do the coffee."

She watched in amazement as he walked over, studied her big expresso machine, gave a clipped nod, and immediately made coffee. "It took me three months to figure out how to use that machine," she said crossly.

"Well, if you had called me in"—he gave her a knowing look—"I could've told you in twenty minutes."

By the time the spaghetti was warmed up, she'd already had her first cup of coffee. They took their heated plates and a second cup over to the table set up by the big window, where she normally had her breakfast. The two of them sat opposite each other.

She looked down at the spaghetti. "You're very pushy, you know? But I forgive you because I'm facing the very same spaghetti I had last night."

He chuckled. "I'm pushy when I need to be because, the bottom line is, if you want something in life, you have to go after it."

She froze, looked up at him, and said, "Are you saying that I'm something you want?"

He gave her a droll look. "What do you think?"

"I don't know what to think," she said. "Did you plan this last night?" She attacked the spaghetti in front of her.

"Partly," he said, "if it makes sure that you eat before

you head off to your full day, then yes."

"I have to interview those models today." She looked at her watch and grimaced, as the phone rang beside her.

He looked up at her.

"I have to at least tell her that I'll be on my way in an hour."

He gave a clipped nod. She quickly answered Anita's call, saying that she just woke up, was eating now, and would be over there soon. When she hung up the phone, she said, "And I still feel bad."

"Are all these models hopeful of working with you?"

She nodded. "Yes."

"Then I'm sure they'll be happy to wait. You didn't cancel. You just postponed."

"I know," she said, "but—" Her attention was quickly diverted back to the spaghetti. She was shocked when she realized she'd eaten the whole thing already. She stared up from her empty plate and looked at him. "How did that happen?"

"Well, for starters, some leftovers are still on the counter," he said, "but that's a decent amount you've eaten this morning. Come on. I'll give you a ride."

"You can't just spend your life taking care of me," she muttered.

"Yes, I can," he said. "Are you painting today?"

"Only to get an idea of skin tones," she said. "It shouldn't matter, but, with some of my images, it does."

"An extra layer of paint?"

"Oily versus dry, extra layers, darker skin versus lighter skin, all of the above." She hopped up, walked over, grabbed a pair of light sandals, picked up her purse, and said, "Let's go."

He smiled at her. "While you were doing that, I put your dishes in the dishwasher."

"That's probably no help," she said. "I haven't turned that sucker on in forever."

"Which is why it was empty," he said with a laugh.

"Exactly," she said, chuckling.

Shortly afterward, as they walked into her gallery, he stepped back and watched as she proceeded to first apologize for being late and then immediately got down to business.

"Morning, Anita. Where are the models?"

"They're in the back room, having a cup of coffee," Anita said. She stood with her pad of paper and a pen and asked, "What do you want me to do?"

"One at a time in my office, please," she said.

"Do you want the images too?"

"Of course," she said, nodding. She walked into her office, turned, looked back at Richard, and frowned.

He grinned back at her. "I'm just watching." He pointed at her office and said, "Am I a problem?"

"With the models?" She thought about it and shook her head. "Particularly if you can find out in any way, shape, or form if any of these potential models would also be potential victims?" she said in a low voice. "The last thing I want is to bring in new models and have any of them be injured."

He very carefully didn't remind her that *injured* was one thing; *dead* was another entirely.

She pointed to one of the bigger chairs on the side of her office and said, "Why don't you just park yourself and pretend to be busy."

He gave a bark of laughter. "I'm doing what I'm supposed to be doing," he said, "and that's keeping an eye on you and the energy around you."

At the word *energy*, she froze, slowly lifting her gaze, and looked at him. "What's that about energy?"

Just then Anita walked in. He motioned and said, "Later."

She nodded, and he watched as the procession started. She asked the first model several questions, checked on her skin tone, got up, walked around, looking for tattoos. Of course she was looking at auras, emotions, darkness. Looking for ones she could work with.

This one asked, "Do you want me to strip down?"

But Cayce was completely nonchalant when she said, "No. I have the full front and back photos," she said. "That'll be fine." She held out a tiny paintbrush and said, "I need to check the skin tone and oiliness."

"Where?" the model asked.

"Your back. And I promise. I'll clean it off."

The girl looked at him nervously and then looked away.

"I can leave if you're uncomfortable," he offered gently.

She looked at him in surprise. "God, no," she said. "I'm a body model. It's what I do. I just don't know if you're here judging too."

"Neither of us are judging," Cayce said. "It's just important that I have what I need," she said. When she was done, she took some cream and a Kleenex, walked over to the model, snapped several photos, and then quickly wiped off the sample that she had done. She smiled at the young girl, liking her innocence and lightness. "Thanks."

The girl looked disappointed, turned, leaving Cayce's office, putting one foot on top of the other. "Is there any way to know when you'll tell me?"

"Not just yet," she said. "I have four today, and another one I have to look at."

"So, is this just for one job you're looking to fill?"

"Not necessarily," Cayce said, easily, gently. "I do these types of things on a regular basis. So, it's a matter of having a couple regular models and a couple standbys."

The girl looked relieved. "I'd be really, really happy to work with you," she said impulsively.

Cayce's face split into a wonderful warm smile. "Thank you," she said. "Now, go off have a coffee, enjoy life, and I'll get back to you."

The girl ran out, laughing. She left a lightness in the room. Cayce looked at Richard, a smile on her face.

"Is that what you're looking for?" he asked curiously.

"Not necessarily for this one," she said, "but, in certain pieces, yes. That energy will shine through."

He nodded slowly and watched as she repeated the exercise with three other models. She quickly tested the skin on each of the models with a paint that, to him, looked like white, but he had to admit that she was right. The color was coming off differently on each of the models. He frowned, fascinated.

The fourth one caught his breath in the back of his throat. Her skin was almost caramel. She was stunning, and she knew it. Yet it came across as self-confidence, not arrogance. Cayce was not in any way looking at her face. The woman stood completely still, while Cayce walked around, did a test sample, looking at the model's skin, asking a few questions, which the model readily answered. When she stepped back, the model looked at her and asked, "Do I pass?"

"You definitely pass," she said. Cayce stood off to the side, tapping her lips, as she considered what she apparently wanted out of this. When she finally dismissed the model, she turned to Richard and frowned. "Some of them are close, but not one is exactly right."

"But will one do?"

She groaned. "That's the thing about art," she said. "There's no such thing as *will do*. It's either good or it's bad." Then she stopped, frowned, and said, "But I'm out of time, so I need to choose."

Her expression said she just remembered something. She walked over to her monitor and clicked the keyboard.

"Did you remember something?"

"One of Frankie's friends," she said. She brought up something on the screen, and the look on her face said she had it. She sat back at the same time as he leaned forward.

"Does this one look better?" he asked.

"Well, she's interesting," she said. "The thing is, my mind is caught with the planes of her face and her collarbones and the way she stands. There's a confidence in her that would be very easy to impart into the body-paintings. The same as the last model."

"So that's good, right?"

"Well, it means that she, they, have something," she said, "that's indefinable. But I'm not sure it's malleable. So each would work for some jobs but not likely for all jobs."

"Maybe it's time," he said, "to not look for someone perfect for all jobs but to have a pool to add something fresh and different every time."

"Right," she said. "So, pick one for this next job, pick one for the job after that, and see how I like them." She brought up the folders, quickly flipped through them, pulled out two, and said, "We'll start with these two." She called out to Anita. "Here."

Anita walked in and said, "Did you make a decision?"

"These two," she said, and she wrote something on a sticky note and stuck it on the top folder. "This is for the ice installation, and this other one will work for next week's forest scene."

"Does she look like a wood sprite?" Anita asked with a smile.

"No, but I think I could turn her into one," Cayce said seriously.

"Do you want to put out the call for more?"

"No," she said. "I have another one on my screen. I'll bring her in too."

"Oh." Anita looked down at the folders in her hand. "Not one of these?"

Cayce shook her head. "No, this is another one." But she didn't elaborate.

Richard watched the byplay and noted Anita's irritation at not knowing anything about the third model. As soon as she left, he leaned forward and said, "What was that all about?"

"Just a little bit of a problem between Anita and Frankie," she said with a smile. "Even artists have to deal with other people. It'd be nice if I didn't, but I do," she said. She pulled out her phone and called Frankie. As soon as he answered, she said, "Can you come in here for a minute, please?"

Richard sat back and watched and waited. As soon as Frankie walked in, she said, "Tell your friend I want to see her."

His face lit up with joy. "She'll be thrilled!"

Cayce looked at her watch and said, "As soon as possible. She probably won't be for either of the next two jobs, but I would like to see about maybe giving her a try. But I want to see her first."

"I'm on it," he said, beaming.

But, at that time, something caught her attention right behind him.

"What's going on?" Anita asked, poking her nose into the room.

Cayce gave her a look. "I'm having a private conversation."

Anita looked quite disgruntled, but she backed out. And it gave rise to the first inclination that all was not well in Cayce's world.

Richard stood, waved at her, and said, "I'll just do a walk around."

She nodded and kept on talking to Frankie.

He left her inner office, stepping into the gallery, but, after another step, he stopped, pissed to see at least a dozen people milled around. He didn't look at Anita before he asked, "What are all these people doing?"

"Could be anything," she said. "It's a bloody open-door policy around here."

Richard nodded and decided to go check that out for himself.

HE WANTED TO see the model lineup. To see Cayce's choices. He knew good ones. Had been around beautiful women all his life. His sister, for example. She'd been a model in her prime time. Unfortunately she had breast cancer, and those beautiful boobs had disappeared, along with the rest of her, forming this wasted landscape of organic material. He couldn't stand being around her anymore. She was this rotting piece of flesh that just couldn't seem to die fast enough. She and Elena had been close friends. He knew that Elena and his sister had both been really bothered by his attitude toward his own sister. It really bothered him too. But he could do nothing about it. He thought about trying to preserve her flesh, but he didn't see what the point was. The light was gone. She was no longer a masterpiece. She was this crippled caricature.

He got up, left his apartment, walked into the big gallery, and perused the huge images that showcased Cayce's work. He just couldn't even imagine the kind of money renting this space cost. These people were absolutely fanatical about having that art gallery look.

His heart gave a happy sigh when he wandered through her art on display here. She was incredibly talented. He kept striving for that. It was the one thing he wanted to achieve for himself. But a part of him wondered if he could ever make it. Finally realizing that he'd been all the way around yet again in her gallery, he turned, walking toward the exit.

Somebody else was in the room, studying him. He quickly picked up his pace; by the time he got to the front door, he was almost running. As he bolted down the sidewalk, he then dodged through the traffic, heading across the street to the little magazine stand. His hands were shaking. He stared down at them, swearing under his breath. When a hand reached out, grabbed him by the shoulder, he freaked. And, sure enough, he turned to see the detective standing there. Staring at him.

He bolted. He heard the shout behind him, but he ignored it. No way he would go back in there again, at least not without making sure that this guy wasn't there. Jesus Christ, where the hell had he come from?

NAOMI STARED IN outrage as the models came out one by one. She sat in a coffee shop just fifty feet away and could see clearly what was going on, which just hit her, like a red-hot poker to the skin. *How dare that bitch do this to me*, she screamed in her head, but outside she smiled a bitter, vengeful smile and whispered, "Bitch, you'll get yours."

"Stop," Derek said, in a soothing tone.

She turned and glared at him. "No, I'm not stopping," she snapped. "Do you see what she's doing?"

"No," he said, "I don't see what she's doing."

"She's checking out other models," she snapped.

"Well, of course she is," he said. "Elena is gone. She has to have new material."

"I'm the next Elena," she sneered.

He sat back and looked at her, his long elegant manicured fingers thrumming out a beat on the table. "Obviously not," he said gently.

"Don't say that," she said, in a tightly controlled voice. "That email means nothing."

"That email means that your services are not wanted for the next show."

"So what?" she said with a toss of her head. "When she has a chance to think about it, she'll realize she needs me."

Derek said, "I don't think so. I think she's moved on. What was spoken between the two of you anyway?"

"I was tired, hungover, and she was taking all day. It was obvious that she shouldn't have been painting that day in the first place."

"Well, I do hope you didn't say anything to her about it," he said, in a horrified fascination, "because she's all business. She has installations scheduled with public showings. She has to be here and to do them."

"Well, her damn hand was shaking," she sneered. "What difference does it make?" she said, finally noting the horrified look on his face. "Anybody can paint this shit. At a certain point it doesn't—"

He reached across, grabbed her hand in a surprisingly steely grip, and said, his voice hard, "Stop. You're heading down that self-destructive path again."

She pulled her hand free. "Who cares?" she said. "That bitch needs to know exactly what she'll do for me." She got to her feet and raced across the road. As soon as she got to the front door of Cayce's gallery, she slammed it open, only to see poor hapless Anita sitting there. Mousy little Anita. Naomi sneered at her. "If that bitch thinks she'll be using models other than me, you can sure as hell forget that idea."

Anita looked at her in surprised shock. "What?"

"You heard me," she snapped. "I'm the one replacing Elena."

Anita looked past Naomi.

She turned, expecting to deliver a full-flight explosion on Cayce. Only it was Richard, the detective, staring at her.

In a mild, yet very interested tone of voice, he said, "Yeah, and just how will you do that?"

She immediately put on the brakes. But it was hard. It was damn hard. She took several slow, deep calming breaths. "She owes me," she said tightly. "That's my job."

"What job?"

"The arctic one."

He shook his head as he said, "Seems to me that Cayce has the right to pick her own models. She already picked one—"

At that, Naomi said with a flick of her hair, "When she picked me."

"And I also unpicked you," Cayce said, coming out from the door behind Anita. "I also told you that in my email to you. So why are you here now?" she asked.

Naomi stared at her with such hatred that even Richard stepped closer.

"I think you've said enough," he said.

"I haven't said anything," she said with the curl of her lip. "Wait until I tell everybody that your models are dying at the hands of a madman."

At that, the detective immediately swung her arms around her back and clipped them together with handcuffs.

She spun around on him, her fury so huge that she could feel the spittle coming from the corner of her lips. Humiliation, fury, and frustration boiled out of her as she screamed at them all. "You can't do anything about this," she roared. "That job is mine. No way any of those other models are safe. I'll make sure that they're not," she screamed.

Just then the detective clapped a hand over her mouth and said, "Stop it. Now you'll get to ride down to the station with me."

And then she stared at them. "Take the handcuffs off."

"Oh no," he said. "You can bet I'll make sure that they all see you like this."

CHAPTER 15

C AYCE STARED IN shock as Richard led Naomi from the gallery, outside into his vehicle. And, as he promised, he did march her past the big bay window for everybody to see.

Cayce walked back into her office and sank down again. "Good God."

Just then Frankie came rushing inside. "What the hell was that?" he cried out.

"Everybody's worst nightmare," she said simply. "Naomi in her rage, threatening everyone, including destroying my business, telling everybody that a serial killer is targeting my models."

His face fell. "She's just vindictive enough to do it."

"Yes," she said, fatigue in her voice, "she would." She stared down at her desk. "She even said she'd make sure they weren't safe, which earned her the trip with Detective Henderson. God, what next?" She'd only been here for four hours, and she already wanted to go home. She looked around and realized she really had no reason not to. She straightened and grabbed her purse and said, "I'm heading home after my next meeting."

He stepped back wordlessly, just watching as she walked past him.

She could see the understanding in his expression, but Anita, on the other hand, said, "Dear God, please don't let that happen again."

"Models can be just as obnoxious as artists." She gave a finger wave and said, "You may want to take the afternoon off."

"I can't," Anita said despondently. "Too much work to be done."

Cayce couldn't deal with that either. She just nodded and kept on walking. She stood outside the gallery, taking several deep breaths, not even sure what the hell had just happened. Something was so cringe-worthy about Naomi, which was just another reason why Cayce had chosen not to use the woman in any more of her pieces. But, of course, there was a certain cachet to being one of Cayce's models, and obviously Naomi had just now figured that out. Which was sad, but, at the same time, what else was Cayce supposed to do about Naomi but fire her? "It is what it is."

She headed out, not sure what she was supposed to do at this point, but she needed to know that she was free. She turned and walked back home.

This was something she could do.

She walked aimlessly, her mind spinning from Naomi to the guy that she had watched Richard chase across the road, to the poor victims, wondering if maybe she should just shut it all down until the investigation was over.

As she headed across the street, just a half block from her apartment, the blow came out of nowhere. She fell to her knees and cried out. Somebody was after her purse, and she tugged back hard on it, and the young male grinned at her and bolted. She struggled to her feet and sat down on a bench close by to catch her breath.

She didn't recognize him. She thought she knew the local pickpockets in the area. But that was not classy, that was not smooth, and that would not get him the money that he wanted.

She sat, shaking on the bench for a long moment. Then she saw Frankie racing toward her. He sat down beside her, grabbed her hand, and asked, "Are you okay?"

"I will be," she said, and the damned tears welled at that.

"Come on. Let's get you home."

"Did you see that?"

"Yes," he said. "I just caught it out of the corner of my eye and saw you go down." He checked her purse. "Did he get anything?"

"No," she said, "but I think he said something as he raced away, about payback from a friend."

Frankie stared at her, a tick in his cheek flicking. "That bitch Naomi."

WHEN RICHARD LOOKED down at his phone to see Cayce was calling, he answered it immediately. "Hey, you okay?"

She hesitated.

He repeated his question with a sharper tone of voice.

"I just wondered," she said, "if you already knew about it."

"Knew what?"

"I was just attacked on the street," she said, taking a slow breath.

He could hear her shaky nerves in her words. "How?" he asked, bolting from his chair, his mind racing to the homeless guy he'd seen at the installation.

"I think just a pickpocket," she said. "He grabbed my purse. I pulled it back, and he ran, tossed me a grin, and said 'payback from a friend' for some reason."

"Payback?"

"Yes, but I don't know what that means. Frankie thinks it's a message from Naomi."

"I'll ask her. But it could be nothing, could mean that you deserved a tumble to the cement because you wouldn't let him have your purse. Providing you kept your purse?"

"Yes," she said, in a stronger, almost relieved voice, "that I did. And that makes a lot of sense. He was such a punk-looking kid."

"Good." Or not so good as that meant it was someone other than the homeless character. "How are you? Are you okay?"

"Just a little shaky," she said. "But that's to be expected. Frankie is here now, and he's taking me home."

Richard swore softly under his breath. "Good. That's where you need to be."

"Yeah," she said. "At the same time, I don't know if it's related or not, but Frankie thought I should tell you."

"Definitely should tell me," he said forcibly. "I'll come over when I'm done at work."

"No," she said hurriedly. "You don't have to."

"No, I don't have to," he said, "but I will be there none-theless."

"Does that mean I'm to wait with the rest of the spaghetti?" she asked in a teasing tone.

Just hearing that tone made his heart lighten. What a fool he was, but he said, "Unless you want me to pick up Chinese."

"You can't just sit here and feed me all the time," she exclaimed.

"Sure I can. Listen. I'll be there in a couple hours, and I'll bring dinner. So, if you're hungry in the meantime, have at the spaghetti."

"I thought I'd have a shower and maybe a nap," she said.

"That works for me."

As soon as Richard hung up from that phone call, he looked over to see Andy walking toward him, his face grim. Richard's heart sank. "What?"

"We've got another one. Not sure what plans you just made with the artist right now," Andy said, his tone matching the look on his face, "but you won't make it."

He sagged in his chair. "When you say, *another one*—"

"*Another* one."

"Do we know who it is?"

"No," he said. "At least I don't. I haven't gotten an ID on the victim yet."

Richard reached down, grabbed his jacket, and said, "Let's go."

FAILURE WAS NOT an option. But it's all he seemed to churn out. How did that work? He stared in frustration at his canvas in front of him. He used to do the same kind of artwork that she did. He just needed to get it back again. Then he could be on top of the world too. If it hadn't been for that time of his life, he would have been there.

And he knew everybody else would say it was just an excuse to get out of it, but he couldn't. He just couldn't. He was completely frozen every time he tried. It sucked. He looked up as a woman walked into the room. "Hey, Bellamy, how you doing?"

"I'm thrilled," she said, walking closer, throwing her arms around him. "Thank you, thank you, thank you."

"For what?"

"For looking after me," she said, as she squeezed him tight.

He wrapped his arms around her and held her close.

"I hope you're feeling okay now."

"I feel much better," he said.

"Do you think so?" She walked around, took a look at his painting, and smiled. "It's getting better," she said.

He knew what she was trying to do, and he appreciated it, but she was lying. "Sweetie, I know it's not."

"No," she said, in a firm voice. "It is getting better."

"And that's a long way from what I was."

"It takes time," she said. "Remember that."

"Yes, I know," he said, "but it's still frustrating."

She kissed him gently on the cheek and said, "Of course it is. Come on. Let's get to it."

"I don't know about dinner tonight," he said.

"You need to eat," she said. "Come on. You can't just keep this up."

If only he could get back the talent he had lost.

"Come on. Forget about it for now," she said, tugging him toward the kitchen.

He glanced to the other room that she never went into, wishing he had time to go in there and to work a little bit more. But he didn't dare. He turned, smiled at her, and said, "You're right. Let's get something to eat."

CHAPTER 16

W HEN RICHARD DIDN'T show up in the two hours he'd promised, Cayce finished off the spaghetti. She couldn't hold off anymore. She realized that his job would probably keep him away from her on a regular basis. And there wasn't as much spaghetti as she had thought, so she was happy to polish it off.

She curled up in front of the fire with a glass of red wine, thinking about her day and Naomi. Surely Naomi wouldn't have done anything for that *payback* comment from the thief. And it could just as likely have been his version of payback because she managed to keep her purse, but she took a tumble. Any and all of it was possible, and that was the problem.

When her phone rang, she looked down at it, not surprised to see it was Richard. "Hey," she said. "I gather you got detained."

"We have another one," he said, his voice grim.

"Shit," she said, putting down her wineglass before she spilled it. "Who is it?"

"I don't know," he said. "I'll send you a photo."

"Do I have to?"

"Unfortunately, yes. I'm sorry," he said. "We need an ID, and this is the fastest way to get it."

She took several deep breaths. "Fine," she said. "Send

213

it."

Sure enough, he sent it. Staying on her phone, she brought up her email and looked at the photo. "That's Liana," she said softly. "I used her on one project about eight months ago."

"Why?"

"Because the person commissioning the art piece asked me to," she said. "Where did you find her?"

"In a dumpster between the other two," he said.

She winced at that. "So somebody really thinks she's just a piece of garbage to throw out. Is that it?" she snapped, her voice gaining strength.

"Some people do look at it that way, yes," he said. "And, no, I'm not one of them."

"No, of course not," she said, hugging her knees to her chest. "No forensic evidence? Nothing?"

"No," he said, his voice even darker. "Once the media gets hold of this, it will get nasty. I think you should avoid going to work tomorrow."

She gave a startled laugh. "What am I supposed to do instead?"

"Are you ready for the next installation?"

"Because I needed something to focus on," she said, "I am a little ahead."

"Then please stay home," he said urgently.

"But it doesn't make any sense that he would be targeting me. He's after my models."

"Do you remember what you body-painted on Liana?"

"Of course, dolphins," she said with an aching sadness. "Turtles and dolphins."

"So, a waterscape."

"Yes," she said.

"And how did it work?" he asked.

She frowned at that. "Meaning?"

"Did it have something special in it, like on Elena? Was it something that this guy would be looking for?"

"But it would have been six or eight months ago," she said, bewildered.

"Yeah," he said. "We need to contact her next of kin."

"I'm not sure there is any," she said slowly. "She was a talker and was friends with the investor. But there was something about not having any family. Or at least nobody nearby."

"Do you have a last name for the investor?"

"No, but I will phone Anita and find out." With that, she hung up and quickly called her assistant. When it went to voicemail, she groaned. She sent him a text. **She's not answering. I'll check my records to see if I have any paperwork for it.**

Good. And that was all he wrote.

She went into her home office and went through her emails. It was probably the fastest way. The company was called Waterscapes. With that in the search box, she quickly pressed Enter, found what she needed, and texted Richard back. **Phil Hennessy**, and she gave him the phone number.

She got a thanks back and that was it.

She slowly made her way back to her couch, where she sat on the floor, this time in front of the fireplace, just rocking in place. "Poor Liana," she whispered to herself. It made no sense that she'd worked for her all that time ago. Where had she been since?

She frowned, wondering if Liana had been doing other modeling or something else since then. A short time later, when Hennessy called her, she stared at her phone and frowned as she answered. "Hello?"

"I haven't seen Liana for months," he said preemptively.

"When did you last see her?"

"I think when she did the modeling for me," she said sadly. "She wasn't my regular model. I put her in the picture because of your request," she said, "and I don't know what happened after that."

"That's what I was afraid you would say," he said. "The cops just called me."

"Yes, I'm sorry. I had to give them your number. Do you know where she's been these past months?" she asked him.

"No clue. She was here one day, had been back and forth, around a lot prior to the art thing," he said, "and then she wasn't. And I realized what a fool I was."

"Meaning that, by giving her that body-painting gig, you thought she would stick around and pay more attention to you?" She kept the judgment out of her voice. She knew a lot of these men with money just didn't seem to care about helping young people, as long as they stayed with them. It wasn't always about sex. It was often just about companionship.

"I guess," he said. "Maybe I'm just a fool. But now I'm really hurt to think that she's been murdered."

"Me too," she said. Her intercom buzzed. She stared at it and said, "I have to answer the door," she said.

"That's fine," he said. "We should get together and have coffee sometime."

She responded in kind, knowing that he didn't mean it. As soon as she hung up, she walked over to the intercom. "Hello."

Graham called out, saying, "A package is here for you."

"From whom?"

"No sender is noted," he said, "and it doesn't have your apartment number on it, just your name."

"Interesting," she said. "Somebody'll come by and pick it up. Just keep it off to the side, will you?" She couldn't understand what upset her about this delivery, but she just knew it was bad news, whatever it was. She didn't want anything to do with it. She quickly dialed Richard's number.

"What's up?"

"A package was delivered downstairs," she said, "without my full address."

"Have you looked at it?"

"Hell no," she said. "I don't even want it up here."

"Good decision," he said. "I'll swing around in about thirty minutes."

She smiled, and hung up.

When her doorbell rang close to thirty minutes later, it startled her because she'd been sitting in a daze in front of the fire, trying to remember the beautiful model Liana had been. And it was sad that she could barely even remember her features. She had pictures of her from the art installation, but not of this young woman who she was at her core.

She walked to the door, opened it, and there was Richard. He looked at her and said, "You get a houseguest tonight."

Her jaw dropped. "Why the hell would I need that?"

"Because that parcel wasn't anywhere near innocent. I can't stay though. I'm heading back to the station."

"Who's coming to stay with me?" she asked in confusion.

"I have a security guard coming."

"And that won't make any bit of difference," she said.

"You saw that Graham kept that package from getting to me."

"It doesn't matter," he said. He turned to motion behind him.

She saw a big man in a police uniform. "Who is he?" she asked in a soft voice.

"Your guard," he said, "until I get back."

She glared at him. "Will you tell me what was in that parcel?"

"Do you really want to know?"

But something in his gaze made her wince. "I gather I don't want to know."

"Let's just say, it's a piece of the last victim."

The breath washed out of her all at once. "Oh, God," she said.

He leaned forward, kissed her hard, and said, "Stay put."

As he walked away, she could hear him giving instructions to the guard. When he was gone, she stepped out, looked at him, and said, "I'm so sorry. This is not a good way to spend your evening."

The guard looked down at her, grinned, and said, "Standing at your door is a lovely way to spend the evening. It's what I do. Now please go back inside and stay there."

She frowned up at him. "Fine," she said, "but tell me if you want tea, coffee, water, bathroom, et cetera."

He gave a clipped nod of his head and said, "Not to worry. I'll be just fine, ma'am."

She had to be satisfied with that. She didn't like it, and there wasn't a whole lot she could do about it. She walked back inside, sat down again, her mind tumbling, yet avoiding the one topic that she knew she needed to consider, which was, *What was in that damn box?* The thought that somebody had sent her a *gift*, or was it another *payback*? Or was it something else? She just didn't know. It was seriously difficult to understand anything at this point.

Knowing that she was struggling, she headed upstairs and had a long hot bath. As she got out, she checked her phone, but she still had no messages from anybody, so that suited her. She got dressed in her nightie, and, with her wine, sat down on her bed and picked up the book she'd most recently been reading.

Just as she finally got into the story, even though it took her several minutes to reread the same page over and over again, her phone buzzed. Instantly she snatched it up. Sure enough, it was Richard.

"On my way," he said.

She shook her head. Now what the hell was she supposed to do? She glanced at the massive bed that she took up only a small portion of. She didn't think he was planning on sleeping with her. But that thought sent her out of her bedroom and over to the spare room, wondering just what shape it was in.

As soon as she opened the door, she realized it was neat and perfect as it always was. She turned back the bedding and walked over to check that towels were in the small bathroom. She didn't know how long it would take him to get here, but she put on a robe and wandered back downstairs anyway. The stars were out tonight, and the city lights burned bright in the darkness. She stayed downstairs, until the doorbell rang. Finally.

She raced to the door and, when it opened up to reveal Richard, she threw herself into his arms. He hugged her close and whispered, "It's okay."

"It can't be okay," she said, tears blocking her sight of

him. "Three people are dead."

"And all connected to you, yes," he said. He quickly ushered her in and closed the door.

She looked at the door, then at him. "Is the security guard still there?"

"No, he'll go home now."

"Meaning, you're staying?" She could barely get past the relief in her voice.

"Yes," he said, "I'm staying." He opened his arms; then she stepped right into them. "I know it's tough. I know this is really a difficult time," he said, "but I promise. We will get through it."

"I don't know how," she whispered. "How is that even possible?"

"Because, unfortunately—"

She shook her head wordlessly and just pressed tighter against him.

He held her close. "You were in bed?"

She nodded.

"Any chance I can have a shower?"

She nodded again, turned, shut off all the lights downstairs, and led the way upstairs. She motioned to the spare room. "This is your room," she said. "There's the bathroom, and towels are in there."

He nodded.

That was the first she noticed that he had a small overnight bag. He dropped it on the bed, turned, and said, "Can you sleep?"

"I don't know," she said. "In all of this, I've never been worried for my own safety. It's all been about my poor models."

"Any thoughts about putting a halt on everything until

the investigation is closed?"

"As soon as you tell me that's what I need to do, then I'll do it," she said instantly. "In the meantime, an awful lot of money is hanging on some of these installations, and I don't know what would happen if I'm not on time."

"A criminal investigation is usually a good excuse," he said.

"The ice show is next week," she said. "Saturday."

He nodded. "Let's hope we can get it done by then. Did you pick out your model for that one?"

She nodded. "You were there with me. I also want to see Frankie's girlfriend."

"Girlfriend? Or friend?"

"Girlfriend," she said. "He told me that they were lovers."

"Interesting. I picked him as gay."

"I think he's whatever. The young people have a new term for it. He does both."

Richard just nodded and pulled his shirt from his pants.

She stepped back, her eyes going wide.

He grinned. "Not to worry, sweetie. I won't jump you."

She flushed. "That's hardly what I was thinking."

"Well, I might strip," he said, "at least as long as you're here. But I will have that hot shower. Nothing quite like death to leave a smell in your nose and on your clothes."

At that, she immediately backed up several more steps. "I'll leave you to it then," she said in a rush.

"I'll take a shower, then come and speak to you. Go get back into bed."

"Hell no," she said with spirit. "That's just way too dangerous."

"In what way?" His gaze was steady.

She crossed her arms over her chest and frowned. "We are not lovers."

"We're not lovers *yet*," he said cheerfully. "That's okay. Go run away. There will be another day."

"I'm hardly running away," she huffed.

He leaned over, kissed her on the cheek, and said, "You better though. Otherwise you'll get more than you're looking for." His hands went to his pants, where he quickly undid the zipper.

She gasped, turned, and raced from the room. Back in her own room, with the door shut firmly between them, she put her hands to her hot cheeks, wondering why the hell she was shocked, when he'd been making moves the whole time. She was just out of practice, not sure she wanted to do this, and then she called herself a liar flat-out.

"Hell, yes, you do," she said. The trouble was, she didn't want any of this other stuff around them. She didn't want their personal relationship to be confused with the case, and she wanted to find out who had killed her friends.

She clambered into her large bed, determined to put him out of her mind, where he truly belonged. She pulled the pillow up, punched it once or twice, and closed her eyes. She'd be damned if she'd let him know that she wasn't sleeping.

RICHARD HAD TAKEN a couple steps in the right direction today. He didn't want to lose the advantage that he had slowly gained. He wasn't so sure about the slow part, but she was as touchy as a doe. After his shower he stepped out in just his boxers, wandered through the downstairs, checking security, making sure that everything was okay, then went upstairs, doing the same. When he got to her door, he hesitated.

"What are you doing?" she demanded.

"Checking your security," he said. He reached for the doorknob and pushed it open and said, "Do you have alarms on your windows?"

"I'm on what, the eighth floor?" she said in exasperation. "Nobody will get at me from here."

He hesitated, then shook his head. "I need to check," he said in a firm voice. "Otherwise I won't sleep tonight either."

"Fine," she said, "but leave the lights off."

"As you wish," he said. He walked through the room, checked the bathroom first, relieved to see it had a good locking mechanism, and then headed out to the bedroom.

As he walked to each of the windows, checking that they were locked, she said, "You're really serious about that, aren't you?"

"About what?"

"About somebody getting in."

He turned, looked at her, and he leaned forward as he answered her. "I've never been more serious about anything in my life."

"It doesn't make any sense," she said gently. "He's after my models, not me."

"He's after possessing a piece of you," he said with brutal clarity. "So, what's to stop him from wanting the whole cake?"

She stared at him.

He could see the whites of her eyes in the dark. She was sitting up, her covers to her chest, but it was the look on her face that broke his heart. He went to her side, wrapped her up in his arms, and whispered, "Sweetheart, I'll make sure he doesn't get in here to you."

She shook her head. "You can't promise that," she said. "He's already gotten three people."

"Which is also why we're rather desperate to find whoever else may have worked for you in all these years."

"Didn't Anita give you that list?"

"Just now," he said, "and we're working on it, honest. But it'll take some time. In the meantime, I want you safe."

She stared up at him. "When will this be over?" she asked in a low voice.

"Soon," he whispered. "I promise. It'll be soon."

Her eyes were so big and revealed her exhaustion. He walked around to the other side of the bed, threw the covers back, and, hearing the silent gasp of her breath, he climbed in. He slid over to the middle of the bed and said, "Go to sleep, sweetheart."

She glared at him.

He shook his head firmly. "No," he said. "Just go to sleep."

When she didn't do anything, he tucked her in gently, her body unresponsive, yet fighting him underneath the covers. He wrapped an arm around her, tucked her up close, and whispered, "Just sleep now. I promise I won't do anything in the night." A note of humor was in his voice. He could feel her starting to relax little by little, and then she chuckled. He smiled, having gotten the reaction he hoped for. "I don't think that's very funny," he said in mock humor.

"Well, it depends," she said. "Are you referring to the fact that you won't do anything during the night, or that you could do it and I might sleep through it?" And she giggled again.

He chuckled and, with an exaggerated macho voice, said, "Honey, no way you'd sleep through that."

"Good," she said, "because I want to enjoy it too." She yawned, curled up against him, and sank deeper into the huge soft mattress.

He smiled as he listened to her steady breathing as she slumbered away. He loved her response because they both knew where they were going with this relationship.

Andy had taken him aside earlier today and again told him, "God, man, please wait until this case is closed."

"She has nothing to do with the murders," he told his friend and partner confidently.

"It doesn't matter," he said. "You know it won't go well if you have a relationship with a suspect."

"We're friends," he said. "That's all it is."

Andy looked at him distrustfully. "I don't know about that," he said. "I know your reputation."

"And that's all it is, a reputation," he said. "And she is not a woman to be trifled with."

Andy thought about it, then nodded. "No, she's a keeper," he said, "so you need to be prepared for that."

"I struggled at the beginning," he admitted. "And then I just gave up. I guess it's a case of finally meeting somebody worth keeping."

"I can see that. But you really, really need to make sure that you don't let this develop any further until after the case."

"I know," he said. "I know."

And it didn't take very long before her breathing became slow, deep, and rhythmic. He knew that she had dropped right out. He lay here—calm, quiet, and peaceful—in a place he hadn't expected to be so fast but delighted that he was.

This woman never took care of herself, and that was something she needed to do, particularly now.

As he drifted off, he sensed something different, something unusual. He didn't open his eyes quickly. He laid here quiet, his eyes closed, figuring out what was bothering him. And then he opened his eyes just a hair, wondering if there was an intruder, but how could that be?

And that's when he saw the black tendril wrapping him around the base of the bed. He stared at it in shock. *What the fuck is that?*

Exactly what I told you to look for, Stefan said.

He froze, as Stefan's words slammed into his mind.

It's all right, Stefan said, the fatigue in his voice evident. *If it wasn't for the fact that I'm looking for this actual energy, I wouldn't have heard you in the first place.*

And you're talking to me in my head?

Yeah. It's much easier sometimes, he said. *Although, if you keep fighting me, it won't be easy at all.*

Right, he said. He was dealing with the fact that this other voice rumbled through his head, and he couldn't tell if it was real or not.

My voice is real, Stefan said. *So take a look at that energy, and try to move slowly so you can see it full-on. See if anything is distinctive about it.*

Distinctive about energy?

Yes. Don't mock it, Stefan snapped. *Just do it.*

Richard took a look at the tendrils. *It's hooked on her ankle. It's black, fading to a light gray on the outside. It's pointed at the ends.*

How long is it?

I don't know. Maybe a foot, a foot and a half. If you can talk to me in my head, can you see it too?

No, he said in frustration. *I can't see through your eyes. Sometimes I can, but, in your case, I can't.*

Well, I won't be too upset about that, Richard said.

Can you see any other energy there?

You said there was a lot.

I also said a lot of them weren't a problem.

Okay, so I see the black one. Something really light, a pulsating gold energy is up around midchest, he said. *She's not sleeping deeply. And these are just like hazes.*

Yes, that's exactly what it is, he said. *She's not sleeping well because she's probably got too much going on in her head. If you reach out mentally, think to pull out the black energy. And I'm not talking about the black energy at her ankle, but something up into her head. Pull it out, and she should start to ease down and sleep better.*

Even as Richard reached a hand up to her head, following Stefan's instructions and pulling out these invisible black threads, he could see that her restlessness was calming, and she slipped into a deeper, more intense sleep. *Well, that's quite nice*, he said. *I don't know what we're doing here, but it seems to be working.*

Now is the gold haze over her chest raspy or soft and smooth?

Sandy looking, he said instantly. He couldn't believe he was seeing any of this anyway.

And you may never see it again, Stefan said. *I'm trying to help you to see it, so that would be one of the reasons why it's as clear as it is, but, if you wanted to, you could see this all the time.*

Following Stefan's instructions again, Richard drew his gaze ever-so-slowly down past the gold, finding some redness at her belly, and a little bit below, a grayer energy. *Some of the colors are intermingled*, he murmured.

Think about her, how you feel for her, and place a hand over the gold energy, Stefan said, *and just smooth it gently*.

Feeling like a fool, his hand six inches above her body, he gently soothed and stroked the golden energy that looked more tarnished and sandier than anything. *For how long?*

Is it making a difference?

He studied it and then realized it was. *It's becoming softer, smoother.*

So, do it a little bit longer, until you can't see any more improvement. That's probably all you'll get done today. And then we'll take a look at the other energies.

What is that gold one?

All the people who she's lost and is holding dear to herself.

Not currently alive people?

No, he said. *She had a very close connection to Elena, and I'm sure you'll find that's one of the main elements of that gold.*

Also a little bit of an orange is in there.

A note of humor filled Stefan's voice. *Yeah, so any idea what that yellowy-orange is?*

No clue, he said.

Can you lean up and over her a little bit to take a better look?

It's all over her.

You mean, all across the torso and or all the way up and down?

Or it's just like between her and me.

So, now look down at yourself, Stefan said, that same humorous tone in his voice that made Richard frown.

Yeah, it's all over me too, he said. *What the hell? Is this dangerous?*

No, not at all, he said. *That's your energy.*

Richard froze. *What are you talking about?* he asked, his voice harsh. *I would never do anything to hurt her.*

That's exactly right, Stefan said gently. *That orange energy isn't trying to hurt her, though is it trying to protect her. It's fading up and down over her body, but mostly from her hip bones to her neck, correct?*

Yes, he said, *but it's also on me too.*

That's because you're trying to protect her, he said. *You're also trying to create a relationship with her, one that will stand the test of time. So that orange energy is both of you playing that relationship dance, both of you putting out the same energy to see if you can meet, mingle, and be special to each other.*

Does that happen with every relationship? he asked in shock.

Looking at your misspent youth? Stefan asked.

Maybe, he admitted. *It wasn't that misspent, but it certainly makes me wonder.*

But, in most cases, when you break up with somebody, that orange energy fades. And it appears only if you really, really care and have developed that shared energy system.

This has developed faster than I had expected, he said.

Because it's coming from the heart, Stefan said. *You weren't trying to have a hop-in-bed relationship quickly with her. You care about her. And that's where the relationship has started.*

Right, he said, *so it's completely different this time.*

Exactly.

It was all too much information to absorb.

The black energy is reaching for me or toward me, he said, shaking his head and sitting up in the bed. The black energy immediately slid backward. *If I move toward it, it retreats.*

You can see it clearly?

Yes, it's much darker. It's not hazy or faded, like the other colors. It's crisp, kind of like the gold that I saw that I helped make smooth.

Interesting. When you look at it, do you get a sense about what it is, who it is?

Is it a who?

It's absolutely a who, Stefan said.

No, I just get this malevolence from it. I want it off her ankle, he stopped. *It's like a ball and chain around her.*

Yes, often energy like that finds a part of the body that's weak. Do you know if she has a weakness?

Like old injuries? I have no clue, he said. *I'll ask her when she wakes up.*

I think that energy has probably been there for a long time, Stefan said. *So that'll be a little bit of an issue for you.*

I don't even know much about her history.

I'm pretty sure you can look that up in your files, Stefan said mildly.

He sank back down in the bed. *Do these energies hurt her right now?*

No, Stefan said. *She's been living with most of them for a long time.*

Jesus, he said. *Does everybody have this?*

Yes, he said cheerfully, *to one extent or another. Not necessarily bad. We keep friends and family close, so what you'll end up finding is that lots of people the world over have energy from those who they care about. When you have somebody who hates you or somebody who is envious of you or somebody who wants something of you, it becomes a different kind of energy.*

That black?

Yes, Stefan said. *When you move toward it and when you reach up a hand to her ankle, what does it do?*

Steadily he stared at the malevolent force that had suddenly appeared clearer to him. *It's retreating.*

Put your hand over where her ankle is. Does she have covers on?

Yes, he said. *It's sliding to the other ankle.*

The question is, does it leave?

It's getting very, very thin, he said. *It hasn't disappeared, but it's very, very thin.*

Reach out and touch it, Stefan said, curiously. *Tell me what it feels like, and be very aware of any images that flash in your mind.*

That stopped Richard in his tracks for a moment, and then determinedly he reached out and grabbed for the black tendril around her ankle. *I don't get anything but cold,* he said in astonishment. *It's really, really cold.*

That's fairly common too, Stefan said. *Now what you need to do is get a feel for that energy there. See if you can recognize who it is when you meet the person again.*

Meet the person again? he asked, hating that all this was happening in the middle of woo-woo land, and nobody was here to confirm that it was happening at all. He had never felt so alone.

And yet you aren't alone at all, Stefan said. *I'm here.*

That's not exactly reassuring, Richard said in a dry tone. *How do I do that recognizing part?*

Pull your hand back and then slowly reach it out, as if you're being absorbed into it or as if you're taking a piece of it for yourself.

Do I want to?

If you want to find out who it is who's targeting her, yes.

Again he froze. *Are you saying that black energy is my killer?*

No, I can't guarantee you that, Stefan said. *But it is con-*

nected to an old case of mine and it's obviously not a good, positive energy for her.

Right. So regardless of whether it's part of this current nightmare, it's not something we want to have there.

So reach out, sink into that little bit of energy, he said, *and try to sense what it is, who it is, male/female, old/young, angry/dark.*

Okay, here goes. He reached out a hand, closed his eyes, and mentally saw himself sinking into this black energy. Immediately he was caught up in a vortex. Anger, pain, and frustration swirled all around him. *Jesus,* he murmured.

Remember. I can't see it, Stefan said, *so tell me what you feel.*

Anger, frustration, pain, mostly frustration though. He *wants something from her, and he can't get it.*

Right, Stefan said. *Can you figure out what that is?*

No, Richard said. He quickly dropped the energy. *Jesus, it feels dirty, like I want to get up and have a shower right now.*

And you can bet it gives her an icky feeling every single day of her life. It's probably been there for a fairly long time.

And she wouldn't have noticed?

Have you noticed that it's now around your ankle?

Richard stared down and swore. He reached down with both hands, ripping it off, tossing it to the ground.

Rather than tossing it to the ground, Stefan said, *wrap it up in white light.*

He immediately threw a white blanket on it, tucked it up in his mind, and said, *Well, now that I have a blanket with this bloody black energy, what do I do with it?*

Don't give it back to her. You've already got that imagery, so send it out the window. Send it back to its owner.

He got out of bed, needing the visual of the window,

and going over, opened up the window, and then ordered the energy out the window and back to the owner.

Now what would be an interesting test right now, Stefan said, *is to watch where that blanket goes.*

He froze. *You're telling me this image and this conversation I'm having with you could lead to the person who put that black energy around her ankle?*

Stefan chuckled. *Absolutely.*

He watched as this figment of his imagination sailed across the city, heading over toward the far north, where the Olympic Coast was. *You know how bizarre this is?* he asked.

Stefan chuckled. *Most of my world is bizarre,* he said. *I use all kinds of methods to find serial killers and pedophiles, all the sludge of the earth. But more than that, we have people who can use energy to help us.*

The criminals also use energy to help them find all this?

Yes, Stefan said. *Think about it. If they had the ability to slide under a door, unlock a door, and get into where somebody was sleeping, how would you feel as a cop?*

As the women who are likely the targets, very violated, he said. *How come we never hear about this?*

Because you don't want to, Stefan said simply. *It's bad enough that I have to deal with it, and I step in when the cops can't do something. Sometimes I can't do anything. Sometimes I can't help at all. Those cases are when I get very frustrated. I put all my time and effort into connecting with a killer or pedophile, and I can't find him. Those are the cases that drive me nuts. It's also why I don't have a 100 percent record. And why some cops don't believe in me. But, when I do find the criminals, and I do bring them down, it's a satisfaction that's hard to explain.*

No, not at all, Richard said quietly. *Because that's what I do all the time.*

Imagine if you were doing that, Stefan said, *but on an energy level as well.*

So, can I use any of this in my day-to-day work?

Absolutely, he said. *If nothing else, it helps you to understand your suspects and your witnesses.*

By looking at the energy on their system?

Absolutely.

Like the gold and the red?

Yes, Stefan said. *And often, with battered women, you'll see a lot of black. Their partners will often have tentacles that go deep into their chakras, and they're so emotionally frozen and paralyzed by the abuse that they can't get out of their relationship. It's only when they're severed by death that the women are freed.*

God, that seems like a jail cell.

Well, isn't it? Look at that black energy from Cayce's ankle. The bottom line is, there's a reason that's around the ankle. It's exactly like a ball and chain.

Richard turned to look at Cayce still in bed. *She looks more at peace.*

That's the black darkness that you pulled from her brain. Her fears, her thoughts, her worries about her other models.

Right, to be expected. He walked back over, crawled into bed, and said, *Now what?*

Now, Stefan said with a smile, *you get to sleep.*

And, just like that, he disappeared from Richard's mind. With a smile on his face, Richard wrapped an arm around Cayce's waist, tucked her up closer, listening. Immediately she snuggled backward, until they were spooning from knee to chest, and, with that same smile on his face, he fell asleep.

"IT WASN'T WORKING. It's never working."

"Forget about it," she said in a firm voice.

He glared at her.

She shook her head. "Stop. This will just drive you crazy."

"I'm already crazy," he said.

"I don't want you to think that your talent is gone," she said. "I just don't feel like you're in the right space."

"Is that how you view it? As my talent being gone?" He slowly straightened and stared at her in full awareness.

She shook her head immediately. "Of course not. I don't know that this medium is the right one for you now." She walked back into the kitchen, put on coffee, and said, "Come on. Let's have a cup of coffee and sit down and relax."

He wasn't sure if she was mollifying him or what, but it was pissing him off. He strode into the kitchen. "Do you believe my talent is gone?" he snapped.

She stared at him, turned her back as she ground up the coffee beans, and said, "As I've told you time and time again, no."

He grabbed her shoulders, spun her around roughly, and pinned her against the counter. "Say it," he said. "Say it."

"No," she said. "I won't say it. I'm not getting sucked into that."

"What's wrong with me?" he asked, sinking down on the nearest kitchen chair. She didn't say anything, and he wished she would. He wished she would fight back. He wished that she would do something.

She brought the coffee over to the table and nudged a cup in front of him. "Enjoy your coffee," she said.

He lifted his head and stared at her. "I told you that I

love you, right?"

She gave him the ghost of a smile. "I love you too," she admitted. "I'm just not sure I can live with you anymore though."

He stared at her in horror. "Please don't leave me," he cried out. "Dear God, please don't leave me."

"It's not what I want to do," she said, "but your frustration is driving me batty. It's making you much more aggressive and much more unpleasant to be around."

"I'm sorry. I'm sorry," he said. "I'm so sorry." He reached across the table and grabbed her hands. "Please, don't leave me. Nobody else understands."

She gripped his fingers and said, "I know that." She squeezed his fingers. "But either I walk away from this, or you find another way to make that outlet happen because I can't keep doing this."

"Nobody else understands," he kept whispering. "I'm a different person than everybody else."

"Of course you are," she said, "because you don't dare let them see that you feel like you're a failure."

"No, I don't let them see. I *can't* let them see. They would never, *never* let me keep doing the work I'm doing," he said.

"Of course not," said this woman, who was the most special person to him, reaching out and gripping his fingers again. "But you're telling yourself that you're a failure constantly," she said, "and that's really hard for me to keep rebutting. You won't listen to me, and you won't listen to yourself. Who will you listen to?"

They both looked at each other, and the word came out immediately. "Cayce."

CHAPTER 17

WAKING UP AS Cayce was, warm, cozy, and being cuddled, was not what she expected. Her eyes flew open when she realized somebody was in bed with her. Richard's electric blue eyes met hers.

"Oh, my God," she said.

He leaned a little bit closer, kissed her on the tip of her nose, and asked, "Did you sleep well?"

She slowly sat up, stretched her arms over her head, while she tried to collect her wits, and nodded. "You know what? I think I did." She frowned. "I hate to think it's because you were here, but I feel pretty decent."

"Perfect," he said. "Do you mind if I have a shower?"

She nodded right away as he got up and strode from her bedroom in just his boxers, heading over to the room she'd unsuccessfully assigned him to last night. He was so nonchalant, so casual, about his heavily muscled body. Not a bodybuilder's body, but the body of a working man. Just a little bit of extra skin around his waistline made him all the more endearing.

When he came back twenty minutes later fully dressed, he raised an eyebrow. "You staying in bed all day?"

She gave him a lazy smile. "I'm pretty sure you gave me orders to not go to work today."

"Absolutely I did," he said with an approving smile. "But

I hadn't really expected you to stay in bed."

"Well, maybe I will," she said. It was starting to sound like the best idea yet.

"That's fine," he said. "I'll go see what there is to make for breakfast."

"Delivery service?" she said in a cheeky tone.

He turned, flashed her a bright smile, and said, "Oh, I don't think so. Maybe a cup of coffee to get you going, but for breakfast? You'll have to come downstairs."

She pouted, loving the interplay between the two of them. "Well, you get the coffee going," she said. "I'll jump into the shower."

"Perfect," he said, as he headed downstairs.

As soon as he was gone, hearing his footsteps running down to the first floor, she hopped out of bed with a laugh. She didn't know why she felt so good, but she did. She twirled around in place, then danced her way to the shower. As soon as she stepped under the hot water, she worked on her hair, wondering if she should get it cut super-super short, so it'd be that much easier to keep clean of paint, then decided she loved her long blond tresses and didn't dare part with them. She shampooed and conditioned her hair, then worked her body over with a loofah sponge from top to bottom. When she was finally done, she stepped out into her bedroom with her robe on, seeing him standing there, holding a cup of coffee.

He made a bow in front of her and said, "Ma'am, your coffee." He walked over and put it on the night table. "Bring it down with you. Five minutes until breakfast." And, with that, he disappeared.

She stared at the empty doorway in amazement. Then she walked over to her closet, figuring out what she wanted to wear. If she was staying home, she wanted to be cozy. She pulled on leggings and a nice soft tunic. Skipping socks and shoes or heels, she picked up her coffee, took a sip. Then she stepped back into her bathroom to run a brush through her hair, quickly turned the wet strands into a braid, popped an elastic at the end of it, and curled it around her shoulder. She picked up her coffee and walked downstairs.

As she walked into the kitchen, she lifted her nose. "I don't know what you're cooking, but it smells delicious."

"Good," he said. "You want to set the table?"

She looked over at her little table, nodded. She put her coffee down there and quickly brought over knives, forks, and juice glasses.

As she walked to the stove, he said, "With that braid, you look about eighteen."

"Well, that's a number I'll never see again," she said.

"Would you really want to?" he asked.

She shook her head. "Eighteen wasn't a good year for me."

"Is that when Elena returned the favor?"

She froze, turned to look at him. "I did mention that, didn't I?"

He nodded slowly.

She smiled. "Yes. That's when Elena returned the favor."

"I'm sorry you lost her," he said, in the softest of tones.

Her smile turned sad. "I am too," she said. "But I also have to remember that we had the time that we did, and that's got to be worth a lot too. And I'm really, really happy that I got the chance to know her."

"Exactly," he said. He brought over two plates to add to the table.

She stared at mushroom omelets with some bacon on

the top, all with a cream sauce drizzled over that. "Is that hollandaise sauce?" she asked in amazement.

"Absolutely it is," he said. "I hope you like it."

"Interesting that you just went ahead and cooked and didn't even ask."

"See? The thing about asking is," he said, "that it leaves you open for people to say no or to get fussy. I find it much easier to just make a meal. Then you'll either eat it or you won't." He didn't appear perturbed either way.

"Well, that's a direct way to do it," she said with a smile. She sat down, took a bite, and smiled even bigger. "My God, it's wonderful," she said. "You really do cook, don't you?"

"Well, I've cooked a couple meals for you now," he said. "How were they?"

"Delicious," she said faintly. "I can't do anywhere near as good as this."

"I think that's because you're off in your own world most of the time," he said.

She nodded. "Exactly. I live in my own world, but this is divine. I don't think I could ever make it."

"I'm pretty sure you can." His phone rang just then. He frowned at her.

"Go ahead and take it," she said. "We never know when it'll be one of those important things we need to hear about."

"Exactly," he said. He checked the ID, lifted his phone to his ear, and said, "Andy, what's up?"

"That present—it belonged to Elena."

The breath left his chest as he whispered, "Jesus Christ."

"We also have the autopsy report," he said. "She was poisoned to death. Likely in her drink."

"Of course."

"It was a fatal dose of ketamine."

"Wow." He glanced up at Cayce.

As soon as he hung up, she stared at him. "What was that all about?"

"WHAT WAS THAT?" Cayce asked harshly, her gaze shying back, as if against a coming blow.

He reached across the table, slid his hand over hers, and said, "Finish eating. We'll talk about it afterward."

She stared down at the last of her omelet and shook her head.

"Three more bites," he said with determination.

She glared at him, quickly shoveled three bites in her mouth, swallowed, got up, and asked, "What is it?"

"The box that was downstairs, that I came and picked up?" he started with, putting it in her mind. "I didn't tell you at the time, but it was a piece of skin—and not from Liana, as we'd assumed. It was from Elena."

Her face paled, and she felt the world spinning around her, as she took the impact as a visceral blow to her stomach. She whispered, "Dear God! How is that even possible?"

"It's obviously from the killer. What I don't know is the why? To scare you? To hurt you? To show you something?"

"Was there a message? Was there something, anything to make sense of this?"

"There was a message," he said. "It said, 'A gift for you to keep forever.' They are working on analyzing the handwriting now. I'm really sorry, Cayce. I know that's the last thing you needed this morning."

She just stared at him and slowly sank to the single chair in the living room. "*A gift to keep?*"

"Yes," he said, "and that brings up all kinds of possibilities."

"Like?" she said softly.

"Like maybe he was preserving her," he said.

She winced at that. "That doesn't sound any better."

"No, it's not meant to," he said, "but I don't think he was trying to destroy her. I guess a fine distinction is here. I think he was trying to keep the masterpiece intact."

"And giving me a piece was for what?"

"Maybe giving you a chance to keep a part of her safe forever too."

HALO COULD FEEL the vibes tightening around them. Mommy was getting mad. They were all in hiding. When Mommy got mad, bad things happened.

And before she got mad, bad things happened.

That made Mommy madder.

He tucked his knees up to his chest, shaking as the evil walked by.

An evil he knew well.

Crying in his mind, he shoved his fist into his mouth to keep as silent as possible and rocked back and forth.

Please leave me alone.

Good boy. Bad boy.

CHAPTER 18

I T WAS BRUTAL news to impart.

"Does that message mean anything to you?"

Cayce gave a broken laugh. "How could it mean anything to me?" she snapped. "None of this makes sense. I mean, obviously I would love to have Elena be with me forever, but I don't want a piece of her organic body. I already have her soul with me."

He slid his head to the side. "Meaning that your friendship will still cross the barriers of life and death?"

"Something like that," she said with a nod.

"What happened when you guys were around eighteen? Could it be pertinent?" His gut said yes. "I'm pretty sure it is."

"I don't even know what to say," she said. "I was stupid. I was young. My ex-fiancé was an older man."

"He beat you up?"

"If you want to put it that way. He beat me up and put me in hospital. Elena came, swooped into the hospital, checked me out against doctor's orders, kept me at her place until I healed, and set the cops on him. He committed suicide soon afterward. Couldn't stand the publicity was my take on it ..." She found it hard to talk about still—yet, when she got started, she couldn't stop. "My stepfather was a nasty piece of work. He beat up my mother a couple times before he got caught for his lovely criminal activities. I swore I'd never be with a man like that, but somehow that's the same place I ended up."

"Oh, God," Richard said. "I hate men like that. Where is your stepfather now?"

"Back East, rotting, I hope. Last I heard he was still behind bars. His last name is Brogan, Walter Brogan. My mother never changed our names when she married him."

"Good. Hopefully he doesn't get out—ever."

"That's my wish. We all hate men like that," she said. "The problem is, I have to accept that part of me that went through that experience because it spawned my artistic side. For days, weeks, months even, I just painted red and black and ugliness. Then slowly, over time, I began to paint light and sunshine. I realized that I had a decision to make. I could live in that darkness and fear, or I could live in the lightness and joy. And, with Elena, who had already seen more than her fair share of evil at the hands of her own stepfather, we formed a bond to never get into that situation again. And every time we met thereafter, it was like meeting some part of my soul. We were so much alike. Our relationship was much closer than any others I had had."

"Did you ever do any weird incarnation or something like that?"

She smiled and looked at him with one eyebrow raised in question.

"You know? Like, go to some tarot card reader and have your futures read or anything like that? I'm not sure what I'm trying to ask."

"We didn't have to," she said simply. "When you save a person like that, you become a part of them. I have always carried Elena in my heart." She instinctively placed a hand on her heart. She stared down at it, patted it, and said, "And Elena feels more at rest right now."

He nodded, but his throat closed up as he remembered what he'd done during the night. "I'm really happy you have her close," he said, "because that's huge."

"It is," she said, managing to smile without the tears. "Do you have to go to the station now?"

He nodded. "I'm waiting for a buzz to tell me the security guard is back again."

"I'm pretty sure that's not necessary," she said.

"I'm pretty sure it is," he said. "So we won't take a chance."

She sighed. "Fine. I just think it's overdoing it."

"Let me overdo it then," he said, reaching out to gently touch her nose. "You've become very special to me, very, very quickly. I don't want anything to happen to you."

She smiled. "Ditto. So maybe you should keep safe yourself."

"Do you think he'll come after me?"

"I don't know, but if you're an impediment to him getting at me," she said, "then maybe."

He nodded. "I hope he does. I really hope he does."

RICHARD GOT UP and left soon after verifying the security guard was out front and Graham was downstairs. With a smile and a wave, he walked out and headed to the police department.

Andy was there waiting for him. "How is she?"

"Traumatized," he said. "She has no idea what the message means, and, of course, she would never want to keep a piece of Elena's body like that."

"They're analyzing the note. Apparently, the skin was treated with something to keep it from decaying."

"That would make sense," he said. "Do we know what that was?"

"Ivory Snow."

Richard stopped in his tracks, looked at Andy, and said, "What?"

"It's full of Ivory Snow. The soap. It's used to preserve rawhide."

"And did it? Preserve it, I mean."

"A little bit, but it's starting to deteriorate."

"I wonder if he's struggling to preserve the other pieces that he's collected," Richard said.

"Probably. There's also something else about the latest victim, Liana."

"What's that?" The two of them talked as they walked into the station. "Her body was kept frozen for many months."

"Shit," he said. "What do you want to bet that she's our ground zero victim?"

"Exactly. So we're to follow Liana's life today."

"Good enough for me. Why did it take so long for anyone to know she was missing?"

"Because Liana was living with other people, and, when she said that she had a new gig and was moving out, nobody even questioned it. And no one knew she was missing."

"So, we don't know where she's been living."

"Not at all."

"Great," he said. "That's not helpful."

"It never is," he said.

"Any analysis on the handwriting?" Richard asked.

"We don't have anything to compare it to yet," he said,

"but we're assuming it is that of the killer."

"Something was almost feminine about it, wasn't there?"

"Yes," Andy said. "That was what I thought immediately." He checked his email and pulled up a couple reports. "Let's go to Liana's last known residence." They turned and headed back out.

Liana had lived in the artist section of town but in the cheaper digs, where multiple artists crowded together and lived the hippie lifestyle for much less money.

As soon as they knocked, the door opened. A kid fell out, getting on his shoes. "I have to go, man. I don't know who you're looking for. They're all asleep." And he bolted out the door.

Richard grabbed him by the arm and asked, "Did you know Liana?"

He looked at him in confusion, shook his head, and said, "I replaced Liana." He pulled his arm free. "I have to go. Otherwise I won't have a job." After those words, he was gone.

The two detectives stepped inside and called out, "Hello. Anybody home?"

A young woman with purple hair, groggy and looking like she just woke from a heavy hangover, popped her head around the corner, and said, "Yeah, who's asking?"

They both pulled out their badges and showed them.

She frowned. "Cops?"

"Detectives," Andy said. "We're asking about Liana."

Her face immediately crumpled up. "We just heard," she said. "My God, who could have ever hurt her?"

"Did you like her?"

"I loved to sleep with her," she said. "She was always up for anything I wanted to do."

"How long did you know her?" Richard asked.

"She lived here for a few months," she said. "I probably slept with her half the time. Well, maybe not. Maybe a third. The others did too."

"I thought she was gay," said another guy, his sleep interrupted by the conversations.

She frowned, looked at him, and said, "You know what? I think she slept with the guys half the time." She shrugged. "We don't really keep count. We go with whoever we want to go with."

"Interesting lifestyle," Richard said.

"Absolutely," she said. "And a healthy natural one. But I can't help you."

"What about her room?"

"The kid who just left has her room."

"Any chance we can see it?"

"We put her stuff in storage," another guy said, as he walked into the kitchen, his hair spiked up in some kind of gel, probably done up the previous night, and he was looking much older now that the night had passed. He held a cup of coffee like it was a lifeline.

"That would be good to see," Richard said. "And do you know where she went from here?"

"She said she had a new gig, and it was the best deal ever. She wouldn't tell us where."

"Of course she wouldn't," Andy said.

"We just heard what happened to her," he said.

"I need everybody who knew Liana to wake up and to make statements. Otherwise we'll have to do it downtown at the station. So, can you go get your friends up?"

It took them hours to get the very groggy, hungover, drugged-out artists to sit down long enough to give their stories. Basically they all said everybody had been friends. With each of them, Richard heard the same thing about Liana. She had told them that she was taking off to live the good life because she got a perfect opportunity, and she was leaving them all. *Sorry, suckers, but sayonara.*

"And where are her things?"

The first guy they talked to hopped up, walked to the front closet, opened it, calling out from there.

Richard looked at him. "Is this all hers?"

"No, no," he said. "This is." He pulled out a duffel bag and another bag, dropping them at Richard's feet. "We'd be really grateful if you would take this with you. We're short on space."

"Why would she leave her stuff behind?"

"Well, the way we figured it, she probably had a sugar daddy who would buy her all new stuff."

"Wow," Richard said. "You guys have so much that you just leave it all behind?"

"It holds us down, holds us back," said the woman with the purple hair. "You really have to let all that go."

"We need your contact information, all of you, in case we need to get in touch with you."

Multiple groans came around the room. "Man, we've cooperated. Why do you have to get our cell phone numbers?"

"Because it's the law," Andy said. He stopped and slowly walked around, grabbing everybody's name and phone number. When they were done, he looked at Richard and said, "Let's go."

He nodded, and they headed out. "Did we ever get any forensics from the dumpster?"

"No," he said. "Well, nothing we've heard back on anyway."

"Wouldn't it be nice if it was like TV," Richard said, "and we could just put it in and get it back within a day or two."

"Wouldn't it," Andy said with a sneer.

Back at the police department, they walked into one of the interrogation rooms, opened up the door, placed the bags on the table. They both put on gloves and slowly went through everything here. The bag was filled with clothing; that was about it. Including dirty socks, dirty jeans, and, unfortunately, dirty underwear.

"Does this make any sense to you?" Andy asked Richard.

"Well, there are two theories," Richard said. "Either she didn't bother coming back because her good deal would replace it all, or she couldn't come back to grab it."

Andy nodded. "Sucks either way."

They checked all the pockets. And they suspected that the others had already done the exact same thing, so not even a quarter was found in the pockets and certainly no money in the wallet.

"What do you think? Did the kids strip it?" Richard asked.

"Absolutely they did," Andy said with a chuckle. "Did you see that group?"

"I wonder how much they make on their art."

"I doubt very much," he said. "Probably nothing at all."

"Right."

"Let's check the duffel bag."

They moved all the clothing off to one side. It would go to forensics anyway, and they brought up the larger bag. It was filled with notebooks. Richard opened one to see sketches.

"She's an artist," Andy said, staring at it. "It always comes back to art, doesn't it?"

"Yes. They're either wearing it or producing it."

"Or both."

"Exactly. Interesting thought."

They quickly flipped through all the sketches. "This is nothing like Cayce's work."

"Everybody there is an artist," Andy said.

"Right. So, it makes sense that we have sketchbooks." He frowned at Andy. "But not that she left these behind."

They quickly pulled the rest of the stuff from the duffel bag. They went through everything intently, but nothing gave them any answers.

When Richard picked up another sketchbook, he noticed that the back cover was thicker. He checked it out and found a pocket. Slipping his fingers underneath, he managed to pull out a note that had been stuck in there. He opened it up, took a careful look, and said, "This might be interesting."

"What is it?"

"Declarations of love," he said quietly.

"Any date on it?"

"No," he said, "but the handwriting looks familiar." He turned it so Andy could see.

Andy's eyebrows shot up. "Don't quote me on this, but it's likely from the killer."

"Thorne's, Liana's, or Elena's?"

"A shared lover?" Andy just stared at him. "We never considered that concept."

"And I don't want to consider it now either," he said. "We need to get this stuff to forensics and especially get this letter looked at."

They quickly packed everything back up, moved it all down to the forensics team, and Andy told them, "I don't know if any of this has what we want, but this note that we found is the most interesting."

The forensic team looked at it, nodded, and one said, "Just leave it all here. We'll go through it."

"Good enough," he said.

As Richard turned and walked out, he asked, "Did you find anything on any of the crime scenes?"

"Not much. Nothing on the bodies either," he said. "The one was definitely frozen. The others were fresh."

"That's always disconcerting," Andy said.

"Do we know how long she was frozen?" Richard asked.

"A few months," he said. "Hard to say any closer than that."

"So possibly as soon as she went missing."

"Do you have any idea who she was with?" the female tech asked.

"No. Somebody new, who would make her life perfect."

The forensic tech just rolled her eyes, nodded, and said, "That's what they all say." She waved him away.

Andy asked Richard, "Do you want to talk to the coroner?"

"I've checked the autopsies that we have so far, and, of course, we're still waiting on the drug tests."

"We also need to confirm that the others were drugged as well."

They made their way to the coroner's office. When they knocked on the door, the coroner called out, "Come in." He looked up and frowned at them both. "I don't like this much work," he said, snapping at them. "So would you find this asshole before I get a fourth body?"

"We'd love to," he said. "Do you have anything for us?"

"They were all drugged. The lab tests are out until we get it back, but I'm suspecting it was something like ketamine, like the first one."

"Right. And it was served in alcohol?"

"Yes, and their stomachs were full. They all ate their last meals, but nothing was tremendously different about any of them. Mostly burgers."

"Burgers for all three of them?"

"Elena had a salad."

"Which makes sense. She was a model," Richard said.

"The other two had burgers," he said.

"I wonder if a burger joint is close in the area where these bodies were found."

"That's your job," the coroner said. "Go." He shooed them out of the room.

They headed back upstairs to their desks in the communal bullpen and looked up any restaurants in the area around where the three dead bodies were found. Armed with the photos of the victims, they both hopped up and headed out to walk the streets. As soon as they got into the general five-block radius that they had picked to search, they went from restaurant to restaurant, asking if any of these people had been seen.

Almost immediately they got a hit. "Hey, that's Liana," one guy said. "She was in here all the time, and then I never saw her anymore."

"When was this?"

The guy shrugged. "Must have been a couple months ago at least. No clue." He looked at the photo, frowned, and asked, "She's dead, isn't she?"

"Sorry," Richard said. "Yeah. Did you recognize who she

was with?"

"She had one guy toward the end," he said. "Up until that, she was almost always with a group. But then it became just one guy."

"Any idea who it was?"

The waiter shook his head. "No," he said. "I got so many people who come and go from here, it's almost impossible to tell you who was who."

"But it was a guy?"

The waiter looked at him in surprise. "Well, I mean, from the surface, I'd say it was, yes."

He nodded. "Okay," Richard said. "And no chance of a description? Have you seen him since? Have you seen that other guy with anybody else?"

"No," he said frowning. "I only recognized Liana."

"We need something to go on," Andy said. "It might have been our killer."

The waiter looked at him in horror. "Jesus, if that would ever make me remember, you just shocked it out of me."

"Well, think a minute. Think about the two of them together. Was he taller than her? Was he skinnier than her?" Richard asked.

"Nobody is skinnier than Liana. The drugs took their toll on her. Another year or two, she probably couldn't model anymore."

"So, physical description?"

"A little heavier, a little taller, a little darker." He frowned.

They waited, hopeful that something would trigger in his memory.

And then he shrugged and said, "I really don't have any more. I got to get back to work. I need my job."

They thanked him, got his name and phone number, and then left.

"Well, if he was seen at one, chances are, he was seen at multiple places."

Andy said in agreement, "Let's go."

After going to several more restaurants, they found another one, a little corner marketplace that served subs. Several workers looked at the photos and recognized the victim immediately. One said, "Yeah. She used to come in here for a sub."

"Did you recognize who she was with?"

The Italian-looking woman and another one frowned at him. "Why are you asking?"

Richard gave her a bit of a smile, pulled out his detective badge, and said, "We're investigating her murder."

Immediately she clasped one hand over her mouth, the other over her heart. "Oh my," she said. "That's terrible. But I don't know anything about it."

"Which is why we're asking," he said. "Somebody knows something."

She nodded. "Yes, yes, yes. Somebody knows. But I don't know anything."

"Did she ever come in alone? Did he ever come in with others?"

"She came in with people, and then once she came in with a boyfriend."

"Did you know her boyfriend?"

"Yes. He comes here too."

"What's his name?"

She frowned. "I don't know his name. He wasn't friendly like she was."

"So, you have no clue who he is?"

"No," she said. "It's not my business."

"I get that," he said, "but we're trying to find out who killed Liana."

"Are you thinking this man did it?" She looked horrified and enthralled at the idea.

"No, not necessarily," he said. "Remember? We don't know anything yet."

"You should know something," she scolded him. "She was a nice young woman."

"Which is why we're trying to do something for her."

"No," she said, raising her voice. "You should have done something for her before."

"Why is that?"

"She had a rough childhood," she said. "With a better start, she'd have done well in life. Been more normal."

"In what way was she not normal?"

"She was just different. She was too shy, too quiet. People took advantage of her. It was easy to tell her that the sky was falling, and she would believe it."

"And you still don't remember what the guy looked like who was with her?"

"No, no," she said. "He was tall and better dressed. He was classy looking. Always well-manicured."

"And he comes in here for subs?"

"No, he comes in here to get a few of my specialty sauces," she said. "He's a connoisseur."

"But you don't know his name?"

She shook her head. "No, I don't."

"Okay," Richard said. "If you think of anything"—he pulled out his card—"anything at all, or if you see him come into the store, please contact me right away."

She frowned at him.

"I don't want you to be in any danger either," Richard said.

Her eyes widened. "You really think it's him?"

"No, I don't," Richard said, "but, until we talk to him, we can't take him off the suspect list, so we're wasting time."

She nodded. "Okay," she said. She immediately put the card down, off to the side, then she added, "You better leave. You're not good for business."

And, just like that, they were sent to the street.

"Too bad," Richard said. "Their sandwiches look decent."

"Right," Andy said. "It should have been an easy thing to do. Just buy a sandwich, ask a few questions, and get out. But we're not exactly getting a good reputation doing this."

"No, we sure aren't."

"That's okay too. Locations, like this, they stick together. Rather than call us, I suspect she'll tell him that we were asking about him."

Richard looked at him, looked back at the store, and nodded. "My feelings exactly."

NAOMI WALKED INTO her apartment, frustrated and angry. "It's that bitch's fault," she said, talking to herself. "I shouldn't have to work for a living like this as it is. But now I can't seem to get any jobs." And that bothered her. She stormed inside her apartment and slammed the door closed.

A voice, calm and controlled, asked, "What's your problem now?"

She spun on him. "Why are you always here? Even when I don't know it?"

"You told me to come and go at will," he said, in a mild

tone. "Plus I do own this apartment, as you know."

"I know that," she said, "but that doesn't mean that you just get to come and go."

"Interesting," he said. "Because, up until now, I've paid an awful lot of the rent on this one."

She groaned at that reminder. "I know that," she said. "I'm just really having a shitty day. I can't get any work. I've just been turned down on two other art jobs."

"Normal," he said. "Just stay calm."

"Easy for you to say," she said, glaring at him. "You don't have to work for a living."

"No, I don't," he said cheerfully. "And that hasn't changed in all the time we've known each other."

She threw herself down on her couch. "I was heading to the top. What happened?"

"You probably pissed off the artist," he said.

"It's that bitch Cayce," she said. "I don't understand why she doesn't like me."

He gave a chuckle that she had heard often.

"I know. You keep telling me to be nicer. It's not part of my DNA."

"It might need to be something that you cultivate," he said mildly.

She wondered at the silkiness of his tone. Just something about having a friend who had more money than you all the time, that dressed better than you all the time, that made friends better than you all the time, that just seemed to get everything handed to him all the time. He had been very generous over the decades. "Why do you even like me?" she groaned.

"You amuse me," he said.

She sat up and glared at him. "That's not funny."

"I thought it was," he said. "You're obviously in a bad mood. I did bring you some Chinese food. It's over on the counter. But I really don't want to hang around while you're like this." And he sauntered toward the front door.

She should call him back, but he was right. She wasn't in a good mood.

As soon as he was gone, she raced over to the Chinese food and crowed in delight. It was her favorite noodle dish. She immediately put it on a plate and stuck it into the microwave.

It might be the only meal she got for the next twenty-four hours. She was no good with money. It was always a case of what she could buy instead of planning or saving. She wanted what she wanted, and she was no good at denying herself.

When the Chinese food was warmed up, she sat down at the table and shoveled the food in her mouth. When she was done, she could feel a warmth taking over her.

"Thank God for a hot meal," she said. She yawned and whispered, "But now it's really nap time. Then I'll go out and party!"

She got up, stumbled into her room, and threw herself across the bed. She was asleep almost immediately.

CHAPTER 19

"**H**AVING A DAY to myself at home really means catching up on paperwork," Cayce whispered to herself. But then that was okay too. She didn't know if Richard was coming back tonight, but she couldn't get the idea out of her mind that maybe she should cook a meal for him.

She had two steaks in the freezer, which she took out to thaw, and she sliced some potatoes, thinking to make scalloped potatoes. She put the slices in a bowl of cold water, added salt, and let them soak. As soon as that was done, she went back to the paperwork with a cup of tea in her hand.

Just about the time she sat down, Frankie called her.

"You were supposed to see my girlfriend," he said, and his voice held a little bit of panic.

"I know. I took a look," she said. "I also told you that she wouldn't be a good match for the first job, so there should be nothing to panic about."

"I know. I know." He took a deep breath. "I'm just afraid that she'll break up with me if I don't get her this spot."

"And you know perfectly well that, if that's the case, you don't need to have anything to do with her."

"Easy for you to say," he said, reining back in the emotions. "But it's much harder for those of us who don't attract people all that easily."

"Maybe," she said. "I'm having a day at home. It's just been a little bit too rough lately."

"Right," he said. "I'm sorry. I should have thought of that."

"Actually, I've been ordered to stay home," she said, "whether I like it or not. But I'm finding that I do like it."

"Interesting. The detective again?"

"Yes," she said.

"Something is going on between the two of you, isn't there?"

"I'm not sure," she said. "It's okay. I'm just catching up on paperwork and taking a bit of a breather."

"You definitely need it," he said.

"I'm sorry. I'm being selfish. I promised. I did say I'd see her, and I will keep my promise," she said. "I will look at your model. But you have to understand that if it's a no, it's a no. And I can't keep her just because your relationship might depend on it."

"I know," he said. "It sucks."

"Then why is your relationship on the rocks over it? She didn't know who you were before, did she?"

He sighed. "We've been off and on for a while, and then, you know, after my accident, I didn't know what to do, and I took the wrong path to get back."

"I know it's been tough for you, Frankie," she said, "but you're doing so much better."

"I know." His voice held a slightly forced strength. "I just thought, you know, if there was one thing I could do to help her for having been at my side all this time ..."

"I get it," she said, "but that can't be based on the decision that *I* make."

"I know," he said. "I promise. I'll back off."

She chuckled. "And I already made a promise I would look at her, so don't worry about it."

He smiled. "Thank you." And he hung up.

She brought out the pictures of his lover, going through them. Frankie had been in a car accident a few months ago, maybe eight months ago. He'd struggled with some of his recovery from it.

"I am at loose ends," she whispered to herself. It was a stolen day and a gift in itself, but it felt odd. Like she was playing hooky.

Just then Anita called. "Hey," she said. "I've got a couple signatures I need from you."

"You want to send them over?" Cayce asked.

"Or I could run them up," Anita said. "It's probably faster if I just bring them to you."

"Maybe, if you're up for a walk," she said.

"I am," she said. "I'll be there in ten minutes."

When a knock came at Cayce's door ten minutes later, she looked up, having finally gotten into some of her invoices. She hopped from her chair, walked to the front door, checking the peephole. There was the guard, and there was Anita, flirting with him. Cayce opened her door with a smile.

Anita stepped inside. "Wow," she said. "If you have to have a gilded cage, that's one hell of a guard to have around you."

"Well, you're single and looking for somebody new, so maybe he is too," she said, to her longtime assistant and friend.

"I doubt it," she said, "I'm still reeling from the rebuff from Frankie."

"That was a long time ago," she said. "You need to move on."

"I know," she said, "but I just—" And she stopped talking. After a moment, she shrugged. "I know you've heard it all before."

"So, what are we looking at?" Cayce asked.

Anita held out the folder in her hand. "This." It was a stack of papers.

She walked over, placed them on her desk, and threw herself down onto the seat.

"Why don't you just work from here all the time?" Anita asked. "It's beautiful."

"If I thought I could, I would," she said, "but I've got to keep a gallery to exhibit my work, which takes up a ton of space, and I may as well have my little office tucked in a corner there anyway."

"I wonder if you really need two offices," Anita said. "I could come here and work."

"But I think it is smart to have some separation between home and work," she said, "so I don't know that I want to do that."

"Makes sense," Anita said.

"I agree." And she grinned. As she picked up the invoices, she looked at them. "Man, some of this stuff is just getting so much more expensive."

"The paint came in a lot higher. We had to use a new supplier because the last one had that weird overlook to the paint you didn't like."

She nodded. "Yes. So, it's almost 20 percent higher. Eighteen point five percent or something like that."

"Crap," Anita said.

"But then"—Cayce shrugged—"it is what it is. What am

I supposed to do, not use the right colors?"

"Right. Not much to be done about it anyway. So just do what you do," she said.

The two women sat going over each of the invoices. They were swinging their feet as they concentrated.

"Did Frankie come by here at all today?" Anita asked her boss.

She was working on the invoices, so wasn't thinking about it. When she looked up, she said, "No, I just talked to him on the phone." She caught the same disappointed look on her friend's expression. "Remember. You have to let it go."

"I don't want to," Anita said, getting to her feet. She stormed around the small office space. "I just can't stop thinking about him."

"He's moved on," she said.

"I know that," she said, "and it's just devastating that he has."

"But he has to. It didn't work out between you and he's trying to get his life back again."

"That damned accident messed him up," she said.

"It doesn't matter," Cayce said patiently. She finally finished signing everything, handed Anita the folder, and said, "Thanks for bringing it over."

Anita hopped to her feet again, having just sat back down. "What about lunch? Are you going to eat lunch?"

"I had a big breakfast," she said, "so I don't know. Maybe just a salad."

Anita frowned. "Are you looking after yourself?"

"I am," she said.

"*Hmm.* I wonder." She seemed to will herself to turn and to walk away.

When she finally got Anita to leave, Cayce headed back to her home office to do more work. The whole apartment seemed surprisingly empty.

Her phone rang, and she reached for it, realizing how many times she'd been expecting Richard to call. This time it was him. She smiled at the phone and said, "Hello?"

"Now that sounds much better. A little more life, girl, than I've heard in the last few days."

"Girl?" she said with asperity.

"Right. I hate to insult you. Woman, then."

"Why did you call?"

"And just as bright as ever," he said with a laugh.

"Absolutely. Any progress?"

"No, nothing. Liana had just moved in with a special partner. I wonder if you had any insight as to who that might be."

"No. I haven't had anything to do with her in eight months."

"We're working on the forensics. They were all drugged first," he said. "Liana's body is the anomaly, having been frozen for several months."

"Now we're assuming that she was the first victim?"

"I really like that theory," he said. "We're working on the time line right now. The problem is, that's a lot of months between the first and second victims, and then no time at all between the second and third victims."

"On the police shows," she said quietly, "they would say he was escalating."

"And that's quite possible. We just don't know that for sure." He cleared his voice. "How are you feeling now?"

"Fine," she said. "I'm not sure why or how, but I slept beautifully, woke up well, and it's been a good day."

"Good." There was such a note of satisfaction in his voice that she became immediately suspicious. "Are you claiming that as a success for anything that you did?"

"No clue," he said. "Don't know what I could have done, except maybe that I stayed with you." As he checked his watch, he groaned. "I'll be back when the day is done," he said, "but that could be late, depending on work."

"I understand," she said. "However, it'd be nice if we could have a nice steak dinner together when this nightmare is over." Seemed now that she would be alone while eating the steak and scalloped potatoes sitting in her fridge, ready to be cooked.

"I'm not sure," he said in a teasing note. "Does that make it an actual date?"

"I'm not sure it does," she said, laughing, "but I think we're past that point."

"We're never past the point of having a date," he said. "And I don't want to skip any steps in our relationship."

"Yeah, it's probably also not very wise of you to get involved with somebody until this case is over with."

"Oh, don't worry. You can bet I've been warned about that," he said.

"Oh? I'm so sorry," she said. "That sounds terrible."

"It doesn't matter," he said. "It is what it is. Anyway, I'll be there soon." And he hung up.

She smiled and put her phone down.

As soon as she did, she heard a knock on her door. As she walked over, she said out loud, "Being at home is almost as busy as being at work." She checked her peephole and opened her door.

The guard stood there with a box in his hand.

She looked at it and recoiled. "You need to tell Richard

about that," she said, "because absolutely nothing in me wants to open that box."

"Is it that bad?"

"The last one had body parts in it." She immediately backed away and closed the door, locking it. She ran over to her desk, picked up the phone, and called the detective, but only got his voicemail. "Shit, shit, shit," she said. She curled up in a ball on the couch and kept trying Richard's phone over and over again.

Finally, after about the fifth time, he answered. "What's the matter?"

"Another package," she said.

He swore. "Be there soon."

"The guard has it," she said.

"It should never have gone upstairs," he said. "Dammit."

"Don't talk to me about it," she said. "I just slammed the door in his face."

"Good enough," he said. "Stay calm. I'll be there soon."

"Yeah, will do," she said.

But she wasn't calm at all. Frustrated, uneasy, and hating that this evil was once again infiltrating into her world, she hopped up, poured herself a glass of wine, and turned on the fireplace, even though it was only two o'clock in the afternoon. She could feel everything inside herself tense into this tight little ball, until finally she heard voices outside her door.

She huddled behind the couch, until she heard Richard's voice. Suddenly her front door opened, and he stepped inside. She popped her head up over the couch, saw him, put the glass of wine down on the coffee table, and raced into his arms, throwing herself against him, her arms wrapping tight around him.

He held her close and whispered, "It'll be okay. *Shh*, it'll be okay."

"No," she said. "It'll never be okay at this rate."

"I have to take this to the station, okay?"

She took a deep breath. "That's fine," she said. "Go. Take that nasty thing with you."

"It does look like the other one," he admitted, "and we'll do more testing this time."

"It was tested last time, right?"

"Of course," he said. "I'm just hoping that maybe this time there will be a fingerprint."

She nodded. "Just take it." She took several deep breaths. "I'll be fine. Just go."

"You're obviously not fine," he said, frowning at her.

"I'll be much better when you get that thing away from me."

He nodded, stepped out the door, turned, and said, "Lock the door behind me."

She immediately threw the bolt and then collapsed back down on the couch in tears.

"How did you get this?" Richard asked the guard.

"The front desk called me," the guard said, "and then they sent it up."

"This is the second such delivery. I should have briefed you on that, but I don't think I had a chance to," he said, as he studied the box. "I'll be back in a little bit." He headed straight to the station, texting Andy in the meantime. Andy met him at the front, and they took the package to forensics.

Very carefully, they clipped the twine that wrapped it up and then opened up the paper wrapped around it. Each piece was sprayed and checked for prints. Nothing was found. Every corner and crease was checked, and finally they turned their attention to the box itself. Nothing was found on the outside, but they kept on working.

Finally the forensic guy said, "It's clear too." He opened the box carefully. The smell immediately wafted toward them. Only this time it smelled of formaldehyde. "He's changing his preserving methods," the forensic tech said. "This time it isn't Ivory Snow. That's definitely a preservative, like formaldehyde."

"That's used in all kinds of things, isn't it?" Richard asked.

"Yes," he said, "it is."

"So it's not that unusual to have."

"Nope."

"I gather the other method didn't work very well."

"Or this is a particularly interesting piece," he said, as he studied it.

"What is it?"

"Another chunk of skin and fat. But this time the artist's signature is on it."

Richard stared at it and realized for the first time that she signed each of her pieces, even the body art. That fascinated him too. He took a photo of it, shook his head, and said, "That's not what she'll want."

"How did it arrive at the building?" Andy asked.

"A courier," he said. "He'd been slipped twenty bucks to deliver it."

"Right. Of course. We need to track him down."

"I'm already working on it," Richard said, in a hard voice. Just then his phone rang; it was the doorman from her building.

"The courier is here."

"Hold him there," Richard said. "I'll be there in five." He turned and said to Andy, "We've got the courier." And with that, he bolted, Andy close on his heels.

HE DIDN'T KNOW why he felt compelled to share his work with her. Maybe because she'd been so generous sharing hers with everybody else. He didn't know if she would appreciate what he'd done.

But it was something to see her signature and to see her work as he developed his own skills, which were slow to come, but he would give himself time. He could recreate her masterpieces too. To think that she could take a van Gogh and put it on the body model was absolutely unbelievable.

It took body-painting to a whole new level. One that he appreciated and yet, at the same time, admired and resented. There, he'd said it. He resented her because she could do it so easily, so flawlessly, so effortlessly. He'd stood there watching her, as she stroked a great big six-inch-wide paintbrush. She saved the fine details for the end, but, even then, she managed to do it with big four-inch-wide brushes. He'd been amazed at the contrast because then, when she worked on the body model, she did it with tiny brushes. It was a skill he knew he would take years to refine. But he was working on it.

He kept bolstering himself up with that. *He was working on it.* He settled back and smiled at his latest attempt. It was close, surely it was close. He poured himself a glass of whiskey and lifted it in the air, and said, "*Salud.*" It made him feel like he wasn't so alone when he shared his skills with her too. And he took a sip of his whiskey.

NAOMI WOKE UP, and the inside of her mouth was thick, plugged with something. Her jaw throbbed, as if she'd been slammed with a fist. She twisted, shifting her body, but it wouldn't move. She laid back, wondering what the hell had just gone on. She opened her eyes, and darkness was all around her. In the far corner was a small task light, and she could see somebody working away over there. She spat out whatever was in her mouth and said, "What's going on? Where am I?"

"You're my visitor," he said. "My guest. Just lie there quietly. I'll get to you eventually."

"Quietly?" She pulled at her hands and realized that she couldn't get free. She was tied up. Not only was she tied up, but she was tied up, nude, and her arms and legs were spread wide on a weird frame.

And some of her body had been painted while she had been unconscious.

CHAPTER 20

C AYCE OPENED HER apartment door and asked the guard, "Do you know if they located the courier?"

He looked at her in surprise. "They just told me that they have him downstairs."

"Perfect," she said. "I want to see him."

"Oh no, you don't," he said, immediately putting an arm across the front door. "You're not going outside."

"Seriously? Am I a prisoner?"

"No, you're not a prisoner," he said, "but my job is to keep you safe and to keep you here."

"Says you," she said. "Why don't you come down with me then?"

He frowned at her.

"Well, I'm going," she said. "So you'll either come along, or you won't."

He rolled his eyes.

She stopped, nodded, and said, "Yes, I'm one of those women. I'm difficult and obnoxious, and I like to get my own way."

He laughed. "But you stay at my side."

She nodded. "Fine."

They took the elevator down. In the front lobby, she saw the same courier she'd seen many times before. "Hey, Lenny. How are you doing?"

He looked at her. "I don't know what's got everybody rattled," he said, "but, when it came to that last parcel I gave you—"

"Don't worry. It's part of a police investigation," she said comfortably. "How is Trixie?"

"She's doing good," he said. "So is the baby." He beamed with paternal pride.

"Of course." She smiled. "So, who gave you that parcel?"

"A guy at the pizza shop. He gave me twenty bucks to deliver it, and I was coming this way anyway. It's an easy twenty bucks."

"Do you remember who it was?"

"The guy at the counter," he said, "but it wasn't from him. It was given to him by somebody who was getting it to you because everybody knows you're around here, and he was happy to help out."

"Great," she said, "thank you."

Just then the front entrance doors opened, and Richard and Andy came flying through. Richard stopped when he saw her and gave her a good frown.

She in turn gave him a big smile. "I came down to chat with Lenny," she said. "He delivers all kinds of stuff for me."

"She's a good client," he said.

"Well, I need details," Richard said. "Who gave it to you and why?"

Lenny went through the same conversation he'd already gone over with Cayce, and, in a few moments, the two detectives were running out the door to talk to the pizza man.

Lenny turned to look at her, shrugged, and said, "Man, you command all kinds of attention these days." With that, he gave her a high five and took off.

The guard looked at her and asked, "Can we go back upstairs now?"

"I guess," she said, "but I'd much rather stay and see the world."

"Five minutes," he said, "but that's it."

She laughed. "Do you always follow the rules?"

"Nope," he said, "but you're in the wide open, and I don't like it."

She looked at him, startled, and then looked at all the windows. "You mean that somebody could see me through the windows?"

"You can bet somebody is watching you right now," he said.

She winced. "That is not what I want to think about."

"Maybe not," he said. "So, do us both a favor. Let's go back up."

She waved at the doorman and the desk clerk on the main floor. "Have a good afternoon, you two."

They lifted a hand and smiled at her.

And she headed upstairs, determined to accomplish something, despite the unsettling drama her life had become. Once there, she locked herself in. She brought out her designs for upcoming installations and started working. She needed to meet Frankie's model girlfriend after having to reschedule earlier but she wanted to get some work done first.

As she worked on one design, she remembered another. From long, long ago. She got up, walked over to the safe that held her old designs and pulled one out. As soon as she saw it, she took a photo and sent it to Richard. He called her just moments later.

"What the hell is that?"

"It's a design I did a long time ago," she said, still confused as she tried to work this out in her mind. "Like Elena as art, this was a similar idea I had way back when to body-paint models with my own paintings, not the masters. What struck me is how the cutout border of this design compared to the cuts that were done to Elena. From that autopsy picture of her torso that I saw. Which is burned into my brain. Except I can't confirm these cuts truly match without seeing her body in person, which I cannot stomach."

"Well, I can," he said, "and I concur. That is exactly what happened to Elena's body. Who would have seen those earlier designs of yours?"

"I'm not sure anyone has," she said. "They're in my safe here. I've had them for years."

"Did you ever paint them?"

"Not this one," she said, "it was a little too dark for the mood I was going for. But when I was depressed and tired and lonely, I used to draw these darker things."

"So, when your stepfather abused your mother and when that guy, your fiancé, hurt you?" he said.

"The dark artwork was part of my recovery," she said instantly. "I painted dark, designed dark, in order to purge all that turmoil inside." Her smiled slipped. "It was very therapeutic."

"What if they are models for the murderer?"

"Well, that would be pretty upsetting," she said. She sat heavily in her chair, dropping her head into her hands. "Please tell me that it's not."

"Then you tell me who would have seen these designs because they'll be my number one suspects."

"Nobody," she said instantly. "They couldn't."

"Who is they? And why not?"

"Because the designs were in the safe the whole time. No one has seen them," she said.

RICHARD SLAMMED DOWN the phone, then scrubbed his face with both palms. Shit was hitting the fan, and they were close to figuring this out, but close only counted in horseshoes. And this was no game.

He packed up an overnight bag and walked out of his apartment. He stopped to pick up a coffee at the service truck he'd been at several times to see if the homeless man had returned.

Hildie looked up at him, smiled, handed him his cup of coffee wordlessly, then motioned around the side of her truck. In a low whisper, she said, "He's there. But go easy. He's really fragile."

Surprised, but his heart slamming against his chest, Richard shifted to the picnic table close by, where he could see his quarry.

Sure enough, a disheveled-looking man in an oversize coat huddled on the ground, hugging a cup of coffee. His eyes were runny, as if he were fighting a cold. And a blank stare filled his gaze. Instinctively Richard knew this couldn't be his killer. Not enough cognitive function was evident there to kill and then to skin his victims, like their killer had. But Richard had been wrong before.

"Look at his energy," Stefan murmured at his side.

Richard turned to look, then realized he was alone. Using his peripheral vision, he could see the glowing gold at his shoulder.

"Now that you've seen my energy, look at his."

Slowly, keeping his head lowered to not scare off the

homeless man, Richard lifted his phone and used it as a distraction as he studied Halo's energy.

It was dark, snaky, fragmented. Broken. Like the man inside. Richard took several photos of the man, who sat frozen in place, staring at something lost in time. Along with his coffee, he clutched what looked like a large cross—among many around his neck—muttering something to it, almost like a litany of prayer.

"Can he be fixed?" Richard muttered to Stefan.

"Maybe," Stefan said. "But those bits and pieces of displaced energy? … That's what his mind looks like too. Past trauma he can't deal with."

"Poor bastard. Why is there never any help for people like this?"

"Because it happened a long time ago. We all have coping methods that work for a while, but slowly those barriers they erect start breaking down, and we see things like this."

"Can you see into his childhood?"

"Do I have to?" Stefan asked, fatigue in his voice. "It's abuse as a child. Mother and father. Possibly a brother. Hard to say. The images are all torn apart, and the pieces bundled together for safekeeping."

"You'd think he wouldn't want to keep any of these memories." Richard sure as hell wouldn't.

"It's all he has of his childhood."

Then, without warning, in a voice that made the hair on the back of Richard's neck rise, Stefan and the homeless man started to sing at the same time.

"Good boy. Bad boy. Good boy. Bad boy."

LATER THAT EVENING he asked if she'd shown up for her

new appointment today with Cayce. She nodded and said, "It went well."

He smiled.

She looked at him and said gently, "I'm not leaving you, you know?"

He sagged in place. "You probably should."

She walked over, gently reached up a hand, and said, "Frankie, an accident caused this. As soon as you heal and are relaxed about it, your art will come back."

He leaned into her hand. "Maybe," he whispered. "But it feels like I'll never be as good as I was before."

"You will be," she said gently. "You just need time. And I don't really care about being a body model. I'm doing this because you feel like I need to."

"I just know that Cayce made Elena's career, and maybe she could make it for you too."

"I get the idea that Elena and Cayce shared a special bond," she said.

"But you did see her today?" he asked anxiously.

She chuckled. "I did see her. She was just walking out of her gallery with some guy, but she stopped, came back in, and said that what she was doing was a favor to you. I don't need you to do me favors. I want to make it on my own."

"But—"

He froze when she put a finger on his lips. "No buts," she whispered. "Just let it be."

"She did say that she's got the next two art pieces picked out. Yet she'll be trying a bunch of new models," he rushed to add.

"And that's good," she said comfortably. "I also have a photo shoot tomorrow. Remember?"

He beamed. "You'll make it. You'll be famous," he

whispered.

"I don't want to be famous," she said. "I'm happy where I am now."

He shook his head. "I don't even see how that's possible. I couldn't even begin to be happy with where I'm at now."

"Because you know that, prior to your accident, you were something different," she said. "And I think that's where the problem is. You're trying to recapture something that maybe is gone, but you're not willing to try something that's very new and different."

"I don't know," he said, his gaze darting to the side and the door that he kept locked.

"Anyway," she said, "I'm going to bed. I'm really tired." She got up and turned to look at him. "Are you coming now?"

"I'll stay and work for a little bit," he said. He stood, walked over, gave her a gentle kiss and a hug. "I'm so blessed to have you in my world."

"Just keep remembering that," she said with a laugh.

He watched as she walked out, headed to the bedroom. He'd have a good couple hours in order to make some of whatever it was that he wanted to produce now. The trouble was, it was just so damn hard to produce when he wanted to.

He waited until she was through in the bathroom and then listened as she got into bed. Afterward he turned and headed to his locked room.

Just as he reached for the doorknob, she called out, "Maybe you shouldn't work tonight."

"Why is that?"

She said, "Because I'd much rather have you spend that time with me."

He froze, chuckled, and said, "Does that mean you want

some nookie-nookie time?"

She chuckled. "I've never known you to refuse a bit of cuddling."

"Hell no," he said. "I'm coming right now." He turned and walked away from his locked door. Whatever was behind that door could wait. At least for tonight.

IT WAS GOING better. It was going much, much better. He smiled in joy as he looked at his paintings. He almost had it. Another few days, few weeks, few months—it didn't really matter because he had improved so much that he clapped his hands in joy.

Finally dropping the paintbrush into the large jar that he kept for just that reason, he stepped back, wiping his hands on this smock. She would love it. He just knew she would love it. He didn't know if she got the message over the signature or not. He often found that women didn't have the connective brain matter to understand the importance of such slight differences like that. Did she understand that she was improving his work and that soon she would be the next? He hoped so. It would make the transition that much easier for her.

The ice show was only two days away. Time had passed at an incredible pace. But he was ready. He was so ready. He just needed to see her amid her artwork one more time. He figured that would do. Maybe one more model, one more opportunity.

He glanced around his room, shadowy dark, full of myriad paintings and attempts. He could see and track his progress as he moved his gaze from wall to wall to wall. It looked so damn good, and he was so proud and so happy with what he'd managed to get done already. He walked to the sink and washed his hands. He straightened, stretched, and rolled his shoulders.

In the background he could hear somebody crying out. But he ignored it. There were always odd sounds. He ignored them. He would have to deal with them soon. But that wasn't his problem right now. With that big rosy glow of accomplishment filling him, he turned and headed to his bed. Of all the things he needed, most of all was sleep.

CHAPTER 21

AN UNEASY TRUCE and a weird atmosphere to the air seemed to hang around Richard and Cayce for the next couple days. Their relationship was moving forward as close friends, really close, but not yet lovers. The entire time Richard stayed with her at night, sharing her bed. She looked forward to seeing him at the end of the day. She looked forward to waking up and seeing his face the next morning. Since that first night when he had moved into her bed, he'd shown no inclination to leave. And she was just as guilty of letting him stay. She should never have let it happen in the first place. Yet she was happy that she did.

So far, their relationship was platonic, as if realizing crossing that line right now was something neither were prepared to do. She wanted him to focus on the case, and she didn't want him to get in trouble for any relationship that the two of them had. Their relationship was friendly, intimate, and yet on the edge of being more. It gave her time to get to know him. It gave her a chance to spend time with him without the added pressure of dating and/or sex. She was really enjoying that.

Something was really special about a man who moved in to care for her without pushing her on a completely different level. Even though she was so ready for that next part of this relationship.

After her second day off, she was completely bored, and, on day three, she headed back to her gallery. The guard walked with her then left her there. "I'll leave you here as long as you stay inside. And I'll let Richard know you're here."

"Sounds good, thanks."

She knew Richard really wanted her to stay home because he wanted her to stay safe, and he equated the two. But that wasn't something she was prepared to believe.

When she walked into the gallery, Anita looked up and smiled. "I wondered if you were ever coming back," she teased. "I was wondering if I needed to cancel the arctic piece."

"Absolutely I'm here," Cayce said with a bright smile which fell away at the mention of cancelling the show. She shouldn't have taken off as much time as she had. "I'll have to get over to the arctic installation and take a look." All thoughts about her promise to the guard forgotten."

"Good point," Anita said. "I also need signatures, and you have a pile of messages."

She looked at the stack and groaned. "Maybe I'll do the installation first," she said, backing out of her gallery.

Anita shook her head. "You can't walk away from this. I need to deal with them today."

"I'll be back in an hour." She checked her watch, shook her head, and said, "Make that two." And, with that, she bolted from her gallery.

As she stood outside, she took several deep breaths, wondering if there was another way to run her life that didn't involve having an office where she was forced to deal with this stuff; yet she really didn't want Anita or anybody else in her house on a full-time basis. And she definitely needed full-time staff to handle the bulk of the business affairs, so her options were limited. Rather than drive again, she walked a little farther than she was comfortable with, but she hadn't been outside for a couple days and wanted the fresh air.

She shoved her hands in her pockets and kept on walking, her mind thinking about her office problem. She didn't have to have quite the same size gallery, if that's what bothered her. She thought it was just the business side of life that irritated her. Was there any way that Anita could do some of this and take it off Cayce's plate? Maybe that was something Cayce needed to look at. But then that also meant handing over control. Although Anita had worked for her for a couple years, if she ever quit, it would leave Cayce completely clueless as to what Anita did for her. The more control Cayce handed over, the harder it was to regain it.

As she made her way to the arctic project, she heard a call from behind her. She turned to see Frankie racing to catch up. She stopped and waited for him.

"Good to see you," he said, in a breathless voice.

"I wanted to make sure this installation was ready to go," she said.

He nodded. "As far as I know it is."

"When were you there last?"

"Two days ago, with you," he said.

Something about his words made her insides a little bit unsettled. "And there's no reason that we should have posted security for it, right?" she asked hesitantly.

He looked at her curiously. "We never have before."

She nodded and hurried faster. The thought of redoing a background of that size made her heartsick. It would take her days. She didn't want to think about something like that.

But it was a possibility.

When she got to the art center and stood before the wall that she had been busily working with over the past week, she was relieved to see that it was still covered with canvas and that the scaffolding was still in place.

Frankie looked at it as well. "Did you really expect it to be damaged?"

Her shoulders sagged with relief. "It's so beautiful, but I had never contemplated vandalism on these pieces until just now. And these sites for my installations all have insurance coverage through their owners, but that's just about money. It's not about my time and my creativity invested already in these," she said, shaking her head. "I should probably have my own security on these pieces from now on, while the artwork is in progress, even starting with this one. I'll get with Anita to set that up." She let out a huge sigh. "All I can say is, I'm just grateful that it seems fine." But, just to be sure, she walked over, opened up some of the canvas coverings, and looked underneath. As far as she could see, the painting appeared to be fine. Her painting seemed unaltered.

"Do you want me to take off the coverings?" he asked. "Would you like to take a complete look at it?"

"No, it's probably okay." But then that inner voice of hers urged her to say, "No, we need to check it."

He didn't say a word. He just popped onto the scaffolding to the intricate set of ropes and wires that kept the sheets over the wall. When he finally had everything rolled up, she stepped back and nodded. "It looks fine."

"Check it carefully," he said. "We've only got a couple days."

"I know," she said with a smile. "Let me just stand here

for a moment." She checked each of the quarters, looking at a couple spots that she wanted to touch up on the last day, mentally filing them away. By the time she had checked it over carefully, she nodded and said, "Go ahead and cover it up again."

He quickly dropped the coverings again, but it still took a good twenty minutes with the two of them tugging and pulling sheets back into place. He hopped down from the scaffold and said, "Satisfied?"

"I'm glad I took a closer look at it," she admitted. "Peace of mind is worth a lot right now. Not to mention the fact that I think a couple things need to be tweaked at the top."

He nodded. "I was wondering about that."

"We can do that after we do the model."

"Did you pick a model?"

She nodded. "Somebody I've never worked on before."

"That's taking a chance, isn't it?"

"It is," she said, "but—" She shrugged. "I'll probably give all four of these gals a try, depending on which art piece I'm working on."

He nodded.

"We'll have what, three hundred people in here for this?"

"At least," he said, rolling his eyes. "This is a big one."

"They're all big," she said.

"But this is another huge charity project."

She nodded. "For the animals."

"And I suppose you did it at half price again, didn't you?"

"Hard for me to not help out the animals," she said with a slow smile.

"I get that," he said. "It's just an interesting thing."

"It is what it is," she said.

He nodded. "And you are what you are. Most people don't realize it, and you never advertise that you do a lot of this for a fraction of the price."

"People don't want to hear that," she said with a laugh. "They want to know that it's all perfect and brilliant for right now, and then they yearn for the next moment."

"You've become quite well-known," he said with a laugh. "Famous."

She shook her head. "No, I'm a realist. People want to be entertained for a few hours, and then they want to move on to the next thing."

He nodded but didn't say anything. He stepped up to her side as they walked out of the front door.

She took several slow deep breaths.

"Are you doing okay?"

"I'm doing okay," she said. "It's a process."

"That is so very true, but you're holding up well."

"No, not really," she said, but she didn't want to tell Frankie about the parcels, the security guard at her apartment, or even the development of her relationship with Richard.

They slowly walked back to Cayce's gallery. Frankie stopped and said, "I'll head over to the coffee shop for a few minutes. I see a friend of mine is over there. And thanks so much for seeing Bellamy too. I know you had to move her original appt, but appreciate you squeezing her in."

She waved him off and finished the last few blocks on her own. When she walked back in, she said to Anita, "Before I forget, please hire security from now on for all my installations in progress to protect from any vandalism, starting today if possible at the Arctic Ice project." Anita nodded, frantically scribbling it all down. "Okay, let's get at it."

The next hour flew by as Cayce dealt with the business side of her life.

With all that finally dealt with, Anita hopped off her chair and said, "Now I'm going for lunch because it's late."

Cayce looked at her watch. Already one-thirty. Later than she thought. She groaned. "How is it that time just flies by?" she asked out loud. She headed to her office, realizing she still hadn't heard from Richard all morning. That's how bad it was, for him and for her, dealing with the fallout of Elena's death. Yet she also kept expecting to hear from him, to see him, to be with him because she just plain missed him. It was a very strange stage of life for her.

Just then her cell phone rang. She snatched it up, and, sure enough, it was Richard.

"Did you eat?" he asked.

"No," she said. She settled into her office chair, listening to Anita leave.

"Do that now." Then he was gone.

She laughed. While he did hang up on her, and he did give her an order—and she wasn't good with those—he had at least softened his tone of voice for her.

Now feeling a little weird and outside of herself, as if something was not normal, she got up and walked around, going into Anita's office, and then heading back out to the main gallery area. This space wasn't huge for a gallery, but it was more grandiose than she probably needed.

Something was still off, but she couldn't put her finger on it.

She wasn't exactly sure how she'd been convinced into signing up for this lease. But she had, and this space had a lot of good things going for it. She just didn't know why she felt disgruntled right now.

As she turned around, sensing somebody, she noted the cleaners were here. One cleaning guy looked over at her, smiled, and waved. He had a big rag in his hand, cleaning the walls, doorknobs, etc.

She smiled at him. "How are you doing?"

"I'm good," he said with a happy smile and bobbed his head up and down and kept on cleaning.

She studied him, not sure why she had a weird feeling about him but subtly took a photo and sent it to Richard.

When he called, he said, "Is it the same guy as normal?"

"No," she said, "but we do have a contract with a cleaning company," she murmured, as she walked into Anita's office. "And they send whoever is available."

"I'm sending the guard over to keep you company," he said.

"Doesn't he have anything else to do with his life?"

"No, he's quite happy making sure you stay safe." And then he hung up.

She wished Richard hadn't hung up quite so fast, as she, once again, found herself craving even the sound of his voice. She sat down at Anita's desk and looked around to see if she was supposed to be dealing with something else here. So much of what Anita handled was confusing and beyond Cayce, like bookkeeping, and some ledgers were here. She moved those aside.

As she did so, she caught sight of some papers sticking out from underneath the big desktop calendar pad that Anita always used. Cayce lifted a corner, surprised to see designs. She pulled them out, looking at them and frowning. A lot of them were her designs, but why were they underneath the desktop pad? Unless Anita needed some black-and-white forms of them for some reason. Cayce flipped through them and froze when she got to the last one. She quickly took a photo of it and sent it to Richard.

He called her back again. "What's that, and why is it important?"

She let out her breath slowly. "I'm in Anita's office," she said, "and I noticed a bunch of papers under her large monthly planner thing atop her desk. It's big. Anyway, I pulled these out, and they are my designs. Or at least a form of them. More like a simplistic skeleton version of them, but, when I got to the bottom one, I had to send it to you."

"And it has that weird cutout shape to it that looks like an animal skin. What we were talking about earlier, right? Like the first design you sent me."

"Yes," she said. "But this design was just a part of one of my early works. I was fixated with borders back then. You can see the border here is similar to the one I saw on Elena's body from that horrid picture of her defaced torso. I can't stop seeing that in my mind. Maybe that's why this black-and-white version hit me so immediately. I think the outer edges of this partial design may match the outer edges of the cuts made on Elena's body."

"Right, and who did you say had access to that particular design?"

She took another deep breath. "Not Anita. I'm not sure anyone could have but me."

RICHARD COULDN'T GET to her fast enough. He knew the guard was coming from across the city and was about fifteen minutes away, but it took what seemed like five hours for his own dash there. When he burst into the space and saw no sign of anybody, he raced toward her smaller office, bypassing other doors until he heard a call from Anita's office. He stopped, backed up, and let his breath out with a hard, heavy exhale.

She smiled, got out of the chair, and walked toward him.

He dragged her into his arms and held her close.

"I just don't understand," she muttered. "And maybe it's nothing. But, of course, that's why you're here, right? Having dropped everything because of nothing, right?"

"I don't know what's going on," he said.

"But we can't exactly judge this to be good or bad at the moment."

Just then Anita walked in, catching them still in each other's arms. "And don't you two look so cute." Her voice was sassy and upbeat. Then she must have sensed that something was wrong. "What's the matter?"

"I found some designs underneath your desk pad," she said. "I sat down to see if I needed to take care of something else while I was at odds. I noticed them and pulled them out."

Anita nodded slowly. He watched her face and could see the disturbance in her expression. "And what about it?" Anita asked. "Why would that put those looks on your faces?"

"Well, one of them is a design I didn't think you'd ever seen before."

At that, Anita's face flushed a little paler.

"Where did you get access to that design?" she asked quietly.

Anita, as if holding out hope, said, "I'm pretty sure I've just seen it in the office," she said, looking directly at Cayce and then at Richard, topped by a frown. "I don't know what the issue is, since your designs are everywhere."

"Everywhere inside the office, yes," she said, "but, prior to you working for me, I had a group of designs that were kept in the safe."

"A safe?" Anita asked, puzzled. "I didn't know you had a safe."

"Which is why this design itself is important," Cayce said. She walked back into Anita's office, pulled out the stack of designs, and asked, "Why do you have these? Where did you get them? This one in particular. Where did you get it?"

Anita looked at it, frowned, and said, "That page doesn't have a footer on it with the website and page 1 of 3 or whatever at the bottom. So it wasn't a Printscreen capture. Yet I could have done a Select All and pasted it into a Word document long enough to print off just what I wanted. Still, I'm pretty sure these came off the internet." She faced her boss and the detective. "I meant to tell you about them, Cayce, but I stuck them there as a reminder for one of those many times I had hoped we would have a break, where we could discuss more than just the major emergencies. But this one, I'm not sure. Maybe it came from the same group as the others?"

She sat down at her desk, pulled up her keyboard, and started typing away. Very quickly she had a long list of Google search hits regarding Cayce's designs. She pointed at her screen. "I think people take photos of the original painting, yours and everybody else's, put it in Photoshop, wash out the color, and come up with some basic line drawing underneath it. You know? Dissecting the great art for beginners to learn by?" She pointed at the monitor again. "That's what these look like anyway," she said. "I don't remember which site I got yours off of, but I'm pretty sure that's where they were. I'm not sure about that one in particular." She looked at it, then at Cayce and Richard standing by her, and asked, "Why is that one different?"

"Because it's my early work, only ever been in my safe," she said. "Was too dark for the kind of work I wanted to be known for, so I tucked it away." She stopped, confused. "I don't get it."

Richard filled in the blanks. "Somebody must have access to your safe."

Anita's jaw dropped. "Oh, that's not something I want to think about." She looked at Cayce. "Where is the safe?"

"At home," she said quietly. "At my apartment."

"The same one you're living in now?" Anita asked with a gasp.

Richard gave Cayce a hard look. "How long have you lived there?"

"Eight years," she said. "Before that, I was at another apartment that I shared with Elena."

"You two lived together?"

She chuckled. "Not exactly. Elena had the apartment, but I stayed in it for quite a while."

"Any idea who else had access back then?" he asked, grabbing her hand. "This is really important. This is a design that has great relevance to the case that connects you and Elena."

Cayce stared at him, chewing on her bottom lip. "But it's old. As in a long time ago."

He reached out and gently stroked her bottom lip to both distract her and to get her to stop. "You'll hurt yourself," he whispered. He leaned over, kissed her gently, and said, "I need you to really think about it."

"I need a cup of tea," she said, looking around, clearly flustered. "Anita, see if you can find the site that you downloaded these from, will you?"

Anita, much more subdued now, said, "Will do, boss. I'm sorry I didn't bring them up earlier."

"It's okay," she said. "Who knew it would be something that mattered?"

"Not me," Anita said. "There's an unbelievable amount of your paintings all over the internet, in some form or another. See?" Again she pointed at her screen. "Anybody can copy and do whatever they want based on just these alone."

Richard stared at her, stared at the search engine, his mind running through it. "Are there any of Cayce's that she body-painted on Elena the night she died?"

"Didn't we give you good photographs of that?" Cayce asked.

"You did," he said, "but I want to know what the internet sees."

"I'll look it up," Anita said, her fingers tapping away on the keyboard again.

Within seconds, she had a whole slew of images of a beautiful Elena.

"Damn. My suspect pool just morphed into millions." Richard studied Elena's face, seeing the calm serenity in her gaze. "I'm sorry that I didn't get to meet her," he said quietly, turning toward Cayce. "She looks like a beautiful person inside and out."

"She was," Cayce said from the doorway.

Her voice was thick, and he knew she was on the edge of tears.

"I'll go put on the tea, while I try to get my brain

wrapped around what it is you need to know, and you can look at pictures without me. I'm not in any shape to look at those yet."

He stood behind Anita as she scrolled through all the images.

"Here's one from the night she was killed."

"She was wearing some masterpiece, right?"

"It was masterpiece night," Anita said, and she quickly tapped through it. Then she brought out one image of Elena, wearing the van Gogh painting.

"She's stunning," he said in amazement.

"It's Cayce who's stunning," Anita said. "She could turn Elena into anything. But also Elena had that chameleon ability to be anything and everything to everyone."

Richard heard a jealous note in her voice. "Did you like her?"

Anita paused, then said, "She always highlighted things about myself that I didn't like, so she was difficult to know in a way."

Fascinated and unable to help himself, he said, "Can you give me an example?"

"Just the fact that she was so beautiful and could become anything that Cayce wanted her to be," she said. "If I dwelled on that, I could get quite jealous, but it would only be with her. I'd see a million other models on a day-to-day basis, and I couldn't care less. But something about Cayce and Elena's relationship brought out the worst in me. So, did I like her? Yes. Did I love her? No. Could I live quite happily without her? Yes. I'm sorry for Cayce absolutely," she said sadly. "I knew that something special existed between the two of them that could never be between the two of us."

"I need that picture." He had overlaid the autopsy pictures of the shape that had been cut free with both old designs that Cayce had sent him, and he felt they were too damn similar. He had Anita enlarge the bottom corner, where the signature was, and he nodded. "Interesting."

"Cayce signs everything," Anita said.

And then it hit him. "Right. She always does, doesn't she?" He walked away from Anita, his footsteps rapidly heading toward Cayce's office. He barged right in. "You always sign everything, even body paintings?"

"If it's a particular art piece, yes," she said, staring up at him and holding a cup of tea in her hand. "Why?"

He pulled out his phone and went to his photo gallery and brought up the "gift" that had been delivered to her. "This was inside the second box delivered to you."

She looked at him and said, "I don't want to see it."

"I get that," he said, "but I need you to." He thumbed through his pictures on his phone.

She swallowed hard and looked at it. Her face blanched slightly because it was obviously a chunk of human flesh. And then she frowned.

He watched her as she studied it, her gaze narrowing and becoming more focused. "It's not my signature," she said. "It's been altered."

"That's what I was wondering, when I saw your signature on one of the paintings on the internet." he said. "Has it been altered by the killer, or has it been altered by whatever process the killer used to preserve it?"

"It's possible the killer altered it," she said. "Can you email that to me? I'll bring it up in an art program."

"Do you use software?"

"Absolutely," she said. "Sometimes I just have to get a different visual of what it is I'm trying to do."

He quickly emailed this photo to her. At her desktop, she opened it up and studied it carefully, going in pixel by pixel.

"It's been painted over," she said, pointing it out. "Here is my original signature, side by side with your photo. And you can see that paint has been applied over the top and above here. See these different layers?"

"So, you don't think it's the software process?"

"The software gives it more of a caricature look," she said, "but it was painted over first."

"So, it's yours but not yours."

"Exactly."

"So, somebody's imitating your work?"

"No," she said. "This isn't imitating. This is stealing." And she quickly shut down the program.

NAOMI SOBBED QUIETLY. She'd been in the same damn position for at least twenty-four hours. Her body ached. Her hands had gone numb. Her feet were beyond numb. And she kept trying to figure out if anybody would even report her as missing. She had yet to see her captor. He had come and gone but always on the far side of this room.

As she'd slowly adapted to seeing in the darkness around her, she'd realized just how much of a cesspool of mental sickness she was in. This was unbelievable. She found paintings, artwork of some kind, and these big round stretching boards. She didn't even understand what kind of canvases were used here, but it looked like hides or skin.

She shuddered because she was on a bigger stretching board herself. She'd been given some water, but, even when he'd done that, he had kept his face in the shadows. His body was nondescript, covered in jeans and a long-sleeve shirt. He was slender, tall, and she was pretty sure male, but not enough light was here to make that definitive assertion. All in all, she was just terrified about where she was. Any time she pleaded to be released, he would just say her time was coming.

Only now was she wondering if that meant she was to be released from life into death.

And she cried all that much harder.

CHAPTER 22

TODAY WAS THE day. Cayce's big installation would be open for public viewing. Cayce was up early—six in the morning—and still no further progress had been made on Elena's case. Thankfully no more deaths either. She and Richard had shared every nonworking moment together, and it already had become something so comfortable that having a hug from him was like being wrapped up in her favorite blanket. Cozy and cuddly. And she didn't want to let go of it.

They had breakfast together most days and dinner sometimes too. He'd been called out for other cases, and she found herself worrying that it could be something connected to her nightmare, but he'd always come back with a smile and a shake of his head before crawling into bed with her. That little indication did a lot to stop her worries. And still their relationship was platonic.

She smiled as she remembered the long hard ridge that had been pressed up against her this morning when she woke up. She'd seriously wondered about pushing it further here.

He leaned over, kissed her on the neck, and said, "Dammit. I really want to be here."

She rolled over, pulled him toward her, and had kissed him with all the passion that she'd kept bottled up.

When he lifted his head, his voice was thick and raspy.

"You're packing a heavy punch, sweetheart. But I'm late for work, and I can't be late today."

She chuckled and said, "Well, save that thought."

He'd leaned over, kissed her hard, and raced to get a shower.

She stretched, loving the sexy and invigorating feeling of knowing that a man truly cared for her and was really interested in her. It seemed like it had been a long time coming. For many, many years she had had nothing to do with men at all. But Elena had helped Cayce adapt afterward too. She surely didn't want what was going on here with Richard to have anything to do with her abusive fiancé, which always reminded Cayce of the abuse her stepfather had dished out to her mom too.

Richard was nothing like those two sorry excuses for men.

And such comparisons would bring up all kinds of stuff that she had wanted to keep hidden. Her mind made the leap, now wondering if Richard had found the other two people in Elena's will.

When he came out to dress, his clothes now hanging in her closet, she pushed herself up into a sitting position, leaning against the headboard. "Did you track down the other two people in Elena's will?"

He shot her a glance and said, "One of them but unfortunately also deceased."

"Isn't that a lot of deaths?"

"Three were pretty straightforward, a bad car accident and cancer," he said. "The last one was a drug overdose."

"Oh. That would be Kiddy," she said. "That likely leaves only Kenneth."

Richard looked at her in surprise. "You knew Kiddy?"

She nodded. "Kiddy was a childhood friend. Elena had said that, if she could ever do anything to help her, she would. But Elena figured she was well down a negative pathway. Kenneth was a foster sibling who helped her out, helped both of us," she admitted. "That's a time of life I have blocked out as much as I could."

"Yeah, and that's exactly what happened with Kiddy. She had a drug overdose during that epidemic of bad drugs a few years back. She was found on a street corner already too far gone to save."

"That's just so sad," she said.

"And you're right. We're still looking for Kenneth Lively. Hopefully he isn't dead too."

"I hope not," she said.

"On the other hand, if he is, you get everything," he said, leaning against the doorjamb.

She frowned at him. "First of all, I don't need it. Second, I don't want anybody thinking that I'm behind this. And it's not what Elena wanted."

"Well, the lawyer is still working on all that."

She shook her head. "Whatever."

"Are you taking care of the funeral arrangements?"

She nodded slowly. "I didn't mention it because I was waiting for the release of the body."

"Which we can't do yet."

She nodded. "We'll do a celebration of life," she said with a sad smile. "A lot of body-painting artists have contacted me, and I think I'll host a paint fest, and we'll have cocktails and invite the art world. I will paint something that I painted on Elena to celebrate her life and her own accomplishments."

He looked at her in surprise. "That sounds absolutely

wonderful," he said. "Can you do that, or will that tax you too much?"

"I feel like I need to," she said. "It doesn't matter if it's too taxing or not. I need to give her a send-off of some kind. And that feels right. She would have had fun with that."

He nodded and smiled. "As long as you will too."

"No," she said cheerfully. "I will end up bawling my eyes out from one moment to the next. But I can't bring her back, so it is what it is."

"Good way to look at it," he said. "Have you already set it up?"

"Anita has been working on it," she said. "We're dealing with it one step at a time, making all the prep in the background until we can set a date."

"I'll do what I can," he said, "but no promises of when that will be."

"This investigation is more important," she said, "and we can't say goodbye to Elena until this part is done."

"And you need to know that sometimes it doesn't happen as fast as we want it to."

"I don't think it ever does," she said, "because, if I had a choice, it would already be over with, and we'd have that asshole in jail—or better yet dead," she said.

He nodded. He finished dressing while she watched.

"I guess I have to go to work too." She yawned, pulled herself from the bedding, and said, "I really don't want to."

"It's the polar ice one today, isn't it?"

"Arctic Ice, yes, and I have to be there early." She rotated her shoulders and neck, walked over and picked up a pair of leggings and a loose T-shirt. With her back turned to him, she quickly dressed. She knew he was watching her with great interest when she turned around, catching him in the act, and tossed her nightie on the bed. "Hey, I made the offer this morning, but you turned me down."

He snagged her as she slid through the doorway, pulled her up tight, grinding his pelvis against hers, and said, "Hold that thought." And he kissed her hard. Then he left her limp against the doorjamb as he headed downstairs. "Hurry up," he said cheerfully. "We need to get some breakfast and get out of here."

Almost an hour later she walked into the showcase room and studied the Arctic Ice painting now on full display, all the canvas covers removed, and the scaffolding taken away. She studied the corner that she wanted fixed and realized that it had been.

Frankie came up and said, his tone a little different, "Is that okay, or do you want to get up there and do more?"

She looked at it closely, then turned to look at him with a beaming smile, and said, "Thank you. I think that's pretty good now."

He looked relieved.

"Obviously you're getting better," she said. "I'm really thrilled."

He gave her that sheepish smile and said, "I keep hoping I'm getting better, but I don't think so," he said.

"I'm sure you are," she said.

"I can't help but think you probably should have used Naomi for this. Although she might have been difficult and hard to deal with, at least she was a known factor. A new model will be somebody completely different in that aspect."

"I don't even know how to get hold of her," she said. "That's not my deal at all."

"Right. I guess Anita calls her, huh?"

"Yes," she said, "and I have no idea if that's even an option, but I don't want it to be an option. I just want to try the new people."

As she turned, the new model she had chosen for this job walked in. She looked excited and nervous. She waved and came racing over. "This is absolutely stunning," she said warmly, as she looked up at the huge painting. "I'm not even sure what I'm supposed to be when I'm done being painted."

"You'll see," she said. "First, we'll do the background colors on you, then I'll line you up with the background art, so I can get an idea what I want to do on you. Then we'll go from there."

"Am I the only one?" she asked, staring up at the big painting.

"No, I have another one as well." She smiled at Frankie, like she had a secret.

"Okay, good," the new model said. "I'm just a little nervous."

"You've done this before, correct?"

"Yes, I have," she said, "of course. Just not … for you."

"I'm the easy part," Cayce said gently. "It's the audience that makes it difficult."

"I really like that part," she said, "but I've never been in such a big production, like this. Will I be the one who takes the step out? I worry that, if I do it wrong, the surprise is gone."

"If I do my job well," she said, "you should be able to move restlessly up there, and it would just seem like the water moving around you. It's one of the reasons why I'll paint you where you are, so I can be certain that, if you can't hold the pose very still for very long, it won't look like anything other than the rippling water."

"That sounds absolutely fabulous," she said. "Will you

have cameras and photos? Because I really want some for my own portfolio."

"That won't be an issue," Cayce said. "So, go get ready, and I'll meet you in that far corner of the room."

"She's got an innocence to her," Frankie said, as she darted away.

"She absolutely does. There's also a certain luminescence to her skin, and I'm looking forward to painting her." Not to mention that her open and accessible energy would be a joy to work with.

"And she was just one of the random ones?"

"We get hundreds of portfolio files sent to us," she said. "She's one of the four I initially picked."

"You know something? Now I know why."

She laughed. "I do know what I like. It's just not always that easy to find it." She looked over at him. "Now, what about you? Have you got work to do?"

"I do," he said. "I'm working on the lighting, and I always want to make sure the lights are perfect, but I can't finalize things until the models are mostly done."

"Good thing you've got the lead on that," she said. "My problem is that I know when the lighting is not right, but I don't know how to fix it."

He laughed. "That's why we work well together. You go do your new model, and I'll tinker with the lighting. I'm fascinated by what you said about the rippling water."

"I'll check back in a few hours," she said, "and hopefully we'll pull it off."

He gazed at her, smiled, and said, "You always pull it off."

RICHARD LOOKED UP as Andy approached.

"Somebody just called in to say that Naomi didn't show up for a modeling job."

Richard's gaze narrowed, and he didn't speak for a moment. "*Naomi*, Naomi?"

"Yes, that one."

"Shit. Do we have an address?"

Andy held up a slip of paper. "Let's go." They bolted outside, and Andy said, "We need to find out if anybody has seen her."

"Exactly." They made it to her place within about twelve minutes. As they parked out in the street, they looked around. "This is a pretty high-class area for her, isn't it?" Richard asked.

"Remember what Elena had for an asset base was surprising too," Andy said.

"But it wasn't her money, not originally at least," Richard replied.

"She did make good money though," Andy added.

"Do you think Naomi does?"

"I can't imagine it," Andy said. "Even if she did, how consistent would wealth be with a temperament like hers?"

"Who knows? Honestly, I've felt a little out of my league on this case in terms of knowing much about the people and the work involved."

"Yeah, I hear you," Andy said. "Naomi's been pretty upset these last few days, according to her agent who called it in."

"Are we thinking she might have harmed herself?"

"I don't think so," he said, "but who knows. We've seen stranger cases."

"Absolutely."

As they walked in and headed up to her apartment, they knocked on the door. There was no answer.

After another knock, somebody came out in the hallway and asked, "May I help you?"

They turned to look at a tall, slender, well-dressed male in his mid-thirties, staring at them with a surprised look on his face.

"Do you know Naomi?"

"Very well," he said. "Why?"

"We have a report that she didn't show up for a modeling shoot and that nobody can reach her."

He rolled his eyes and said, "Naomi is prone to drama."

"But doesn't she need to show up for her shoots?"

At that, the younger man frowned. "Good point. She definitely needs the work, and she would never miss that. Not with what the lifestyle means to her."

"What's your name?" Richard asked. "And how do you know her?"

"Derek," he said with a smile, reaching out and shaking their hands. "Naomi and I have known each other for decades. Do you want to go inside and check to make sure she's okay then? I can do that," he said, as he pulled out keys and inserted one into the lock.

"You have a key to her place?" Richard asked, frowning.

Derek looked at him. "It's my apartment," he said in a dry tone. "Naomi likes to pretend it's hers. She does pay me token rent, albeit begrudgingly, but she's constantly digging at me that it's too high and that she should be paying less."

"And what is too high?" Andy asked.

"She pays me twelve hundred a month," he said.

The two men exchanged glances, then looked at him.

Derek nodded. "She has a sense of entitlement. I could

easily get twice that for this place." He opened the door, and they stepped inside to see an absolutely gorgeous apartment, very artistic looking, very contemporary.

"This is your place?"

He nodded. "The apartment is mine. The furniture is hers." The furniture was just a shade less luxurious than the rest of the place.

"What is her money situation?"

"Right now, it's really sad. She can't afford to have lost the job she was offered or to be late for another."

"But she is very temperamental and known to cause issues. Has she been fired from sets before?"

"Unfortunately, all the time."

"So maybe you can tell me why you're still friends then?" Richard asked him.

Derek looked at him in surprise. "My friendship is not dependent on her financial or mental or emotional status," he said. "We were friends in kindergarten. That hasn't changed."

The two detectives stood here in the landing.

Derek said, "I'll be right back." He walked toward the bedroom, calling out, "Naomi, are you here?"

The detectives studied the main area, opened the front closet door, looking for something to say that she had been here recently. They walked into the kitchen to find a mess, not terribly surprised. A take-out container, an empty bag, a plate. Forks.

When Derek came out, his strides were long and purposeful, and a worried frown crossed his face. "She's not here."

"Maybe we could check her bedroom?"

He waved them through. "Yes, of course."

They walked into the bedroom to see the bed was also a mess, with clothes on the floor, clothes on the chairs.

Sounding apologetic from behind them, Derek said, "She was never a neat person."

"What can you tell us about her?"

"She is mean, and other than the fact that she is greedy, jealous, arrogant, and of the opinion that no other woman can do what she can do when it comes to modeling, she hated Elena with a passion, and she hates to see others succeed with an almost equal amount of passion."

"Do you know why?" Andy asked.

"I'm sure you can guess, Detective," Derek said in a hard voice. "I have no illusions about who and what Naomi is. I still don't. The fact of the matter is that she is who she is, and that will never change."

"Why are you friends?" Richard asked again.

"Because I've known her for such a long time, I've seen her evolve," he said. "It's almost amusement at this point. She's like an accident ready to happen."

At that, Richard winced. "That doesn't sound very nice."

"No, it probably isn't," he said, "but it's the truth. Just like the fact that she is only friends with me for what I can do for her."

"And what is it that you can do for her?"

He laughed. "Well, this apartment for one. And I brought her the Chinese food the other day because she hadn't eaten."

"Is she that broke?"

He nodded. "When she is broke, she lives a very dangerous lifestyle."

At that, something else clicked in Richard's head. "Meaning the attack at the bar the other night?"

"Yes, and it's not what you're thinking," Derek said. "It's not that she's prostituting herself. But she's a very adept thief. She is offered lots of opportunities."

"That *can* get very dangerous," he said, "and it also completely opens up a suspect pool for our missing-person problem right now."

"She also has a tendency," Derek said, taking a deep breath, "to disappear for days and weeks on end, particularly if she's gone on a bender, when she gets very sick and depressed."

"So, we don't have any idea if she's missing or if she just chose to walk away."

"Exactly. The fact that the agent called you is something that is unusual in itself."

"I think it was only because we had recently spoken to him," Andy said.

"That makes more sense," Derek said.

"I was wondering if she'd lost some major opportunities because of this or not?" Richard asked.

"All the time," he said with a grimace. "I've been seriously considering just breaking off my almost daily contact because she's on such a self-destructive path. But it felt wrong."

"And your relationship all this time has been just friends?"

"Yes," he said, "just friends. I'm gay," he said, "so we've never been lovers. I never ever went in that direction."

"And who is your partner currently?"

He looked a little startled at that question, but he answered readily enough. "Benjamin," he said. "Benjamin Haskell."

Richard nodded. He wasn't sure what the hell was bothering him, but something was. Maybe it was that little bit of dark energy that he kept seeing, and the fact that he was even seeing it really drove him nuts because a part of him didn't want to. Yet, at the same time, he wanted to see more of it, and he couldn't or didn't know how to. He tried to shift his position to look the way he had originally started this extended aura sight the other night with Stefan, but that didn't work either. He wasn't sure what he was seeing at all.

"And how has your relationship with Naomi been lately?" Andy asked.

"It was normal," he said. "I keep my distance, but I've always been there if she needed me."

"How does she get along with your partner?"

"She has never gotten along with any of my partners," Derek said. "I think she considered them competition for herself."

"So not just women are competition to Naomi?"

"When she loves, she loves deeply. I am hers in her mind, though whether she loves me or not, I don't know," he said. "But I am deemed hers, so anybody else in my world is somebody she has to compete with for attention."

After that, the detectives did a quick sweep around but found nothing to show where she might have been.

"Do you know where she went last?" Richard asked Derek.

He shook his head. "I saw her last when I brought the Chinese food. She was in a shitty mood, so I got up and left. I don't know if she went to bed right afterward or if she went to the bar."

"The bed is messed up, but it's hard to tell if she was sleeping or not," Andy noted.

"Her bed always looks like that," Derek said.

Richard turned, looked at him, and asked, "Do you know what she was wearing at the time?"

Derek looked at him in surprise, frowned, and said, "She was wearing her favorite red slinky top."

"Do you want to take a look in the bedroom with us and see if that outfit is there?"

He nodded immediately. He strode back into the bedroom, stopped, and looked, swearing. "How can you ever find anything in this mess?" He looked down in disgust. "You got gloves?"

Richard looked to see if he was serious, realized he was, and said, "We can take a quick look." He went to the laundry hamper. Nothing red and slinky. Moved a few pieces of clothing on the floor and on the chairs, so he could see what was underneath. Nothing red. He checked the closet. Nothing. "Does she use a laundry service?"

"In her heyday she did," he said, "because she was too good for anything else. Plus, if Elena or Cayce had it, then she wanted it too."

"Why was she so fixated on Elena?" Richard asked.

"Elena had that something special that Naomi could never emulate, and she knew it," he said immediately.

"Is she an artist at all or interested in art or artists?" Andy asked.

"No. Hell no," Derek said. "But, at one point in time, they had a boyfriend in common, and I think that's part of Naomi's ongoing feud."

"And who is that?"

"Kenneth," he said. "He was Naomi's boyfriend first, I think, and then he went out with Elena. Naomi took that as a rejection." But he frowned, as if trying to figure something out.

"Kenneth, the engineer?" Richard asked, taking a stab in the dark.

Derek shrugged. "Not sure I knew his profession. I presumed he was an artist."

Richard shook his head. "I'm not sure he dated Elena—my research and investigation hasn't confirmed that—just that they may have gone out together. After all, Elena and Kenneth the engineer were foster siblings and childhood friends."

Derek looked at him in surprise. "Oh, I didn't know that. I doubt Naomi did either. Too bad. She wouldn't have taken their relationship the wrong way. Still, that was years ago."

"Yeah, plus he's over in Dubai these days," Andy said.

"No, he's not," Derek said. "He's here. At least he was the other day." Then he stopped, frowned, and said, "I think so anyway. My partner saw him."

"Your partner knows him?"

"Well, from photos." Derek shrugged and said, "Look. It probably wasn't even him. Especially if he's supposed to be in Dubai. You're probably right."

"It's hard to say," Andy said, "but we can check to see if he's back in town or not."

"Where was he seen?" Richard asked.

"At the bar we frequent," he said.

When he gave the name of the place, prickles stood up on the back of Richard's neck. *The same bar where Naomi had been supposedly beaten up.* "Interesting," he said slowly. "Do you have a photo of him?"

Derek frowned. "No, nothing here that I know of."

"So how did your boyfriend know who it was?"

"I have no clue," he said. "He just mentioned it in passing."

"When was this?"

"A few days ago. Maybe a couple days before Elena was murdered," he said.

"Did you know Elena?"

"Well, much to Naomi's dismay and anger, yes. We hung out in a lot of the same circles. I really liked her. She was a real sweetheart."

"And again, you were just friends?"

"Just friends," he said. "But she might have been looking at seeing Kenneth again. I don't know."

"Interesting," Richard said.

As the detectives turned to walk out, Derek said, "You could always check with the art world," he said. "A lot of us are connected that way."

"Are you an artist?" Andy asked him.

Derek shrugged, shook his head, and said, "Not really. My partner dabbles though. So does Kenneth."

"What stuff does he do?"

"All kinds," he said, "but I don't think he classifies himself as anything in particular."

"Who, your partner or Kenneth?" Richard asked, a sense of stillness inside him.

"Kenneth. Elena said that he and Cayce used to paint together all the time years ago."

Richard stared at Andy. Andy stared back, and they quickly made their exit.

Richard asked, "What was that look for?"

"I warned you, dude."

"I hear you," he said with a shrug. "It doesn't mean a whole lot though."

As they got outside, Andy said, "Where are you going?"

"I'm going to ask Cayce a few questions."

IT'S A GOOD thing that the police didn't have a clue. "I'd have been taken in years ago." But, hey, this is the way life was now for him. And he really, really wanted to get down there tonight.

If there was a chance of completing this last piece, then he would be a happy boy. He wasn't so sure it would be effective, but hey.

He checked his watch, swore, rose, walked over quickly to shut off the music he had been playing to drown out the sounds behind him. Washing up again quickly, he switched his shirt, and headed downstairs. He lived in a hovel, with no time to clean it or him, but that was expected of an artistic temperament. Nobody gave a shit here, and he liked that.

As he raced down the stairs, somebody called out from above, "Hey, you left your door open."

He froze, turned to look at him, and said, "Pardon?"

The man pointed back down the hallway. "Your door isn't closed, man. Somebody will go in there and steal everything."

He slowly worked his way up the stairs to where the young man stood and asked, "Did you take a look inside?"

"No, no, I didn't," he said, backing up a few paces.

"You did, didn't you?" he said, in a threatening manner, stalking closer.

"Hey, look. Your door was open."

As he walked past, he stared at the door and frowned. It definitely was open. But it hadn't been like that before. "That was you, wasn't it?"

"Hey, I just checked and called out to see if you were

inside," he said.

"Funny, I didn't hear you call out."

"Well, I meant to," he said. "Then I saw you down here and thought maybe I'd check and see if it was you."

"And, if it wasn't me, you would go in there, huh?" He shoved his face right into the personal space of other man, who backed up quickly.

"Look. I don't want any trouble," he said. "I was just being a nice neighbor. Jesus Christ." And he turned to walk away.

Except that he didn't dare let him go. He was too close now to reaching his goal. Tonight was too important. He reached out, grabbed him in a pincher move on the back of the neck, and, with a hard right to the temple, put him down. He quickly checked both sides of the hallway, then dragged him inside his apartment. He tied him up and stuffed a rag in his mouth and left him there to be dealt with later.

Trouble was, he didn't really want to deal with him at all. He just wanted him to go away. If he knew which place was his, he would just dump him there with a warning. As it was, he didn't have time now. Swearing, he closed and locked his door this time and raced out to the street. He wanted to be there before the show started.

CHAPTER 23

A FTER HOURS OF bending and working, it was all due to
start in just a little while. Cayce still had to get dressed,
and she had less than thirty-eight minutes to do it in. Anita
was panicked at her side, but Frankie stood calm and silent
as always. She stepped back and finally told Jilly, her new
model, and the second one she had added, Bellamy—
Frankie's partner—to go stand where they were supposed to.

Frankie sucked in his breath as he saw them. "Wow," he
said.

She stood up, rubbing her lower back, and said, "Okay,
girls. Like I said." And ever-so-slowly they slid toward each
other. One step out, bringing the other foot together.
Against the backdrop but not touching it, and, sure enough,
with every movement they took, it looked like the waves
churning on the mural behind them.

Anita laughed and then cried out, "Oh, my God," she
said. "I didn't know how you could possibly top the last one.
But this, … this is amazing."

Cayce watched her models with a critical eye and then
relaxed. "Okay, girls, you have ten minutes to yourself while
we clean up and get ready, and then it'll be showtime."

The two women just nodded obediently, but you could
tell that they were incredibly excited. "You'll film it, right?"
Jilly asked.

"We definitely will," Frankie said. He looked down at Cayce. "I can't thank you enough."

"Don't worry about it," she said. "You can spend a few minutes with Bellamy while I go get changed, but then, as you know, I'll need your help."

He nodded. "I'm here and ready."

He always was. She smiled, nodded, and headed to the small bathroom on the side of the large room.

There was Anita, standing outside, holding the dress that Cayce would wear for the cocktail hour and for the big presentation. She stepped into the bathroom, quickly stripped down, had a quick shower, and plaited her long hair until she was fully dressed. And then, wearing only her underwear, opening the door just a smidge, she asked for the dress, slipped it on and up over her chest, putting her arms through her sleeves.

Then realized she couldn't zip it. "Anita, I need help closing it."

She heard a muffled sound of voices on the other side of her door. She frowned. She opened the door ever-so-slightly. "Anita?"

Instead of Anita, she saw Richard. He took one look at her in that dress, and she watched his face turn to one of complete and instant lust. He stood, frozen, as was his gaze.

"We can't do this now," she said, her voice thick.

He closed his eyes, swaying in the spot. "God damn it," he said. "You *so* have to wear that dress at home."

"Only when it's over," she said.

He swallowed hard and said, "Turn around."

She slowly turned around and gave him a glimpse of her smooth, clean back as he reached out a shaky hand. She watched in the mirror as he zipped her up.

When she turned to face him again, he said, "I'll be outside." And he disappeared.

Feeling more wanted and sexier than she'd ever felt in her life, she put on her makeup, then unbraided her hair, brushed it out, clipped it back in a sedate ball at her neck, picked up her work clothing to put everything into her extra bag, and stepped out.

Anita looked at her with a happy sigh. "You're stunning," she said. "That dress is so you."

Cayce didn't need Anita's words to build her up tonight. She'd seen the look on Richard's face. And honestly, she was still shaken by it herself. She smiled at her friend. "Come on. Let's make this happen."

By the time Cayce walked back out to the main exhibit again, the doors were just opening to let in the crowd. She stood in the center of the room, a flute of champagne in her hand, as everybody swarmed toward her. She lifted her glass and said, "Welcome."

And, with that, the chaos began. Everybody mingled and looked at the big black silk-covered wall, completely covered before the grand presentation. She'd had the curtain specially made, and the roller too, but, at her signal, the podium cleared, and she stepped up to announce the prelude of what this installation was for and who was behind it all.

Major Robert, her client, came up beside her, holding her hand, then gently bent over and kissed it. "I have never met," he said, in a loud booming voice, "anybody who was so special, so talented, and so beautiful as this woman. The job that she has done behind us is way beyond my expectations."

She laughed and said, "Thank you for that. And now, may you all enjoy it." She motioned to Frankie. "Frankie, if you will." She stepped off to the side, as the curtain was quickly pulled apart, revealing her work.

There were gasps of oohs and aahs as everybody studied the massive painting in front of them. The ice fall, icebergs, the ocean. The audience was given five minutes to stare at the huge painting, and then she signaled Frankie to start the music. The two models—separated from the wall and yet still so close to it—were almost impossible to tell apart. From her angle, she could.

But, as Jilly and Bellamy took their tiny steps across the stage, everybody laughed and cheered because, indeed, it looked like water rippling.

Frankie stepped up behind her and said, "I can't believe you did that."

She gave a happy sigh. "It looks pretty good, doesn't it?"

The major stepped over and whispered, "Dear God, lady. You have outdone yourself."

She smiled. "It's all for a good cause."

"Saving the animals," he said with a nod. "A most worthy cause, indeed. But this, … wow! This is one of those dinners where they'll pay five thousand a plate, and we'll collect an awful lot of money here tonight," he said. "I don't know how to thank you for donating your time and money."

She felt Frankie gasp beside her. She reached up, kissed the major gently on the cheek, and said, "For Elena."

A hand landed on her shoulder. She smiled because she knew it was him. She leaned her cheek against it, and he stepped up behind her, pulling her against him. "I don't think I've ever seen anything like it," Richard said.

When the signal was given, the music and the models stopped, and the crowd could all approach. They stood calm and quiet, and, when the music started again, they moved so that everybody could see how the effects worked.

She looked up at Richard and smiled. "I can't get away from here very early," she said.

Frankie shook his head. "She'll be here right through to midnight."

"That may be," Richard said, "but I'm not leaving here either."

She looked up at him. "Did something happen?"

He reached over, kissed her gently on the temple, and said, "You have your night. I have some questions, but that's all."

"Maybe I can help," Frankie said.

Richard looked at him, and, while she watched, Richard said, "Maybe." He leaned down and whispered in her ear, "I'll be right back." He motioned to Frankie, and they stepped away.

"Do you know anything about Kenneth?"

"HE'S THE BASTARD who beat up Elena," Frankie said.

"What?"

"No, no, wait, that's wrong," he said and then shook his head. "No, that's wrong. Sorry," he said, frowning, as if trying to remember. He took a deep breath. "I had a head injury not too long ago, and sometimes I get things wrong."

"I don't understand," Richard said. "Why would a woman like Elena go out with somebody who beat her up?"

"She didn't. I had that wrong," Frankie said. Then his face lit up. "I got it. Kenneth is the son of the man, the stepson, of the man who hurt Elena."

"Kenneth's stepfather hurt Elena?"

"Yes," he said, "and Elena helped Cayce later, and, as I

understand it, became close with Kenneth."

"Interesting. Well, apparently Kenneth is somewhere around."

"I don't think so," Frankie said, "but then I don't really know. I just know what I heard from the two of them talking here and there. I've been around long enough that, while I haven't been privy to their conversations, they forget I'm here sometimes, and I overhear conversations."

"Right," he said, "that makes sense. Any idea where we would find him?"

"No, I didn't know he was anywhere around here."

"And what do you know about Elena's or Naomi's friend Derek?"

"From money, doesn't really work. He has his fingers in a lot of pots. He is a little bit of an artist but not much. He really cultivates a role in the artist community though."

"And his boyfriend?"

"Well, it used to be Kenneth," he said, "but I'm not sure who it is now."

Richard reached out, grabbed him, and gave him a shake. "What the hell are you saying? That Kenneth used to date Derek as well?"

"Yes, as far as I know."

"And where are you getting this information from?"

"Naomi," he said, "because Derek might be private, but Naomi is anything but."

"Crap," he said. "Let me get this straight. Cayce saves Elena from her abusive stepfather, and Kenneth is the stepson to that man and the stepbrother to Elena too. So Elena and Cayce continued to bond, and the stepson/stepbrother is around, and, somewhere along the line, Kenneth hangs out with Elena and becomes really good friends with the group. But then goes back to school to become an engineer and heads off to Dubai?"

At that, Frankie looked at him and frowned. "I don't know anything about engineering and Dubai," he said. "He was an artist."

"What kind of artist?"

"He used to do big mural-size stuff too, like Cayce," he said, "but his wasn't very good. I don't know how to explain it. It was really dark."

"Ah, crap." Richard pulled out his phone, called Andy, and said, "We need to find this Kenneth Lively, and we need to find him now. Apparently there's a chance he's in town, and he's tied to this artist community. He needs to be brought in for questioning ASAP."

"As in Elena?"

"Absolutely," he said. "Not only was he there when Cayce got beaten up way back when but it was his stepfather who abused Elena, and Kenneth became very good, very close friends with Elena. And he's an artist. He used to do mural stuff. Dark stuff."

"Jesus, that's an awful lot of coincidences."

"Yeah. I don't like any of this," he said. "None of this is a coincidence. I'm not sure if it's his plan, or if there's a devious mind behind him, but something is going on, and it involves this Kenneth guy."

Frankie leaned forward and said, "But Kenneth isn't anywhere around here," he said. "I haven't seen or even heard anything of him for years."

"And yet Derek told me that his current boyfriend saw him not too many days ago."

"Seriously?"

He nodded. "But why would the boyfriend even tell

Derek? That seems weird."

"Because that's the relationship they have," Frankie said. "Benjamin is insecure, so it was probably a poke at Derek to see if Benjamin could get a reaction. See if Derek still cared."

Richard nodded, spoke to Andy, still on the phone. "Did you get all that?"

"Yeah," Andy said. "We're already looking for Kenneth too. I'll be there soon." And he hung up. Richard frowned at Frankie. "Are you going anywhere tonight?"

"No way. Cayce relies on me," he said, "and my girlfriend is one of the models."

Richard stopped, looked at him with a smile, and said, "Cayce did it, did she?"

He gave a sheepish grin and shrugged. "Yeah. I know it's only because I asked her to."

"No way," Richard said. "I may not know her as well as you do, but I do know she would never allow herself to be pressured into doing that. She is true to her art, and your girlfriend either fit the project or she didn't."

Frankie relaxed, nodded, and said, "Thank you for that."

"I want you to stay damn close to Cayce tonight," he said, "and your girlfriend."

Immediately alarmed, the younger man's face clouded. "Why?"

"Because we have two dead models and a third who was in the industry, and I've always felt this was targeted at Cayce. Maybe her artwork. I don't know. But don't let them out of your sight."

But Frankie was already moving by the time Richard finished speaking, headed back toward Cayce. Richard walked up beside her too and whispered into her ear, saying, "I'll be back later. Do not leave here, and stay surrounded by people you trust."

She nodded mutely. He leaned over, kissed her hard, and was gone. He had too many people he had to talk to, and he needed to find them fast. As he headed outside, his phone rang. "Tell me you found one of them."

"Derek is bringing in his partner," Andy said.

"I'll meet you at the station," he said. "Any word on Kenneth?"

"Nothing," he said. "Not yet."

Richard raced to the police station. As he pulled in and walked through, Andy hailed him.

"Over here."

Richard walked into the small interrogation room and sat down. With a look over at Derek, he said, "Thanks for coming in." He shook the boyfriend's hand and said, "We need to know what you know about Kenneth."

At that, the other man's lip curled.

"The truth," Richard said. "Not jealous suppositions."

Surprised, Benjamin looked quickly at Derek, then back at Richard. "Well, you don't have to put it that way."

"Yes, I do," he said. "Three models are dead," he said, "and we need to find Kenneth to see if he's involved."

At that, Benjamin gasped, covering his mouth with his hand.

"No theatrics," Richard demanded. "Just tell me what you know."

"Well, I don't know anything," he said.

"You said that you saw him," Derek said. "Either you did or you didn't."

Benjamin flushed. "I just knew it would bug you."

"So, this is me asking, so you better tell the truth," Richard said. "Did you or did you not see Kenneth?"

He frowned and said, "Well, I thought it looked like Kenneth, but I can't be sure."

"What does Kenneth look like?"

"Oh, I took a picture," he said, as he pulled out his latest model iPhone and hurriedly flicked through his photos. When he found the image he wanted, he held it up.

Derek snatched it from his hands, looked at it with squinted eyes, and said, "That could be Kenneth."

Benjamin looked at him and said, "What the hell?"

"What?" Derek asked.

"How could you possibly recognize him from that?" Benjamin asked.

"You did," Derek said.

"Yeah, but that was my fear talking."

Derek immediately squeezed the other man's fingers and said, "And I keep telling you, you don't need to worry."

"I know that," Benjamin said. "And I need to give you the trust that you deserve, but it's damn hard when that's the reason my last relationship broke up."

"Which is even a better reason not to be dragging it forward."

Richard looked at them, grabbed Benjamin's phone, and said, "Are you two done?"

Derek flushed. "I'm sorry," he said. "We typically don't air our dirty laundry."

"If it includes Kenneth," Richard said, "I want to know every damn piece of it. So we'll be sitting here until we drag out every bit you know." He handed the phone over to Andy. "Email that to George, please."

With that done, Andy got up and left the room.

"Where's he going?" Derek asked.

"To get that photo enhanced and to see if we can get

something that we can go on, so we can talk to people."

"Well, if he'll be anywhere, he'll be at the big centers," he said. "He's all about art."

"Meaning, he'll likely to be at Cayce's big showing tonight?"

Derek looked at him in surprise and said, "That's exactly where he would be."

"Do you know how he feels about Cayce?"

"A love-hate relationship."

"Why the hate?"

"Cayce saved Elena, called out the abuse of Elena, so Cayce's responsible for Kenneth's stepfather going to trial, only he ran away, never to be found again, which then led to the breakdown of Kenneth's stepmother."

"Didn't the stepfather attack and sexually abuse Elena?"

"Yes. He did, and Cayce made sure Elena got help in the hospital," Derek said. "It was pretty ugly at the time. And, yes, the stepfather absolutely deserved to go to jail but disappeared somehow. But it caused Kenneth's stepmom a lot of problems and some very conflicted emotions. Remember now, they were preteens or teenagers at the time, so definitely a love-hate relationship."

"And yet, how did Kenneth end up dating Naomi?"

Derek nodded. "That's way back when he was still going out with women," he said. "After they broke up, he and I hooked up. But it was years later."

"And how long were you with him?"

"Six to nine months probably," he said. "I honestly can't remember."

A sniffle came from the boyfriend.

Richard glared at Benjamin. "Keep it together."

The boyfriend just nodded.

As Richard continued to ask every question that he could—upside, downside, and every other angle—he wasn't getting any new information. "Outside of tonight's show, do you have any idea where else Kenneth might go, or where he would stay?"

"No," Benjamin said.

"He owned an apartment at one time," Derek said.

Richard froze, picked up his pen and notebook, and asked, "Where?"

Derek looked around the small windowless room, as if orienting himself. "I have no idea what the address is," he said, "but it's not very far from here."

"We did a local title search already, and he doesn't own any Seattle property."

"No," he said. "Not him. I think it's in the stepfather's name," Derek said.

"Okay. We'll have to run that up on him too," Richard said.

"I can tell you," Derek spoke out, "that Kenneth will be too unstable to go to trial."

At that, Richard sat back and said, "Now that would make the most sense yet."

"How does that make any sense?" Benjamin asked, in a querulous voice.

"Because whoever is killing these people is obviously mentally unstable," he said. "With three already dead, we don't want a fourth." He stood, ending the interview. "You can leave, gentlemen. Please stay in town. I may have to get in touch with you with more questions."

Derek stood, and immediately the boyfriend did also.

"Did we do okay?" Benjamin asked Derek.

Derek nodded and said, "We did." He stopped, turned,

and looked at Richard. "Detective, do you think this has anything to do with Naomi going missing? I wasn't too worried to begin with but now ..."

"I don't know. But it's very possible that, when we find Kenneth, we'll find Naomi."

"She's not a very nice person sometimes," Derek said. His voice dropped to a quiet tone. "But she doesn't deserve what happened to Elena."

"None of them deserved that," Richard said, and he bolted from the interrogation room.

LOOK AT ALL the people standing in line just to get inside. Look at the accolades she was getting. He sighed with joy and happiness. She was such a success. A success that should have been his and would be again.

He almost had it perfected. He was doing so, so well. He smiled, accepted a glass of champagne—the servers doing their best to keep the patrons waiting outside a little mollified. Putting on airs, he gently walked around, speaking to others, as if he were the artist. Because, of course, he could do this. He'd done things like this many times. He was perfectly capable of it.

He sighed a happy sigh, reached up, and gently patted his hair, making sure that it was as good as it could be.

It was not the way he wanted to leave his apartment, but one had to make do. At the showing, he stood in awe at the turnout. Cayce had done phenomenally well for herself. He could hardly contain his excitement.

When one of the guards walked over to him and asked if he was okay, he gave him a frightened look, realizing he'd shown too much eagerness. "Of course I'm fine," he said.

Then he took his flute of champagne and turned his back to the guard.

He wasn't sure what could possibly have attracted the guard's attention, but he wanted to get closer to see the models and to see the large picture. He also wanted to take photos, and certainly a lot of photos were being taken. He stood in line and took several selfies, acting the same as everybody else.

Then he went inside and hummed with joy. When he looked at the two models, he sighed happily. They were both perfect. Then he contemplated which one. Which one?

Just then, Cayce walked over and talked to one of the models. He saw her, as silver slice against the ice, against the blue ice, and against the white, the light shining and playing across her perfect form, and he sighed as recognition hit him.

He didn't need to choose a model. It was Cayce's turn. He was finally here. She was finally it. Cayce had her grand finale, and that's exactly what this was, her finale. Now it would all be turned over to him. And he was more than happy to pick up the gauntlet.

CHAPTER 24

THE WARM, FUZZY feeling continued throughout the evening. Cayce was really, really proud of this. Proud that she was helping in some way to bring global awareness to help save the animals. She hadn't told anyone she had donated all her time to this. Anita would have a fit. Cayce had told her assistant that she had donated all the materials but not her labor, but she had to do the work that brought her joy. Otherwise there was no point in doing this at all.

So much ugliness was in her life right now that she wanted desperately to have something that made her feel good. It was hard to be upset when such a warm glow of love and acceptance was all around her. She took in the admiration, realizing that the glow would only last for tonight. At the same time, she was sad that Richard had gone. But apparently he had a good reason for it, since Frankie was staying at her side.

"So, are you hanging around me because you want to," she said in a low tone toward him, "or did Richard order you to?"

Frankie looked immediately guilty.

She nodded. "You need to remember it's the models who were kidnapped."

He nodded. "And I'm terrified that something'll happen to one or the other, and I want to bring them both over here and keep them beside you, but you all deserve whatever moments you have tonight."

She said, "We'll be just fine. It's a public place. Nothing'll happen here."

He looked at her, scanned the area, and said, "Please don't say that. That's like poking the devil and daring him to try it."

She laughed.

As the waiter went by, he held out a tray with a single flute. She immediately switched her old glass for the full one and thanked him. She turned to Frankie and said, "It'll be fine. The show was perfect tonight, wasn't it?"

"It is great," he said. "You are great."

"And you will get your painting mojo back," she said to him.

"I was wondering …" and he hesitated.

"Wondering what?" she asked.

"I started doing something very different. I wondered if you would take a look and let me know if it's any good," he said, his words came out in a rush.

"Absolutely," she said. "Is it different than your other stuff?"

"Yes, very. Very different, but it's kind of dark."

"Dark isn't necessarily bad," she said.

He looked at her in surprise.

"When I've hit some difficult rock-bottom times in my life," she said, "it was painting the dark that got me back out of it to the light again."

"You know what? I was wondering about that too because lately I've been reaching for lighter colors." He frowned and shook his head. "That never occurred to me."

She reached down, squeezed his wrist. "Be gentle on

334

yourself. You had a brain injury. There can be all kinds of repercussions from that."

"Not the least of which is my painting," he said in frustration.

"And maybe it's because you're going back to something that can't be had again. Maybe this new stuff is where you truly belong because it's different and fresh."

"That's a possibility. I like that idea," he said. "I think, when I was doing the stuff from before, I always felt like I was competing with you."

She stared at him in shock. "Why would you feel that?" she asked. "And why would you want to do stuff like this? This is a nightmare."

He looked at her in surprise.

She turned cross. "Do you know how much I have to work to get these massive paintings done? Look at the size of my canvas. Stay working on small ones. It's so much easier on your stress level."

He laughed. And he couldn't stop.

She watched in amusement as he bent over, howling. She managed to get the champagne glass out of his hand. And another waiter came and took it away from her. She smiled.

When Frankie calmed down, she said, "Well, I don't know what I said that was so funny but—"

He wiped the tears from his eyes. "You have no idea how much I needed to hear that."

She smiled at him. "We're our own worst enemy sometimes. You know that, right?"

He gave her a genuine smile, full of joy and buoyant laughter, and he nodded. "I think that's exactly what I've been doing." He turned to look at Bellamy, who was up against the mural wall, staring at the two of them. "And now I think my beloved girlfriend is wondering and worried about what's going on."

"Go," Cayce said. "I think she at least deserves to know that she's getting the Frankie she knows and loves back again."

He leaned over, kissed her gently on the cheek, and said, "You are divine." And, just like that, he was gone.

She chuckled. "I can't say I've been called that before."

A gentleman at her side said, "That was a lovely compliment."

She nodded. "It absolutely was." She took a sip of her champagne.

"I can't imagine the scope of the work that went into this," he said, "but I don't see a signature anywhere. Did you sign it?"

"I absolutely did," she said, "but the signature was never meant to be part of my design, so it's up in the cloud." She pointed at the top right corner.

He gasped and said, "I never even thought of that. Most artists are proud to put their signature on a piece of work."

"And I am too," she said with a bright smile. "But it's never intended to detract from the art itself." She turned and smiled up at him. Her gaze narrowed as she studied the man in front of her. "I'm sorry. Do I know you?" She held out her hand, even as she wondered at the flicker of recognition.

He shook it and smiled. "Absolutely you do." He tucked her hand a bit under his arm, moving her farther away from the crowd.

She glanced around and said, "So who are you?"

He laughed and said, "A friend from your past."

She stared at him. "I'm sorry. I don't remember."

"It's not a problem," he said. "It's not a problem at all."

When she ended up slightly away from where everybody else was, she stopped, looked around, and said, "I'm sorry. I need to rejoin the crowd and mingle with all the guests."

"Just a moment," he said. "I don't think we want everybody to hear the details."

She looked at him in surprise. "Details?"

He said quietly, "Do you really not remember me?" And his voice turned sorrowful. "I was there at a time when you desperately needed us."

"Us?"

He nodded. "Elena and I."

She stared at him in shock. "Kenneth?"

He beamed and opened his arms. She threw herself into them, and he hugged her tight. "I didn't think you'd forget me," he said, against her hair.

Tears were in her eyes when she stepped back and looked at him, holding him close. "Dear God," she said. "I haven't seen you in forever."

"I know," he said. "I just had to have a life of my own."

"And how is that?" she asked. "It seems that you dated everybody I know."

"That was a long time ago," he said, "although I have reconnected with a few people since then."

"Such as?"

"Just a few friends," he said coyly.

She chuckled. "I see you're still the same. Untamable, never one to have a relationship for long."

"Is that wrong?" he asked. "I know it's not fair to ask you to ditch all these people, but I was really hoping to spend some time with you before I leave tomorrow morning."

"I can't," she said regretfully. "Are you really. Tomorrow? Where to?"

"Yes," he said. "England."

She took another step back, and a waiter stepped to her side, taking her empty glass and leaving. She smiled up at Kenneth and said, "Come join the party, if you want, Kenneth."

He regretfully shook his head. "I can't quite do that yet."

"Okay," she said.

As she turned to walk away to follow the waiter, Kenneth called out, "Oh, wait."

She turned in surprise to look at him, unhappy to feel the room swaying. He laughed, then reached out, and grabbed her gently. "I think you've had a little too much champagne."

"Oh, I don't think so," she said. "I never drink too much."

He quickly helped her over to a bench off to the side. "Obviously tonight you did."

She sat down with a hard *thump* as she stared up at him. "What did you give me?"

"Just something to help you relax," he said. "Don't you want to join Elena?"

And that was the last thing she heard.

EVIL. EVIL WAS stirring. He could feel it. See it. As if he had tuned in to it.

He watched the man's huge shadow disappear across the street. Recognition hit him.

Evil.

He knew that face. Knew that smell. He'd lived with it

for a long time.

HE had to stop him. Help her.

Pretty lady. Painting. Evil painting. No, pretty painting. Evil woman. *NO.* Pretty woman.

He struggled to his feet and took several stumbling steps after the trail of evil.

It was time. Time to stop this.

Clutching the cross against his chest, he crossed the street and entered the building. There he stopped and listened.

And heard it.

Footsteps on the stairs.

RICHARD ANSWERED HIS phone, hearing Frankie's panicky voice on the other end. "She's gone," he screamed. "She's gone."

"Who? Where?"

"Cayce! She was here. Everybody was around us. It was fine. I went over to check on my girlfriend for a moment, and, when I came back, she was gone. Somebody said they saw her walking toward the hallway. A waiter said he took her empty glass, and there's no sign of her anywhere."

"And where could she possibly be?" Richard asked, already motioning at Andy, as he raced from the station.

"I don't know," he said. "I don't know. Did you find Kenneth?"

"No," he said in frustration. "We did talk to Derek and his boyfriend though."

"And is Kenneth here?"

"Apparently," Richard said. As he hopped into Andy's car, he kept Frankie on the line. "Lock down the place," he said, "and make sure nobody leaves."

But Frankie was past talking.

"Get me security," he said urgently to Frankie.

Suddenly another man spoke on Frankie's phone. "Security here. We've done a full search of the building. No sign of Cayce."

"I want all the camera feeds from inside and outside, available on all street corners," Richard said.

"We're already pulling that together," he said.

"I'll have a full unit down here within minutes. Where was she last seen?"

"On the northeast side of the building. A section where somebody said they thought she was sitting on a bench with a man."

"And we need to know about that man."

"Oddly dressed. In a suit that was slightly wrong."

"Slightly wrong? What the hell does that mean?" he asked in frustration.

"Well, they couldn't quite say, but he didn't look like he quite fit the suit."

"So, like an ill-fitted suit?"

"No, no. Something more than that. But again they couldn't explain."

"I don't have time to talk to everybody there," he said. "When my team arrives, make sure they interview everybody."

"Absolutely," he said. "We've already locked down security and explained what's going on."

"Are people pissed off?"

"No, not at the moment. I think they're all just horrified. Cayce is very special to this group."

"Right," he said. As he hung up, he closed his eyes,

acutely aware of how special she had become to him.

"It's Cayce?" Andy asked.

"Yeah, she's missing. Last seen sitting on one of the side benches, with a man. Next thing they knew, she's gone."

"Drugged?"

"It would make sense."

"How?"

"Champagne," they both said immediately.

"So now what?"

"Redirect," Richard said. "Let's get to Kenneth's apartment. A team at the ice installation will take statements. They're collecting all the video camera feeds they can. We'll get that routed through immediately, but my instincts are telling me to get to Kenneth's apartment."

"And where is that?"

He looked at Andy and said, "Two blocks from here. Just two blocks but he couldn't have carried her though."

"No," he said, "It's not very far but that would be very conspicuous. So, I mean, if he had a vehicle …"

"I don't know how he got her there, but maybe he walked her up here. Maybe it was that simple."

"Only if he had a weapon."

"Cayce would do it in a heartbeat to keep everybody else safe," Richard said. "Plus he's an old friend. Maybe no weapon was needed."

"Yes, I agree with you there. She would cooperate." Andy drove toward the apartment, parking on the street. They both exited quickly.

Richard turned and looked back at the installation, saying, "Wait. It's not two blocks. Look." At that, they stopped and took in their surroundings. They were at the corner at the back of the building. "He only had to get her through the back of the building and down an alley."

Richard raced across the street to the back of the adjacent building, checked to see if the door was locked, but it opened. And right in front of them was a shopping cart, like a homeless person would have. The two looked at each other and raced up the stairs toward Kenneth's apartment. "Let's go, go, go."

"Yes," Andy said, "but I'm calling for backup."

Richard stared at him in frustration.

Andy shook his head firmly. "No point barging in there and him killing her and getting ourselves taken out in the process."

Richard knew his partner was right, but he hated it. He continued up the stairs, and, on the next floor, a lady came out of an apartment on the same floor as Kenneth's. "Excuse me," he said. "Do you know the guy who lives in 224 B?"

She looked back that way, as if mentally counting the doors, and nodded. "Very strange guy," she said. "Kind of getting stranger by the minute too." She laughed. "Those artists."

"What do you mean by *getting stranger?*"

"Well, I mean, getting stranger," she said. "He just, you know, he started off fairly normal, and then he'd come up covered in paint, and then he had an odd smell coming out of there. I thought about calling management about it, but then he explained that he was trying new painting combinations, and that's what was causing the smell."

Richard nodded. "Did he ever appear dangerous in any way?"

"No. God, no," she said. "Although he did surprise me. He seemed like he wasn't very tall, and then, when I saw him the next time, he was rushing across the street, and he seemed like somehow he had straightened up."

Tucking that away in the back of his head, Richard walked up to the apartment. Andy quickly joined him. Richard said, "And?"

"Backup is on the way."

"That's nice." He turned the knob ever-so-gently and found that it was locked. Reaching into his back pocket, he pulled out a small wire and quickly picked the lock. He looked at Andy, and they both pulled their weapons. He inched the door open just slightly.

Immediately the smell wafted toward him. Grimly, the two of them opened the door a little bit wider. In the background they could hear music, eerie instrumentals that set him on edge. As he pushed, the door opened a bit more, something kicked him in the foot.

He glanced down to see a young man tied up and gagged on the floor, his eyes wide and rolling in terror. They quickly picked him up and moved him out of the apartment, cutting his bonds.

"He is crazy, man," he whispered. "He's completely crazy."

"Where do you live?"

"Right there," he said. "I'll be right over there." He bolted to his feet and darted into the apartment and slammed it shut as quietly as he could.

Andy and Richard looked at each other. Richard shrugged and said, "Not exactly our normal procedure, but Cayce is our priority right now."

They stepped back across the hall and pushed the door to 224 B slightly wider, then closed it behind them to stop the light from being detected by Kenneth.

The detectives crept forward, the smell filling their nostrils and making their stomachs heave. As they moved into the living room, they noted that the windows had been covered in some light-blocking material. As he stood in the gloominess, studying the layout, Richard focused on finding where the music was coming from, and he also heard a voice.

"You were supposed to bring me milk for my tea," she said in that querulous voice.

"I did bring you milk, Mom," he said ever patiently. "I brought it to you yesterday, and I brought it to you again today."

"Well, I'm out," she said, in a sad voice, denying the evidence in front of them, which was that she couldn't remember anything.

"Open the fridge, and you'll see the milk in the left-hand door."

He heard her shuffling across the room, heading to the fridge, and the small *click* that said she had opened it.

"Oh, you're such a good boy," she said. "The milk is here. I just didn't realize you came and went without stopping to visit."

"Mom, I came and had lunch with you."

"Are you coming today?"

"If I do, it'll be late."

"That's okay," she said in delight. Her words were followed by the *click* of a phone.

Silence. Then …

"You were supposed to bring me milk for my tea," she said *in that querulous voice.*

"I did bring you milk, Mom," he said *ever patiently. "I brought it to you yesterday, and I brought it to you again today."*

Richard followed the voice to a side hutch where a recording played on infinite loop.

And then, through the multiple layers of noise, another voice came from a different room.

Cayce's voice. And another man's voice. Dear God, how many people were here?

CHAPTER 25

C AYCE MOANED AS she shook her head, getting her bearings. She lay on a floor somewhere, in a room off a kitchen, but it was hard to see without any lights. But what she saw broke her heart and shook her soul. "Kenneth?" Surely not. Surely he wasn't behind all this evil. Yet he didn't look the same from all those years ago. It's as if he'd deteriorated in the last decade to the point where she barely recognized him.

"Yes," he cried out in delight. "You do remember me."

"Of course I do," she said, when, in fact, he looked like nothing she'd seen before. However, his voice, that she recognized. How long had it been? Only eight years ago, when she and Elena had lived together? Or fourteen years ago, when she had been eighteen and attacked by her fiancé? That was a part of her life she'd desperately shut down. "You held me close when I was hurt. You made sure I got to the hospital. That I was taken care of. How could I not remember you?"

Dear God, what had happened to him? Where had he been all this time? Elena had mentioned something about going to visit somebody overseas, maybe in Dubai? But it was a one-time thing, and Cayce had nodded but hadn't asked for details, being busy at the time.

"You went to a home in Washington, didn't you?"

He shook his head. "No that was my brother."

Brother? Stumped, she stared him. "I thought your brother was …" and she stopped. How could she ask about his hospitalization? "Is he doing okay?"

"He should be. I have no idea." Kenneth shrugged his shoulders. "After Mom died, the family broke up."

Duh, his stepmother had been a sadistic bitch, married to an even more sadistic husband. Both had beaten Kenneth and his brother, Heath, from an early age. Elena and the boys had been foster kids to these same evil stepparents. Elena's biological father was a violent criminal currently jailed somewhere or, if they were lucky, had died. Elena's "stepfather," her foster father, had sexually attacked Elena that terrible night so long ago. The two girls had been on the phone, besties forever already, with Elena crying great big sobs as she tried to explain what was wrong. Her foster father had come in, roaring at her.

Cayce had heard through the phone and had raced to her friend's side. She'd rung the doorbell several times, then barged in and dashed to her friend's bedroom to see the foster father pulling his pants on as he left the room. She'd dragged her friend out of the house and straight to the hospital.

Cayce would never forget standing in the ER, two little girls, preteens, Cayce supporting Elena, who was bleeding all over the floor—or the nightmare that came after that. Cayce had no idea her actions would spawn a series of events that would take Elena from her for years. But, by the time the police, the doctors, and social services took over, no one would let Cayce know anything.

Until she'd found herself in a horrible position years later with her own fiancé.

Elena had contacted Cayce one day out of the blue and told her that she needed to get out of that relationship. When Cayce had tried to leave, her fiancé had come home and caught her packing.

Elena had showed up with her "siblings" and had rescued Cayce. The next few months had passed in a blur, but Kenneth had put that paintbrush back in her hand and had painted at her side, while she filled canvas after canvas with black and red as she purged her soul of everything that had gone wrong. She had two broken ankles, compliments of her ex, and had been stuck in bed for months. That's when she'd spent so much time with Kenneth.

It wasn't long afterward that the two women had gone to Dr. Maddy, at Elena's suggestion and with Cayce's money. Not that she'd had much back then, but she'd had more than Elena. And they'd both been in such need ...

Kenneth had had access to her early designs. Not from her safe over the recent years but from many years earlier, as she had created them. "What happened to you?"

He looked at her in surprise. "Nothing. I've developed my skills, the same as you have. Of course I started from a bit further behind, but I'm there now." He sat back, rolled his shoulders, and said, "It was hard after I saw what happened to you. And Elena. I made a point of trying to fix things. But when I killed my stepfather for what he did to Elena and then I killed your fiancé, for what he did to you, I realized that, by doing so, I was bringing in my soul thing, ... people I didn't want to have there."

She studied him closely. She could see flashes of the younger man she'd known and flashes of a strong very together man, but they were hard to see with his fanatical gaze locked on her.

"How did you learn that soul thing?" she asked slowly, not sure she wanted to know. But anything she could do to delay the inevitable gave her more time for Richard to reach her. Surely he'd be here soon. When she heard something from the other side of the apartment, hope surged. Surely that was him?

"Heath showed me the initial path. Then you showed me the rest."

She stared him in confusion. "Heath?"

"Yes, he killed our mother. She deserved killing, you know?" he said in a contemplative voice. "She was worse than *him*. She abused all three of us but only the two of us sexually. Still, she was our mother—or all we knew as a mother. We loved her. After Heath killed her, he kept a part of her soul inside. And she's in his head all the time now. I keep her close but not like he does."

At that, a face appeared around the corner from the kitchen. A scarred face with tormented eyes.

Kenneth turned and said, "Heath, why are you here?"

"Evil," he whispered to his brother. "Evil."

"I know. I'll save her. I don't want you to be a part of this. You've got Mom, and you got overwhelmed," he said crossly. "I've got Dad and Elena and the others. You've got all you can handle with Mom. You don't get Cayce too. I do. And we'll paint together forever."

THOSE WORDS OF reality, Cayce's current reality, repeated in Richard's mind, bringing with it fear but also a wave of relief.

Cayce was still alive and, from the sound of her voice, not badly hurt. But, as his eyes adjusted to the darkness, he sucked in his breath in horror. Andy reached out and grabbed his arm, pointing …

Not only were many stretching bars all around the place but it was obvious that they contained some of the pieces missing from the corpses in the morgue that Richard was looking for. Indeed, he saw far more pieces than he had bodies. He exchanged a hard glance with Andy as they realized just what the hell was going on. When they crept ever closer, Cayce's voice called out, "You didn't have to hurt everybody."

"I wasn't hurting them," Kenneth said. "Not at all. I was capturing them, so they could live forever in their paintings and in me."

"But you killed them," she said quietly. "How was that capturing them?"

"Evil," said that other voice which Richard struggled to identify. Heath? And then it hit him. That ugly dark energy he had seen wrapped around Cayce's ankles that night not long ago. It was close to but not exactly the same broken black energy of the homeless man called Halo.

Was he Heath? Brother to Kenneth?

God. It wasn't hard to see it now, because the darkness wasn't necessarily coming from the closed-off windows but from the energy coming from the man bending over Cayce, who was lying on the floor of a room off the kitchen. The second man was curled nearby on the kitchen floor, whispering in a singsong voice, "Good boy. Bad boy."

That confirmed Halo's identity, and, after what Kenneth had just explained, might even explain the nightmare that had damaged Heath's childhood. Obviously Kenneth was equally damaged.

Richard crept closer, and when Kenneth straightened

and stepped away from Cayce, Richard jumped forward. "Hands up," he said.

The man in front of them froze. Halo's voice rose in a high-pitched song, repeating the same phrase over and over again, adding to the din.

Then Kenneth looked at Richard, dropped to his knees, and held a needle against Cayce's throat. "Don't come any closer."

CHAPTER 26

CAYCE COULDN'T BELIEVE Kenneth was behind all this madness and couldn't believe what he'd done, but her gaze landed on one of the paintings against the wall. Hard to not recognize it, as she'd last seen it at the masterpiece party where she'd painted the van Gogh on Elena. Cayce's eyes filled as she recognized the image and the skin.

But something else was here that neither Kenneth nor Heath could see.

And Cayce could use it right now.

She closed her eyes, hearing the men argue, and reached out with her energy to the painting on the wall. She hadn't been joking when she'd told Richard about the energy of the model being important to Cayce. And blending Cayce's energy with her model's to make the painting come alive.

Just then Richard said, "Oh, I'll come closer," he said to Kenneth. "Then I'll beat the living shit out of you for touching her."

"You can't touch me," he said, in a weird singsong voice. "I'm full of light. Full of people. It's much, much better," he said. "I can show you exactly how good it was." He looked at the detectives, beaming. "My latest paintings prove it."

"What is it I'm supposed to look at?" Cayce asked, as Kenneth pulled her into a sitting position, then up onto her feet.

"Let me show you," he said, "but don't you cops come any closer." He wrapped an arm around her neck and, still clutching a needle there, dragged her off to the side of the room, while Richard watched helplessly. Kenneth turned on a small table light. "Look," he said. "Look. I made it."

And Richard stared in shock because there was Naomi, her carved-up corpse off to one side and a piece missing from her painted body on the other side. It was hung up near the painting that had been taken from Elena.

"See? I did exactly as you did. Aren't they perfect?"

Cayce, in a calm, yet sad voice, said, "You did. Elena loved you so much." Her stomach contents started to climb up into her throat. Nothing was joyous or beautiful at all about what had happened to Naomi's body. Or to Elena's masterpiece, which was completely unrecognizable. Instead, Cayce could see the energy of demons as they crawled from the center of Naomi's skin, the flesh already rotting and decaying. What his human-skin canvases were intended to be wasn't even visible. Madness had completely taken over Kenneth.

"I know," he said proudly. "And now Elena's with me always. That's why I sent you a piece. So she'd be with you too."

Cayce closed her eyes, as tears dripped down her cheeks. Then resolutely, determinedly, she stretched out her energy, blending with the bits and pieces of Elena's energy still left on poor Elena's masterpiece. Not much there to work with but all objects were energy. Even pieces that had been taken from people who were light themselves. She could hear Heath in the background, as he slipped further away into his own darkness. Meanwhile Kenneth was explaining in that earnest voice of his how he was bringing more light into people's lives with his work and how Cayce would help him do so much better once they were all together.

She took a deep breath, and she sucked in *all* the energy she could reach for around her—whether good energy or bad—from the bits left of Elena and Naomi, whatever Heath had too. Then, feeling the energetic power build and grow as she reached for Kenneth, Cayce pulled his energy into her space and away from him. Feeling the power surge into her, ... through her.

Let it go right through. Keep pulling, but release it out the other side, Stefan whispered, calm and steady in her head. *This needs to happen, but you don't need this energy. It's too dark. Too ugly. You need to let it go. Think of a paintbrush, and stroke that energy forward to go around you and to carry on out behind you. Let it all go. Release Elena's energy, keeping just your memories of her. Release your ex-fiancé. Release Elena's stepfather, ... all those ugly and painful memories. Let them go and the people with it. Most of all, let go of Kenneth and Halo. ... They are broken souls. You need to walk free.*

The energy pressure built higher and higher inside her. Stefan was helping her, pulling energy—or maybe blocking her from pulling energy?

I'm only protecting the other two in the room. Pull, he urged, *pull harder ...*

She could see Richard's beloved face in front of her and heard Kenneth's screams in her head.

Pull hard, then let go, Stefan ordered.

She could feel someone else joining her efforts but not with the pulling ...

Dr. Maddy whispered, *I'm helping you to let go. This will kill you if you don't. The brothers are already gone. We need to save you now. Release all this old energy. All the pain. Release the energy from these evil men …*

Blindly aware of Kenneth doing some midair dance beside her and Richard moving closer, his hands out to help, … she reached back.

Reach for a future, Dr. Maddy said encouragingly. *Let go of the past.*

And, with that, she let the tainted energy swoop on past, and she stepped forward, disconnecting from all that had been, collapsing into Richard's arms.

SHE'LL BE OKAY now, Stefan said quietly. *And I realized the connection I was feeling. It was Halo. He was in treatment at one of Dr. Maddy's centers, where she had asked for my help. He showed such initial progress that the foster care system pulled him out against our wishes. He was a broken soul back then and has declined so much since then. The brothers are both at peace now. Richard, look after Cayce.* Stefan's voice faded from his mind.

Richard cradled Cayce into his arms. "God, I thought I'd lost you," he whispered, sending an emotional thanks to Stefan.

She sobbed quietly against his shirt. "You cut it damn close," she whispered.

He kissed her, holding her face close, and kissed her once more. "I made it though," he said. "That's what counts."

She gave him a wistful smile and whispered, "You're right." She looked down at Kenneth, then around at Heath. "Are they dead?"

Andy stood over Kenneth, studying the macabre sight of his severely dehydrated body. "This will be fun for the coroner to decipher." He looked over at her. "Are you okay?"

"I will be," she answered, not prepared to explain what just happened. As far as she cared, these two dead men could be declared as unexplained causes of death. Something for the medical experts to talk about for years to come. As long as they didn't try to discuss it with her, she'd be fine.

"Both men are dead. Same dehydration," Andy said in confusion. "I don't know what just happened here, but I'm glad whatever the hell happened didn't affect us. And what the hell are these?" Andy said, motioning at the stretched skin canvases behind them.

"It was Kenneth's attempt to recreate my work," she said.

Andy looked at her, looked at these pieces, and said, "They don't deserve to be anywhere near your work. These are awful and disgusting, the product of a crazed mind."

"Exactly," she said. "But, for him, this was a success. Because he did what he thought he could do. So, if nothing else, he died a happy man."

"And that's too damn bad," Richard said beside her. "Because all these people didn't."

As she turned to take in the whole room, her skin paled as she stared at the number of canvases laid out in front of her. "Oh, my God," she said. "How many people did he kill?"

"I don't know," Richard said. "It'll take us a long time to find out." He pulled her into his arms again. "But that's not your problem tonight." He looked over at Andy. "We've got a long night ahead of us." Just as the backup units began to fill the apartment, Richard's phone rang. "First, you need to tell Frankie that it's all okay."

She took the phone from him and answered it. "Frankie,

I'm fine."

"Oh, my God," he screamed into the phone. "What happened?"

"Let's just say I came very close to becoming a permanent masterpiece," she whispered. "I'm exhausted but okay. Richard saved me by the stroke of death."

"My God," Frankie said, his trembling evident through the phone.

"Listen. Go home. Take your girlfriend with you, and enjoy life for a day or two. I'll contact you in a few days."

Taking the phone back, Richard said, "Frankie, Andy will cut you loose over there as soon as we can. There will be plenty of follow-up to do, but sit tight, and we'll process everybody out of there."

"Thank you," Frankie said, "for—you know."

"I know."

Andy was off to the side, already on the phone, issuing instructions.

"Can I go home now?" Cayce asked, her whole body shaking.

"Yes, you can."

She walked over and reached out a trembling finger against the piece that held the masterpiece that was once Elena. "I want that piece," she said, "to bury with Elena."

"And you can have it," Richard said. "I just don't know how long it will take to get it all processed."

She swallowed, visibly upset, and nodded. "Please, please just take me home."

He hesitated a moment. "I'll take you home, but I can't stay."

"Of course not," she said, her voice thick. "But that's okay, I understand."

"Do you?" His voice held doubt because he'd been in plenty of relationships where they hadn't understood, not at all.

She stroked his cheek gently and said, "I do understand. And, if you can handle me and my crazy painting hours, I can handle you and your crazy cop hours."

He reached over, and, in the tenderest moment that he'd ever offered to anyone, he kissed her with all his heart. "I'll get there as soon as I can."

"Good," she said. "And, whenever that is, I'll be waiting."

CHAPTER 27

CAYCE HEARD RICHARD come in, but she was half asleep. She could see that the room had some light coming in around the curtains and realized what a long night he'd had. When he slid into her bed and wrapped his arms around her, she murmured something to him, but his warm voice against her ear whispered, "Sleep." And she drifted back under.

When she awoke a second time, she saw him beside her, crashed, dark rings under his eyes, and she realized what a terrible toll the last several days had taken on him. As she tried to sneak out of bed and not disturb him, his arm slid over her, tucked her up against him, and nudged her closer.

She immediately turned over, slid her arm across his chest, and whispered, "I didn't want to wake you. You're exhausted."

He smiled, but his eyes remained closed. "I am," he said, "but it's over. We're here. We're together, and there's an awful lot we have to be thankful for."

She lay her head on his shoulder and whispered, "Thank you for that."

"I didn't do anything," he said, "nothing more than my job."

She gently pinched his skin.

"Ouch," he said. "What was that for?"

"Just wondering if that means, whenever someone is threatened, you'll feel the need to move into their beds."

He chuckled, the sound bubbling up through his chest. "Okay, so maybe it wasn't just my job."

"I should hope not."

He rolled over, suddenly pinning her beneath him on the bed. His eyes were open and a deep, deep blazing blue as he stared down into hers. "That we have shared a bed over these recent days," he said, "you have no idea how grateful I am that you're still alive and here with me now."

She smiled up at him cheerily. "Oh, I think I do," she said. "I'm pretty grateful about it myself." She reached up and kissed him gently. "Do you think it could be our time now?"

"Absolutely," he said, kissing her gently. "We've had a pretty rough go of it."

"Yes, we have," she said, as she kissed him again. "Do you have to be anywhere?"

"No," he said, "not right now. What time is it?"

Just then her phone rang. She quickly snagged her phone, took a look, and gasped.

He looked at the phone with her and said, "What am I looking at?"

She scrolled down to read a text.

I'm terrified to send this, but Bellamy said I had to.

It was a picture of a room with multiple paintings.

She zoomed in and looked closer. "Amazing."

"I don't get it," Richard said, curious at her reaction.

"It's Frankie's work," she said gently. At that, her heart warmed as she thought about him. "He used to paint very differently from this, and then he had a car accident and ended up with a brain injury, and he could never quite get *it* again. So he's been very frustrated and angry."

"What is this then?"

"He finally tried to do something different. He let his hand take care of his heart, and this is the result."

"Wow," he said.

Awkwardly holding the phone, she quickly sent back a text. **Amazing, Frankie. So proud of you. I'll be happy to take a closer look, but it won't be today.** She sent it, tossed her phone on the night table. With a happy sigh she returned her attention to Richard. "Now that is something that really makes me happy."

"You're close to him, aren't you?"

"Absolutely," she said. "He's been a confidant for a couple years now."

Richard gently kissed her on the cheek and nose. "A lot of people are in your life, aren't there?"

She slid her hands to his cheekbones, gently stroking the strong bones under his eyes. "That doesn't mean my life is full," she said. "There's plenty of room for one more, right here beside me."

He smiled down at her, and she was entranced by the insecurities she could see peeking through his gaze. She asked him, "Don't you ever feel that you aren't good enough or that you don't belong."

"How did you know that's what I was thinking?" he joked.

She slipped her finger down to his mouth to stop him from talking. "Because I can see it," she said. "Remember that one thing that I do as I paint? When I paint, I *see* other people. I see inside people."

"I need to ask you a few questions," he admitted.

"I know. There will be lots of questions for all of us for a long time," she said.

"The luminescence, the light."

"It took me a long time to perfect that," she said, "but the answer is so damn simple." She slid her arm up around his neck. "We can talk about that later too."

He lowered his head and kissed her deeply, her body completely melting underneath him. She wrapped her arms around him and held him close, feeling tears welling up in her eyes. She was just so grateful to be alive and to have him in her life.

His hand stroked her breast, and he lowered his head to take the nipple into his mouth, suckling, and she cried out, her body arching under his attentions. When he did the same for the second one, she was already shuddering and quaking at his touch. After all, these past several days had seemed like one long foreplay session. Plus it had been a long time for her. And the fact that being with Richard was so special and so new, just made it all that more poignant.

Her skin was supersensitive, her heart already melting, and her belly, well, everything south of her navel was more than ready for his attention.

He slid a hand over her hip, down her thigh, across her knee, to her calf, only to slide up the inside of her calf and thigh. But to completely miss the tiny triangle of curls that she left there.

When he wouldn't go there, she whispered, "You're a tease."

He chuckled. "Maybe," he said. "But I want to make sure that you're ready for me."

"Are you kidding?" she said. "I've been ready for days."

"I know," he said, "and I'm sorry. I didn't want to drag it out, but I also didn't want to cross a line that would compromise the case."

She reached out, pulling him up to her, and said, "I knew that, and I understood."

He kissed her again and again. "Not many would," he whispered.

"I do," she said.

"You have the parameters of your work, and I have the parameters of my work," he said. "It is what it is on both counts."

"Got it," she said, kissing him on his lips, on his neck, on those incredible cheekbones. "It feels so damn special to be here with you right now," she said. "I just feel so thankful to be alive."

He kissed her again. "You have no idea how I felt when Frankie called and said you had disappeared."

She placed a finger across his lips. "Stop," she said. "We got through it, and we'll get through the rest too."

"Just some questions. There won't be a trial. The suspect is dead."

She winced at that, and Richard immediately kissed her, as if that would heal the wound. She had to admit it went a long way toward making it easier. She slid her leg up his calf, up his buttocks, and noted he had no boxers on. She stopped and stared at him. "Did you sleep in the buff?"

He chuckled. "I sure did," he said, "but then so did you."

She shrugged. "I did, but I'm not sure that it was deliberate. I was so exhausted."

"Well, in my case, it was deliberate," he said. "I've been sleeping this way the last couple nights in your bed next to you."

She stared at him in shock.

He chuckled. "And I'm kind of disappointed you didn't notice."

Her laughter rang out. "You know what? I can understand that." The surety that she was right where she needed to be overwhelmed her. The knowledge that he was hers and that she was his. She couldn't even begin to plan for all eternity, but she was damn happy to take it one day at a time, just as they had been. She tugged him to her and said, "Now, please. I want you inside me now."

He settled back ever-so-slightly and whispered, "I don't think you're quite ready." And he lowered his head to kiss her across her cheek and on her earlobe and down her neck, across to her collarbone. Meanwhile his hand slid across her hip, between her thighs, and just his thumb played with the little nub between the soft folds.

Her hips arched up, and she cried out. "No. That's not true," she said, her head twisting from side to side. "I was ready days ago."

"I know," he said. "I just want to make sure this is all about you."

Her eyes opened, and she stared at him. "This isn't about me or you," she said. "This is about us. This is about us being the best that we can be together."

He aligned his body with hers, sliding in between her thighs. She wrapped her legs around him, high up on his hips, and he stared at her in surprise. "I've never even thought of it in that way before," he said, "about being an *us* in bed."

She slid her arms around his neck, pulled him to her, and said, "Good, that's just between us then."

He lowered his head, kissed her, his tongue plunging deep, even as his hips surged until he was seated right in the heart of her.

She stilled. He lifted his head, looked down at her in worry. She took several slow deep breaths. "I'm fine," she said. "It's just been a while."

He shuffled ever-so-slightly, and she lifted her hips and wiggled. He closed his eyes, reaching for control.

And then she whispered, "Don't worry. I'm good."

He kissed her hard and said, "Are you sure?"

"I said it's been a while," she said. "And that was a little more than I bargained for, if you know what I mean."

He chuckled and said, "As long as you're okay." And he lifted his hips and gently started to ride. Moments later, she hung on, giving as good as she got, and soon wasn't capable of anything but responding blindly to the power, the presence of the moment, and the heat that surged through the two of them.

When she came apart in his arms, she cried out for joy. As she collapsed, he roared above her, and she could feel his own orgasm ripping through her, and her body exploded again. She lay shuddering in shock.

When he finally collapsed beside her, he said, "Good thing we've got a lifetime ahead of us because that went way too quickly."

She placed a finger on his lips. "*Shh.* It was perfect," she said. "And, as you said, we have a lifetime for more."

"But, a lifetime aside, we can do it again in a minute, right?" And he waggled his eyebrows.

She laughed in delight.

Her phone rang, and she eyed it distrustfully.

"If it'll bother you," he said, "why don't you turn it off?"

She lifted the phone and saw it was a message from Frankie. And as she scrolled down, a photo loaded. Then another and another. Close-ups of his paintings. She gasped in shock at the scenery, the soft pastel rivers, almost European settings. She stared at them in delight.

"What are they?" he asked.

She twisted her cell slightly so he could see, and he nodded. "Those are amazing."

She quickly texted him back. **Absolutely wonderful. These are fantastic.** She included a heart emoji to go along with it.

"And that was for what?"

She looked up at him, smiled, and said, "Validation. We all need it."

He nodded in comprehension. "And going back to that question I asked you earlier."

"About my painting?"

"What makes them glow?" he asked. "What is that luminescence that makes them come alive?"

She smiled and said, "It won't make a whole lot of sense to you, unless you understand the energy of things and the colors of energy."

"I'm slowly learning," he said, "particularly after Stefan gave me a few lessons." On that note, he looked down and checked out her ankles, realizing they were completely free of the black bonds. He reached down, pulled her right knee up so that he could stroke the ankle. "The chains, the black energy, was wrapped around both of your ankles."

"Which is interesting," she said, "because both my ankles were broken by my ex-fiancé," she said. "So I guess it makes sense. He liked to tie his victims by the ankle." Her tone turned sad as she remembered it.

He leaned over and whispered, "We'll leave that sadness behind now. But you still haven't answered the question."

She laughed in delight, threw her arms around him, and said, "It's the simplest answer in the world. I use energy, but I use good energy. I use what would heal the entire world, if people would stop and accept some into their heart."

He stared at her, and she could see the confusion in his gaze.

"I infuse all my paintings with love."

This concludes Book 17 of Psychic Visions: Stroke of Death.

Read about Ice Maiden: Psychic Visions, Book 18

Ice Maiden: Psychic Visions (Book #18)

Gabby was loving her winter in Aspen, Colorado, until a dangerous event with a ghost nearly killed her. Not that she was a believer but, given the circumstances, she had to be open to such a possibility. When one of her roommates is brutally murdered in their shared apartment, rumors circulate of a serial killer returning, which just adds to Gabby's pain. Confused and grieving, Gabby is forced to move to a new residence, while the police investigate the death, the crime scene at the apartment, and her.

Detective Damon Fletcher considered Gabby a flighty troublemaker after an incident at the bookstore where she worked and then later on the slopes. But when one of her roommates is murdered, his interest in her grows to a whole new level.

When another of Gabby's roommates is killed, Gabby is caught in the middle, as suspicious gazes turn her way. What had she gotten mixed up in? Even worse how are these deaths connected to several cold cases? The danger escalates as events, ghostly and otherwise, strike closer to both Gabby and all those who she holds dear.

Find Book 18 here!

To find out more visit Dale Mayer's website.

https://geni.us/DMMaidenUniversal

Sneak Peek from Ice Maiden

THIRTY-YEAR-OLD GABBY MULDER called out to her friends, "Go."

They all dove down the ski slope, racing to the bottom of the hill, on the last run of the day. The sun was high; the snow shone brightly on a wonderful Aspen day. Gabby was tired after a long but wonderful day of snowboarding, looking forward to hitting the hot tub. The others had wanted to do one more run, and she'd been willing to go along, knowing she could take it easy. Snowboarding was such a great way to combat stress.

Something she had in spades.

Especially after yesterday.

She worked as a clerk at a local Aspen bookstore. A job she'd quickly fallen in love with, even though she'd only been at the resort town for the winter and planned to leave when the ski season was over. She and her best friend Wendy had been planning a winter here since forever. Now the end of March was near, and she couldn't bear to think about leaving. She loved it here, … the town, the atmosphere, her job. Even her boss, although morose and cranky most of the time, was great.

He had been looking for a gimmick to bring in more customers. As a lark, she had picked up a pack of tarot cards she'd found under the counter, and Gabby had offered free readings. That had been all fun and games, until several people had come back, confirming that her readings had been right on. Then somebody had returned, saying how horrible the message was that she'd been given because it all happened just as described, and now she was widowed and felt Gabby could have done something to save her husband's life.

That was followed by a visit from one of Aspen's finest. Detective Damon Fletcher had definitely not understood nor had he been impressed. In fact, it's almost as if he thought she might have had something to do with the man's death to make her prophecy come true. She wasn't sure whether he thought she was a scam artist or a murderer.

His parting words, "Don't leave town," had been a sobering reality check.

Her boss was furious with her, saying, "Gabby, these readings are supposed to be fun and positive. Nothing else. You don't believe that stuff, do you?"

She just looked at him mutely.

"Stop them now," he ordered. "Our business depends on the goodwill of the community. A bad reputation and ugly rumors will finish us. Your job is on the line over this."

She immediately nodded because she needed the job. The cost of living in Aspen was brutal. She shared an apartment with four other girls, none of whom could afford to move.

Her friends knew about her tarot readings. She'd done several for them in the last few weeks. Had even done readings for them during breakfast this morning and hadn't thought anything of it. When they'd asked her to pull a card for herself, that had been fine too. Until she pulled the one card that made them all gasp. The Death card.

She laughed and said, "Whatever," then tucked it into the box, as they'd all looked at her in worry. She smiled and said, "The Death card doesn't mean a literal *death*, as in I die. It could just mean the death of a relationship or a job even." Although she hoped it wasn't the latter.

Unconvinced, they all headed to the slopes. And now here she was, at the end of the day, happy that the dire card hadn't proven to be a bad omen.

With a pleased smile at the beautiful sunny view of whitecapped mountains around her, Gabby rode the mountain, bent into the next corner, loving the power and the sense of control she had as her board bit into the icy surface.

Just then a hard push sent her careening forward. She cried out as her body instinctively bent and twisted to keep upright, even as she tried to see who'd pushed her. She struggled to brake. She was a good snowboarder, not racer material, but she'd have said better than average at least. Until now. Nothing she did brought her board back under her control. Or her speed. She dug the edge of the board in, her body almost scraping along the snow, but it wasn't working. ... An out-of-bounds marker flashed in warning up ahead.

Panic hit her, as the wind slashed her cheeks and as icy-cold tears stung her eyes. Still her out-of-control board propelled her forward, as if guided by unseen hands.

She hurtled toward the cliff's edge, screaming at the top of her lungs in terror. Her friends hollered and waved at her, telling her to get back over.

In desperation she threw herself to the ground to try to stop. Snow and ice burned into her skin and eyes, as she hurtled downward into a snowball of board and limbs that never seemed to stop spinning.

Splat.

She slammed into a small jut of the cliff, sending a cloud of snow falling on top of her. Gasping for air, terrified to move, she couldn't even see for the instant whiteout. When she finally realized that her world had stopped moving, she peeked through her lashes. The snow was no longer falling, and she could see the ski hill stretch high above her to the right as she laid on her back. That emboldened her to test out her limbs. She moved her fingers and toes, but no pain ripped through her. She sighed softly in relief, rolling her head to the left to see how close to the edge she was.

It. Was. Right. *There.*

The cliff dropped away at her cheek. Her bent left knee suspended over the edge into nothingness.

Oh, hell no. Too terrified to move, in case her small perch gave away, her heart slamming against her ribs, she froze on her tiny perch. It wasn't much more than a tiny jut of rock keeping her from falling to her death below. Her mind couldn't wrap around it. What the hell just happened?

Then she remembered the tarot card. *Death.*

No way was this about the Death card. Couldn't be.

A voice whispered in her ear, *Death comes to us all. Sometimes earlier than we want and sometimes by another hand. You live this time.*

Shocked, she cried out, "Who are you? What do you want?"

The same voice chuckled, a sound of triumph and joy. *You can call me Death. And what do I want? That's easy. I want you.*

And, with that, the voice disappeared.

Terrified, still in shock at how close she came to flying

off a cliff, she lay pinned against the mountainside, afraid to move.

Calls behind her had her raising her hand to let those racing toward her know she was okay. But was she really? She didn't dare check, too paralyzed with fear and cold.

Minutes later Wendy finally reached her, her face red and puffy from exertion. She stood a safe distance back and above her, calling out, "Oh, my God. Are you okay? What happened to you? Ski patrol is on their way. Don't move."

Gabby had no plans to move ever. In fact, the longer she lay here, the more rigid and panicked she became at the thought.

"What happened, and did I hear you yelling at someone earlier?" her friend asked hesitantly.

Gabby rolled her head to look at her best friend in confusion. "I don't know," she said. "I thought somebody just spoke to me." She couldn't very well tell Wendy about the message. She wouldn't believe Gabby. No one would.

"It's all right," Wendy said. "Take it easy. You probably just hit your head."

In truth, Gabby felt fine, which she shouldn't have because that was a hell of a tumble. She could have—should have, in fact—broken several bones. Even her board was still attached to her bindings, her feet still locked into place.

Just then the ski patrol arrived. Thank God. The first man unclipped his skis and made his way down to her.

At her side, he stopped and stared. "You."

She bolstered her courage to smile at the detective, who only yesterday had told her not to leave town while they investigated her and the tarot card mess. "*Uhm*, hi. I'm sorry about all this."

He snorted. "What the hell was that all about? I saw you

start down the mountain. Then you went nuts. That was incredibly irresponsible. You're lucky to be alive."

She shuddered, shrank as small as she could, and said, "I don't know what happened." She could almost see a sneer forming on his face. "It wasn't me," she rushed to add. "I was pushed."

His gaze sharpened. He studied her as she lay here, not daring to even breathe deeply, in case that shifted the balance somehow. "Who pushed you?"

"You won't believe me."

"Try me."

She looked up at him and whispered, "A ghost?"

Find Book 18 here!

To find out more visit Dale Mayer's website.

https://geni.us/DMMaidenUniversal

Author's Note

Thank you for reading Stroke of Death: Psychic Visions, Book 17! If you enjoyed the book, please take a moment and leave a short review.

Dear reader,

I love to hear from readers, and you can contact me at my website: www.dalemayer.com or at my Facebook author page. To be informed of new releases and special offers, sign up for my newsletter or follow me on BookBub. And if you are interested in joining Dale Mayer's Reader Group, here is the Facebook sign up page.
http://geni.us/DaleMayerFBGroup

Cheers,
Dale Mayer

About the Author

Dale Mayer is a *USA Today* best-selling author, best known for her SEALs military romances, her Psychic Visions series, and her Lovely Lethal Garden cozy series. Her contemporary romances are raw and full of passion and emotion (Broken But ... Mending, Hathaway House series). Her thrillers will keep you guessing (Kate Morgan, By Death series), and her romantic comedies will keep you giggling (*It's a Dog's Life*, a stand-alone novella; and the Broken Protocols series, starring Charming Marvin, the cat).

Dale honors the stories that come to her—and some of them are crazy, break all the rules and cross multiple genres!

To go with her fiction, she also writes nonfiction in many different fields, with books available on résumé writing, companion gardening, and the US mortgage system. All her books are available in print and ebook format.

Connect with Dale Mayer Online

Dale's Website – www.dalemayer.com
Twitter – @DaleMayer
Facebook Page – geni.us/DaleMayerFBFanPage
Facebook Group – geni.us/DaleMayerFBGroup
BookBub – geni.us/DaleMayerBookbub
Instagram – geni.us/DaleMayerInstagram
Goodreads – geni.us/DaleMayerGoodreads
Newsletter – geni.us/DaleNews

Also by Dale Mayer

Published Adult Books:

Hathaway House

Aaron, Book 1

Brock, Book 2

Cole, Book 3

Denton, Book 4

Elliot, Book 5

Finn, Book 6

Gregory, Book 7

Heath, Book 8

Iain, Book 9

Jaden, Book 10

Keith, Book 11

Lance, Book 12

Melissa, Book 13

The K9 Files

Ethan, Book 1

Pierce, Book 2

Zane, Book 3

Blaze, Book 4

Lucas, Book 5

Parker, Book 6

Carter, Book 7

Weston, Book 8

Greyson, Book 9

Rowan, Book 10

Lovely Lethal Gardens

Arsenic in the Azaleas, Book 1

Bones in the Begonias, Book 2

Corpse in the Carnations, Book 3

Daggers in the Dahlias, Book 4

Evidence in the Echinacea, Book 5

Footprints in the Ferns, Book 6

Gun in the Gardenias, Book 7

Handcuffs in the Heather, Book 8

Ice Pick in the Ivy, Book 9

Jewels in the Juniper, Book 10

Killer in the Kiwis, Book 11

Psychic Vision Series

Tuesday's Child

Hide 'n Go Seek

Maddy's Floor

Garden of Sorrow

Knock Knock...

Rare Find

Eyes to the Soul

Now You See Her

Shattered

Into the Abyss
Seeds of Malice
Eye of the Falcon
Itsy-Bitsy Spider
Unmasked
Deep Beneath
From the Ashes
Stroke of Death
Ice Maiden
Psychic Visions Books 1–3
Psychic Visions Books 4–6
Psychic Visions Books 7–9

By Death Series
Touched by Death
Haunted by Death
Chilled by Death
By Death Books 1–3

Broken Protocols – Romantic Comedy Series
Cat's Meow
Cat's Pajamas
Cat's Cradle
Cat's Claus
Broken Protocols 1-4

Broken and... Mending
Skin
Scars

Scales (of Justice)

Broken but… Mending 1-3

Glory

Genesis

Tori

Celeste

Glory Trilogy

Biker Blues

Morgan: Biker Blues, Volume 1

Cash: Biker Blues, Volume 2

SEALs of Honor

Mason: SEALs of Honor, Book 1

Hawk: SEALs of Honor, Book 2

Dane: SEALs of Honor, Book 3

Swede: SEALs of Honor, Book 4

Shadow: SEALs of Honor, Book 5

Cooper: SEALs of Honor, Book 6

Markus: SEALs of Honor, Book 7

Evan: SEALs of Honor, Book 8

Mason's Wish: SEALs of Honor, Book 9

Chase: SEALs of Honor, Book 10

Brett: SEALs of Honor, Book 11

Devlin: SEALs of Honor, Book 12

Easton: SEALs of Honor, Book 13

Ryder: SEALs of Honor, Book 14

Macklin: SEALs of Honor, Book 15

Corey: SEALs of Honor, Book 16

Warrick: SEALs of Honor, Book 17

Tanner: SEALs of Honor, Book 18

Jackson: SEALs of Honor, Book 19

Kanen: SEALs of Honor, Book 20

Nelson: SEALs of Honor, Book 21

Taylor: SEALs of Honor, Book 22

Colton: SEALs of Honor, Book 23

Troy: SEALs of Honor, Book 24

Axel: SEALs of Honor, Book 25

SEALs of Honor, Books 1–3

SEALs of Honor, Books 4–6

SEALs of Honor, Books 7–10

SEALs of Honor, Books 11–13

SEALs of Honor, Books 14–16

SEALs of Honor, Books 17–19

Heroes for Hire

Levi's Legend: Heroes for Hire, Book 1

Stone's Surrender: Heroes for Hire, Book 2

Merk's Mistake: Heroes for Hire, Book 3

Rhodes's Reward: Heroes for Hire, Book 4

Flynn's Firecracker: Heroes for Hire, Book 5

Logan's Light: Heroes for Hire, Book 6

Harrison's Heart: Heroes for Hire, Book 7

Saul's Sweetheart: Heroes for Hire, Book 8

Dakota's Delight: Heroes for Hire, Book 9

Michael's Mercy (Part of Sleeper SEAL Series)

Tyson's Treasure: Heroes for Hire, Book 10

SEALs of Steel

SEALs of Steel, Books 1–8

The Mavericks
Kerrick, Book 1
Griffin, Book 2
Jax, Book 3
Beau, Book 4
Asher, Book 5
Ryker, Book 6
Miles, Book 7
Nico, Book 8
Keane, Book 9
Lennox, Book 10
Gavin, Book 11
Shane, Book 12

Bullard's Battle Series
Ryland's Reach, Book 1
Cain's Cross, Book 2
Eton's Escape, Book 3
Garret's Gambit, Book 4
Kano's Keep, Book 5
Fallon's Flaw, Book 6
Quinn's Quest, Book 7
Bullard's Beauty, Book 8

Collections
Dare to Be You...
Dare to Love...

Dare to be Strong…

RomanceX3

Standalone Novellas

It's a Dog's Life

Riana's Revenge

Second Chances

Published Young Adult Books:

Family Blood Ties Series

Vampire in Denial

Vampire in Distress

Vampire in Design

Vampire in Deceit

Vampire in Defiance

Vampire in Conflict

Vampire in Chaos

Vampire in Crisis

Vampire in Control

Vampire in Charge

Family Blood Ties Set 1–3

Family Blood Ties Set 1–5

Family Blood Ties Set 4–6

Family Blood Ties Set 7–9

Sian's Solution, A Family Blood Ties Series Prequel
Novelette

Design series

Dangerous Designs

Deadly Designs

Darkest Designs

Design Series Trilogy

Standalone

In Cassie's Corner

Gem Stone (a Gemma Stone Mystery)

Time Thieves

Published Non-Fiction Books:

Career Essentials

Career Essentials: The Résumé

Career Essentials: The Cover Letter

Career Essentials: The Interview

Career Essentials: 3 in 1

Made in the USA
Middletown, DE
03 October 2023

40022157R00225